THE ETERNAL PRISON

Walking steadily toward the horizon, I wiped My Russian's blood out of my eyes and heard him asking me, *How many men have you killed, for* yen? I shook a cigarette out and placed it between my lips. I didn't know. I'd lost count. I was dead. I'd died back in prison. As I leaned in to light up, there was a deafening boom behind me, and I was lifted up off my feet for a second by a warm gust. I staggered forward and steadied myself with the street, lying there for a moment, my cigarette crushed into my face. When I flipped over, the restaurant was on fire, pieces of its roof sailing down in fiery arcs from the night sky, all of it in strange, muffled silence as my ears rang.

Well, shit, I thought, sitting up on my elbows. *That's fucking strange.*

By Jeff Somers

The Electric Church
The Digital Plague
The Eternal Prison

THE ETERNAL PRISON

JEFF SOMERS

www.orbitbooks.net

ORBIT

First published in Great Britain in 2010 by Orbit

A CIP catalogue record for this book
is available from the British Library.

ISBN 978-1-84149-705-1

Typeset in Palatino
Printed in the UK by CPI Mackays, Chatham ME5 8TD

Papers used by Orbit are natural, renewable and
recyclable products sourced from well-managed forests and certified
in accordance with the rules of the Forest Stewardship Council.

Mixed Sources
Product group from well-managed
forests and other controlled sources
www.fsc.org Cert no. SGS-COC-004081
© 1996 Forest Stewardship Council

FSC

Orbit
An imprint of
Little, Brown Book Group
100 Victoria Embankment
London EC4Y 0DY

An Hachette UK Company
www.hachette.co.uk

www.orbitbooks.net

To my Danette, whose wrath I fear, whose support
I require, and whose affection I treasure

PART ONE

PROLOGUE

SHORT WORK OF A FILTHY JOB

"Stay down," the tall System Pig with the precise, fussy beard said in a reasonable tone of voice. Gentle pressure on my shoulders guided me to my knees, my wrists bound behind me. "Or I will cut a few tendons and hobble you, *capisci?*"

His partner was shorter and older, standing in front of us, cigarette dangling from his lower lip. His face was red and blistery, like he'd fallen asleep in an oven, and he hadn't said a fucking word since I'd been dragged out here. After a moment he scanned us quickly, nodded once to himself, and stepped around to join his partner behind us.

I was soaked and shivering, the steady rain drumming down onto my shoulders and finding its secret ways inside. The street outside the remnants of Pickering's bar was half-flooded, inches of water in spreading pools. I was one of four assholes kneeling in the damp; I wouldn't have suspected four people remained anywhere below Twenty-third Street these days. Not alive, anyway.

The two System Pigs who'd scooped me up with their list of Very Important People had moved on down the block, taking their team of Stormers into a sagging old tenement. Every few minutes there was a gunshot or a shout, but otherwise it was peaceful, kneeling in the water, feeling the cold rain make its way down my back, my hands bound and no more decisions to be made. I'd been ready for my execution, but I was just as happy to kneel here and think about nothing.

I hadn't been myself for a long time. The Plague had sucked everything out of me.

The guy next to me started murmuring something; it took me a moment to recognize it as praying, old ritual language. I remembered my mom praying when I'd been a kid, her sing-song voice, her tightly shut eyes. I opened my eyes and looked at my fellow Very Important People: none of them looked so important to me. They were wet, thin, and all three sported the ugly scars on their necks left by the Plague; a few months before, they'd been coughing blood and croaking, inches from death. And I'd saved them. These three assholes. I'd scratched myself bloody crawling around the fucking world, and it was because of me they were still here, still breathing.

I looked around dreamily, this block I used to know so well. The System Security Force had already torn down half the buildings, flattening everything into rubble and then sending in Droids to crush everything into neat little cubes. I had no doubt more Droids would eventually roll in to collect the cubes, picking the whole place clean until you'd never guess that any of this, any of us, had ever been here.

The thought slipped off the shiny, smooth surface of my brain and disappeared.

A block or two over, a huge Vid screen glowed silently, bright and frantic, beaming the mime-news to everyone within a few hundred yards. The clips were short and edited to convey most of the message without audio. Most of the stories were upbeat testimonials to how the System was recovering from the Plague, but I'd been tuning into the underground Vid nets out of the Appalachians for the last few weeks, and I silently translated as the clips flashed by.

First, fifteen seconds on how casualty numbers from the disease were still going down as more and more surprisingly tough and scrappy citizens emerged from hiding places, shaken but alive. Translation: the entire East Coast of North America was a fucking graveyard, and places as distant as Brazil had seen upward of 10 percent of their population killed. Two more days and the whole fucking world would have been dead, jiving and singing, doing dance moves.

Then, a happy story about the citizens of the System of Federated Nations African Department discovering they had a food surplus and electing voluntarily to send huge shipments of organics and nutrition tabs to other areas of the System more affected by the Plague. This with lots of clips of smiling, celebrating people, people just fucking delighted to be living in the System. Translation: everyone, everywhere was starving *before* the fucking Plague, and the way things were going n-tabs were going to be the new goddamn currency any day now. And if you didn't have any n-tabs, you could cut off a finger and pay—feed—someone with that, and we'd all be eating each other, over and over again, the System gnawing itself raw.

The rotten tenement down the street suddenly exploded, a plume of fire and masonry shooting out into the street below, the world shuddering and leaping. The skinny guy kneeling next to me cursed under his breath. I turned to watch the smoke and fluttering debris for a moment. It was beautiful.

"They're okay, Silvie," Fussy Beard behind me said, getting his report in his earbud. "The rats are holed up in a secret room, packed in like fucking roaches, and blew a charge when Solly came sniffing around, but they tripped it too soon and killed two of *themselves*, and we didn't even get a scratch." The two cops laughed. I smiled, too. This was fine. Everything was fine.

The Vid was now showing Dick Marin, the Emperor himself. Director of Internal Affairs of the System Security Force; no one was telling Dick what to do these days. Dick was discussing the need for a reorganization in the wake of the Plague, in order to make things more efficient. Translation: his nominal bosses the Joint Council Undersecretaries, who thought *they* ran the System, were starting to give Marin flak, and he'd decided it was time to forcibly remind them of the real pecking order. From what I'd heard, he was going to find out they hadn't been sitting on their hands, waiting for him to send his cops after them. I thought about the fucking mess things were going to become soon and for a second almost wanted to stick around, just to watch the fireworks.

"Here they come. Look at those shitheads!"

They came stumbling out of the dust and smoke, three more of us coughing and bleeding, followed by a knot of Stormers in their grimy, flickering Obfuscation Kit that struggled to map itself to the swirling smoke and rain they passed through. Then the two officers, the bald one and the stiff, good-looking smiler that had taken me down and checked me off their list of People of Interest, people too important—for whatever mysterious reason—to just kill.

The three prisoners were young kids, teenagers. They were all wearing long oily-looking coats and bright red pieces of cloth around their necks, black, homemade ink around their eyes melting onto their faces in gummy streaks. I'd seen that a lot recently. It was a fashion. The one in front was tall and skinny, with deep cavernous cheeks and bright, wide-open eyes. He had a big scar on his forehead, old and leathery, and some fresh cuts all over his face. Even with his wrists laced up behind him, he walked steadily and with his head up. He was staring at me, and when the Stormers brought them over to us, he took an extra two steps and landed next to me as someone swept his feet out from under him, sending him to his knees.

"Fucking *manners*," the kid hissed.

"You okay with these chumps?" Baldy shouted.

"Fuck, Mage," one of the cops standing behind us shouted. "*Yeah*. We can handle babies and gramps, here."

The kid next to me sucked in blood from his nose and spat it onto the street in front of us, where it was immediately washed away. "Babies, fuck," he muttered.

This was fine. Everything was fine. I didn't have any outrage anymore. I knelt there feeling nothing but cold and wet. No anger, no sadness, nothing. I was just waiting for the next thing, and not feeling terribly interested about it, either. I wondered, idly, if they would shoot me in the head if I stood up and started to walk, or if I'd just get another beating. I wanted the bullet, but I didn't want another beating.

The two cops in charge signaled their Stormers, and the whole herd of them marched off to clear another building on their list. After a moment it was just the rain and wind again, the sucking noise of the System Pigs' boots as they stepped under a scrap of roof still clinging to the building behind us.

"I've got a blade," the kid said suddenly, his eyes locked on the street in front of us and his voice steady. He knew better than to whisper—the cops couldn't hear him, but I could. He knew better than to look at me or to move or to do *anything* except talk in a steady, controlled voice. "I can get my fingers on it, saw myself loose, and pass it to you." I remembered when I'd been sixteen, running the streets with a blade and nothing to lose. I'd pulled some demented shit back in the day—it had been all about survival, from one day to the next. Then I got some yen and some standing, and it became commerce and reputation. And then one day a pair of System Cops had come to make me an offer I wasn't allowed to turn down, and then I'd been angry. I'd been angry for *years*.

I saw Gleason, cold and dead, changed by the Plague into something terrible. I wasn't angry anymore. I wasn't *anything*.

"My two guys will jump in," the kid said, spitting blood into the street again. "Well...one of them will. I dunno about the other one. We take these two cocksuckers out. Fuck, I was willing to take my chances alone, but you look like you've seen some shit, huh? A player. That's *luck*. I've always been lucky."

I closed my eyes. The kid was probably nicknamed Lucky or Chance or something fucking ridiculous like that, probably had it tatted onto his chest in big block letters with some fucking dice or playing cards or something. He was right, though; the two Pigs weren't paying us much attention—to them we were just shivering assholes who'd gotten a foot up their ass, who'd gotten the point. If we moved slow and secret for ten seconds and then fast and furious for ten more, we had a good shot. If their Stormers and bosses didn't pick that moment to return. If I let the kid take most of the chances. And if our two minders didn't turn out to be like some of the cops I'd known, like Nathan Happling or Elias Moje, mean and tough and full of unpredictable tricks.

Or Janet Hense: inhuman, unbeatable.

All this I thought by rote, mechanically, some programmed part of my brain just clicking and whirring along the usual routes, slamming into hardwired decision trees onto new paths and arriving at the expected destination. None of it was connected to my body. There was no flood of adrenaline, no familiar spark of rage and terror. There was nothing. I knew I wasn't going to move. I wasn't myself anymore: I'd become a ghost. And it felt *good* to be a ghost.

The kid waited for me to say something. He didn't move. The kid had discipline. He wasn't going to be impatient and blustery, wasn't going to threaten me and waste time. I liked him. I wished him luck. I thought about telling him I would go for the smaller cop first, if I were him, because the tall one liked to talk and threaten, which probably meant he was all bullshit. The short one just stared at you, and that made me nervous. But I didn't say anything.

"We got like a minute here," the kid said. "Those other bitches come back here, we got a problem. We gotta move right now." His shoulders rolled, and I could tell he'd sliced himself free. It was impressive. "Here," he hissed at me. "Take it."

I closed my eyes again. *Fuck you,* I thought. *You don't tell me what to do, when to do it, or when to give a fuck.* I'd be happy enough to keep kneeling here until I died of hunger. A few heartbeats ticked by, ragged and lurching. Opening my eyes, I saw the kid turn his head to look at me.

"What the fuck, man? *Take it.*"

A few months ago, I would have reached out and grabbed this hunk of snot by the ear and pinched until he cried, and fuck, I would have *enjoyed* it. Now I just wanted him to volunteer to shut the fuck up and let me die in peace. It wasn't that pinching his ear wouldn't have solved my problem. And I still would have enjoyed it. But it would simply require way too much effort. I was old, and I'd survived things no one should have to. Survive, that is.

"Don't tell me you're going *pussy* on me. Fucking hell."

A spark of something, something molten and corrosive, flared up in my belly, flickering on for an instant and reminding me of…and then it was gone, snuffed out, drowned in a black inky flood of *who gives a fuck* and I just smiled, looking up at the Vid hovering above the rooftops. It was showing a bright, clean, pure white nutrition tab factory in Brazil, smiling tan people in clean white jackets processing raw protein and minerals into tiny white pills that guaranteed no one was going to starve to death. The tag line informed us it was the fifteenth new factory opened this year, and n-tab production was at a record pace.

I closed my eyes, smirking. Translation: you are all going to starve to death, probably sooner than later. Shit was falling apart. Marin's snatch of People of Interest was just the beginning, I figured.

"Shit," I heard the kid mutter. "Fucking *bitch.*"

He fell silent, and then it was just the rain again and the sucking noise of one of the cops behind us on the move. *Bitch.* The word sank into my neck and made swallowing difficult.

"What are you two fags jawing about?"

The cop's breath smelled like dead fish and cigarettes. He

knelt down between us with the casual ease of someone who'd been in charge of every situation he'd encountered, ever, his face almost close enough for his trim little beard to scratch my cheek. He plucked the cigarette, damp and cold, from his mouth and put a hand on each of our shoulders, pulling us toward him.

"No fucking talking, okay? You two want to suck each other off, wait until you're alone. Be decent about it."

I wondered why every fucking cop I'd ever met was afraid of the queers. Me, I'd worked with plenty of them, and they were just as dirty and apt to shiv you in the back as everyone else, but no more so. Then, before I could even think to tell him that this wasn't right, this was too soon, the kid jerked his elbow hard into the cop's face, crunching his nose into a pulp and knocking him back onto his ass. It was an easy move, a surprise move with the cop off balance and in a dumb position, and it had been hard to resist, but I knew better. The easy move wasn't always your best move.

The rest of it happened outside my peripheral vision. I didn't turn my head to see, but I could hear, and I knew exactly how the choreography went—it was a short, unhappy skit. The cop was on his back like a turtle, nose a fountain of blood, and the kid leaped on top of him with the blade, swinging it down in a dramatic, stupid arc to slice the throat presented to him. I could see the kid's face, the same face I'd made a million times—not ecstatic, not excited. Grim. Twisted up in concentration, trying to make short work of a filthy job.

And then the gunshot, and the kid sailed into my field of vision like a cannonball had hit him in the stomach, landing a foot or two away with a big spray of dirty water. He lay there in the street clutching his belly as blood poured between his fingers and blended into the ocean around him.

"Moda-fucka!" the first cop hissed, lurching to his feet and into my sight. I didn't look up at his face. He stood there next to me for a few seconds, just panting through his mouth, and then half twisted around. "Danks, Silbie." He stepped out into the street, sinking into a puddle up to his ankles, and approached the spluttering kid. For a few seconds he stood over him, hands curling and uncurling. "Moda-fucka," he repeated more softly. He breathed in through his smashed nose violently, his whole body shaking with the effort to suck air and blood through it, and then spat a prodigious glob of blood and snot onto the kid, followed by a solid kick to his stomach that made him scream and flip over.

"You piece of shit," the cop hissed, kicking the kid again. "You know what, Silvie? Upon further fucking *reflection*," he huffed, landing another kick to the kid's side, "and study of the fucking *lists*"—another kick—"I don't think this particular shithead is all that fucking important after all."

One more kick. The kid started to crawl, pulling himself feebly forward through the puddle of rainwater with one hand. The cop drew his handgun and pointed it lazily down at him and waited.

From behind me, the other cop, the one with the blistered face, spoke up. "Not to me, that's for sure." He sounded sad, like he'd seen this little play before and hadn't liked it the first time.

With a nod that sent a little mist of blood spray around, the other cop squeezed off a shot. The kid's head did a quiet little explosion and he sank down into the water as if relieved. The cop stared down at him for a moment and then nodded, holstering his gun and yanking a handkerchief from his coat to press against his flattened nose as he stepped back behind the rest of us without even a glance. I stared at the kid, slowly joining his ancestors in the sewers of Manhattan Island.

"There'll be heat for this, because of the lists," Blisterface said without emotion. "*You're* fucking filling out the Incident Report."

"I'll fill out the fucking SIR," Fussy Beard snapped back. "That's you all over, Silvio. Afraid of fucking paperwork."

I kept my eyes on the kid for a few seconds, watching. He was just dead, though, like I should have been years ago, like everyone I'd ever known—give or take a few shitheels I didn't care about—was dead. The cops' talk descended into murmurs behind me, indistinct and predatory. I closed my eyes, and it became just the rain and the wind. I was a ghost.

I

AMERICAN MURDER

Las Vegas was a scrub of a town, an electric grid in the middle of the fucking desert, guarded by the burned-out husks of ancient hotels. You could walk through the inhabited town in ten minutes and be in the extended graveyard that was the old city, and I was getting the fifty-yen tour following the Russian around. You could get anything you wanted in Vegas—easier if it was illegal. There were no cops in Vegas; I wasn't sure if there had ever been, but now that the cops and the Spooks were at war, there wasn't a cop within five hundred miles of the place.

Romanov's was a dump from the outside—pink-gray stucco, bars on the windows, and weak, jittery neon—set between happy-ending bars and burlap-window opium dens. Inside, it was plush, red velvety material everywhere, brass on the bar. Although the waiters were all Droids on wheels, skimming across the floor with terrible efficiency, the bartender was a human in a black suit, bright eyed and pasty faced, speaking English like he'd memorized it off cards. He didn't like the look of me but took his cigarette from his mouth long enough to saunter over and toss a napkin onto the bar. There was music in the air, a tinkling piano, and I could see my Russian in the mirror across from me, which was good enough.

The bartender stopped in front of me, his dark hair hanging

in his face. He picked tobacco off his lip and spat it onto the floor. "You have yen?" he asked.

I smiled, tossing my credit dongle onto the bar. "Sick with it." One thing I still had was yen. Problem was, you needed a fucking wheelbarrow of it to buy anything.

He looked down at the dongle for a second but didn't bother to pick it up and scan it. He sighed, almost in disappointment. "What will you have?"

I liked his accent. It was hard to understand, but it sounded nice. He was Russian, of course, of some sort—maybe he was Bulgarian or maybe he was a fucking Cossack, but it didn't matter: he was Russian for all practical purposes. Everyone in Vegas was a fucking Russian—they owned the city, if you wanted to call it a city. Mainly because no one else wanted the piece of shit out in the middle of nowhere. The Russians were keeping Vegas going through sheer determination, though things had gotten easier recently since the army had moved into the Southwest. I hadn't seen a System Cop in *months*.

"Doesn't matter, I can't taste anything anymore anyway. Gin," I said. "Warm."

He snorted, producing a glass and dropping it in front of me. "Gin. Fucking prole, yes?"

I winked, pulling a cigarette from my pocket. "Fucking right."

My Russian was an old guy, short but broad in the shoulders, with the tight look of a man who'd been lean and tough his whole life. He was old, silvery hair thick and short on his head. In the mirror he was sitting at a table crowded by two tall, plump baldies who sweated freely in their standard-issue leather coats. My Russian was clasping the hands of a tall, thin man with waxy skin and a shiny suit: the owner. They were beaming at each other so forcefully, pumping hands, I wondered which one hated the other more. The dining room was pretty full, lots of swells out for a nice meal, mostly fat men in suits so fucking pretty they were almost gowns. There was a nice buzz of noise in the air.

The bartender poured my drink, and I lit my cigarette, sending a cloud of bluish smoke into the air. I picked up my glass and swallowed the drink in one gulp, ticking my head down toward the glass before he could put the bottle away.

"Another," I said.

"You really can't taste anything, eh?" he said, squinting at me and pouring another.

"Or feel anything."

"Bullshit."

In the mirror, I watched the tall, waxy guy walk away from My Russian and plucked my cigarette from my mouth. I pushed the red coal against the top of my right hand and held it there, white smoke curling up. I counted five, watching My Russian in the mirror sweep the room with his tiny, thin eyes, and then put the butt back in my mouth, waving my hand at the bartender to show off the blackened welt. "Not a fucking thing."

"That's impressive." The bartender nodded, leaving the bottle on the bar as a sign of good humor. "Nerve Augment?"

I shook my head, picking up my glass and staring into the cloudy liquid. "Something that happened to me in prison," I said slowly, one of my moments coming on me, a strange, slow feeling in my thoughts. I shook my head a little and let it slide past me — it only got worse if I tried to force a memory. "I don't like to talk about it." I toasted him and drank my shot off as he spun and walked away. As I was setting the glass down, I felt the air around me getting crowded. In the mirror, My Russian and his two sweaty bodyguards had suddenly gotten much nearer.

"My friend," My Russian said, "I have been seeing visions of you all day." He spoke with the weird precision foreigners brought to English, every word bitten off, newly minted, invented a few seconds ago. "Why is that?"

I returned my cigarette to my mouth. Without looking around at them, I shrugged. "I've been hired to kill you."

In the mirror, My Russian shot his cuffs, and I caught a glimpse of a dark, blurry skull tattoo on his wrist. Fucking Ivans and their bullshit: the Russians had been just about the only organization to survive Unification, and it had made them fucking batty with the symbols and rituals. It wasn't pretty, of course—they made most of their yen through drugs, heavy shit sold to the bottom rung of the System, mostly designer, unstable, and as likely to pop a vessel as get you high. The cops had no patience for narcotics—Dick Marin, the Director of Internal Affairs and pretty much king of the cops, set the tone there—and they beat up on the Russians every chance they got, and the Russians were quick to put a bullet in the head of any-one who looked like a weak link to them.

They'd never made much of a dent in New York, back when there'd *been* a New York. The locals had closed ranks against them, and the System Pigs owned New York the way the Rus-sians owned Vegas. There'd been a couple of attempts over the years, but it had ended in tears. But the Russians had survived.

Everyone in that organization had done terrible things. Ter-rible Things was their fucking initiation rite.

My Russian cocked his head at me for a moment and then burst into laughter. His two bald friends joined in after a second of hesitation. Their boss looked around as if he'd made a terribly funny joke, soaking up the room.

"Come have a drink with me, my ghost," he chuckled, turn-ing away. "Talk to me."

One of the bald giants leaned down, but I forestalled that bullshit by standing up, blowing smoke around. "Touch me, Boris, and I will break a finger."

He grunted, straightening up. "Name not Boris."

I nodded. "Finger will still be broken," I advised, pushing through them. I jerked my head at the bartender, who was back to leaning against the wall, watching me walk by with slitted eyes and smoke curling up from his own cigarette. He flicked his hand from his waistband, and my credit dongle leaped at me. I snatched it from the air.

"*Spaaseeba*," I said, just a collection of sounds I'd learned. I tucked my dongle away into a pocket.

"Nice knowing you," he said to my back.

I grinned.

The place was air-conditioned aggressively, but I imagined I could still sense the heat out in the desert. It had been 113 at noon, though it was expected to cool down to a manageable 104 by midnight. I hated Las Vegas. It was like living in someone's armpit.

They led me toward the back, passing the packed tables, and kept walking past all of the heavy-looking red padded doors marked PRIVATE and took me through the swinging doors into the kitchen. The black, humming cooking unit took up an immense amount of space, swollen within the tiled room, just a cube of rough black metal with neat, tidy conveyor belts inching out of it. It was idle at the moment, there being more activity at the bar than the menus, but I didn't like the way it hummed, an almost silent vibration that reached inside me. I pushed my hands into the loose pockets of my ill-fitting suit, too heavy for the weather and full of my sweat, soaked up lovingly and held jealously. I wasn't made for this town. Too hot, too empty, too old.

My Russian kept walking through the empty kitchen and out the back door into a fenced-in lot that smelled like rot, the wet, heavy smell hitting you in the face and settling down to soak into your clothes and skin. Weeks from now I'd be smelling like this fucking parking lot. I kept smiling, though, trying to look my new friends over. All of us thought we knew exactly where this social call was ending, and all that remained was to see who was right.

I put my eyes on My Russian and ran them up and down his shiny suit, deciding he wasn't carrying a barker. The Russians—the higher-ups, at least, the real old-school Ivans—had a fetish for strangulation, a wire shining out in the darkness. I'd heard they regarded any murder that didn't require you to get right up close to the mark—a knife, a piano string—as pussy work. American murder.

Pussy or not, the two bald mountains had two guns each, big ones, under their arms. They didn't look fast, and their coats were too tight for that kind of move—it would bunch up if they tried to pull both at once, and if they were going to pull them one at a time they were fucking morons for carrying two anyway. The two bodyguards stopped and let My Russian and me take a few steps more, so that I ended up between him and them, the two huge balls of flesh between me and the door.

My Russian stopped and turned to smile back at me. I squinted around, the dark heat settling on my shoulders and pushing. It was bright out, a big moon shining down onto us. The fence looked high, a serious fence. Not impossible to scale, but not something I was going to leap over while people shot at me. The sky was a dark blue canopy over us, empty, clear, just filled with evaporating heat.

"I take meetings here," My Russian said, spreading his hands and grinning. His suit shone expensively in the dim light leaking from the sky. "It is quiet. So," he said. "You have been hired to kill me, yes? Who has hired you? Why?" He cocked his head. "I know your face. I know your name. New York, yes? Lots of you New Yorkers out here these days. Rats fleeing the sinking ship."

"New York's gone," I said. "They're tearing it down and replacing it with a goddamn shopping mall."

"Yes. I know you—a big gun, yes? How many men have you killed, for *yen?*" He said it as if there were better things to kill for. Then he squinted one eye at me owlishly. "You were in Venice recently, yes? The World Banker. I forget the name."

I shook my head. "Haven't been to Europe in years, Boris. You're thinking of some other desperate old man."

My Russian frowned and pushed his hands back into his pockets. From below his collar a smudge of ink was visible—a star atop what I assumed was a crown, the symbol of high rank. I reached up and scratched my shoulder where my own prison tattoo used to burn. Prison had been good for me. I didn't like to think about it too much, about Michaleen and Bartlett and the others. It hadn't been a good time, an *enjoyable* time, but it had been a *necessary* time, for me. It had boiled me down, and I'd come out of it the better man.

He saw me looking and smiled. "You know what it means?" He suddenly jerked his sleeve up, revealing two and a half of the blurry skull tats on his arm. "And these?"

"Prison work," I said, keeping myself still, feeling the bodyguards' eyes on me. "Where'd you get the art?"

"You know what it means, my friend?"

I smirked, figuring that would annoy him. "I know what it's *supposed* to mean, Boris. Anyone can slap some ink on you."

"My name is not *Boris*," he complained. Maybe he wasn't as smart as me after all. I wasn't used to being the smartest guy in the room. "And where I come from, they kill you for false emblems like that. Buy you a drink somewhere and slit your throat, you fall back onto a plastic sheet, five minutes later it is like you were never there."

"Yeah," I said. "How many? Five? Ten? You think *ten* is a big number?" If I'd had a skull for every person I'd killed, I'd be a fucking shadow. I'd be nothing *but* ink.

"Numbers do not matter. You New York boys, always counting." He peered at me. "You are sure you did not work the Venice job? I heard your name, very clear."

"Then someone is lying to you," I said. I'd been sucked into Chengara Penitentiary and hadn't made it too far away since getting out. "The last two times I made it to Europe, things didn't go so well for me." The two big boys behind me hadn't moved, not even to loosen up their coats.

He nodded, crimping his lips as if to say, *yeah, okay, whatever.* "You know my people?" he said suddenly, voice soft and casual, like he was asking me if I liked his shirt. I didn't. My own shirt was white and scratchy and a little tight around the neck, like it'd been made for a different man. "You know who I work for?"

"Sure," I said, nodding. "You're connected. You're a high roller. You run this town—for your boss. You live in a fine suite in an ancient hotel; you go from an air-conditioned room to an air-conditioned mini-hover—it's fucking cute, like a little toy—to an air-conditioned room every day and probably haven't sweated in ten years."

He chuckled, nodding and stepping around me. "*Da,*" he said jovially. "*Da!* And you were sent to kill me. It is funny. Now, if you will excuse me, I must have my dinner. Lyosha and Fedya will finish our conversation."

I turned to watch him walk back into the restaurant, the door shutting behind him as if on a motor of some sort. I looked at one of the big guys and then at the other. They were slightly different in the shape of their rounded heads and the angle that their mouths hung open but were essentially the same person occupying different space. I wondered idly if there would be an explosion if they accidentally touched.

The one I was looking at—I thought he was Lyosha but wasn't sure why I thought that—grinned. "You break my finger now?"

I sighed, feeling tired. "Sure, why not," I said. I could do the math: two of them against one of me, alone in a back lot, their friends inside and everywhere, fuck, the whole damn city. They hadn't frisked me or tried to take my own gun away. I chose not to be insulted. I reached up and took my crappy cigarette from between my lips and held it carefully between my thumb and forefinger.

Lyosha flicked his own cigarette into the air and exhaled briskly, shrugging his shoulders, getting loose. The butt fell limply to the ground as if the air were too thick to travel through, the coal bright on the dark, shadowed ground. For a moment we all stood there, hands hanging free, each of us waiting to see who would move first. First move was a losing move—it telegraphed your intentions, and when you had more than one person to deal with, it guaranteed at least one gun was going to find its way onto you and make some painful alterations. The air around us was completely still, like hot jelly, and I was reminded of the yard back at Chengara, where I'd gotten a free but excellent education on how to fight when outnumbered.

Rule number one was, sometimes making the first move made sense.

I launched myself at the one I'd decided was Lyosha, tossing my cigarette into his face with my left hand as I pulled my gun with my right. He cursed in Russian, all consonants and fucking phlegm, waving his hands in front of his face and dancing back. As I crashed into him I brought my gun up and fired twice into his belly, falling down on top of him and rolling off to the side. I wasn't worried about the noise; My Russian expected a few shots. A few more and he might send the waiter out to see if we needed anything, but not yet.

I came up into an unsteady crouch and fired three times, quick, where the other bodyguard had been a second before. He was still there, for a moment, and then toppled over, hitting his knees and then falling over face-first. I stayed low, listening to the sudden silence, feeling the heat on me, straining my senses.

Rule number two was to never assume. It wasn't nice, but I turned and found Lyosha, put my gun against his head, and made sure he was dead. Then I stepped over to his buddy and did the same, warm blood spraying me lightly. You assumed people were dead, they had a habit of coming up behind you at the worst times. I'd been assaulted by dead people so many times I'd become paranoid about it.

I turned and jogged back toward the door in a wide arc, approaching from an angle, taking soft, easy steps. I knew I didn't need to worry about getting the door open—I had magic. By sheer force of will the door was going to pop open. After five steps it did just that, and a big, thick-necked woman with a god-damn shotgun held across her body, a streak of absolute dark-ness, stepped halfway out into the yard. She peered out into the lot, muttering to herself, not seeing me coming at her. I just kept approaching, holding off; you couldn't shoot someone in the back. I wasn't a big believer in justice, but everyone deserved to at least see it coming.

I was just a few feet away when she suddenly turned, hiss-ing something I couldn't make out and swinging the shot-gun around, slow and clumsy. I squeezed the trigger, and she whipped around, sending one blast from the shotgun into the night air and falling awkwardly against the door, propping it open with her body. I leaped forward and plucked the shotgun from her loose grip; studied the wet, ugly wound I'd created in her chest; then looked into her staring eyes. With a quick glance into the bright, empty kitchen, I broke open the shotgun and let the shells drop out, then tossed it away to my right, the shadows swallowing it. After putting an insurance shell into her, I edged into the humming kitchen. The crank air being pushed out of the vents above rushed past me like someone had opened an air lock out in the desert. I stopped right inside and wasted a moment or two, listening, watching the swinging doors that led to the dining room.

As I stood there, the doors swung inward and admitted a pair of serving Droids, skimming along the floor bearing dirty dishes. As the swinging doors snapped closed, I caught a glimpse of the busy dining room, all reds and browns, plush fabrics that looked heavy and old. My Russian was sitting back toward the front of the place, laughing and holding a drink up as if making a toast. I looked straight at him as the doors swung shut again, gliding slowly on their tiny motors, but he never looked up at me.

I raised my gun and let the clip drop into the palm of my hand; it was difficult coming by hardware these days, most of it coming out of scavenge yards down south, Mexico generally, where the SSF's grip was getting a little sketchy under pressure from the army. For six yen a week kids sorted bullets into calibers and hand-filled clips, which were then sold to assholes like me for a thousand yen a clip. I wasn't sure where the fucking bullets came from, loose and sometimes ancient as hell, and I generally expected my gun to blow up in my hand every time I pulled the trigger. It kept things exciting.

I exchanged the old clip for a fresh one and snapped it into place as quietly as I could. I wasn't paid to scamper around waiting for the safe moment—I was paid for results, and now that My Russian was aware of me, there was no better time than the present, before he called his people and brought the hammer down—a wall of fat guys in leather coats, a team of idiots with garrotes in their pockets and my picture on their little handhelds. Besides, my instructions had been pretty clear: My Russian had to die *tonight*. I'd agreed to terms, and terms had to be upheld. I took a deep breath and racked a shell into the chamber gently, deciding that the best way to do it would be to be fast—no wasted movements, no wasted time.

I put the gun down low by my thigh and pushed my way into the dining room. I walked quickly and steadily toward My Russian, my eyes on him the whole time. Momentum was the key—no one paid me any attention as I crossed the room, just part of the blur of motion around them.

When I was halfway to his table, My Russian glanced at me, then looked away, his face a pleasant mask of polite enjoyment. Then he snapped back to me, his expression tightening up, his hands jumping a bit on the table like he'd thought about doing something and then killed the idea. It was too late by then; I was at his table. I should have just brought the gun up, killed him, and walked out. But I stood there for a moment with my gun at my side. I wasn't sure he could see it.

"Lyosha and Fedya will have some explaining to do, yes?"

I shook my head. "No. And neither will the kitchen help." I gave him another second, but he just sat there staring at me, his hands balled into fists. Macho asshole, no gun because he was *tough*. Fuck tough. Tough got you killed.

I raised the gun and there was no reaction at first—I'd expected a hubbub from the crowd, some noise, chaos. But I'd been away from civilization for so long I guess I'd forgotten the rules, how it worked. I raised the gun and put it a few inches from My Russian's face—not close enough for him to grab it easily or knock it aside—and nothing happened. There were people just a few feet away, eating their dinners, but no one was even looking at me.

My Russian stared at the barrel. "You know who I am, my friend," he said slowly, licking his lips. "Maybe you wish to be rich?" His eyes jumped up to my face and then tightened up. "No, I see you do not wish to be rich. Perhaps you don't wish to *live*, either. You are not a young man. You know who I work for. This will not be forgotten."

I nodded. "You draw a lot of fucking water out here. And now it doesn't matter. I don't know what you did, but you pissed off the wrong people, and here I am." Talking was for amateurs, but I wanted to give him his say. When you killed a man, you had to let him have his last words, if you could.

He was shaking now—with fear or rage, I couldn't tell. "You do not care who I work for, then? But you do not understand.

It is not like the old days, where we run from the fucking cops and they chase us behind the furniture. We are *part* of things. We are *partners*. You do not fear *us*, but do you fear Cal Ruberto? Ruberto, the Undersecretary."

I blinked. Now there was a sudden shout from across the room, and the whole place got quiet for a second, followed by a hissing wave of whispers. Cal Ruberto was Undersecretary for the North American Department and, nowadays, a major general in the New Army. The Undersecretaries had been running things—as much as Dick Marin and the System Cops would let them—since the Joint Council had gone senile years ago, but now they had some muscle. Ruberto wasn't just an Undersecretary anymore. He was a fucking *general*.

"You do not fear my boss," My Russian continued. "But maybe you fear Ruberto. Maybe you fear the whole damn System behind him."

I stared down at him a second longer, then cocked the hammer back. "Cal Ruberto," I said, "is *my* boss."

I squeezed the trigger, the gun making a thunderous crack, My Russian's face imploding as he was knocked backward, spraying me with a fine mist of brains and blood. I stood still another moment, thinking that I was almost at the point where I felt nothing when I admitted that.

Then I spun around, bringing my cannon with me, and stood there dripping blood, running my eyes over the crowd. Most of them ducked down as I looked at them, crouching in their seats. There were some shouts, but no one was moving. I let my gun drop to my side again and stepped quickly toward the entrance. There would be no cops, but you didn't kill a man with a crown on his chest in this town and just walk away whistling.

I crashed through the doors and into the hot, empty desert night, slipping my barker into my pocket. I imagined My Russian's blood baking onto me, turning into a shell. The street was busy, crowds of people who made up the infrastructure of the

Russians' private city out for the night. I just pushed through
bodies, looking up at the dark, hulking shapes of the ancient
hotels on the horizon, huge complexes rotting in the sun, mark-
ing the outer edge of a rotting city slowly filling with sand and
choking sunlight. A man could get lost in the darkness there
forever, if he wanted. In the heat, forever was a lot shorter than
you might imagine.

Walking steadily toward the horizon, I wiped My Russian's
blood out of my eyes and heard him asking me, *How many men
have you killed, for* yen? I shook a cigarette out and placed it
between my lips. I didn't know. I'd lost count. I was dead. I'd
died back in prison. As I leaned in to light up, there was a deafening boom behind me, and I was lifted up off my feet for a second by a warm gust. I staggered forward and steadied myself
with the street, lying there for a moment, my cigarette crushed
into my face. When I flipped over, the restaurant was on fire,
pieces of its roof sailing down in fiery arcs from the night sky, all
of it in strange, muffled silence as my ears rang.

Well, shit, I thought, sitting up on my elbows. *That's fucking
strange.*

II

JUST STILL ALIVE

My leg ached.

I figured it would ache for the rest of my life. It was amazing I could even walk on it, really. My lungs still burned when I walked too fast or if I smoked, too; the fucking Plague was going to be on me forever.

The Plague. I thought of Gleason, saw her face, smudged with dirt and giving me that sarcastic smile. At first I couldn't quite place the feeling that soured inside me, and then I realized that I *missed* her. I missed her making fun of me, and I missed showing her things, teaching her. Thinking of her made me angry, so I pushed her away.

I wanted to shift my weight, ease up off my bad leg and let the blood flow a little, but I couldn't move. I was strapped in standing up, inside a skeleton of blackened metal that smelled like rust, held stiffly and painfully upright. I could move my fingers some and my toes and my eyes. Not that my eyes were much use to me. I had a half million subtle angles of the sweating head strapped down in front of me, about two inches between us. The whole train car was packed with bodies, each of us pumping unhappy heat into the air. Sweat poured down my face into my eyes, making me blink madly.

"This is why," someone muttered from a few spots behind

me. "Democracy. Fucking democracy. Revolution. This shit right here."

"We *got* democracy," a deep voice boomed from further back. "No one's got a vote. We're all equals."

There were some subdued snickers at that, and then the first voice came back, screeching at throat-searing volume. "*Fuck you, you fucking Pig! I know you're a Pig! Burned Pig! I'm gonna slit your fucking throat!*"

I closed my eyes as everyone on the fucking train started shouting, the noise blurring into a sludge of hoarse white noise. I was thirsty. I'd woken up strapped in and had no idea how long I'd been here, smelling my fellow prisoners and wishing I could somehow will my own leg to just wither and drop off. Every now and then there was some indication of speed, a sudden yawing as the train took a curve, but for the most part it was as if we were standing still. From what I could tell we were moving just slightly slower than the goddamn speed of light.

After a moment the voices all shut off at once, leaving behind a trail of dry coughing and muttering. I kept my eyes shut and enjoyed the relative peace for a moment.

"Cut your fucking throat," the first voice muttered again, sandpaper on rotten wood.

We'd all been collected in the cleanup of the East Coast after Squalor's Plague. I didn't know how many people had died—if New York had been any indication, it was all of them—and the cops had brought in reserves from every tiny little shithole of the System and banged on every door left standing in the whole fucking city, putting bracelets on wrists and bullets in ears, following an executive order by Dick Marin, Director of Internal Affairs. Some of us had been shoved onto the trains. Whatever the reason, instead of an execution in the ruins of Pickering's bar, I'd been checked off a list and loaded onto transit. I guessed Marin was still my own personal guardian angel.

"We got a fucking cop here?" someone new shouted. "For fucking real?"

"Not anymore, he ain't," croaked a woman who sounded like she breathed whiskey and cigarettes.

"That's what stinks in here," another one bellowed. "I thought it was *me*."

Laughter, rusty and weak, drifted past me. I opened my eyes again, sweat immediately flowing into them, stinging. The head in front of me hadn't changed. It was a little shorter than me, round and bald with a fuzz of fresh whiskers growing on it. The upper edge of a dark tattoo appeared just above the neck restraint, a complex pattern of swirls and crosses. I'd been staring at it forever and I had no idea what it meant, if it meant anything.

"Hey," the man behind me whispered. "Hey, what's your name?"

I blinked, unsure if he meant me.

"*Hey*," he hissed again. "What's your *name*?"

I licked my lips with my dry tongue. I'd give all the yen I still had in anonymous accounts, trillions of it, for a fucking drink of water. "Cates," I said, my own voice thick and raspy, unfamiliar. "Avery Cates."

There was a pause. "No shit? Damn, I thought you was fucking immortal."

I tried a grin as an experimental expression. "Nope. Just still alive." I thought about asking his name but discovered there was nothing I cared less about.

"How'd they get *you*, man? Shit, it must have been a fucking bloodbath."

I smirked for my own amusement. "Yup. A bloodbath." I remembered sitting there, letting them put the bracelets on, feeling the gun against my head and *wanting* it, just feeling so tired.

"Were you sick?" the chatterbox came back. "Hell, I almost

shit the bed. Lying in the street just fucking *bleeding out of my ears*, you know? I thought I was dead."

I didn't say anything to that. I couldn't take a deep breath without pain, but I didn't need to prove anything to this guy. I could feel a change in our momentum, a slight pressure against me. We were slowing down. For a second, I wanted to move so badly I would have kicked and screamed and rattled my cage, just to stretch my fucking leg out for a second. I'd heard stories about Gunners standing still for hours, for days—all bullshit, I'd decided. No one could do it. Not even Canny Orel, who if you believed just half the shit about him was the baddest ass there ever was. Even *he* had to scratch his ass now and then.

The deceleration was getting more pronounced, pushing me forward, and everyone noticed all at once, a buzz of chatter sweeping up and down the train car. They all sounded excited, like this was some fascinating trip. Like the bracelets and the gun barrel against your head, the sap against your skull, and the involuntary train ride where you couldn't even stretch your fucking bum leg was all the System Pigs' way of telling you you just won the fucking lottery.

Everything started to happen fast.

The lights came on, super bright and terrible, clicking on with a sizzle, one bulb exploding into sparks just about over my head. The light burned my eyes, making me squint and try to turn my head as much as I could.

A door far up at the front of the car snapped open, a fat man framed in the entrance. He was tall and round and wearing a baggy police uniform, a Crusher, a low-level cop. A gun was strapped to his hip, riding low because he had long arms. I peered at him with dry, scratchy eyes and considered: his face was flat as if he'd been stepped on in the womb and outlined by a black beard that was trimmed to a neat point.

He stepped into the car and stopped. He looked around, his

expression gaining a hint of amusement. The train was moving so slowly now I could feel every bump and twitch.

"Welcome to Chengara Penitentiary," the not-Crusher said in a booming voice, a great voice, deep and rounded and with precise, particular enunciation, like he'd been to school. This was, I thought, either the System's most overqualified Crusher or not a Crusher at all. Or something else that I'd never encountered before. The thought was depressing.

"This is your orientation," he continued, putting one hand on the butt of his gun, an easy, nonthreatening gesture that drew my eye and made me nervous. I stared at his hand for a moment and forgot my fucking aching leg and remembered I couldn't move, not even to turn my head away. "It will last thirty-six seconds and will not be repeated."

He looked around again, satisfied with the impression he was making.

"Chengara is an EOT installation. EOT stands for end of term. You do not get released from Chengara; you do not move on to any other location."

He smiled. "There is no escape. Should you choose to take your chances, we will not break much of a sweat to stop you. There is a wall and towers, and we will snipe your ass in a second if we can, but if you scale the wall and run for it, good for you! There is nothing but hundreds of miles of desert around you, and you will be dead within a day. This is not idle bullshit. One day. It's even *worse* in the winter.

"No one is being paid to protect you or keep you alive. You want to fight each other? Kill each other? Go ahead—I don't get paid enough to stop you." He shrugged. "We log you in alive when you get here, and it's just paperwork for me if you die. A Standard Incident Report. I can fill one of those out in *one minute*. So feel free."

He paused to look us all over. "Some of you think, I'm sure, that because some cunt of a paper-pusher put your name on a list, because some asslicker in an *office* somewhere decided to classify you as a *Person of Interest,* you have achieved some sort of protected status. Indeed, some of you may have been spared execution on the spot precisely because you are POI. Well, fuck that, and fuck you: there are no interesting people on this train."

He drew his gun with impressive speed and flair. Before I could shout or twitch or do anything, he turned to the poor sap strapped in to his left and shot him three times in the goddamn face. I saw the guy's arms and legs jiggle with each shot, and then he just hung there, the liquid sound of blood dripping onto the floor clear in the sudden, mean silence.

"There are no fucking *paper-pushers* here. None of you are special, and none of you will be seen outside of this facility again. Remember that, punks."

And with that, the non-Crusher smiled, holstered his gun, and turned for the doorway. It snapped shut as he stepped through it. The silence clung to everything. When the train stopped moving altogether, the restraints all snapped free at once, and everyone sagged to the floor with a groan. My legs buckled under my sudden weight, and I went down onto my knees, catching myself on my palms, my face staring into the asscrack of my fellow prisoner. I spent a profitable few seconds staring at the rubbery black material of the floor. It felt damp and smelled like piss.

"Everybody up!"

The voice of our new friend, the non-Crusher, crackling and tinny over the train's PA system. I looked up, my head shaking slightly, my neck cramping up. We all struggled to our feet, shaky and rubbery, stretching painfully. Both my calves seized up into iron-hard cramps, dropping me back to the floor. I bumped the guy behind me as I curled up, grabbing my legs and massaging the muscles, grimacing, clenching my teeth.

"I said everybody *up*," the voice snapped.

Panting, I rolled onto my knees and slowly got to my feet. My calves ached to match my leg, each flaring up in a distinct rhythm. The moment I was upright again, the PA clicked on.

"Good. Row by row, exit the fucking car."

No one moved for a moment, and I knew we were all thinking the same thing, thinking maybe we *don't* move, maybe we put a stop to this taking-orders bullshit right here. But there was no play there—we were on a bullet train car, with no access to the pilot's cabin, rubber legged and unarmed. You could almost see the realization going from head to head: *we're fucked.* Someone near the front of the car started moving, and one by one none of us could think of an alternative. When the guy in front of me started to stagger forward, I twisted my head until my neck gave me a satisfying pop and staggered after him.

"Hey, Cates," the guy behind whispered. "You remember everyone you killed?"

I blinked. "Yes," I said, without hesitation. I saw them all, flashing through my head. I saw them with perfect detail, every pore, every blown pupil and ruptured vessel. I didn't know all the names, but I knew enough of them.

The end of the car was an impossibly bright square, just pure white. Heat blew in, a dry steady wind. It felt good after who knew how long being frozen in the train's crank air, and I shambled toward the exit with something approaching enthusiasm. At the edge of the train car, I stopped and squinted around, reaching up to shade my eyes from the bright, painful sunlight, my throat deciding it didn't like the hot, dry air and seizing up, making a choking noise that fell dead at my feet.

We were in the desert all right. A few feet down, the ground was sandy and cracked, with little scrubs of sad-looking grass here and there. In the distance I could see mountains, so far away they looked like a painting, a backdrop. The sky was a pale, light blue that looked thin and delicate. Sweat popped up all over my body. I forced a breath into my lungs and it burned all the way down.

The train had stopped inside a gated area, the chain-link fencing rising up on either side about twenty feet, topped by barbed wire, just wide enough for the train to pull in with an inch or so on either side for clearance. The only way to go was forward, and I saw the prisoners who'd exited ahead of me stumbling, blinking, and panting, along a path that forced you into a spare-looking cinder block cube looking like a single room, no windows, just a small, darkened doorway. Stretching off to the left and right of the structure was a massive wall of the same material, as tall as the chain link and with its own barbed wire. Glancing up, I could see a tower in the near distance, blank and gray and topped by a railing. A single figure stood atop it, tiny and vague.

Suddenly, I was pushed hard from behind. I stumbled, lost my balance, and fell, hitting the hard, hot ground hands first, scraping skin and sending a shock of pain down my back and leg. I shot my breath out of my nose and blinked my eyes to clear them, listening carefully, all my old instincts rushing to the fore. Running with the snuff gangs in Manhattan, I'd taken plenty of beatings, but you learned over time how to give as good as you got. And you never forgot.

I took a handful of the warm dirt in one hand and started coughing, stretching it out until I heard the scrape of his shoes as he dropped down and stepped toward me. I stopped coughing and waited for instinct, then whirled, sweeping my bad leg out as I did so and catching his ankle. I didn't knock him down, but I threw him off balance so he was backtracking as I lurched upright again, swinging my arm around and aiming the dirt for his face. I didn't get a bull's-eye, but I made him turn his head away long enough for me to rush forward and crash into him—a tall, wiry Asian guy with tan skin like coffee and long black hair tied back into an impressive tail. He went down and

I went down with him, landing with my knees on either side of him and showing him a close-up of my fist, asking his opinion on it. He didn't like it and spat a bloody tooth back at me, grinning nice and red.

"You fucking remember them *all*, Mr. Cates?" he slurred, laughing. "You are *sure?*"

I stared down at him, running his face through my memories, trying to match him up with someone. What were the fucking odds? But I guessed we'd all been sucked up out of New York, and I'd killed a lot of people in New York.

I rolled off him, and he was up immediately, spitting a glob of red phlegm onto the ground and walking off without a glance back, strutting. I lay there and watched him go, perplexed, and slowly climbed to my feet, dusting myself off. After a moment, I realized someone was standing on the other side of the thick chain-link fence. I looked over at him, squinting against the glare. He was the shortest man I'd ever seen, old and wrinkled, his snow-white hair wispy and thin and dancing on top of his head. He wore a bright orange jumpsuit of sorts, grimy and tattered, and grinned at me, yellow teeth and chapped lips. He was so small I thought I could slip him into my pocket. He nodded at me, smiling.

"Welcome to Chengara, Mr. Cates," he said in a rolling accent, stressing all the wrong syllables like he was reciting a poem. "You'll do well."

III

I WASN'T SURE I WANTED TO RESIST

"Walk with me, Victor."

Vic rolled the toothpick around in his mouth for a second or two, thinking it over, and then sighed heavily and peeled himself from the wall. We took a few steps along Las Vegas Boulevard in silence, Victor's sweaty, broad brow wrinkled up in anxiety, and his yellowed eyes shifting from side to side.

"You sure it's a good idea to be walking around?" he said in a low whisper. Victor whispered everything. He figured that by whispering and not looking at anything directly, he was sort of invisible—and the strange thing was, it seemed to work. Victor knew everything, because people forgot he was there and talked in front of him. "Word is you're a dead man. Word is, you popped someone high up on the ladder, and the whole fucking organization has your DNA in their handhelds."

I shrugged. "I have friends, too."

He snorted derisively. Vic was shorter than me, but his torso was wider and deeper, and he lacked a neck. He was just naturally burly. He wasn't much of a fighter, but you wouldn't know it to look at him. Vic's first choice of self-defense was to run away and find a nice Dumpster to hide in, but he *looked* tough, and most people didn't mess with him. "I don't have your friends, man—why come here and make me be seen with you? The fucking Ivans sometimes get crazy ideas."

My hands twitched at my sides, but I forced myself to be calm. I wanted badly to grab Victor's nose and remind him what our working relationship was, but I needed Victor's goodwill. I was on the Russians' shitlist, and Victor was one of the few people who hadn't just walked in the other direction when I'd shown up.

"I need a loan, Vic," I said simply, trying to sound casual. "I need to get out of this shithole."

Vic snorted again. "You're loaded, man. I've seen your credit."

I nodded, keeping my face a mask of good humor, everything pleasant. "No one wants my credit next to their name, Vic. I've been blackballed. Someone sells me a seat on a hover out of here, next week *they're* being tuned up. I need insulation."

Vic's head was aimed toward the cracked, baking sidewalk. I was wearing my suit, stifling, so hot I was like an oven at night, radiating the day's heat I'd absorbed. Vic was in a lightweight shirt that gave you a misty view of his hairy, blubbery chest and belly, and a pair of loose dark pants that had been cut off above the knees unevenly. He was a hairy man, coarse dark hair overflowing every part of him, and looking at him made me itch. His eyes flicked this way and that, and when he responded, he didn't look at me or move his lips, pretending to ignore me.

"So *I'll* end up getting tuned up."

I shook my head. "Cover your tracks."

"Shit, the Ivans hear you've skipped town, they'll just find out everyone who bought a fucking trip out of the desert recently and have a chat with each of us."

I nodded, keeping my cheerful mask in place even though he hadn't looked at me. "I'm laying off the risk for you, so stop worrying."

What the fuck. It was only yen. It cost 200 yen for a cup of coffee these days. I braced myself for his price while he considered, chewing his lip and pretending to read the strip-club ads pasted on the plywood wall between us and a deep, ragged pit where a building or buildings had once stood.

"Three and a half, then," Vic finally said, flinching away from an imagined blow.

I clenched my teeth and counted three. "Three and a half," I said slowly, stopping and letting him twitch a few feet ahead of me, "is fucking *murder,* Vic, and you know it. You're gonna step on my balls, Vic? I'm in a jam, and you're gonna charge me three and a fucking *half?*"

He flinched again, even though my hands were still in my pants pockets. I'd known Vic as long as I'd been banging around Vegas, ever since I'd crawled out of the desert mostly dead and burned to a crisp, my yen—linked to me by fingerprint scan no matter what else happened—the only thing that kept me alive. I'd twisted Vic's nose a few times, so I didn't blame him for acting like I was a live grenade next to him.

"Three, okay?" He turned away from me suddenly and stared at the ancient wall. "Come on—you're making me a fucking target if I help you out. I've got to—"

We both stopped as hover displacement boiled up around us, like someone had turned a knob. We both twisted around to look over our shoulders and squint into the blast of hot air sent our way by the shiny silver hover—a small, compact model with military markings—that was sinking down into the street. The people on the sidewalks didn't run or even look particularly concerned; they just watched blandly.

"Looks like you got a free ride, huh?" Vic said.

I nodded without looking at him. "Okay, Vic," I said, turning to face the hover as it settled onto the street. "We'll finish this up later."

I glanced over my shoulder, but he was already gone, ten

steps away from me and hustling, head down and eyes everywhere. I watched the hover come to grips with gravity, settling
into an impressive hold about one foot off the street, the ground
under me vibrating with a rapid, subtle rhythm. The three massive turrets mounted on the hover's chassis were aimed at me,
each one firing an armor-piercing shell about the size of my fist.
I decided not to move. For a few moments it was a still life, me
standing there and the hover just floating a few feet away, and
then it slowly set itself on the street, neat as a pin, impressive flying. There was an electric sizzle in the air and a curt, electroni-
cally filtered voice boomed out in a low, reasonable volume that
pinned my ears back against my skull.

"Approach the vehicle," it suggested.

I sighed, looking around. As I walked over to the hover, I
shook out a cigarette and put it in my mouth. I had the lighter in
my hand when the hatch slid out and up, revealing a tiny cabin,
big enough for maybe three or four people if they didn't mind
touching knees. In the tiny cockpit, separated from the cabin by
a half wall, there were two men in the bright white uniforms of
the shiny new System of Federated Nations Army. They looked
like twins with their shaved heads, big mirrored sunglasses,
and humorless expressions. You couldn't tell by looking at them,
but they were both Augmented to the hilt—night vision retinal
grafts, ultrasonic auditory implants, bone-strengthening DNA
treatments, Sleep-Deprivation Neuron Stimulators—shit, they
were more gadget than human. The SFNA spared no expense, but
they'd had to get up and running fast, and they'd skipped training
in favor of the best Augments yen could buy, even though almost
all those Augments were still illegal for regular citizens.

I leaned in and lit my cigarette, putting one hand on the hull
for balance. You couldn't afford to look weak, especially when
every other person you saw on the street was probably plotting
to kill you for reward money. "What can I do for you, buddy?" I
said with a puff of smoke.

The copilot turned his head toward me for a moment, held those mirrors on me, and then looked straight ahead again. "Ruberto," he said tonelessly, jerking a thumb over his shoulder. Sometimes I actually preferred the psionic whiz kids who made up the high bureaucracy of the civilian government. The Spooks were creepy with their ability to Push you into doing things or lift you off your feet with just a thought, but at least they weren't half-robot and crammed full of designer DNA.

I took my cigarette from my mouth and squinted down at it. I didn't have any choice, of course; Ruberto was sitting on top of the pyramid these days, and the turrets, I reminded myself, fired shells that would turn me into something resembling powdered milk. Besides, I wasn't sure I wanted to resist—I needed out of Vegas, and here was the safest ride you could get.

Taking a deep drag from my cigarette, I flicked the butt into the air and swung myself into the rear of the cabin. "He have you flying all over the goddamn city this morning looking for me?" I said with a grin. Neither one responded. The hatch slid shut with a hiss of pressurization, and the hover immediately powered on, lurching up into the air.

I settled back in my seat and studied the symmetrical backs of their heads, a hole opening in my stomach as we rose into the air and then the slight push backward as the little hover leaped forward, cutting through the overheated air. It was cool inside the cabin, and I was about as safe as it got as long as we didn't cross paths with any cops. The whole System was a patchwork of authority now, with things shifting slowly one way or another. New York had changed hands five or six times in the last year, from what I'd heard.

Ruberto was Undersecretary for the North American Department, of course, which was a lot of territory, but the front line in this hemisphere was pretty much Mexico and the Southwest, so he'd set up camp near Vegas, out in the desert. It was a short, quiet flight, and when my two new friends wordlessly

opened the hatch again, we were on the roof of Ruberto's temporary Southwest headquarters, a six-story building in the center
of a Second Army encampment, powered by sixteen generators.
It was airtight, climate controlled, earthquake resistant, and
rumors said it had been built with walls thick enough to with-
stand a direct missile hit or two. They'd built it in six weeks,
prefab.

I pulled myself out and stood on the roof for a moment,
looking down at the camp, ringed by a tall chain-link fence.
Ten thousand troops, divided among armored units and hover
squads, all at Ruberto's command. The camp went on and on,
tiny people moving this way and that. I lit a fresh cigarette and
contemplated having the power to just summon something like
this out of thin air. Two years ago when I'd been scooped up
and sent to Chengara, there hadn't *been* a System Army—Earth
was unified, after all. Ruberto and his fellow Undersecretaries
waved their hands, and here the army was, as if it had always
been.

I headed for the elevator, where a broad-shouldered black
man with shiny, curly hair stood stiffly in a decent gray suit,
deep sweat stains the only sign that he must have been suffering.
I nodded at him, but he ignored me, gesturing the elevator doors
closed and then just standing there with his big hands folded at
his groin. We rode it down one floor in companionable silence.
I studied him, and he studied the opposite wall of the cab, both
of us sweating freely in the heavy air it had brought down from
the roof, and when the doors split open again, admitting a blast
of frozen air, I simply stepped into the foyer without a word.

Two soldiers with gleaming, polished sidearms stood on
either side of the formidable-looking black door. They didn't look
at me or appear to move at all, even to breathe. I didn't waste any
time playing with them—I knew from experience there was
nothing I could do to them that would get a reaction. I just blew
smoke around and stepped up to the fingerprint scanner bolted

in next to the door and jabbed my thumb onto it. After a moment it lit up green, and the door clicked open. I pushed it open just enough to slip through it.

It was frigid and white beyond the door, holographic projectors making the office appear to be snowbound, huge drifts of snow blown gently around by the wind. Springing up in the midst of this winter scene was a long white bar, without stools, that stretched off to my left, ruining the illusion. The wall across from me was a huge window, floor to ceiling, in front of which sat the only furniture in the room, a massive dark wooden desk, a plush-looking black leather chair gleaming behind it. Two deep upholstered chairs faced this, the sort of chairs you sank down into and never escaped. The sort of chairs you got killed in, struggling halfway up out of the pit before they got the wire around your neck, the knife into your belly, the gun against your skull.

There was no one else in the room. There was one other door off to the right of the desk, and I could hear water running. Ruberto loved his water. He had it hovered in every day from up north and used most of it in the fucking bathroom. Feeling gritty and suddenly chilled in the crank air, I reached over the bar and retrieved a bottle at random and one of Ruberto's cube glasses, the glass thick and custom cut. I poured a few fingers of something brown into the glass and turned to lean back against the bar, swirling my drink around and enjoying the scene. If you stayed still and just used your eyes, the trick was pretty good.

The door opened, admitting a thick cloud of steam into the room, and then the Undersecretary himself emerged, a tall black man with a round head shaved close, his feet emerging from beneath a thick, white robe at a sharp angle to each other, duck feet. He was rubbing his head with an equally bright white towel, his belly jiggling impressively. I could smell him from where I was, like he was perfumed. The bit of chest exposed by the robe was puckered and scarred, an old wound that looked like it had taken years to heal completely.

"Ah," he boomed, his voice deep, like it was coming up from the floor, like lava. "Good. I see you've made yourself at home."

I pushed off from the bar as he headed for his desk. "I see you're still a fat fuck."

He laughed. Cal Ruberto's laugh started in his belly and erupted upward until he threw his head back and let it burst out of him, his whole body shaking. He tossed the towel onto the desk and dropped heavily into the plush chair, sweeping his arm at the chairs across from him by way of invitation. I ignored him and sipped my drink: rum, it turned out.

"I enjoy that sort of ribbing," the Undersecretary said, patting his midsection. "Keeps me honest. I started out in the force, did you know that? The SSF. I didn't do well and mustered out. At any rate, I got quite used to friendly abuse. Police are a rough sort." He glanced up at me. "Oh, for heaven's sake, is there some sort of Gunner's code that you can't sit down?"

I shrugged, swirling my drink like I'd seen some of the swells in Vegas do it. "You going to tell me everyone who's come into this office has walked out?"

His smile thinned out, and he leaned back, lacing his fingers across his stomach. "Someday we will have to teach you how to behave, my friend."

I winked. "If I behaved, I wouldn't be useful to you. Thanks for getting me out of Vegas."

He looked down at his desk and began gesturing busily, the surface glowing softly with awakened data streams. "I didn't do you any favors. I have a new assignment for you."

"A new job offer, you mean," I said, draining my glass and heading back for the bar. "I'm not on fucking salary, Cal. I take your jobs because you pay well. And I enjoy my work."

Behind me, he chuckled, sounding distracted. "Of course. Now, would you kindly attend to me? I don't have much time."

I refilled my glass and knocked it back, tasting nothing. I could drink all day and not feel a thing. I filled it again anyway and took it with me back to the desk. "Go ahead, Cal. I won't be much use to you in Vegas anymore, though. I'm burned in that town after the Russian."

He didn't look up from his desk, his fat hands moving in intricate patterns, his eyes following the glowing icons and text streams. "Not Vegas." He suddenly looked up and smiled at me. "Rejoice, my friend! You're going home." His hands finally stopped, and he cocked his head as if considering something. "We are at war. With the police, the SSF. And, frankly, it's not going as well as I would have hoped—it is taking too much time. So a drastic, dramatic act is required." He looked down again, hands moving. "And I wouldn't worry about being burned—if you pull this one off, despite your small role, you'll be burned *everywhere*."

I watched his hands in fascination. "Uh, yeah? Who is it?"

This time he did pause and look at me from under his thin eyebrows. He didn't say anything for a second, and then he smiled a little—a tiny, cold smile that conveyed exactly the opposite of what smiles usually conveyed. "Dick Marin, my friend. The King Worm himself."

IV

EVERYONE ELSE WAS JUST CROWD

"Oh, now, this is a fucking shame, a fucking shame," Michaleen muttered, handing me a cigarette produced from some secret place as we watched Bartlett.

I accepted the cigarette wordlessly with a sweat-slick hand. I was already thirty-nine cigarettes in debt to Michaleen. Who knew where he got them from, and so far they'd been offered freely, but I was waiting for his pitch. Michaleen Garda was the name he'd given, and he had adopted me. Why the little man had so much pull in Chengara was still a mystery, since as far as I could tell, he was a funny little guy who kept book on anything with doubt in the outcome. But he pretty much ran the fucking prison.

Bartlett was a tall black guy, old but still in good shape. He stood in the middle of the yard, shirtless and shining with sweat, surrounded by a screaming crowd and taking on all comers. He turned his head a little and spat bright red blood onto the sandy ground, his swollen face twisted into a mask of purplish rage. He stared around at the crowd of inmates and extended his hand, curling his fingers in invitation. I could see his tormentors pretty clearly; the only one that caught my eye was the girl — tall and burned to a crispy red by the sun, which just made her body art look like complex veins of green rot crawling through her skin. She wasn't pretty—no tits to speak of, and a nose that should have been broken a few more times in an attempt to get it back to its roots—but she was *interesting*, the way she'd sold off every acre of her skin for ink, all the way up to her neck and down to her ankles. Her face, unfortunately, was free and clear, and her broken, snaggly teeth crept out in a sneering grin far too often. She was wearing a pair of super-short pants and a top of stretchy material and nothing else, barefoot, her short, self-cut black hair tied up in several messy knots. I wanted to ask her what all the art meant, but I hadn't gotten a formal introduction yet, and I didn't know if she was the sort to kick you in the balls for asking.

Everyone else was just crowd.

"Come on!" Bartlett shouted, his hoarse voice like molten lead bubbling up out of that barrel-chested body. "Come on, you fuckin' dogs!"

I leaned over and let Michaleen light my cigarette. "The Pig's got heart," I said. "You got to admit it."

"Fucking cop has heart, yes, yes." Michaleen nodded, lighting his own cigarette, his sharp eyes squinted and hidden beneath his bushy white eyebrows. "Heart indeed. I have no sympathy for the System Police, you know, Avery, but this is uncivilized. No one can take on five hundred men and live. They want the cop dead? Fine, fine—but do it civilized-like, you see?"

I nodded. I agreed in principle. Bartlett had been a captain in the System Security Force, burned for some unknown crime against Internal Affairs—the Worms, the cops called them. For some reason known only to Dick Marin and his gear-and-silicone brain, Bartlett had been sent here instead of just being killed. Though the way things were going, it was going to turn out to be pretty much the same thing. I held Michaleen's cigarette in front of me as we sat on the dirt, watching the festivities.

"You want to help him out?" I suggested, curious where

the little man was going with this. "You think he needs some friends?"

The little man turned and offered me a comically horrified face. "Help out a fucking Pig, man, are you insane?" He jerked his head toward Bartlett, who'd fought six men bare fisted so far and put them all down, and now stood panting and sweating, arms up weakly while the crowd voted who took him on next. "Whatever he did to bring Marin's ire down on him, that's on him, eh?"

I shrugged, looking around. "Okay."

Chengara wasn't much of a prison, I didn't think. It was basically a huge yard surrounded by admittedly high walls. In the middle were two simple, cinder block buildings: a big cavernous one filled with cots and some tables where we lived, and a smaller one where the administration offices were. I'd never been inside the smaller one, which was a pretty formidable-looking structure, complete with some serious security systems—it didn't even have windows. Each corner of the wall had a guard tower, where a single Crusher was always stationed with a high-powered rifle. The only thing that made Chengara hard to get out of was the desert. Just sitting there next to Michaleen, the heat was wearing me down, beating me into the ground. We received a nutrition tab and four pints of water every day, which meant we were all more or less dying very slowly as we baked in the sun—the idea of walking any distance without more water, food, or shelter was madness.

"You're a bloody pill, Cates, you is. You want to help the Pig? Go ahead." He swept a tiny hand around the yard. "No one's stopping you."

I shrugged. "It's a fair fight," I said. "He takes his chances, just like the rest of us."

"Very wise, kiddo. That's what I heard when I heard the name Cates, out of New York: Smart. Smarter than your average Gunner at least, which maybe ain't saying so much."

I nodded absently. Michaleen liked to talk. I was already bored with listening to him all the time. He was an endless stream of information, though, about the prison; over the last few days he'd filled me in on the way things were in Chengara Penitentiary. He'd told me there was no program or schedule—the Crushers barely appeared, and if they did, they did so in force, overwhelming and unforgiving—that we were more or less left to shift for ourselves, with no work, no activities, no structured time at all. And he'd told me that if you misbehaved enough to bring the Crushers out of their hidey-holes, you were carted off to solitary. And so far no one had ever returned from solitary.

"Let me ask you something, Mickey?"

Out of the corner of my eye, I saw him shift and squint; he didn't like being called Mickey. "Certainly, Mr. Cates," he said, exhaling smoke through his wide, flat nose. "I am at yer service."

"Why are you treating me like your long-lost son? Ever since I got here you've been fucking glad-handing me."

He sat smoking, and I turned my attention back to Bartlett, giving the little man time to consider his answer. A new champion had been elected from the crowd, a broad-shouldered white guy with the flabby look of an Augment junkie who'd been away from his stabilizer meds, long dirty hair hanging down past his shoulders. He looked like he smelled pretty bad, and I considered it a rare talent to *look* like you smelled a certain way. The crowd of identical orange jumpsuits was shouting a hundred things at once as Bartlett watched the new guy circle around him, waiting for the first move.

As I watched, something in the longhair's hand glinted brightly in the sun, and I narrowed my eyes, my heart picking up speed. He was taunting the ex-cop, circling around like a moon caught in the black man's orbit, but he was keeping his hands down and back a little. I saw the glint again and struggled to my feet, my bad leg reluctant to move. I plucked the cigarette from my mouth and walked in my uneven roll toward the scrum, trying to will some life back into the leg, some flexibility. The longhair kept circling and shouting abuse, a fucking punk, trying to look tough but afraid to lean in and start it off unless he saw an opening for him to use the shiv. The crowd got louder as I got closer, and when I reached its outer perimeter, I took one last deep drag off the cigarette and tossed it aside, grabbing two shoulders in my hands and pushing my way through.

As I stepped into the empty space around the two men, the crowd noise died off, collapsing into a low murmur and then whipped away by the dry wind. The sun was like a lamp held over my head, an inch away, burning a circle onto the thin skin of my skull.

The punk noticed the silence just as I got to him and half turned as I reached out to grab his arm. He cursed in some language I didn't understand, all consonants and clearing his throat, and tried to dance back from me. I caught hold of his jumpsuit and yanked, smacking my fist into his stomach as hard as I could and snatching at his wrist as I let go of his suit. His breath exploded out of him with a grunt and he tried to go down to his knees, but I twisted him around—liking the familiar feel of the move, like pieces of me dropping back into place—until his arm was bent back toward me and he was hanging from his wrist. I reached up and took the shiv from his weak grasp, a pretty thing made from a piece of sharpened stone and some dark, coarse fabric.

He smelled as bad as I'd expected.

I leaned down and put my mouth next to his ear. "You want to fight, you fight," I said, panting. "You pull a pot sticker like this, you better be sure no one can take it away from you." I gave his arm a yank, and he screamed, dropping limply to the ground when I released him. I turned, and there was Bartlett, staring down at me. He was fucking enormous. I'd never seen a bigger un-Augmented man in my life.

"Thanks," he said, a grunt of a word, and spat at my feet, just missing my cracked boots.

I looked him up and down. Behind him, I could see a fresh trainload of Interesting People being unloaded behind the thick, electrified chain-link fence, including a tall, fragile-looking old woman with white hair cut very close to her pink scalp, her face deeply wrinkled, her eyes tiny, unhappy slits. Her black coat was too heavy and looked expensive, though it had seen some rough treatment on the train. For a second I imagined our eyes met, though at that distance it was impossible to tell, and I thought I recognized her—a face from the Vids. She was ancient and looked like a strong wind would blow her away, but in that instant I had an impression of strength that disturbed me. I wasn't used to old ladies freaking me out.

"Fuck you," I said to the cop without looking back at him, and stepped around. The crowd didn't exactly part, but it was easier getting through it the second time. As I walked back to Michaleen, I examined the homemade knife and liked it—it was light and looked lethal, decently balanced, and easy to hide. I slipped it into the big pocket of my jumpsuit and resumed my seat next to the little man. A new combatant had already stepped forward, and Bartlett was beating him to a pulp with brutal, red-eyed efficiency.

Michaleen turned to squint at me, his fleshy face folded up into a mask of perplexity that was almost amusing. "That was an odd decision, Mr. Cates," he said.

I shrugged. "He deserves to get killed in a fair fucking fight," I said, accepting yet another cigarette as it was held out for me. "Besides, I spent years killing cops, and look where it got me." I ignored the proffered lighter and slid the cigarette behind my ear. "Maybe I'll see what happens when I save their lives."

"Well, you've brought attention onto yourself, ain't you?" he said after a moment. "You've led a blessed life, Avery, my boy—not a lot of prison time logged. Let me give you a lesson: attention's the last thing you ever want."

"I don't learn easy," I said with a sigh, feeling tired, sweating freely. Fuck his tiny air of midget wisdom.

The little man cackled. "Oy, that's right, ain't it, ain't it. No one tells the great Gunner what to do, eh?" He sobered and looked down at his feet. "Which is why, Mr. Cates, I ain't gonna *tell* you to do anything. I'm gonna *ask* you to listen to a proposition."

I cocked my head but didn't look at him. This was it; this was the pitch. I had a feeling my first three days in Chengara had been softened quite a bit by Michaleen, in unseen ways. I was interested to see what he thought all that was worth.

"What can I do for you, Michaleen?"

"Oh," he sputtered. "What can you do for me, you murderous bastard. Why, you can help me break out of this shithole. That's what you can do for me."

V

HARD PEOPLE DOING A HARD JOB

I awoke suddenly, opening my eyes and completely online in a split second. It was always like that now; I'd never been a heavy sleeper—heavy sleepers woke up with empty pockets and slit throats—but now I lit up from a complete blackout kind of slumber like a switch had been flicked. I'd gotten paranoid back in prison, where I'd been a pretty popular target, but I didn't think I'd ever get used to it.

"Welcome back to the land of the living," I heard Ruberto say. "Did I tell you this guy could sleep? If I had that much blood on my hands, I would lie awake screaming all night. Mr. Cates shuts down like he doesn't have a worry in his head."

I blinked around. I was sitting in a comfortable leather seat that spun silently in response to any shift in weight. As I was turned around, I saw I was in a sumptuous hover cabin done up to resemble a luxurious hotel room—wood paneling on the walls, expensive furniture bolted into place, low music in the air. When the two men came into my view, I stared at them stupidly for a few seconds before I recognized Ruberto, sitting plump and primped in a beautiful pink suit behind a tiny built-in desk, his fucking lady hands still moving in silent, complex patterns over his work space.

The other man I'd never seen before. He was deeply tan,

with shiny black hair cropped close to his head except for the top, which flopped around in an uneven wave. He was tall, too, uncomfortably squeezed into the seat, his legs stretched out as far as he could get them. His suit was dark blue and just as snazzy, a few ten thousand yen of fabric on his back shimmering in the light, and he wore several gold rings on his long, slow-looking fingers. He had a familiar young-old look about him, and piercing, unblinking eyes that were familiar to me. A psionic, I decided. I'd seen enough of them to know, and they all worked for the civilian government—the Spooks. For a moment we sat and stared at each other.

"Maybe he cries himself to sleep," the psionic said.

I smiled. "I cried, once. Didn't enjoy it."

This earned me a smirk, which I also didn't like much.

"We are currently over Ohio," Ruberto said distractedly, not looking up. "We will be near New York City in about half an hour." He looked up at me from under his eyebrows. "Can't get you too close, unfortunately. Director Marin *owns* New York, and we won't get into its airspace without an incident. Neely, give our boy the rundown."

Neely and I looked at each other again. I didn't recall agreeing to the job, but of course, I had: I'd been hoping to have a shot at Dick Marin for years. Problem was, most of the Dick Marins you ran into on the street were avatars, Droids with digital brains, controlled like smart puppets from diverse locations. I didn't even know if there was a real, human Richard Marin left or if he was totally digital. You could kill hundreds of Marins and he'd still be there, like mold.

"This is the guy?" Neely said, staring at me. "He looks like a fucking slug, boss."

Ruberto smiled down at his desk. "Play nice, please."

Neely shrugged, arching his thick black eyebrows. The hum of the hover was lulling, a steady rhythm that tugged at you. "Okay," he said, turning back to me. "Marin *is* the cops, right?

I mean, we don't have anything against the System Security Force—good people, just about every one of them."

I smiled wide. "Speak for yourself," I advised.

"Hard people doing a hard job," Ruberto murmured softly, like he was cooing to his lap desk.

Neely spread his huge, supple hands, the sort of hands that would be good at strangling you. "It's Marin. He's the poison. He's the problem here. He's fucking power mad—excuse my language, boss."

Ruberto nodded absently.

"He thinks he got elected mayor of the whole fucking System," Neely went on, shooting his cuffs and shrugging his shoulders inside his expensive suit. "Cut that motherfucker's head off, and the cops go back to just bein' cops, right? Sorry again, boss."

I leaned forward, putting my elbows on my knees. "You can't kill Marin," I said slowly. "You kill him, three more crawl out of the shadows to shoot at you."

Ruberto chuckled, but Neely just gave me those blank eyes. "Right, if you go after the fucking avatars like an asshole." He leaned over to his side and extracted a sheet of shiny electric paper from a thin briefcase. He handed it over to me, the sheet catching the light and reflecting a shimmering silver back at me. As I took it in my numb hands, it made a metallic, flexible noise, the print blurring and refreshing at odd angles. I snapped it back into shape but didn't look at it, keeping my attention on Neely, who was the sort of guy who lunged at you when you were distracted.

"You need to go after the Prime," he said, nodding at the sheet. "Kill the Prime, and every fucking avatar on the streets of the System will hit the bricks."

"Problem solved," Ruberto said, nodding his head slightly.

"The avatars have a complete template of the controlling intelligence, of course," Neely said. "But they don't have any kind of real-time backup—they're flat templates. Snapshots. Everything gets fed back to the Prime, and the Prime issues all the commands. The avatars can function on their own, of course, but without the Prime there is no coordination. You'd suddenly have a thousand Director Marins scattered everywhere, little puddles of authority."

"Chaos," Ruberto murmured.

"Anarchy," Neely echoed.

I glanced down at the sheet, flipping through the specifications quickly with curt gestures. "Why can't you go after the Prime remotely? Hack it?"

"Independent network," Ruberto muttered, hands moving delicately.

"Independent network," Neely echoed, spreading his hands, jewelry flashing. "Dedicated infrastructure; unique handshakes and encryption; heavy-duty, rolling security. The rest of the System could go dark, and Marins would still be running around. Marin doesn't share bandwidth. You have to take out the Prime." He leaned back. "Take out the Prime, and the SSF is headless."

"Order is restored," Ruberto said quietly.

"Problem solved," Neely finished.

We all sat there in silence for a moment. I flipped through the specs again. "This Prime unit is in Moscow. Fucking *Russia?*" I was never going to be free of the Ivans.

Neely nodded. "Fucking Moscow. SSF HQ is New York; Marin decided it was best if Internal Affairs was headquartered as far away as possible. The Kremlin was fortified during Unification; it's as tough a nut to crack as you'll find, so he settled in there, when he's not on the move."

"A man after my own heart," Ruberto muttered.

My eyes kept sweeping the sheet. "That's a huge storage and UPS. I've never seen an uninterrupted power supply that heavy."

"The Prime is not mobile," Neely said immediately. "Its hardware demands keep it stationary."

I nodded and looked back at them. Ruberto was smiling and nodding his round head a little, as if something on his desktop amused him a great deal. Neely had his dark little eyes locked on me, those brutal hands steepled in front of him. Fucking government. They all thought they were civilization itself, salvation in human form—the cops, the Undersecretaries, and now their fucking flunkies the Spooks. They were all just gangsters.

"How do I kill the Prime, then?"

Neely gave me a flat, unimpressed stare. "You can't just waltz in, put a bullet into some black box, and that's it. The Prime is a fucking complex, it's a building unto itself, several floors below ground. Server banks, big pieces of tech. Generators, signal boosters, an army of Techies. The Prime *is* Moscow, practically. There's, of course, ancillary security." He shrugged. "In the form of his Worms, the Internal Affairs elite officers. The *Worms*."

"Also avatars," Ruberto said softly.

"Also avatars," Neely agreed without expression, his dead eyes staring at me. I stared back for a moment, the words hanging there between us.

"Excuse me?"

"That's what Marin's doing. That's what this is all *about*," Ruberto said, his eyes popping open while the rest of him remained perfectly still. Around us, the whine of displacement shifted down a bit, which meant we were near our destination. "That fucking insane dictator is making the System Security Force into an army of avatars—digital intelligences ripped right out of the brains of real, actual cops. He can mass-produce copies, each one with all the skills and memories of the original. Plus—"

"Programming," Neely said.

"Programming," Ruberto echoed. "They're like the original cops—look the same, act the same—but the fucking maniac can insert instructions into their templates. So not only are his cops—his fucking *army* of cops—inexhaustible and replace-able, but he can *control* them."

"This is what the prick's doing," Neely interjected.

"We estimate that about half the force has so far been trans-formed," Ruberto said, suddenly standing up, his plump little body almost bouncing as he began to pace, his hands pushed deep into his pockets. "This is what we're *fighting* against. He has displayed bad faith."

Neely stared at me for a moment, silent. I looked around, knowing this was not going to end well for me. They weren't going to send any of their own into the saw blade—why not send Cates? We keep throwing him into the fire, and he some-how crawls out.

"So the Prime is the installation," I said slowly, feeling my way through it. "It's not just a single fancy avatar. It's the whole fucking—what, building? City block? *City?*" Silently, I fervently hoped they did not tell me Marin's Prime was an entire fucking city.

"The Kremlin," Ruberto said, sounding distracted as he paced.

"The whole building," Neely offered. "Whole thing has to be fucking nuked to take him out."

"We're launching an offensive to take Moscow," Ruberto said briskly, returning to his seat. "The general staff is not optimis-tic. Moscow's defenses are extensive, and it's historically been a tough nut to crack."

I took his word for that.

"So you're insurance," Neely finished. "We'll try to get in, bomb the fucking place to hell. In case we can't, you go in, tear him down local."

It was curious, how stupid they thought I was. "And if I'm sitting there with my thumb up my ass when you break through the lines and start bombing?"

"You are being *compensated*," Ruberto said, sounding exasperated. They always thought it was all about yen.

Neely smiled as if it were all settled. "Marin's in the process of converting his cops into *avatars*," he said. "It's not complete yet. He's started with the street cops and now he's moving into the upper ranks—and he hasn't touched the Technical Associates at all. He's worried."

"The spark," Ruberto said, standing up.

"Whatever," Neely said, sitting forward and clasping his hands in front of himself. "He's moving slow, being careful. This guy, name's Gall"—he reached over and tapped the sheet of paper, making it shimmer—"is in charge of Marin's Kremlin security. Internal Affairs, old-school, one of Marin's original recruits. Draws a lot of water, gets a lot of leeway from Marin, and pretty much does what he wants. He gets around, has his fingers in a lot of pies, most illegal, but Marin gives him a pass. You name it, this bastard does it: protection schemes—"

"Large scale," Ruberto said, pacing.

"On a *huge* scale. Political favors, fuck, he even bodyguards VIPs for a million yen a week. This guy directs all Kremlin security. Get to him. That's step one. Get to him before Marin tin cans him, and you'll know everything there is to know about the security situation."

I studied the digipaper for a moment. A big-shot Worm, all right, living the high life. Not easy work. I snapped the sheet again and the data flowed up from the bottom, his public SSF record—more fucking redactions than text—a grainy old picture that almost looked pre-Unification.

"You in, Cates?" Neely spread his big hands, each finger like a limb of its own. "I know you suffered terribly in prison, assrape and silent, private tears and all that shit. You don't have the nerve for this, just say so."

Ruberto crossed over to stand behind Neely and put a hand

on the sitting man's shoulder. "Trust me, Neely, this man has
done amazing, terrible things. This is our man."

I looked up at the fat Undersecretary, numb and feeling one
of my fuzzy moments coming on like glue filling my head. "Why
are we going to New York if my mark's in Moscow?"

"Gall is in constant motion; we don't know exactly where
he'll be," Neely snapped, sounding impatient. "You'll need to
make contact, get some fucking intelligence, not just go tearing
ass into the wilderness."

Ruberto looked down at his small feet for a moment, then
directly at me. "Well, what do you say? I realize this is a bit
more complex than our usual arrangements, and once you're
behind their lines in New York, we can offer you no more direct
resources, unfortunately. Here and there we may be able to pass
information or other aid to you, but it will be unpredictable."

"The fucking cops kill our people when they find them,"
Neely said. "But there's one name we can give you: Krajian. Cop,
but she's clued in on what Marin's doing—"

"First the cops, then *everyone*," Ruberto said. "All of us, taking the King Worm's invisible orders."

"—And she ain't happy about it. We don't manage her as an
asset, so you take your chances, you contact her. But it's all we
can give you for now, as long as the city's basically under siege."

"So!" Ruberto snapped, suddenly jolly. "Name your fee. This
is an unusual assignment. Name your fee for your assistance."

I looked from Ruberto to Neely and back again as the hover
began to slow. I figured my odds of death had just shot up tre-
mendously, but felt nothing. "My fee? Shit, Cal, if this puts Marin
in a grave, I'll do it for free."

Neither of them seemed surprised.

VI

A HEAVY BOLT OF FABRIC STRETCHED ALL AROUND US, SUFFOCATING

I was dying of thirst, and I was about to be stabbed.

I hadn't been in prison since I'd been a kid, three months in a juvie center in New York a lifetime ago, before the rules had changed removing the juvenile distinction. I'd been lucky, then, caught out by some loafing Crushers instead of some hardcase System Pig — it was the difference between juvie and just being beaten to death, or worse. It had been easy time, and I'd made my first big-deal contacts back then, older kids on the cusp who introduced me around, put the first knife in my hand, pointed me at someone's jugular and the big money. Easy as it had been, there'd been chores, and bored Crushers with electric prods to get your ass in motion, and I'd gone to bed every night sore and exhausted from cleaning the fucking bathrooms until they glowed and a million other backbreaking chores.

Chengara Penitentiary was something completely unexpected. I'd been in-house for a week and so far hadn't been given a single chore, command, or beating. There were Crushers around, sure, but we only saw them when something went seriously off the rails, when a riot seemed to be brewing. Then they were everywhere, all at once, but only as long as it took to get things back in order, and then *poof!* They were gone again.

Mainly, they used water to keep us quiet.

The heat was like a heavy bolt of fabric stretched all around us, suffocating. Twice a day we got our nutrition tab and water ration. We lined up, meek and quiet, took our share, and did our best to make it last, to make it seem like it was enough. It wasn't. It was just below *enough*, making us all shrink. And when we acted up, the next ration got canceled, and you spent a sleepless night feeling your own body chewing on itself. In my week it had happened twice, and already I'd been trained to just get on line and keep my mouth shut.

Meanwhile, there was no work detail, no required activity, no schedule at all aside from the dole. We lounged around, we got into fights, we worked a primitive economy, and we talked a lot about the jobs we'd pull when we got out, and the Crushers let us. As long as we didn't cause too much trouble, they let us do whatever we wanted and didn't seem to care.

I eyed my two admirers while the dole line moved forward a step. In front of me were five or six soft-looking middle-agers, two men and a woman in their thirties who'd aged considerably since arriving, their faces haggard, their posture slumped. They wore their jumpsuits like they hurt them. When they'd arrived a week before they'd been plump and sleek, if a bit ruffled. Politicos, support staff for some Undersecretary—now just People of Interest, like the rest of us. It was the strangest prison I'd ever heard of, but some things were universal, like having people who wanted to kill me.

The skinny Asian kid who'd jumped me off the train and the long-haired asshole I'd disarmed out in the yard a few days ago had made friends and were out of line a dozen feet ahead of me. They leaned against the wall in their bright orange suits, staring at me. When I'd first noticed them, I'd been incredulous—was their plan *really* to just stand there waiting for me to come within reach and then jump me? It seemed impossible. The line moved a foot at a time toward the little booth where the single Crusher stood, taking his damned time about issuing each prisoner's ration. I kept my hands in my jumpsuit's pockets, one wrapped around the shiv I'd taken from the longhair, the other curled into a fist.

The line lurched forward, and suddenly someone was at my side. Since he only came up to my elbow, I knew it was Michaleen, and didn't even look down at him.

"Fucking morons," I muttered. "You see this?"

It was amazing how quickly I'd taken to the little man. His wrinkled, loose face was folded around an unlit cigarette, as usual, and his hairy, short arms disappeared into the deep pockets of his own jumpsuit. "The youth of today," he said, shaking his head. "It's a fuckin' tragedy."

I nodded. "Give me some room, Mickey."

He pulled one short arm from his suit and laid a calloused, gentle hand on my arm. "Not here, Avery, not here. You can get away with a lot, but you don't fuck with the dole. Copy? They get all bent out of shape if you mess with the dole. You fellows start a scrum down here and you'll end up in solitary."

I turned my head until my neck cracked. I couldn't just let it go. I was an old man, and I'd been pinched. If I started to walk away from fights, I was as good as dead. "I can handle solitary."

"Avery," Michaleen said in a low, intense voice. "Listen to me. I've been here in this fucking hell a *long* time. No one ever comes *back* from solitary."

I took my eyes from the geniuses and put them on Michaleen's upturned face. I wondered how exactly he'd managed to remain here a *long* time. Everyone else seemed to be here on a strictly temporary basis. He gestured and a stooped, round-shouldered man with peppery hair and nervous, quick eyes that tried to be everywhere at once stepped forward.

"Avery, this is Guy," the little man said, pronouncing it,

unfortunately, as *Gee* with a hard *g*. "He was in the banking line until a few weeks ago, when the Pigs plucked him outta his plush little apartment in Washington. He's graciously agreed to take your place in line and collect your ration in exchange for some...considerations."

Guy didn't look at me, though he flinched away from me as if I'd made a move at him. "And you said I'd be *protected* on line," he whispered.

"Yes, yes," Michaleen said soothingly. "No one'll touch you because I say not to. Now, you've heard of the right honorable Avery Cates, yes? So you know what happens if you screw him out of his ration, yes?" He leaned in to mock-whisper in Guy's ear and winked at me. "Here's a hint, boyo: he kills people. Yes?" The little man slapped him on the shoulder and waggled his eyebrows at me. "Okay?"

I glanced at the geniuses again, still glaring at me with undiminished hatred. Where'd they get the energy? How in the world did they just keep it up like that? I wasn't where I'd been back in the ruined shell of Pickering's when the cops had picked me up—I'd come back up for air. But I still wanted to nap half the fucking time, just let everything wash over me.

"Why do I want to leave the line, Mickey?" I said, letting the knife slip from my hand inside my pocket. "I like it here." I realized that I was still holding on to one thing from the Plague, from shuffling through the burned remains of New York: I didn't care about dying. Everything else had come back to me, but I thought of dying and felt nothing.

Michaleen nodded as if he agreed with everything I'd said, wholeheartedly and without reservation. "We're havin' a meeting, concerning the escape project."

He started walking away at as brisk a pace as his short legs would take him, and I cursed a little under my breath, stepping out of the line to follow him. "All right," I muttered, falling into step beside him. "All fucking right, you little runt, is this

question-and-answer time? We're gonna talk?" A lump of corrosive anger formed in my belly, suddenly there fully formed.
I reached out and grabbed the little guy by the shoulder. He
paused and...almost moved, his body twitching familiarly
beneath my grip. Then he went still and closed his eyes.

"All right," he said after a moment, opening them again and
looking at me. "All right, Avery. You are irritated, I can see. Let's
have a quick chat then, on our way to the others."

I stared down at him. I'd had the craziest feeling—an
instinct, feral and speechless—that he'd been about to turn on
me, to come *after* me. A man two feet shorter than me, a hundred pounds lighter. Thirty years older, if not more. For a second, every alarm in my head had lit up bright and worried, and
it didn't make sense—I wasn't worried about *Michaleen*. I could
fit Michaleen in my fucking *pocket*.

We looked at each other for a long moment. It was a familiar flat stare, one I'd shared a million times: Michaleen was a
pro. He was an old hand, and suddenly, we understood each
other perfectly. I let my eyes slip past him, and there was the
old woman I'd seen arriving the other day, sitting fiercely erect
at one of the bare metal tables provided. Her hair was mussed,
standing up crazily in several directions, but she didn't look too
bad for an old bag in prison. She was smoking a cigarette and
looking right back at me. I still couldn't place her face.

"All right," I said, nodding and looking back at Michaleen.
"Let's go." He turned to start walking, and I put my hand out
again, once more feeling him stiffen in that oddly familiar, pri-
mal way, like he was forcing himself to stay calm, let it pass. I
grinned suddenly. I *wanted* to see this little man go apeshit. I
wanted very badly to see what the old bastard could do.

"No more fucking cigarettes," I said. "I'm not your fucking
performing monkey, and I'm not being trained to drool every
time you whip one out, okay? If I'm in, I'm in for myself."

He stood there for another moment and then nodded, turning his familiar, fake-as-hell grin on me. I saw through it now. His eyes were hard and dead, even if his face was twisted up comically. "All righty, then, Mr. Cates. You fucking owe me three packs of good cigarettes. You can work it off, eh?"

"Fine. Why are you my best friend, Mickey?"

There was some movement behind my shoulder, and I cursed myself for turning my back on my two fans. As I started to hunch down and move my shoulder to take whatever impact was coming, Mickey dived under my arm.

The tall, skinny prick from the train was right behind us. A grin spread across his face as Mickey stepped up to him, but the little man didn't hesitate or say anything, lashing out a solid punch right at the kid's balls with one calloused hand. The kid's breath shot out of him, and he bent over double with a grunt, cupping his crotch. Michaleen slapped an arm around his neck and jerked him up, hooking one little leg around one of the kid's and bending him backward harshly. The kid seemed to swallow his own tongue, his face instantly turning a shade of purple I found worrying.

"Lad," Mickey said in a calm voice, not sounding out of breath at all. "I see your shadow again today, and you won't be waking up tomorrow, eh? If you understand me, roll your pretty eyes for me."

The kid's eyes began rotating spastically. Mickey nodded and released him in a graceful motion, spinning away as the kid, hacking and coughing, fell to the floor like a sack of shit. The whole thing had lasted ten seconds and produced almost no noise or fuss. I stared at the kid, replaying the scene—it had been a professional little takedown, the sort of ballet moves that took skill and lots of practice. Michaleen, I realized without too much surprise, was a fucking dangerous man, and I felt like clown shoes next to him.

And then the little bastard was on the move, and I had to hurry a bit to catch up.

He led me out into the yard. The Crushers on the towers were distant, but I could feel their tiny eyes on me. My second day some asshole who referred to herself as a Master Thief, whatever the fuck that was, started scaling one of the walls like a fucking insect, somehow finding cracks in the mortar and clinging to it, rising up incredibly fast. One of the Crushers had taken his time, making a show of setting the rifle against his shoulder and taking aim, and then the Master Thief's skull had exploded silently, a neat little plume of red. She'd left a nice red stain on the wall. It was brown and flaky now, slowly eroded by the endless sandy wind.

"Didja know your father at all, son?"

This with breathless casualness, like it had just occurred to him. A thrill went through me, and I grinned at the air in front of me.

"He's dead," I said. "This I know for a fact, so don't tell me you're my dear old pa, okay?"

He laughed—and I thought it was probably the first real laugh I'd ever heard the little bastard allow, his head shooting back and his shoulders rolling joyfully. "Oh, Mr. Cates, I got hundreds of 'em. Bastards, I mean. I been doin' my part. But"—he bent over briefly, guffawing, staggering as he walked—"but none of 'em are as fucking *gigantic* as you, yeah?"

I couldn't stop a smile from twitching onto my face. "All right. What about him?"

He straightened up, wiping one surprisingly small hand down his face. "I knew him, a little. Not long and not deep, but I knew ol' Aubrey."

The thrill kept vibrating within me, becoming a buzzing electrical current making my skin itch. I had very few memories of my father. I remembered him in a greasy black uniform, a waste disposal worker, and I remembered him shrinking in a huge hospital bed, getting smaller every time I looked at him. A few other random things—him drinking beer from a bottle, a fucking bottle. Him laughing, missing one tooth. Him screaming at my mother, once, terrifying. That was it. "Bullshit," I said. "He worked. He had a job."

"Shit, Avery—before Unification, *everyone* worked. At some-thing." He waved one hand in front of him. "I'm not saying we exchanged love letters and shared our deepest souls. Our paths crossed. We shared the neighborhood for a while. That's all. I just wanted to say, he was a good man, Avery. Every son deserves to hear that. He had his opportunities to turn away and sink low, and he resisted."

I swallowed thickly. "And?"

He sighed. "Where I come from, Avery—the *time,* you understand—knowing someone from the neighborhood meant something. It was a bond. It wasn't just a grudging greeting when you passed in the street, it was being from the same area."

My mind was suddenly racing, flipping through my small stash of memories. "You don't sound local to me," I said, licking my dry lips.

"I didn't say I was born there, Avery. Anyway, I can't con-vince ya of shit if you're suspicious. Just wanted you to know. You want to know why you. Two reasons. The first is because I knew yer people, okay? I ain't leavin' you behind, Avery, and I ain't gonna stand by while Aubrey Cates's son gets his brains sucked out of his skull, okay?" He looked down at the dirt for a moment, grimacing, and then glanced up, sunny again. "Now, here we are."

I wanted to ask him questions, to grill him about it all, the fucking liar. Because I *wanted* to believe him. But he'd stopped purposefully where three other prisoners sat baking. A few pockets of prisoners sat around here and there in the sun, suck-ing down their water rations, chewing their nutrition tabs, look-ing weak and dejected. Every day weaker and more dejected, I guessed. Nearby, the cop, Bartlett, sat gleaming, his jumpsuit undone to his waist, his torso and face a maze of fresh scars and ugly, purple bruises. We looked at each other as I approached but said nothing.

The two of us stood there for a moment with nothing but the sun burning us to ash and the hot, heavy wind pushing lethargically against us. I wasn't impressed. The toughest one of the trio was definitely the illustrated girl I'd noticed before. Her ink was faded and blurred, amateur prison work all of it, but it was colorful and it was *everywhere.* Birds and dragons with long, stretched-out feathers of green and red and gold intertwined with each other, circling around her limbs and up her torso to her neck, where actual figures were abandoned for a more monotone set of bluish patterns that crawled up and disappeared beneath her short, dark hair. Only her face, sharp and angular, was spared. She was scrawny-thin and looked older, I guessed, than she actually was.

She eyed me up and down in a frankly sexual way that made me a little nervous, lingering on my crotch with a raised eyebrow. I gave her a steady look until she brought her eyes back up to my face, but then she held my gaze with no hint of worry until I looked away. She reminded me of the tough broads that had always hung out in Pickering's in the good old days. I felt like I knew her immediately.

Sitting on the hard-packed sandy ground a little removed from her were two others. The first was a skinny older man in affected, ancient wire eyeglasses. One of the lenses was cracked, and he looked about as tough as a flower.

"This is Grigoriy, Avery," Michaleen said.

The old man grinned. "Call me Grisha."

I grinned back. "Fuck, what in hell did *you* do to get in here?"

"I stole some things," he said in a thick Russian accent. He smiled at the floor. "They would like them returned but cannot get to them." He tapped his head.

To the side, Bartlett suddenly guffawed, rich laughter booming into the still air. We all ignored him. He was a burned System

Pig in a prison. He was already a ghost, and we were treating him accordingly.

A Techie, I thought. *Hell, the old man's putting together a* team. Like he'd been hired to do a job.

"Grigoriy also has a knack with explosives. I see you've introduced yourself to Marlena Niks," Michaleen continued, gesturing at the illustrated girl. She twitched and a knife was in her hand, a real knife, smuggled in somehow. She danced it across her knuckles once, showing off perfect balance, and then it disappeared again. I nodded, more impressed that she'd gotten it inside than with her bullshit tricks.

"I've heard of you," I said, memory blooming. "Niks, out of Philly. Call you Skinner. A Taker—you find people."

She grinned. "People who don't want to be found. Wanna fuck?"

Michaleen and I ignored her with the same slight tick of our heads, turning to regard the third of the little man's recruits, a young black girl who was lying back on her elbows, basking, her dark skin gleaming with sweat. Like Bartlett, she'd stripped down her jumpsuit to the waist, unconcerned about her tiny, bare breasts. She looked like she'd last eaten about a year ago and held herself with an exaggerated carelessness that told me she was terrified.

"And this is the Christian," Michaleen said. "I don't know her real fucking name. She's—"

"She's our Snake," I said, eyeing her skinny, flexible body. I let the question of why Michaleen thought he needed someone skilled at squirming through small openings and getting out of locked rooms drift, and kicked the kid lightly. "What's your name?"

The Christian opened one eye and studied me for a moment, then closed it again and stretched luxuriously.

"She don't talk," Michaleen said. "Only heard her once, and she was fucking *praying*. To *god*."

I nodded at her. I'd never met anyone who believed in a god before. "What are you? Catholic?" It was a word I'd heard, long ago, in ancient times. Had it been my mother? A female voice. *Catholic*.

She just stared at me. I gave her a few seconds and then sighed. "All right," I said, losing patience. "You want to break out of this hellhole. Fine. You've got yourself a Taker to steal necessaries and find out info for you, a Techie to hack security systems, and a Snake to get inside tight spaces—pretty fucking handy for an escape, and glory be it's like a fucking criminal hall of fame in this place, so recruiting's easy." I jerked my thumb back at myself. "I'm old and stiff, I don't move fast anymore, I need a lot of space, and I don't make friends easy. Why am I here?"

Michaleen smiled, putting a cigarette into his mouth, his eyes dead and flat as always. "Well, shit, Avery. That would be reason number two, as we were discussin'. Escapin's likely to be a messy business, and no doubt we'll need to kill a few people." He winked. "And no one in this place is better at killin' people than you."

VII

YOUR ONLY CHANCE OF SURVIVING ME

I watched the kid sprint out of The Rock like she was being chased by a swarm of bees. I didn't blame her; I didn't want to be that close to the System Pigs, either. I couldn't enter SSF HQ easily; my face would be scanned upon entrance and moments later I'd be flagged—I was supposed to be in prison, or dead, not standing outside with a cigarette and a fairly new set of clothes.

I watched the kid duck the rare pedicab and the thin foot traffic, running at me with the sort of malnourished energy I hadn't felt in twenty-five years. Her features were vaguely Asian, and she had pale, fish belly skin, tight against her bones. She was wearing an old coat too large for her but in decent shape. Compared to Vegas, New York was fucking *freezing*, though I couldn't feel it. And empty. And smelled vaguely like something was burning in the distance.

"They take the message?"

She nodded, her round face grim and serious. I'd found her down near the old Stadium—one of the last bits of old New York, of *my* New York, that was still there. Squatters were still living there, if you called that living, but even I could tell their time was coming. Under the Emergency Powers Act that had been in force since I'd destroyed—or thought I'd destroyed—Dennis Squalor and the Electric Church, Dick Marin had ordered most of downtown bulldozed since the Plague. It was a wasteland, rubble and cleared lots, some with the beginnings of new construction in place, some just weeded and abandoned. Fresh, new Vid screens proclaimed new luxury homes were coming. As soon as Marin could get the pesky civilian government and their not-so-civilian army off his back, I guessed.

Who was going to live there was another question, since New York was pretty empty. The Plague had killed three-fourths of the old population, rich and poor alike, and the cops had cleared out most of downtown enthusiastically afterward. Even standing right outside SSF Headquarters, in the center of everything, I thought I could hear my steps echo against the buildings.

"Fucking Pigs," the little girl snarled, wiping her nose. "Lookin' at me like I done somethin'. I'll cut their fucking throats." She squinted at me. "Fifty yen. You said."

I nodded. At first I'd thought she reminded me of Gleason, but she didn't. I held out my credit dongle, and she stared at it suspiciously before producing her own. We swiped and she glanced at the tiny indicator on hers, finally nodding. "Okay," she said and took off at a run. I didn't blame her. She stood out uptown—and shit, *all* of Manhattan was uptown now. I watched her dashing through the dribbling traffic until a roar of speeding hovers took my eyes up to the gray sky, a formation of a dozen silvery bricks busting ass overhead.

Uptown wasn't the same anymore, either. As empty as it felt, there was still a crowd—but it was all cops. Cops everywhere, all of them—even the officers—in riot gear, big sweaty gas masks and shiny black armor that made them look like bugs. You could pick out the Crushers, still; they slouched and held their shredding rifles like they were afraid they'd explode in their hands. If you squinted you could pick out the pips on the officers' collars: One for a lieutenant, two for a captain, three for a colonel. Four, I assumed, would mean a major, but you didn't see many of those on the ground. Pairs or triplets of cops were on every corner, and I figured they had Optical Face Scanners wired into their masks, passively snapping every face that came into range and running it by the SSF database, just in case. There were no *people*, just cops, scanning each other. I kept my head down and my sunglasses on and tried to keep moving, to keep transporting my cigarette from my mouth to my hand and back again. Mobile OFR scans were state of the art, but they needed precision. Give 'em blur and they spat out garbage.

I waited, pacing and staying in motion. It was exhausting.

It was a wide avenue, the pavement cracking and a couple of sinkhole-sized ruts threatening the spokes of all the pedicabs. There were still some posh restaurants spilling out onto the street, sparse groups of bored-looking pretty people in expensive suits toying with a glass of wine or a portable Vid. Interspersed were some empty buildings; one narrow sliver of old stone had gray boards stamped over all the windows, making it look blind. Some of the restaurants had signs posted announcing shortages—one had no more coffee, another could offer no fresh vegetables. I stared at that one for a moment, trying to remember if I'd ever eaten a fresh vegetable in my life. I didn't think I had.

The people, what was left of them, had changed a little, too. Right outside Cop Central, Rockefeller Center, and some of the folks staking claim to a few feet of pavement were a little rough around the edges. Not exactly my sort of folks—not downtowners, most of whom had died in the Plague—but still, not the shiny, artificially young swingers who usually populated uptown. I watched one skinny guy on the other side of the street for a few minutes—he was professionally eyeing everyone who walked by, performing thirty-second appraisals. His coat was pretty nice, expensive and in good shape, but his shirt was ancient and patched, and his shoes had no soles. I stared at his feet for a while—the illusion was fucking amazing as long as he stood flat-footed, but every time he lifted a foot there was a flash of bare, tough skin. A Pick, I decided, looking for someone with a loose pocket and a credit dongle they wouldn't miss for a while. I smirked and looked around more carefully, smiling to myself when I spotted his partner, who was actually wearing the same coat, standing just halfway up the block, engrossed in the Vid screen looming over the intersection. Soleless Joe snatches the dongle, walks briskly past his handler, and drops it into a pocket, and even if the Pick gets sussed he walks away, blameless. Unless the System Pigs wanted to get some exercise. Uptown had alleys, too.

I looked around again and had to force myself not to stop and stare at the two men casually not enjoying cold cups of coffee while sitting on the very edge of a café half a block from me. Even if their supernaturally calm, stone-faced demeanor hadn't screamed *cops*, the fact that they were identical twins in every way, including their striking, overtailored suits, would have caught my attention. The fact that they performed every gesture, movement, and weight shift almost simultaneously, one lagging a second or so behind the other, just strummed my alarms a little harder.

On a street that boasted about two dozen System Pigs of various ranks standing around, these two were suddenly the only ones I was worried about.

They were young, good-looking men, hair cut painfully close, square faces red and clean shaven. White, generic, with decent builds—though their suits had so much padding in the shoulders it was hard to judge—and big, nimble hands. I watched them both spinning their coffee spoons with dexterous twitches of their fingers for a few seconds, entranced. They each wore narrow tinted glasses with lenses that glinted purple in the hazy, cloudy light.

For a moment, I thought they might be after me, but I was clearly in their line of sight, and if they'd been looking for me it seemed likely I'd already be in the back of a hover with plastic laces around my wrists and a hood over my head. They were staring fixedly at Cop Central, watching everyone come and go, so I concluded that I was the last thing on their mind.

As I turned away, imagining myself innocent and preoccupied, my contact stepped out of Cop Central, moving fast. At first glance, she was your typical old-school System Cop: all slick clothes and hard edges, moving arrogantly and gracefully down the street. She was wearing a purple pin-striped suit, with matching long coat perfectly cut for her lithe figure. Her dark hair was swept back and up in a complex, fashionable style, and her face was made-up, porcelain in appearance. She wore a simple black patch over one eye, her one good orb glinting with a soft golden glow—an Augment. System Pigs with Augments—the fucking world had turned while I'd been in prison and then in Hell, Nevada.

She turned her head once to scan the street as she walked, and for a quick moment she was looking right at me. She turned away and kept walking, but in that flash I'd seen her face full on. She was terrified.

When the fucking *Pigs* were frightened, I started to worry.

As one, the twins stood and started after her, moving past me without a second glance. As they passed they each produced cigarettes and placed them between their lips with one hand while flipping open a lighter with the other, then cupping their hands around their mouths to light up, all in sync. It was like an invisible mirror followed the one around, reflecting him back to us.

I gave them half a block and watched my contact turn west down Forty-ninth Street. Moving fast but with controlled, easy motion—nothing tight and worried that might trip a crowd analysis Droid—I cut across the street and then in the opposite direction toward Fiftieth Street. If the city hadn't changed too much, I'd beat her to our rendezvous by half a minute or so.

The cops were everywhere in their riot gear. I was used to

cops layering uptown Manhattan like a fine grit, but this was
beyond my most paranoid imaginings: blobs of them every half
block or so, standing around with their faceless masks on or
pushed up onto their heads while they smoked. They didn't chat
or interact, they just watched everyone as they passed, silently
staring at you with those blank plastic goggle eyes. I kept moving past boarded-up storefronts; even the businesses that were
open were festooned with multiple signs concerning what they
didn't have, squatting empty and ominous on the sidewalks,
often with gangs of Crushers hanging about outside. Overhead,
every few minutes I could hear displacement as hovers sailed
by, and I looked up at each and every set, keeping my face in
motion.

A block and a half down Fiftieth Street, there was a narrow alley between buildings, not even wide enough to spread
your arms across. I sidestepped into it in one fluid motion, then
pressed myself back against the wall for a count of five, listening carefully for any sign anyone had taken notice of me. Satisfied, I sprinted down the length of the alley and found the old
fire escape ladder, rusted and creaky but still attached to the
masonry. It shuddered and lurched as I jumped onto it, but I
pulled myself up rapidly, crawling onto the gravel-lined roof.

I paused for a moment. Sitting with its back against the lip of
the roof was a Monk.

You didn't see Monks much anymore. After the Plague the
System Pigs had made it a special project to clean up the Electric
Church's mess once and for all, and for a few months all you saw
were Monks getting flushed from their hiding places and exe-
cuted. They were still *people*, in a sense, still had human brains
inside their chassis, still were citizens of the System, technically.
But where once that had meant something to Dick Marin—back
when he'd been controlled by the programmed limits of his own
digital existence—it hadn't stopped him from ordering their

mass execution. Every now and then a Monk showed up somewhere, and it usually ended with a bullet in its brain. And most people shed no tears.

This one was obviously out of commission: rusted and tattered, it slumped there with both arms stretched out at its sides, stained white palms up. My guess was it had been there for a year or two.

I turned away and ran for the opposite edge. I leaped the gap to the next building easily and took that roof running as well. Three jumps later and I was descending another rusted ladder, this one missing several rungs and leaving me dangling off the ground a good eight or nine feet. I dropped into a steady crouch and popped up again, sprinting for the edge of the alley and skidding to a halt before stepping calmly out onto Seventh Avenue, thirteen steps or so from the huge Vid screen bolted to the side of a run-down old brick building. The reporter on it was a plastic-faced blond girl whose cheekbones were so sharply defined they would cut your hand if you tried to touch them, and the scroll beneath her cleavage was informing us that—in case we hadn't noticed—the illegal siege of New York by forces under the command of Joint Council Undersecretaries continued. It then segued into a lengthy list of shortages and associated conservation edicts that had been enacted. I took up position under the Vid and watched my cop approaching. When she moved past me, I didn't turn or look at her.

"Any reason you've got two Worms on your ass?"

She fooled me. For a second she kept moving forward, just long enough to lull me, and then she whirled viciously, snapping out a telescoping prod and slapping it hard against the back of my knees. I didn't feel a thing, but the joints buckled and I went down onto my knees with a teeth-chattering thud. She was already coming down hard for my head with the rod; I dodged to my right and took the blow on my shoulder, reached out and gripped her ankle with my left hand and yanked, throwing myself off balance but knocking her onto her ass in the process.

I twisted myself up onto my knees again, and she hit me on the nose with her fist, cracking something and knocking me onto my back, my vision flashing purple. I still didn't feel anything, my consolation prize from the System for stealing six months of my life, but I put out a decent muffled scream and played dead, slumped on the cold, damp sidewalk. I snaked my hand under myself and took hold of my Roon automatic, the best handgun ever made. I heard the scrape of her boot and the snapping sound of the rod shrinking back to handheld size, and I let instinct direct me. Springing up, I grabbed blindly, finding a handful of her coat. Pulling as hard as I could, I let my own weight take her down until she was lying on top of me, my gun jabbed into her chest. *Her* gun was thrust painfully into my belly.

All around us, shouts and boots on the pavement.

"Ruberto," I hissed into her ear. "I'm from Ruberto."

She smelled good. Light perfume—not perfume, I decided. *Soap*. She smelled clean. She panted into my neck once, twice, and then she was pushing herself up, staring down at me, her Augmented eye flat and artificial, like it had been animated on her face. She still looked terrified.

"I know what you are," she said. Then she climbed off me, dragging out her gold shield and whirling, showing it to the Crushers who'd surrounded us, shredders aimed, impassive plastic faces steamed from their heavy breathing.

"Back the fuck up," she hissed, spinning, holding her badge out like a talisman. "I'm Captain Helena Krajian, and I said *back the fuck up!*"

The Crushers hesitated. I lay panting on the ground, numb, and my head swam for a moment. I never thought I'd see the day Crushers didn't shit their pants when an officer told them to. It was fucking disturbing.

Krajian didn't like it, either. She paused and then took two fast steps toward the nearest one and reached out, tearing his serial number from his uniform with one violent yank. She held the hunk of fabric out toward him.

"What's your name, asshole?"

The Crusher looked around, but the moment had passed and his buddies were all lowering their weapons. He reached up and popped his mask up onto his head. His face was red and unshaven, with dark, thick eyebrows. He licked his lips two, three, four times. "Mikkels," he said, his voice phlegmy. "Andrew—"

"You're a fucking dead man, Mikkels," Krajian hissed, stuffing his serial into her pocket. "I'm filing a nine eighty-nine on you and you *will not survive*, understood?" She glared around as Mikkels stood there looking stupid. "Anyone else? Any other of you *mental giants* want to defy an order from an officer? This man," she said, gesturing at me, "is my prisoner and you will not do even a fucking OFR scan of him without my permission. Now back...the fuck...off."

The world snapped back into normal focus, and the Crushers fell over each other to spin and vacate the area. Krajian stood there for a moment, panting, her gun in one hand pointed at the ground. Mikkels stood there gaping at her.

"Sir," he started to say, but Krajian raised her hand and he shut his mouth.

"Your only chance of surviving me," she said in a suddenly low, tired voice, "is to walk away right now. I make no guarantees."

He blinked once, suddenly startled as if someone had poured invisible cold water down his pants, and then turned and jogged after his comrades. Krajian stood for a moment with her back to me and then turned, slamming her gun back into her holster and stepping past me. I didn't feel anything, and my nose didn't even seem to be broken. Everything was coming up Avery.

"Come on," she snapped. "Surprise me again and I'll blind you."

Dripping blood onto the sidewalk, I struggled to my feet and holstered my own gun. "I think I'm in love," I said, limping after her.

VIII

THIS WAS ENTERTAINMENT

"Slow down, you fucking cable runner," I groused, dragging my stiff leg in the sandy dirt, blinking sweat out of my eyes.

Grisha spun and walked backward for a few steps, peering at me through his stupid, affected glasses. His narrow face was bright red and his jumpsuit sported a dark V-shaped sweat stain that appeared to be more or less permanent. He had his hands thrust deeply into his jumpsuit and a damp-looking cigarette, unlit, clenched between his teeth.

"You look like shit, yes?" he said without a grin. "Look like you fell into a bucket of razors, huh?"

I nodded, panting. "I'm popular around here."

He nodded, swiveling the cigarette to the other corner of his mouth. "Yes, popular. I see." He shrugged. "Someone does me dirt, my friend, I do not forget. I have my revenge. I do not forget." He winked. "So please remember this, yes?"

I frowned. "What did you steal, Grisha?" I liked the skinny little bastard. He was unlike any Techie I'd ever met. "To get here, I mean."

"As opposed to bullet in head, yes? It does not matter. It is worthless now, though apparently this fact escapes Director Marin's attention. This data that has ruined me is safe anyway. In The Star."

The Star: I'd never been in it, but of course everyone on the streets of New York knew of it. A star-shaped building a hundred feet high, solid stone, on an island off Manhattan. A data haven, now—for a few million yen you could store all sorts of things in secure servers. Some people even maintained entire labs inside it. Miles Amblen, maybe the most famous Techie in the System after Dennis Squalor and Ty Kieth, had done a lot of black market work in The Star, or so it was said.

Rumor was it had been a fortress before Unification, but rumors were worthless—whatever it had been, it was long gone. Some people liked to say the SSF couldn't breach it, which was why someone like Amblen could hide up in there, but that was bullshit. If the System Pigs wanted inside a place, they got in.

Grisha spun around again and didn't slow down. All at once every fresh cut on my body stung me, my own sweat sizzling on my skin like alcohol. My two new fans had woken me up right before sunrise, trying to stab me with the most pathetic shivs I'd ever seen. As a professional, I'd been offended, especially since it would have taken them a couple of really irritating, painful hours to actually kill me. As I walked, I jiggled my three shivs in my pocket and scanned the yard. For some reason I hadn't killed them. It would have been easy, but I just…walked away.

Grisha led me out into the sun, making for the walls in the distance. "This place," he said, spinning around again, "is very strange. A prison, yes?" He smirked. "Worst fucking prison I ever see. And I see a few, unfortunately. The Pigs, yes, they send you to prison, it is usually for one of two reasons: One, you irritate them, piss them off, so they want to kick you in the balls for a few months. Two"—he pulled one hand from his pocket in order to thrust two fingers up into the air—"they need something from you. Otherwise, just a shell in the ear, yes?"

He twisted his head around to squint back at me, and I gave him a curt nod. It was one thing we all had in common here, that memory of a cop's gun barrel against your head.

"This place," he continued, facing forward and pushing his hand back into his pocket. "This place is strange. Oh, yes, basic security. Walls, yes. Razor wire on top, of course. Guards with amazing skill in towers, able to put a hollow point into your eye from this distance—superhuman. Electric fencing that will turn you nice and crisp if you try to cross. Anti-tunneling measures—the usual. But, nothing *special.* Nothing *good.* Nothing I could not get around easily, with a few weeks to study and plan." He shrugged. We were halfway to the walls. I raised my hand to shield my eyes and squinted up at the tower, the sniper on station there a black dot. I imagined I could feel his red eye on me.

"Ah." Grisha stopped and turned. "But then there is the sun." He looked up into the sky. "Based on stars at night, Cates, we are in fucking Death Valley, desert. North of Mexico. Hot. Nothing nearby for a hundred miles. This is the true prison. The rest is for show, the rest is just crowd control, to keep us in manageable spaces, yes? I could get out of here—my goodness, Cates, I could slip out for groceries and be back before dole and no one the wiser, yes? Except, then what. Then I die in the desert. I starve; I dry up."

I nodded, turning to look back at the main complex. "What's your point, Grisha?"

"Michaleen asks me to give you the rundown, since you are latest recruit to our little team." I turned back to the Techie, who grinned again. "He is a very smart man, in his way. He is going to get us out of here."

I nodded, hearing the little man saying, *Not long and not deep, but I knew ol' Aubrey.* "Mickey's a genius, okay. What about getting everyone else out?"

"Everyone else? Fuck everyone else."

I nodded again. "Okay, so run it down." I turned back to him, a man who looked so thin and dry he couldn't possibly exist out here in the sun. "Where do the Crushers come from?" I'd seen two disturbances so far, fights that had pulled dozens into their gravity, threatening to become bedlam. Each time, the guards had been there instantly, dozens of the fuckers, as if they'd been hiding under our fucking bunks, ready to spring. I'd seen the fat, bearded man from the train, the non-Crusher, each time, looking fresh and clear, like he'd been napping and eating right in preparation for just such a contingency.

Grisha shrugged and started walking back toward the main complex. "That I cannot explain. Where do they live? There are no guard quarters. Under our feet? Possibly. There may be a huge complex underground, yes? That is the most likely explanation. But I cannot say for *sure*."

I nodded. We barely saw guards when things were quiet. There was the one at the dole, there were the five or six we could see on the towers, and that was it. No one walked the yard to keep order; no one made sure we weren't conspiring or plotting.

"This is mysterious," Grisha muttered. Four people had emerged from the main prison building. I recognized the broad-shouldered form of my admirer, the longhair, and the skinny brown shape of my first-day attacker. There were two other men with them. I played with my three pot stickers and tried to make my leg bend a little as we walked. The thought of beating those two idiots off one more time almost made me want to lie down in the sun and bake until I passed out.

"This whole place, mysterious," Grisha continued. "Why bring us all here? For what purpose? This is why we must escape. Before we discover the purpose the hard way, yes?"

I nodded absently. A crowd was forming behind my two idiots and their new friends, a casual, spotty crowd moving slowly and easily. An audience. I closed my eyes and imagined myself in the desert, empty and vast, the wind the only sound. I imagined a distant roar, so loud the sand vibrated beneath my feet. It felt good.

Opening my eyes, I blinked the glare out of them and took another look at my fans. The skinny kid had gotten improbably skinnier, shrinking under the murderous diet and smothering heat. The longhair was still limping from our last encounter, his jumpsuit spotted red. Their new friends were big, tall Augment freaks—bigger than the longhair had been but looking a little saggy after their time in Chengara. I wasn't sure why all Augment addicts looked exactly the same, but they did: stiff and bulging, almost hairless, with thick, ropy veins traced under their thick, leathery skin. These two were burned pretty dark, so I figured they'd been here for a while. I ran the numbers in my head as we closed the distance: malnourished, bird boned, and willing to kill someone in return for a fucking nutrition tab and some cigarettes.

"Ah, you have some business, yes?" Grisha said, sounding almost happy. "Michaleen says you are a Gunner. That you have killed many people. That you are skilled."

I took a deep breath of hot, dry air. It hurt my throat. My leg hitched painfully. "What I am," I said with a slight smile I couldn't suppress, "is old."

"Yes," Grisha said. "As are we all."

My new friends had stopped about twenty feet away. Behind them was most of the prison, I thought, spreading around us to form a loose circle. There were no Vids; this was entertainment. It was difficult to be sure, but I thought some of the faces I'd gotten used to seeing were gone, disappeared. It seemed like each morning there were more missing faces, but new trains arrived every other day, so it was impossible to say for sure.

I kept walking as Grisha veered off and joined the crowd. With the sun like a fist pressing down on the back of my head, I continued until I was a few feet away and stopped.

"Well—"

They came at me all at once, all four just charging at me. Our audience let out a cheer, and I leaned down over the hot ground, putting my head down and my stiff leg in front of me, letting the longhair crash into me and rolling him over my back. Taking a fistful of sandy dirt almost unconsciously, I pushed myself up and tottered backward, off balance as the four skidded to a halt, spinning.

The crowd let out a cheer. I heard my name.

They came at me again, without even a hint of finesse or plan, just superior numbers. Assholes always thought superior numbers meant everything. I forced myself to stand still until they were right on top of me, then spun to my left, tossing my fistful of dirt into one of the big guys' faces and bringing one of my shivs from my pocket. He cursed and went down onto his knees in a stumble, and I fell against him, my leg screaming out in sharp, sudden pain, and dragged the blade across his throat.

"Asshole," I muttered, pushing myself back onto my feet.

The crowd cheered.

The other three spun and then stood there, staring from their dying fellow as he choked up blood into the thirsty ground to me. For a second, none of us moved, and then the other big guy let out an anguished screech and leaped at me. The crowd roared—but the roar transformed into something else. A puff of dust erupted silently at my feet, a sniper's bullet.

The big guy suddenly jerked backward, a spray of blood hitting me in the face as his head turned into a sculpture of blood and bone. The crowd erupted into noisy chaos as the Crushers appeared, Taser sticks in hand, shouting and smacking everyone in sight. Again, they'd come out of fucking *nowhere*. If someone told me they'd blinked in from thin air, I'd fucking believe it.

I hesitated, picturing the puff of dust. I could feel the sniper on my back, but I didn't know if he wanted me to stay put or get moving. Just the day before I'd been Tasered until my stomach had tried to crawl up my throat, and I didn't want to repeat the experience, so I chose to move. I dodged clumsily to my right and then threw myself into a stagger to the left, my leg sending a sharp stabbing pain up my side. I scrambled for the edge of the crowd, hoping to skirt around the main body of ass-kicking and limp into the shadows. Fuck it. I was an old man, and there was no glory in pissing your jumpsuit twice in two days.

Panting and wincing, I swung through the thick cloud of hot dust and then skidded to a halt as my favorite Crusher, beard as neatly trimmed as always, loomed up in front of me. As I tried to shift direction, my leg twitched painfully and went dead under me, spilling me onto the ground.

The non-Crusher grinned. "I knew we'd manage to train you soon enough," he shouted, raising his stick up dramatically. As I lay there trying to decide if I should just piss my jumpsuit now and get it over with instead of waiting for my nervous system to be lit up like a fucking power grid, someone appeared behind him and grabbed him around his thick neck. With a jerk, the non-Crusher's head was twisted around much further than I thought possible as his legs left the ground. He kicked and jiggled for a moment and then there was a sudden violent stiffening of his limbs, and he dropped like a rag doll and lay still.

I stared at Bartlett for just a second, and then struggled back to my feet. The big black ex-cop surged forward, and before I knew it his bruised, sweaty body was right on top of me, his big hands wrapping themselves in my jumpsuit and lifting me up off the ground. He fucking *carried* me about twenty feet through the dust and noise and then slammed me down into a shady spot where the ground sloped downward, forming a shallow trench against the cinder blocks of the bunkhouse. A moment later he slammed against the wall next to me, panting.

"Gotta make sure you twist 'em *all the way*," he huffed. "Gotta keep it up until they disconnect."

"So we're even?" I breathed.

"Even?" It was the first time I'd heard him speak at a normal volume. He had a deep, rich voice that sounded like a minor earthquake going off next to me. "Fucking rat. Fucking copkiller. You think you lift one shiv off an asshole for me, and now we're fucking *buddies*? Motherfucker, I'd slit your throat right now—I'd probably be avenging what, a dozen—*two dozen*—dead cops just like that."

I blinked. "Then—"

"She gave the order."

I followed his jerking thumb. Sitting calm and composed in the narrow shadow of the dorm wall, her ridiculous, heavy coat still hanging off her thin shoulders, was the old woman I'd seen getting off the train. She stared back at me with those clear, dry eyes and then looked away. I felt the dismissal like a physical force buffeting me.

Before I could ask a question, the tide of the scrum intervened. I turned and Bartlett was gone.

IX

IF YOU WANTED TO KILL ME . . . THERE ARE FASTER WAYS

I stepped into the bar and stopped, the hair on my arms standing up. Krajian kept walking, the smoky gloom swallowing her, and I forced myself back into motion, stepping down and letting the door swing shut behind me. The sounds of the street disappeared, instantly replaced by the buzz of conversation and the clink of glasses.

I forced myself to keep moving and stay calm. It was a small, old place, sunk into the ground and almost windowless, the gloom feeling permanent, smeared onto everything like a stain. The walls were rough stone and the bar and tables were substantial, huge hunks of wood, polished with use and expensive looking. Everything felt close together, as if the furniture shouldn't have been able to fit through the door. No one looked at me, but they didn't have to—every cop in the place had noticed me the second I appeared in the doorway.

I followed Krajian to a table in the back with my head down. It was one thing to have half the System Pigs in the place know you were a criminal with just a casual glance; it was something else to have your face scanned by a fucking OFR handheld and have a dozen open cases pop up like hot coals, along with your name.

Sliding into the booth across from Krajian, I kept my coat on and hunched my shoulders to try and minimize my profile. Everyone seemed to be laughing.

"If you wanted to kill me," I said slowly, growling, "there are faster ways than parading me through a fucking *cop* bar."

She leaned forward savagely, putting her face near mine. "The fucking Worms won't come in here, okay? It's the safest spot for *me*. I don't recall giving a shit about you, Mr. —"

Before I could stop myself, I pounded the table with my fist. "Do *not* say my name here."

She leaned back, and for a moment we just stared at each other. In the dim light her patch melded in with the shadows, and her exposed eye glowed dully as if some nonexistent light was shining behind me. She wasn't a bad-looking woman, though her face was hard and angular, with a sharp nose and prominent cheekbones. She had a mean mouth, thin and severe, probably turning cruel when she smiled. I wasn't sure if I would ever see her smile. I *was* sure I didn't really want to.

"I thought Augments weren't allowed in the SSF," I finally said.

She started to respond just as a serving Droid arrived at our table on its silent wheels. It placed a gleaming glass of something clear and flat in front of her and then sat politely, waiting.

"Gin," I said. "Warm."

The Droid rolled away, and she leaned forward. "Don't presume to ask me questions," she said, suddenly calm. "You're here from our mutual friend, yes?" Her eye locked on me; she picked up her glass and took a sip, surprisingly dainty. "Call me Krasa." She leaned back, seeming to fold herself up into half the space, one leg curled under herself. "You do not look as I expected."

I grinned as my drink was delivered. "Better looking?"

She snorted. "Shorter." She leaned forward again, but this time there was an air of intimacy about her, as if we were about to share secrets, as if we were on some sort of horrible date. "What do you want, then? I'm about three days from following my partner down Marin's fucking rabbit hole. Better talk fast."

"What'd you do to get the Worms upset at you?"

She squinted at me and leaned back, regarding me with a slight kinking of her mouth that I decided had to be her smile. It was every bit as heartless as I expected. "I didn't *do* anything, did I? I learned something I'm not supposed to know. My partner and I. Look around—every cop in here is still a fucking human being. I think. The new and improved ones don't drink anymore." She nodded her head toward the crowd around us. "Avatars. *That's* what we found out. My partner's gone. Burned." She winked. "I will be going, soon."

"So you just sit around and wait for it?"

She shrugged, leaning back again, settling in as if the booth had been molded to her body at the factory. "I'm a cop. Where the fuck do I go?"

I let that hang for a moment, letting it breathe. Then I looked up at her from under my eyebrows. "Can you get me inside The Rock?"

Her smile dripped over her face in stages, widening and getting colder as it went, until I thought my eyebrows might catch fire. "Why?"

I tried to match her smile, but I suspected I was completely outclassed in the fucked-up department. "I need information. Our mutual friend asked me to do him a favor."

For a moment she kept that crazy grin on me, her patch a black hole that was sucking at me, making me lean forward slightly. Then she put both hands flat on the table, making our glasses rattle. "Okay," she said brightly. "What the fuck. I've got nothing to lose. These cops in here"—she jerked her head to indicate the rest of the bar—"are maybe the last fucking real cops left in this city. Who knows? Maybe the world. We're being burned, one by one, carted off and never seen again." She winked. "I'm on the short list. So what the fuck. You want in The Rock?" She nodded once, curtly, and then stood up.

"You're under arrest," she said, loud, snapping a pair of silicone bracelets from her coat with a crack. I hadn't had time to process this before she leaned in and grabbed hold of my arm, pulling me up with surprising strength and bending it back behind me, shoving me down until my head cracked against the tabletop. With a practiced, efficient jerk the straps were around my wrists and pulled numbingly tight, and then her fist was curled in my hair and pulling me up. I was spun around and found a silent bar of shadowed, soundless men and women staring back at me.

This had taken a second. This had taken *no fucking time at all*.

I closed my eyes and tried to be outraged, but it wasn't in me. I was amused. I'd let my guard down around a fucking System Pig, after all, and this is what I got—I *deserved* this.

She frisked me professionally—one hand on my neck the whole time, in case I got ideas, one hand pushing and patting, checking every possible spot for a concealed weapon. She took my gun and blade immediately and eventually found the small pot sticker I kept in my boot, snorting in triumph.

I kept my head down, smiling at the floor, to try and stop any of her colleagues from getting a good scan of my face. I took a few glances around, to see how we were playing to the audience, and was surprised—they all looked bored, unhappy. Like none of it mattered anymore. I could hear distant rumbles, like thunder but more regular: bombing. The Undersecretaries were doing their usual announcement of intent, endlessly softening up New York's defenses. The low wail of an alarm rose up, distant and everywhere, making my ears twitch.

"Move," she snarled, giving me a good shove. I stumbled

into motion and walked toward the exit. Behind me, I heard her talking low into the air, her earbud catching everything.

"Control, this is Krajian H-U8-9 calling in an OFR negative for peace violation," she said, giving me occasional encouraging taps on the back. "I need a transport."

At the front door I obliged by pushing it open with my head. Outside it had gotten darker. The rumbling of big guns had joined the bombing, both fat and faint, a little twitch beneath your feet. People were moving rapidly up and down the narrow street, well-dressed folks obviously in a rush to get off the street before whatever was happening in the distance got any closer.

"What the fuck do you care why?" Krasa hissed, yanking once on my coat to make me stop moving. "Control, I need transport home. Since when do I have to explain why? I have a fucking shithead in custody. I need transport, and I need to book a Technical Associate consult with badge number 7-OI-4. Read that back? Confirmed.

"There," she finally said, her voice falling to normal volume. "You wanted in The Rock? Easy fucking peasy."

I turned to say something, but her fist, traveling at approximately the speed of light, changed my mind. And whipped my head around, knocking me off balance and sending me staggering into a small knot of horrified swells, most of whom ended up with a little blood splatter on their nice clothes for their trouble. A woman shrieked, and I was pushed roughly back at Krasa by several sets of hands.

I probed a loose tooth with my tongue, feeling nothing. "What the fuck was that for?"

Krasa's smile was equal parts cruel and hopeless. "Realism."

Our hover, a dented, rusty piece of shit from another century, rattled and wheezed its way through the air, low to the ground due to wartime airspace restrictions, and set us down on the roof of Rockefeller Center without any serious mishaps, which I attributed to the skill and patience of the pilot. Krasa pushed me very realistically into a large elevator that smelled like a magical combination of blood and piss. There was a large, crusted bloodstain on one wall of the elevator car, a dent in the exact middle of it as if some overenthusiastic System Pig had once literally beaten someone's brains out on that spot. I stared at it as the door shut behind us.

"Ten, check in," she said in a monotone. "Krajian H-U8-9."

The elevator started to move. "You're checking me in? Isn't that a little too much goddamn *realism?"*

"Don't cream yourself," she said without looking at me. "I'm checking you in as an OFR negative, no positive ID. Gotta check you in. New directives—no one enters unless they're checked in. Apparently there was an embarrassing moment a year or two ago."

I nodded. I remembered it well. "Why are you helping me?"

She shrugged, still staring ahead. "This time next week, I'm disappeared. If you're going to shove something hot and sharp up the King Worm's ass, it'd be something to keep me warm wherever I'm going."

The elevator doors opened, and I squinted into the bleached, bright light. The elevator disgorged into a small, shallow room, all white. There was room for maybe four or five people to stand uncomfortably in it. There was a round indentation in the wall, the only feature I could see. The light was eye searing.

"Krajian H-U8-9," she said, and there was a soft *ding* in the air.

"Place subject's face in scanner," a feminine voice said softly. I glanced at Krasa. She didn't look at me but shook her head.

"Wait a sec," she said. After another moment there was a flat, unhappy sound.

"Scan failed. Place subject's face in scanner."

The unhappy sound rang out again. *"Scan has failed."*

"Override, enter as negative ID," Krasa said. The happy *ding* sounded again, and suddenly a panel in the wall snapped open with an automated, smooth motion.

"*Entered,*" the voice responded. "*You have been assigned Interview Room seven-seven-eight-nine. Technical consultant is en route.*"

Krasa jerked me into motion again, pushing me through the narrow doorway, and we were inside The Rock proper. It was just as I remembered it: white corridors, harsh lighting, near-complete silence. A short corridor led to another elevator. Krasa dragged me into it with such vigor I thought she'd probably be able to just carry me the rest of the way; I slammed into the back wall and stayed there, breathing the heroically filtered air and studying her back. She had good posture.

Then another of those antiseptic halls, this time with a few helpful signs posted here and there, too small for me to glimpse. More people, too—desk cops, they looked like, their knuckles free from scabs, their clothes a little finer. Some were even carrying metallic mugs of coffee, like they lived in this whitewashed building. This while getting a cup of coffee on the streets of New York was almost impossible, even for the richies. We cut through them easily enough—none of them paid any attention to me at all, even when they gave Krasa a curt nod of recognition. At what appeared to be a random door, she jerked me to a stop and gestured. The door unlocked, drifting inward slightly.

"All right," Krasa said. "You're in."

She shoved me against the door and it gave, admitting us into the familiar sight of a Blank Room, shielded from all signals and devoid of any kind of recording equipment, the System Pigs' favorite place to encourage their prisoners to do some talking. I'd been in plenty of them. It was home.

For a second, I had one of my moments—my mind going blank, everything seeming to recede into shadow. It only lasted a second, and then I was blinking my eyes and trying to focus. Sitting at the small table that adorned every single Blank Room I'd ever been in—simple metal table, scuffed and scratched—was a pudgy young guy in a pricey but ill-fitting suit, his face just small, nervous eyes and a long, thick beard that completely covered his neck. He glanced up from his handheld as I entered and froze for a second. Then he shot up onto his feet, the handheld dropping to the floor with a crack, and staggered backward until he hit the wall.

"Fuck *me*," he said in a tight, dry voice.

I smiled and stepped aside to let Krasa in. "Relax, Mr. Marko," I said, feeling good. "I'm not here to kill *you*." I winked. "Yet."

X

THE LITTLE MAN AND HIS FREAKS

I lay half-upright on the cot and stared at the ceiling; the moon was bright and shadows pushed their way around, fading whenever one of the high clouds passed overhead, then clarifying silently. Marlena snored softly next to me, naked, her inked flesh black and gray in the weak light, her mouth open and slack. She always fell asleep next to me, snoring to make my teeth rattle. I wanted her to go away because I was getting to like having her next to me.

My shoulder ached a little where she'd inked me up. It was a surprisingly detailed sketch of a skull in profile, all black and gray, a garish black crown sitting on top and a cigarette burning between its grinning teeth. Underneath she'd laboriously spelled out TEMPUS FUGIT, MORS VENIT. I'd asked her what it meant and she'd said, "Time passes, death comes.

"Alcatraz tradition," she'd explained. "I don't know where it comes from, but when I was penned up there a few years ago, that's what they gave anyone in for murder. Murder a cop, you got a crown on the skull."

Skinner had been getting around. If you were sensitive you'd say she was hooking, selling off sexual favors in return for whatever she needed that day. I got the feeling, though, that Marlena just liked sex, and getting something in return was incidental, something she did when she thought about it. I was turning out to be the only one she spent the night with, though. I liked her. She didn't take any shit, and I'd never known anyone more comfortable in their skin. Just looking at her and you relaxed, felt normal.

It never got quiet. We didn't have a lights-out—there were no lights—or a curfew. Half the people I'd arrived with were gone, and I had no clue how it happened. I would suddenly realize that I hadn't seen a face for a while, and that was it: they were gone. Before they got vaporized or whatever, they were free to do whatever they pleased at night, which mostly meant gambling. Everyone had something they'd managed to smuggle in or take from someone else. I had six shivs already, taken from people who'd tried to stick them into my guts—my only possessions. Others had mysteriously brought dice or knives or cigarettes. One good-looking kid with perfect skin had brought his credit dongle, like a talisman. After he'd been beaten into a coma and left out in the sun for a few hours, it had been passed around, amusing everyone to discover that he had fifteen thousand yen in his account, enough for a good meal or maybe a haircut.

He'd been gone the next day, as mysteriously as everyone else.

"You ever know your father?" I'd asked once, surprising myself.

"No," she'd said immediately. "Mother, either."

Above the usual hushed murmur of games, fights, and conversations all around, I heard the unmistakable rhythm of a confrontation. I ignored it at first, two tight voices hissing like snakes and weaving in and out of the other sounds, two more assholes impatient to get wherever Chengara was taking them. Then I heard one word in another voice, impossible to catch but the voice was clear enough: an older woman's voice, uneven but the syllable bitten off fiercely.

I sat up, Marlena sliding down from my shoulder and grunting. I listened for a moment, but it was just the first two voices again, jumping all over each other.

Swinging my feet onto the still-warm floor of the dorm, I eased up off the cot and stepped as lightly as I could toward the voices. My leg throbbed suddenly, making me hitch as I walked. The old woman was sitting at the same table I'd seen her at before, still painfully straight, her hands clasped tightly in front of her. A touch of bright red had come to her old, dry cheeks, but she sat perfectly still, her eyes flashing from one of the men leaning over her to the other in rhythmic, mechanical ticks.

"C'mon, ya hag," the one on the left growled.

"Give it or we cut it off," the one on the right finished.

She pulled the coat tighter around her. I'd never seen her take it off, despite the soul-crushing heat. Her friends weren't anything special—two kids, teenagers, shaved heads growing in, scars on their arms, and deep curves to their spines. Clouds of kids like that had infested New York at one time, and you had to swat them off you like flies.

"Oh, for fuck's sake!" the one on the left hissed. "It's just a fucking coat!"

I cleared my throat. "You all right, lady?"

"Who the fuck—" the one on the left started to bark, twisting around. He stopped when he saw me, his right eye sagging under a thick yellow scar. His friend turned, and for a moment they both stared at me.

"Uh," the one on the left said, blinking, his whole face twitching. "This ain't your worries."

The other one just stood there mute, mouth hanging open.

I had one of my confiscated knives palmed and crossed my arms to keep it obscured. I looked at the woman. She stared back at me, her hands still clutching the damn coat tightly to her throat. "I worry about a lot of things. The worries of the world keep me awake at nights." I shifted my eyes to look back at the two kids. "You want me to worry about you?"

They looked at each other, and then the one on the right closed his mouth, turning fully around to face me. For a second or two we studied each other. I had a foot or more on him, and I'd managed to eat better for the past two decades. He didn't know I had the blade, but I'd already been forced to kill a few assholes since my arrival, and my name still had a certain weight to it, even to people who hadn't lived in New York. It was painful to watch him think—and he was clearly the brains of the operation.

Still, I was on the balls of my feet, ignoring the pain in my leg, my wrists and elbows loose and ready. We were all People of Interest. Even Slackjaw here was in for a reason. I didn't want to find out his reason was because he could pop blood vessels from fifty feet away with his mind; people had always made the mistake of thinking Kev Gatz was a harmless idiot, and that had turned out wrong—at least the *harmless* part.

"No, Cates," he finally said in a marble-mouthed mumble. "No." He started forward, then paused to tug forcefully at his friend's arm. They both launched into motion, moving rapidly past me. I turned my head enough to keep track of them until they were swallowed by the gloom, and then I looked back at her.

"You okay?"

Her eyes squinted up a little, making her already stern face almost fierce. "Do Gunners with over seventy confirmed murders—at least thirty-seven of them officers of the System Security Force—normally make a habit of saving old women from thugs? Or is being in a penitentiary a tonic of sorts for worthless scum?"

I put one eyebrow up, racking my brain to try and remember where I knew her face. "I save one old woman for every ten people murdered." I shifted my weight to try and ease off the dull ache in my leg. It didn't work. "And your numbers are a little out-of-date, lady."

She nodded. "It's been a while since I've had access to SSF

dossiers." She leaned back a little, letting go of her coat and folding her papery hands on top of the table. "Last time I saw yours was when Marin was pushing his little Squalor project and plumped you as a candidate."

A memory clicked into place. I pointed at her. "You're an Undersecretary." I reconsidered. "*Were* an Undersecretary."

She nodded, her face impassive. "Dolores Salgado," she said crisply. "And I *was* Undersecretary for the Australian Department." She shrugged and busied herself lighting a cigarette. "I happened to be in Baltimore when the tricky bastard made his move, and I got caught up in the sweep."

"His move?" I stepped over the bench and sat down across from her.

"Marin. Your patron." She looked down at the table. "Worst decision we ever made, raising that half-dead simp from his hospital bed to the directorship." Her eyes jumped back onto mine, startling, so alive and energetic in the midst of that tired, thin face. "I can still see him, dark and pudgy, broken. Harmless!"

I tried to imagine Dick Marin as *dark and pudgy*, and couldn't.

"But we wanted to test the technology, of course." Her smile was hollow. "He turned out to be smarter than we suspected, eh? First the state of emergency you helped him engineer. His programmed limits lifted, just like that. But he has no budgetary control, we told ourselves. We starved him of funds and poured everything into our shiny new army. Thirty years without a standing army, Mr. Cates, and now we have a *huge* one, ready to move. But Marin's still smarter than us. They told us that being digitized in no way altered your natural intelligence or abilities, but I think Director Marin is proving us all wrong."

I scratched my leg absently, trying to push down hard enough to get at the never-ending ache. "I had a friend once, got turned into a Monk. Not the same thing, but he said it...clarified him."

She squinted and ticked her head. "Yes, perhaps. *Clarified*. I like it. Perhaps Marin was clarified. At any rate, he has moved first—thrown the weight of his police against us, without warning. It's a civil war, Mr. Cates."

I nodded. Even in here, this was old news, brought in stutteringly by the new arrivals every day. "What do you know about Ruberto? Your counterpart?" He was the only other Undersecretary I knew by name, I realized. Ruberto had authorized a government Spook—a psionic—named Bendix and a team of Stormers to come snatch me up in Paris during the Plague, a lifetime ago.

Tilting her head, Salgado smoothed her coat, studying it apparently for lint. "Not much before his inexplicable rise. He doesn't have much history. He wasn't an original Undersecretary—his career's been guided by powerful friends. He came to significance shortly after we elevated Marin, springing up like a weed in Chicago." She shrugged, returning her eyes to me. "Aside from sharing a title with him, I don't have much in common with or opinion of Mr. Ruberto. He is, however, the power broker of the Undersecretaries at the moment. He will no doubt be a very powerful figure in the new army, and the New Order it ushers in." She sighed, but it was theatrical and there was nothing sad or wistful about it. "I am afraid, Mr. Cates, that the System as we knew it is now a memory, and something new will be taking its place."

I gave her a small smile. "I'm not afraid of that at all." I kept the smile simmering in place. "Why are you here, then?"

Her face remained blank, but she lifted one skinny arm and tapped her head. "The same reason we are all here, Mr. Cates. Though I suspect even Director Marin does not know what a treasure *my* brain will prove to him." She looked down at her lap and sighed again, and this time I thought it felt real. "I wish I were brave. I could cheat him." She looked back up at me. "But I am not brave."

I studied her. I liked her calmness, her poise. "I could do you a service," I said steadily, keeping my eyes on hers. "If you want." I shrugged. "I've got nothing but time here. And it's what I do."

Movement made me turn, startled, and I found Bartlett, bare chested as always and gleaming with a million fresh scars on his massive chest, standing just a few feet away. He looked like he was glaring angrily at us, but he always looked that way and I didn't pay him much attention. He and Salgado exchanged a stare, and after a moment he snorted and walked off.

"You know him?" I asked.

She nodded. "I know every cop ever detailed to me. Espin Bartlett, Captain, originally Detroit until Detroit got shut down and evacced. A hothead, but a good man. He was on my bodyguard detail for three years some time back. Before the SSF decided it had better things to do than keep Undersecretaries alive." She shook her head. "Espin's had a hard time these past few weeks."

I considered. She sounded almost motherly. I remembered her from the Vids—always painfully erect, those eyes glaring at you from the screen. "You've got to be more valuable to Marin than some of the shit kickers we have here. Why let you rattle around here?"

She shrugged. "Marin is still bound by his limitations, Mr. Cates. He's one man—or one intelligence, I suppose, is more accurate—processing the data streams of hundreds of avatars, not to mention the snail streams of his assistants and secretaries. It's a volume of information the human mind was never designed to handle, and even if he is operating on clockspeeds, now he's slow and sloppy." She shrugged again, putting her cigarette into her mouth and taking a deep drag. "They are pulling tens of thousands of people through facilities like this. He just hasn't noticed me yet. By the time he does, I'll probably have been sucked through here and processed, so no harm done, yes?"

She smiled, and at first I thought she was laughing, her face reddening. Then I realized she was coughing. I watched her without moving, and she waved her bony hands at me.

"Damn," she panted, cigarette wobbling up and down between her lips. "A hundred and seven and I'm on my fourth lung. I may cheat Marin after all!"

"What do you mean, processed?"

She was gasping like a fish, but stole little nips of smoke in between. "Mr. Cates, I have a favor to ask you. I've read your file. You're a man of honor, in your way."

I shook my head again. "You're thinking of someone else, mother. Someone who didn't make it through the Plague."

Her eyes stayed on me. I didn't like it and struggled not to let it show. "I'm nearly dead, and high time," she said. "I've done what I could to . . . never mind my ridiculous justifications. I am a corpse. My brain and heart just haven't figured it out yet. I'm too cowardly to just end it, so I'm taking my chances here and hoping I keel over before they process me."

Process. I didn't like the word. Monks had been processed.

"I hear you're getting out, you and the Freak Show — the Little Man and his Freaks, yes?"

All of my attention narrowed down to her for a moment. There were no secrets in prison, of course, but this bothered me for some reason. That *she* would know about it, with her voice so used to command it just oozed out of her, her eyes sharp and disappointed eternally. I decided not to say anything, but she nodded and looked down as if I had and she was satisfied.

"I'd like you to take Espin with you," she said.

I blinked. "The *cop?*" I blurted, and then to try and sound semi-intelligent, I added, "Not you?"

She crushed the cigarette out on the table and stood up laboriously, her breathing ragged and rapid. "I am a dead woman, Mr. Cates. Though I may," she said with a sudden smile that made her look impish and feminine for a second, "live on in this hellhole, yes? Perhaps." She winked. "If so, look me up someday, Mr. Cates. I may be of some use to you." She turned and walked slowly away. "I feel I owe Espin a debt, Mr. Cates, and this is my only chance to offer him something. You can trust him, Mr. Cates. You have my assurance on that."

I watched her inch away from me. The strange thing was, I believed her.

XI

IT'S ALL RIGHT. YOU *DID* LOOK KIND OF SAD ABOUT IT

"Don't open your fucking mouth," I advised Marko with a raised hand. "I might have the urge to put something in it."

Marko appeared to be trying to push himself into the far wall. He'd gained some weight, his hair had swallowed most of the rest of his face, and his affected glasses had gotten smaller and more stylish. He bent slowly, his eyes locked on me, and retrieved his dropped handheld. Instead of the old Technical Associate jumpsuit, he was wearing a moderately luxurious suit and held the handheld in front of his belly as if it were going to protect him. I gave the device a few extra seconds of my attention—for all I knew about tech it just might shoot energy beams at me.

"Mr. Marko is a friend of the cause," Krasa said from behind me, slicing my bracelets off with a jerk. "He saved my life."

I gave Marko a merry wink. "How's that?"

"He's been farming the SSF network," she said, stepping back around me. "Keyword searches dumped to a private net of his that he's walled off on his own. I was chasing down my partner, trying to figure out what had happened to him, and Marko saw the Worms red flagging all of my Standard Incident

Reports and activity logs. He cleaned up my files and passed the word to me."

"I, uh," Marko said slowly, licking his plump lips, and then his eyes, tiny in the midst of so much hair, flashed to me in apprehension.

"Oh, for fuck's sake." I sighed. "Speak."

"I've been evolving my opinion of the System Security Force."

I nodded. "Okay. Marko's a revolutionary. Fucking fantastic. Why hasn't Mr. Wizard been processed himself?"

"The Technical Corps is still largely untouched, for some reason," Krasa said.

"Marin's worried about complex and creative thought," Marko said. "Worried that the algorithms won't capture it. He's afraid to process the Technical staff and some of the higher Worms until he's more sure of himself." He licked his pink lips. "Unfortunately, most of the Tech staff is voluntarily working on this for him."

I pulled the one chair out from the table, and Marko made a low, whimpering sound, putting his hands up a little higher. Krasa lit a cigarette.

"You two know each other?" she asked. She sounded like this was the least surprising thing she'd ever heard.

I grinned. "Mr. Marko left me for dead not so long ago." I winked at Marko as his eyes popped open. "It's all right. You *did* look kind of sad about it, as I recall." I spread my hands. "Calm down. You had Hense up your ass and what the fuck were you going to do?" I remembered Janet Hense, avatar, sailing around Bellevue, kicking the entire world's ass. "Okay. Forget it. Zeke, you're not high on my list, okay? You're not even in the first *volume*. Sit down, relax, and let's help each other out."

Slowly, he nodded and peeled himself from the wall. I didn't feel anything for Marko—no hate or anger; although I did feel mean, grim satisfaction that he'd apparently spent the last year and a half terrified that I might come back to kill him. He slowly approached the table, shooting his cuffs and adjusting his collar. He glanced at his handheld and gestured at it before setting it on the table, his hand lingering on it for a moment as if reluctant to let go. Then he pushed his hands into his pockets.

"Okay," he said, licking his lips. "Okay. Let's."

"He was slipped under the door by our mutual friend," Krasa said.

Marko blinked his tiny eyes. His lips were permanently wet, glistening under the harsh light. "Ruberto sent you?"

For a second, my mind was blank, and then I was irritated. "No one *sent* me, Mr. Marko. He *asked* me to come here." I found my smile again. It felt fake on my face, but I put it on anyway. "He asked me to do him a favor."

"Kill Marin," Krasa said, her voice flat. "That's the fucking *favor*."

Marko's face tightened up, his nostrils, bits of pink flesh in the midst of his jungle of hair, flaring anxiously. "You're aware of Director Marin's special…attributes?"

I nodded. "Hard to kill the Man of a Million Avatars, yeah, I know. That's why I'm here, in this room, Marko: fact-finding. I thought I'd have to *look* for you—but figured if I could find you, I'd have a source of information." I nodded, spreading my hands. "I am a genius."

"Hard to kill," Marko said musingly. He started to pace. I got the impression he was slowly forgetting there was anyone else in the room. "That's nice. You can't *kill* Director Marin."

I nodded impatiently. "You can turn the fucking Kremlin into dust," I said forcefully, trying to will Marko to stop speaking. "I need information, and I don't think we can just buy it. I've been given a target, one of Marin's key lieutenants—"

"Gall," Krasa said immediately. "Horatio Gall. Marin's right hand."

I glanced at her but didn't say anything.

"Gall," Marko said. "Jebus, you mean Gall. *Major* Gall. Oh, fuck, Cates—why *not* go for Marin himself? You think you're saving yourself trouble by going for his fucking *right hand?*"

I shrugged. "Gall is just the first step. Information, then we make a plan."

He shook his head, suddenly confident and animated. "You want Gall, you *still* need Marin. He's so close to Marin—he's Marin's *moon.* His itinerary, his security protocols, the officer assigned to his personal valet—you need information. Information that you only get from Marin's network."

He smiled suddenly. "Mr. Cates, you don't need a Gunner, you need a *hacker.* Marin is a *cloud,* he's a network unto himself. What you need to do"—Marko suddenly resumed, twirling his hand again—"is get a world-class Techie type, someone who can understand the algorithms and encryption, the nanotech and spider-busses. Someone who can hack the Prime's cloud, extract the data without tripping alarms. Sure, sure—nothing simpler. The System is *crawling* with guys of that caliber." I found I didn't like Marko when Marko got sarcastic. "You'd need someone like Squalor. Or Miles Amblen."

No one said anything for a moment. Every Techie I'd ever met used Amblen's name half a dozen times in the first five minutes of a discussion—the Amblen Protocol, the Amblen Theorem. Amblen was a typical old-school Techie, like Squalor: Pre-Unification he'd been famous, too, a brilliant academic. After Unification he hadn't been able to work on the System's leash and had gone underground.

I leaned forward. "How would you even access the *cloud?*"

Marko started pacing again, shaking his head. "That's easy, easy. The avatar architecture is two-way. Marin—any avatar—has to be able to collate new information from his avatars. They have to be able to interact with the control node, to supply information, and the control node needs to be able to take direct control whenever it wants. Any avatar could be made into a two-way gate to Marin's network. Then you'll be able to access Marin's data, including Gall's file."

I nodded. This was getting exciting. "So you'd need to snatch one of Marin's avatars."

Marko was pacing so fast, tight little bustles back and forth. The fabric of his suit made a distinct dry sound every time his legs scissored. "You'd need to have full physical access to it for some time. I've never seen a spec for the avatars, so who knows what kind of fireworks would be waiting for you—it's quite possible—strike that! It's almost *certain* that taking an avatar off-line would cause a panic response, most likely a complete data dump into the pipe and a hard wipe of the memory, probably triggering a scratch and shuffle of the handshake keys. So the chances of being able to put this plan into effect are slim."

"I assume every Marin avatar has a security retinue?"

Krasa nodded, staring at the thick blue smoke of her cigarette. "Like each and every one was the Emperor himself."

I turned to look at Marko and tried the grin again. It flashed onto my numb face, trained and compliant. "To get close to Marin you don't need a hacker, Marko. You need a *Gunner*."

He stared at me for a moment and then strode forward so quickly my alarms almost went off. Stopping myself from hurting the Techie, I let him lean down into my airspace, all that heroic hair rippling in the scrubbed air of the Blank Room like grass in a wind. "You're in for this? Three-fourths of the SSF are avatars by now, more every day. I have one, maybe two people in my department I can trust. Marin's security is going to be *heavy*, and I doubt Ruberto can get you any help here."

I nodded. "We don't need to do it *here*," I reminded him. "There are fucking Marins everywhere, all over the System. Open a drawer and a dozen spill out."

I should have been thrilled—my heart should have been pounding, my skin electric—this was the ultimate cop kill, this was the King Worm himself. This was what I'd wanted all those years ago, panting outside of Westminster Abbey. This was my revenge—this was bringing the whole damn poisoned System down, and I'd just talked myself into believing it was possible. Get to Gall. Map the security. Find the weak spot and tear it all down. Why not? But I felt nothing. I was calm; I was dry as paper.

Marko started nodding, and it was like his head couldn't stop. "Okay." He looked at Krasa. "What do you think, Captain?"

Krasa looked at me for a moment like I was an interesting equation Marko was forcing her to appreciate. She sucked in smoke with a squint and then shrugged. "What the fuck," she said, smoke dribbling from her lips limply.

This was not exactly the inspirational speech Marko had been hoping for, but he nodded as robustly as he could. "Right."

I stood up, pulling my Roon from its holster and checking the chamber. "Okay—so where do we get this Miles Amblen–level Techie, Mr. Marko, since you're apparently not the right man for the job?"

He blinked. And then he smiled. His smile was awful—yellow teeth, one broken, and angry red gums. "Well, why not make it Miles Amblen himself? We've got him downstairs in the lab, in a drawer somewhere."

XII

SOME MIRACLE OF SHITHEAD PHYSICS

I heard her approaching my bunk—her steps light but with no real effort at concealment. I came fully awake and opened my eyes, finding Marlena crouching down so her face was on level with mine, her inked-up skin kind of frightening in the sapping moonlight. We stared at each other comfortably for a moment. It was a relatively cool night, hinting that maybe it wasn't always broiling in the desert, that maybe, if we lived that long, we might even see a time when you didn't contemplate suicide every time you took three steps.

Chances were slim we'd last that long.

"You up?" Skinner finally said.

"No, this is a dream," I said. "You here to seduce me?" The moonlight softened her face a little. I wondered when I'd decided I trusted her enough to let her sneak up on me at night. I tabled the thought for future contemplation. Marlena was easy to talk to, and so far she hadn't fucked with me. That was enough, for now.

A faint smile eased her face a little. "Not this time," she said. "The little man's holding a meeting."

I raised my eyebrows. "Now? Fucking hell."

The little man was special, that was for sure. Michaleen was setting a record every day he remained walking around—he wouldn't say how long he'd been interred, but my best guess from the scraps of evidence I'd been able to gather was several months. I'd asked him how he'd avoided being disappeared like everyone else, and he'd just winked, saying that he knew when to stand still and make like a rock. Whatever the fuck that meant. The average for those of us without mystical rock-making powers seemed closer to three or four weeks, tops.

She shrugged, standing up, her knees giving off soft cracks that sounded loud in the near silence. "Just the messenger, Cates. Maybe when we're done listening to the midget, we'll see about *seducing* you." She pronounced the word like it was a prim curiosity, the sort of thing assholes said. I didn't like that, but swallowed it as I sat up and started to push myself to my feet.

Marlena put a hand on my shoulder. She didn't push, just laid her calloused, bony hand there, and I sat back down, looking up at her. She stared down at me steadily.

"You really think he can get us out? Michaleen?"

I considered, keeping my eyes on hers. Her face was impassive, but her eyes burned down at me. I knew the look: desperation. She was a pro and hiding it well, but there it was.

I pictured the little man. I'd seen him just that morning, sitting in the sun out in the yard, alone except for three rations of water—how he'd gotten them I didn't know—sipping and sitting still. Perfectly still. I'd watched him for half an hour from the shadows of the dorm walls, and the little man hadn't moved so much as an eyelid except to drink.

"Yes," I said honestly. "I think that creepy little bastard can do it."

She nodded. "Yeah, okay. But I don't trust him. I think he's using us."

I smiled. "C'mon, Lena. Of *course* he's using us." A flare of anger lit up inside me, a tiny ember flickering. The man had invoked my father, had used his name. I knew it was bullshit; I knew it was just to make me soften a bit, old Uncie Mickey from the neighborhood. And yet I hadn't called him on it. I'd let it sit there between us, unchallenged.

She nodded again, her face still composed. "I think he'll leave us behind if he can. Don't let that happen. If he comes to you with some story about how I got left behind, *don't let it happen.*" Her mask fragmented for a second and she looked away, the muscles of her throat working. "I don't want to die here, Avery."

For a moment I just looked up at her, fully awake now and unsure of what to say. I knew if I made a promise of any sort it would complicate things. You didn't make promises, you didn't accept responsibility for anyone else, because in the midst of a plan you were usually lucky to be able to take care of yourself.

"We all get out," I found myself saying, amazed. "Or none of us get out."

Without another word, she nodded and turned, walking away. I shook my head and swung myself into motion after her, watching her hips sway under the tight fabric of her short pants—one of the only prisoners who'd ditched the orange jumpsuit, opting for a perpetual sunburn.

"Wait a sec," I said, turning to cross the dorm, stopping about ten feet away from where Bartlett sat on his bunk, a dark form with a bright cigarette coal dancing in front of it. "You coming?"

Behind me, I heard Skinner hiss, "You have *got* to be shitting me," but I ignored her. Bartlett swung his legs off the bed and stood up. I'd never seen the ex-cop sleep. I supposed if I'd been thrown in with a few hundred folks who wanted me dead, I'd probably have learned to do without as well. As for me, my two admirers had been disappeared a few days ago—*poof!* they were gone, and I hadn't had any trouble from anyone else since.

Skinner hesitated as we approached, then shook her head and spun away, muttering. She led us into the yard and over to the debarkation area, where a train had arrived and was disgorging a fresh bunch of People of Interest, all of whom looked a little stunned and horrified. Mickey, Grisha, and the fucking *Christian* were already there, a few feet from the sturdy chain-link, electrified fence. The little man was sitting with his back to the train, cross-legged, eyes closed, hands clasped in his lap.

"Good evenin', Avery," he said without opening his eyes. "Thank you, Marlena."

I watched the newbies being detrained, moving stiffly through the cool air. I startled when I saw him: the bearded fuck, the non-Crusher, my old friend from my first day. I'd seen Bartlett kill him, I *knew* I had. But there he was, barking at the newbies like he felt better than ever. As I stared, he glanced at me, then did a little double take, and grinned.

I looked at Michaleen and watched him for a moment. He was sitting perfectly still, a statue. I let a few heartbeats go by, watching, but he didn't twitch or even seem to be breathing.

"All right, *Uncle*," I said, stretching, several things in my back popping. "What's up?"

He opened his eyes to look at me and then closed them again, settling himself. "Somethin' on your mind, Avery?"

I twitched. It might be true, who the fuck knew. I *wanted* it to be true. "Not yet," I said.

He didn't open his eyes. "Time's running out, Avery. We need to get a plan in place and start moving, before members of our merry band start vanishing, yes?"

I was irritated and tired. I'd been tired for days, feeling gravity get a little stronger every minute. "Why out here, little man?"

"No bugs out here, Avery. The cots're full of 'em."

"You have a pretty broad skill set, Mickey," I said slowly. "Maybe I'd like to know a little more about who I'm getting in bed with."

He sighed, producing a cigarette from behind his ear. "I'm nobody, Avery. I was a clerk. I was sent to collect debts. I must have seen somethin' along the way." He grinned. "Don't kick my balls, Avery."

I decided to let it go, for now. I didn't know if he was lying to me about my father, about any of this, but I did know I was going to stick next to him when we got out, and if he was lying about anything, I was going to make him eat it. I nodded and shrugged. "O-kee. You're a clerk who has magical knowledge of the SSF's listening devices—a clerk in the Listening Device Office."

He smiled. "That's the ticket then, Avery. Now"—he nodded past me—"why bring the Pig? He's not pop'lar here, you know."

I spread my hands. "He says he wants in, and he can buy a ticket." I turned to Bartlett, who stood like a small mountain, his eyes bright white. I swept my hand toward the rest. "The floor's yours, Espin."

He glanced at me and then back at the group. I sauntered over to sit down next to Grisha, who greeted me with a nod, and then we were all staring at the ex-cop in silence, the shouts and insults of the Crushers unloading their cargo behind us.

"All right," he grunted, nodding. "You all want out of here. Good. Every single *one* of these shitheads ought to be digging tunnels with their *hands* to get out of here. Flappin' their arms like wings to fly out of here. Fuck the desert, man. Take your chances."

We stared at him. None of us said anything.

He sighed. "Any of you know what an avatar is?"

I let a few seconds go by. "A mechanical ghost," I finally said. "A Droid with an uploaded human brain—a digital recording of a human brain. Made to look like the human, so it goes around looking just like whoever it's supposed to be, acting like him, talking like him." I nodded, reaching down and taking a handful of still-warm dirt. "Used to be they had no eyes—just cameras for eyes, like the Monks. Same technology. But not too long ago I saw one that could've passed for human."

Bartlett nodded. "One of the *new* models. A cop, yeah?"

I nodded back without looking at him. I saw Janet Hense, a pretty little thing. I could remember how she smelled. I could remember the stillborn smile on her face when she left me for dead. I could remember her flying through the air, taking bullets, and not batting an eye. "A cop."

"Reason I'm here, that rat-fuck Marin is replacing cops with *avatars*. And it isn't voluntary, you get it? Your partner goes on assignment, comes back, acting a little wiggy—fuck, his brain's been sucked out of his head and a copy put into storage, a copy put into an avatar. He goes back to the beat; you can't put your finger on why, but you don't trust him anymore. Then, a few weeks later, *boom!* Happens to you. Marin's doing this on every single cop in the force. That's why I'm here—I found out; I started making some trouble." He hung his head for a moment. "Shit, I should have known better."

I kept studying the dirt. None of us said anything until Michaleen cleared his throat. "I don't give a fart about the fucking cops getting theirs," he said amiably. "You got a point?"

Bartlett stared at the little man for a moment and then nodded. "Yeah, I got a point. I said they store a copy, right? Process kills you, but no matter—Marin gets your brain on a quantum drive and it gets stored, and they can make as many of you as they want. Manufacture the body, upload the brain, done. That one gets killed? Do it again. Storage is no problem—you could store the entire force, all seven fucking million cops, in one building." He paused and took his eyes off Michaleen to look at the rest of us. "Could do the same thing with *Persons of Interest*, huh?"

A sharp sense of dread bloomed inside me; rusty blood dripped into clear water.

"They're makin' *avatars* outta us?" Marlena said with a snort.

"No," Bartlett said. "They don't bother. We're all here because we all got something in our heads Marin wants or thinks might be useful. We *People of Fucking Interest.* But he don't need us wandering around in souped-up Monk bodies, passing for human. He just wants what we know. So he rips your brain, puts it on a drive, and stores it. You die, but whenever he gets around to seeing what you got, he just pops you into the Big Iron and pokes around until he finds it." The cop grimaced. "It's called a fucking *economy of resources.* Us sitting here in this prison, it costs money. It costs resources. Sticking us in a solid state storage brick? Cheap."

Grisha sat forward. "So they make a redundant brain wave imprint—using Amblen algorithms, I assume?"

Bartlett shrugged. "Fuck if I know that shit. What I do know is, the assholes they have patrolling this place? That pop up out of nowhere and kick balls?" He nodded. "Avatars. You take one out in some miracle of shithead physics, they're back in an hour, shiny-new. They do real-time incremental backups over the air, so the avatar loses no memory. You can shank the guards here all you want. They'll make more."

Michaleen had closed his eyes again. "So we move soon, or we end up quantum ghosts, eh? All right, *Officer,* I'd be moved to say you've acted in good faith and given us valuable information." His eyes popped open, steely and hard in the midst of his jowly, smiling face. "But how do we know you aren't here to fuck us? A mole? Undercover?"

Bartlett stared for a moment and then sort of deflated. "I guess you don't. Sure, could be, if you think that highly of yourselves." He shrugged. "If that's so then your little escape plot's borked anyway, right?"

Michaleen smiled. "Sure, sure—ruined in any event." He looked around. "I'd take him along. Anyone object?"

The rest were staring at Bartlett but said nothing. The Christian, who I'd never heard speak, shifted lazily, stretching her thin, long limbs.

Michaleen nodded. "All right, Mr. Bartlett—you're in, on fucking sufferance. I don't like the way Pigs smell, so stay upwind, y'hear? Don't irritate me. But you can crawl up our ass when we make the move, providing I don't change my mind."

Bartlett didn't say anything. He just stood there, hands slack at his sides. I wondered what he planned to do, where he planned to go—if there was an Island of Burned Cops out there, somewhere. "Mickey," I said, dropping my handful of dirt and scrubbing my hands. "Speaking of our *move*, what's the plan? Murder an infinite number of avatar-Crushers and die of thirst being cooked and frozen out there?"

Michaleen didn't look at me, but his flattened face turned sour. "I swear, Avery, if I didn't have the tenderest feelings for you as if you were my own son—all right. That's why we're here tonight, isn't it? You're right, we can't just walk out of here. Even if we scale the walls without takin' one in the back, we're wanderin' the desert like fucking assholes. Won't work. So we're not going to *walk*. We're going to *fly*."

A faint rustle of movement swept through everyone, but it died fast and no one said a word. I studied Michaleen's smug, satisfied face, old and leathery, and thought again, *Who the fuck are you, little man?*

XIII

A LITTLE GOD

I twisted my hands in the bracelets, checking them. They'd been put on loosely, but I estimated it would still take me a minute, maybe two due to rust, to get out of them.

"I don't like this," I said.

"So you said," Krasa replied over her shoulder, not slowing her pace. "But fuck you. I can't explain you running around inside here armed and uncuffed. I'm hours away from being burned as it is. We need to maximize that time, not shorten it."

I looked around the corridor. Other cops stalked past us, glanced at Krasa, and ignored Marko and me like we were freight. Krasa swaggered ahead of me like she didn't have a worry, gesturing us through a series of doors with a negligent sort of assumption I admired. She was a cop on the verge of having her file pulled, and she was burrowing into Cop Central with me in tow, unprocessed. She was not fucking herself—she'd been fucked a long time ago. What she was doing was digging up her own body and enthusiastically re-fucking it, and it was kind of exhilarating to watch.

I slid my eyes to Marko, who was holding on to my right arm and trying to look tough. His ID was turned inward inside his jacket, obscuring the blue border that proclaimed him Tech Services. He seemed to enjoy playing the role of ass-kicking cop, though anyone with street eyes would peg him for a paper-pusher at a hundred feet, with his soft posture and off-balance walk, his cheap fucking clothes. He was sweating.

"Tell me about it," I said quietly.

He blinked a few times rapidly. "What? The technology? What Marin's doing? It's elegant."

He turned to look over his shoulder, the fucking asshole, looking guilty. He leaned in close, smelling like bad cologne, the sort of stuff that went bad in the bottle, getting fishy. "Digitization of the brain used to cause unstoppable neuron-mapping corruptions in about ninety-nine percent of subjects, because the original algorithms were based on the assumption that it was the physical makeup of a brain that dictated how it was wired, you know? Instead of realizing that people's brains wired up based on a lot of experiences. But it used to be a ninety-nine percent kill rate—digital copy came out as noise, and noise left behind in the host. It scrambled them. When the Undersecretaries worked on the project that eventually gave us Dick Marin, man, they went through like two hundred candidates before they got one that took. Marin was on like the frickin' tenth list or some shit. They'd hoped for better—Squalor's project, of course, wasn't going to work, but everyone wants to fucking live forever. We solved the problem, though. You can't predict the mapping—you just have to follow every connection, one after the other. Takes fucking *hours*, but it leaves a perfect copy. The host, uh, well, the host still always dies."

He sounded vaguely embarrassed, but I suspected he was only embarrassed to have to *admit* it. "Does sound elegant," I said. "Sort of a zero-sum equation, huh?"

"It *is*," he enthused. "Think about it—four hours and you're digitized, and you can be slotted into an avatar over and over again, or exist in quantum space as a floating intellect. It's *immortality*, you know?" He nodded, his grip on my arm becoming annoyingly tight. I considered teaching him a lesson in shitty fucking police work but decided it would be counterproductive to cause a scene when I was supposed to be wallpaper walking around, just another subdued shithead being escorted to a tune-up.

"What's the scope?"

Marko coughed, and now I thought he *was* actually embarrassed. "Global," he said in a low voice.

"You're fucking kidding," I said, frowning. *Global.* Fucking hell, the whole world, sucked up into a mainframe, dancing to Marin's tune, the avatars equipped with controlling circuits that would force them to do whatever Marin thought was important. Everyone dead, walking the earth. I wondered why it was that the three or four madmen who'd been tearing shit up the last few years were always intent on *killing* everyone.

I felt tired for a moment, then realized I didn't actually feel anything.

"That's why I'm *here*," he said quickly. "Risking my neck. To be fair," Marko went on in his lecturing voice, "there would be advantages. No more violence, no more disorders. Great minds could communicate and collaborate easily, at faster-than-light speeds."

My urge to do some violence to Marko was almost blinding. "Captain," I said in a low voice. "Tell your partner here to shut up, or the prisoner might show him how to break an arm when your hands are secured in front of you."

"Mr. Marko," she said immediately without turning or stopping, "shut the fuck up until spoken to or I might give the prisoner permission."

I didn't look at the Techie, but I heard the satisfying click of teeth as he shut his mouth. Fucking *advantages.* I felt him shift away from me, putting some daylight between us, and felt a little better.

We turned a corner and headed down a dead end that terminated with a door that was exactly like the others except for a thin blue border around the frame. Krasa stopped and let us catch up to her.

"How do you find your way around this place?" I asked, twisting my wrists again.

She didn't look at me. "You memorize everything," she said flatly. "Mr. Marko?"

I frowned a little. "You can't open that door?"

She shrugged her coat onto her shoulders. "Colonels and up can," she said tightly. "Too many lower ranks were barging in and beating the tar out of the Technical Associates."

We stood there in an odd awkward silence for a moment, and then Marko stepped forward, gestured, and the door popped open with a soft click. Krasa immediately shoved him aside and led us through.

"Didn't really stop them," Marko muttered as I stepped past him.

The blue-framed door led to a small room with barely enough floor space for the three of us to stand comfortably. Another handleless door that might have been an exact copy of the first faced us. Wordlessly, Marko stepped forward.

"You got a promotion, huh?" I said to the bush of hair threatening to envelop Marko's neck.

He half turned his head, looking down at the floor with his hand raised. His jaw muscles bunched. "Hense wrote me up, a commendation," he said. "I'm assistant director of Technical Services for the Northeast Administrative Division."

I gave Marko a low whistle, admiring his broad shoulders and impressively curly hair. "Assistant fucking director, huh?"

He snapped his head forward again and gestured the door open. "Fuck you," he muttered.

My hands twitched. Krasa barked a laugh. "Fuck *you*, he says, bold as fucking brass." My arms started upward, and her hand lashed out and took hold of one wrist, stopping me. "Don't assault the assistant director," she said, and pushed Marko roughly toward the door. "Technically, he outranks me."

I put a small, inoffensive smile on my face and offered up the low, impressed whistle again.

The *assistant fucking director* led us into a lab setup, white walls and floor, black ceiling, counters and equipment lining the walls. It wasn't a particularly large room. The far wall was dotted with dozens of input jacks.

Marko swept into the room fluidly, stretching and pulling off his jacket, his sleeves already rolled up. He looked bigger suddenly, like a guy who'd found his scale—like the room had been built around him, perfectly proportioned to him. I let my hands rest and just watched him as he crossed over to a bank of cabinets and began searching through them fussily, gesturing open the locked drawers with perfunctory, well-learned movements. His hands looked like they belonged on someone else, like they weren't really part of his short, chubby body. Like he'd stolen them from someone else.

"Let's see, I know I had him down here. A copy of him, I mean."

"An unauthorized copy," Krasa said softly, sounding bored.

"Yes, yes," Marko muttered, opening drawers and peering into them in rapid succession. "Ah! Here he is."

He turned, yellow teeth ugly in the midst of all that hair. He was holding a slim white rectangular box in one hand, thin and stained with several dark fingerprints. A short cable hung from one end, dangling in the air. "Meet Dr. Amblen. Or a simulacrum thereof." The smile disappeared, snapping off his face instantly. "I'm never clear on the terminology."

"Uh-huh." I gave my wrists a twist, feeling nothing. "And what do we do with him?"

"Ah!" Marko snapped his fingers and turned, striding for the far wall. "We plug him in, of course. The bricks are set to go into sleep cycle when disconnected and to wake up on plug in."

With his back to us, he took the dangling cable in one hand and shoved it into a jack on the wall, apparently at random. Then he took a single step back.

"Dr. Amblen?"

Nothing happened. Marko turned to flash us a politician's grin, holding up one hand to signal patience. I investigated and found I didn't have any, but I did have a strap around my wrists so I didn't do anything about it.

"Dr. Amblen?" Marko repeated, at the same volume.

There was a curious humming sound, tuneless and irritating. It went on for a few seconds, and I wanted to cover my ears or walk out of the room, the sound getting under my skin somehow and scraping along my nerves. Then it was gone, and there was a hollow sense of someone on the line, as if we'd made a particularly long-distance connection to someone.

"Who are you?"

Marko turned around and gave us his political grin again. "He doesn't retain much from session to session, due to limited storage and low voltage in the brick. We actually didn't expect *any* retention when in portable storage—we expected them to boot up back in their initial states every time. But he does remember certain things. He sometimes thinks they're dreams."

"I said...who are you?"

The simulated voice was elderly, shaky and dry. It pumped outrage and anger into the room. I immediately formed a mental image of Dr. Amblen, who I'd never seen: white and pale, with skin like paper, white haired and severe, a long, sharp nose cutting through the air disdainfully. I hated him.

"I'm Dr. Ezekiel Marko, Dr. Amblen," Marko said, still grinning at us as he shoved his hands into his pockets. "We've spoken before."

"We have not," the voice snapped, swelling up suddenly, as if the bits and bytes inside the brick had finally gotten their shit together and formed up into an actual intelligence. His frail voice

quaked through the air as if he were the room, or the shell—but I'd never heard a shell with that much cranky, pissed-off personality. *"I'm not feeling well."*

I wondered, for a second, how they came up with the voice—and *why*. Why bother giving him a voice that approximated his own, or did they just have a generic old-man voice?

"Dr. Amblen," Marko continued, still grinning, like this was a pattern, something he'd been through many times. "I'd like to ask you a few questions. About the Deva Project. You freelanced on it."

There was a pause, the only sound the steady hum. *"I do not wish to talk about that. Who are you?"*

Marko's smile was painted on, painful to look at. "I'm Dr. Ezekiel Marko, and I need to know infiltration vectors for the consciousness matrix you helped design. I need to know data flow patterns, handshake codes, and security layers."

That hum again, edging into my organs and making them swell.

"You're looking to hack, naughty boy," Amblen said crisply. *"Don't you pups know anything about social engineering? You don't just* ask *for such things. You provoke them. You trick, you charm."* He sounded peevish. *"Everything went to hell during Unification. Straight to fucking hell."*

Marko nodded. "I need infiltration vectors for the Deva Project, Dr. Amblen. Will you help?"

"All the information I could give you is outdated. Keys changed, numbers resifted, new layers added. This was years ago, son."

Marko kept nodding. "Yes. Will you help?"

Another pause. *"The Deva Project. Hmmph. You're going after that son of a bitch Marin, yes?"* There was a blast of weird static, as if Amblen had tried to make a sound the rendering software couldn't interpret. *"Then yes, by god, I'll help. Where...where am I? I need my lab. Take me...what...take me to my lab."*

Marko was smiling and nodding, but his eyes were suddenly locked on Krasa. I followed his gaze, studying her for a moment before realizing what he'd noticed: Her gold badge, the pocket-sized hologram that made her a *cop*, a little god, was no longer gold. It glowed a bloody, rusty red.

"You've been burned," he said to her, his voice somehow containing wonder.

She tore at her coat and stared. I looked back at Marko and smiled at him. "So have you!" I said cheerfully, enjoying it for some reason.

He lifted his jacket and stared at his own ID badge, which had transformed from a soft hazy blue to the same shade of angry red.

"Oh, *shit*," he said softly.

XIV

ROLLING ALONG TO SOME INEVITABLE DISASTER

Everything was fucked.

I stared down through smoke and sweat at the body of the Christian—shit, I'd never even learned her name. We were in the yard next to the fence around the arrival area, down in a hastily dug pit that gave some cover from the snipers on the towers. Not enough cover; the Christian's head had popped in a silent explosion, as if someone had planted a bomb inside her brain when she'd been born and waited, patiently, until the right moment to press the button.

Reaching up, I wiped her warm blood from my face. It was gritty with the sandy dirt we'd been excavating. I blinked my burning eyes and sat back for a moment. The Christian stared at me, one eye red and blown. I still didn't mind dying. Michaleen's plan was a good one, and I'd been entertained to take my part in it, but if it all ended with my own skull exploding in a sudden burst of bone and blood—well, I figured I wouldn't even know it. And no one would deserve it more.

It was a strange, quiet spot—I could hear the roar in the distance, but it was a mile away, distant in space and time, something that was going to happen in five minutes. Shouts and screams and gunshots and a disturbing booming sound I couldn't figure. Michaleen had been right: starting a riot in Chengara had been about as hard as starting a fire in a gas can. The trick was keeping it going long enough, and the little man had assured me he had his end covered.

I looked around. The yard was blanketed with thick, gray haze pouring from a few dozen smoke grenades. I wasn't sure how, but the Crushers—avatars with whatever gadgetry came standard—were able to see right through the smoke and nail anyone scampering along the ground. I figured if I stayed low in my little ditch I'd be okay, and a thick, insistent urge to do just that weighed me down. I wasn't afraid, but the effort of moving just seemed incredible, impossible.

I looked back at the Christian. Her ruined eye glared at me. I'd never spent so much time right next to a corpse—usually I needed to get away as quickly as possible, and most times I'd been dodging bullets and trying to remember floor plans, desperate. Her absolute stillness was fucking annoying. I wanted to stretch out a leg and jostle her a little.

Thinking of my leg made it ache. I looked away from the girl. Michaleen wouldn't know my end had gotten sticky—he'd be proceeding with the plan, stoking the fire until the walls blistered and peeled, until the Crushers started boiling into gas around us. Until it got so bad they sent in the fucking cavalry. Until the hovers, stuffed full of Stormers or avatars or whatever the fuck Marin sent in the hovers these days, floated down from the sky, death and terror. Our ticket out.

"Never the easy way," I muttered.

The easy way would be to just lie back and let it wash over me—or, better, to stand up and wave my arms until suddenly—lights out.

I looked over her body at the edge of the chain-link fence separating the yard from the arrival area. We'd feverishly dug out underneath it, bullets and smoke grenades flying, until the fence could be lifted up a few inches, enough for the skinny little girl to wriggle under, our Snake earning her way. The plan had been for us to duck under the fence and wait for the hover that Michaleen guaranteed would land, apart from the others, in the arrivals area. "Standard fucking procedure," he'd said. Didn't matter that no one much cared if we all scattered into the desert to die; the SSF had a standard response to prison upsets, and part of it was securing the arrivals area.

"They maybe have shiny chrome brains," Michaleen had said, "but they're still the same fucking assholes as ever, and they will follow standard operating procedure."

The rest had been pretty simple: let the bulk of the crew disperse to their postings, and when the skeleton crew was alone, I kill everyone. The genius details of how that was accomplished were left to me. The hover pilot would lock down his brick, and then our Snake would crawl in through the obscure, vulnerable maintenance hatch under the hover's belly, release the drop-bay hatch, and I'd finish the job. Then we'd wait for everyone else to crawl in and be on our way.

Simple. Stupid simple. But I'd had nothing better to do.

I eyed the fence. I thought I'd be able to pull myself under it in return for some of the skin on my back and arms. As far as dealing with the hover, that would require just one slight adjustment to the plan: I'd have to kill the pilot first.

Behind me, there was an explosion.

I whirled as the fireball shot upward, swelling and fading, heat and wind pushing against me. I didn't know what had gone up—if it was one of Michaleen's little surprises or just a fluke—but it was a sign. No one was looking at my dark little square of the world for the next few moments, and I thought, fuck, I didn't want to die sitting in a dark hole, unnoticed. I was Avery Fucking Cates. If I was going to die, I wanted at least to tug a bit on Marin's tail, let him know how I'd gone. Maybe drag him down with me.

I pushed at the dead feeling in my limbs, poking it, testing it. I knew I was just a piece of the machinery, a ball bearing in a machined trench, rolling exactly where the universe wanted me to go. I'd been on a rail, my whole life. I figured, what the hell: if the universe had me on a rail, then it didn't matter what I did or didn't do; I'd either die or live or burst into flames or grow wings—whatever the universe had waiting for me was going to happen, probably. So I was either immortal—if it wasn't my time, nothing was going to kill me—or I was fucked. Might as well cause a little damage while I skittered down the trench, rolling along to some inevitable disaster. Either way I was never going to be free.

The thought got my heart pumping. *Why not?* I thought, and took a deep breath, diving for the fence, getting my fingers under its bottom edge. It was thick, stiff wire, and getting it up just a few inches was hard, arm-trembling work. I twisted around and pulled my torso through, suddenly desperate to get moving, to start doing something. Months spent drifting fell away, and I was frantic to get some momentum going. The sharp ends of the fence tearing up my stomach and legs, I pulled and wriggled under it and lay on the other side in cool, deep shadows. I lay for a moment, panting, looking up into the smoke-filled sky. I could see lights, the gem of a hover floating above us, and then there were several in the sky, and the distant hurricane of displacement made the cooling ground tremble beneath me. They were beautiful.

As I lay there, they spread apart, five or six of them heading for the yard and, sure enough, one right above me. Fucking Michaleen—whoever, whatever he was, he had good intel. He'd said he could prod the prison into a storm, and so he had. He'd said one hover would put down in the arrivals area, and so it was. Except for not foreseeing the Christian's head exploding from a sniper's bullet, he'd been spot-on so far.

For some reason the Christian made me feel better about

Michaleen. It was good to know the fucking dwarf could make
a mistake.

The hovers dropped like graceless rocks, making me brace
for an impact, but then touched down as soft as dust, one after
the other, weightless bricks. Mine hit the ground just a foot or
two away from me, filling most of the fenced-in space. The drop
bay was on the opposite side; I lay very still and listened to the
familiar sound of Stormers being screamed out of their hovers.
I waited for the universe to tilt the board and send me rolling
again. The Stormers poured out of my hover in a brisk, orderly
formation, so close they could have smelled me if they'd paid
any attention. I watched the majority of them double-time it into
the prison area proper, leaving three behind to guard the hover,
plus the pilot, unseen inside his shell.

I wondered if these were humans or avatars.

I didn't know how to kill an avatar. My hands curled up into
fists, tight against my bleeding belly. I knew how to kill people,
how to make it fast or slow, with their breath in my ear or from
across a dark room. It was—had been—my profession. I even
knew how to kill Monks—

I remembered someone saying the avatar tech was based on
the Monks, a new generation. A refinement, not a new technology. I knew enough about tech to figure they wouldn't reroute
every bus, wouldn't be able to overhaul the whole design. They'd
simply replace the one thing in the Monk design they no longer
needed: the brain. A headshot would probably be enough. Do
enough damage to anything and it stopped working.

I was no Techie, but I didn't have time to investigate. Taking a deep breath, I counted to five and slowly rolled out of my
shadow.

Noise wasn't a problem—another explosion made the ground
vibrate beneath me as I rolled, and everything else was a formless
swirl of noise, displacement and gunfire and shouts. I put myself
under the hover in a fast, continuous roll. Stopping and starting

was what drew eyes to you; with everything else moving around, the Stormers, even if they were avatars, would be more likely to ignore more motion than they would something that kept jerking to a halt and then moving again. *Keep moving*—the fucking story of my life. Under the hover, at the bottom of a pool of shadows, I stopped and closed my eyes, listening for any sign that the Stormers had noticed me.

Three, four heartbeats—nothing.

The pilot had to be first. Without our Snake to wriggle in through the redundant maintenance hatch, if the pilot sealed the hover, the big turrets mounted under its nose would pretty much spell the end of our little escape plan. I'd wriggled *out* of a hover not so long ago, during the Plague, but Ty Kieth had cleared out the hatch by then and gravity had done the rest. Forcing my way up, bum leg and all, sounded like the perfect way to get stuck like a cork and then shot in the ass. Even if it was what the universe wanted, I wasn't going to shuffle off that way, shot in the fucking ass.

I opened my eyes and counted feet. Six in view, two sets in front with their backs to the hover, one by the drop-bay hatch. I considered human psychology as I knew it—and even if these were walking quantum hard drives they were based on human brains—and figured the Stormer by the drop bay would be a little less on edge, a little less worried; after all, they thought we were all shitheads. We'd all been rounded up and taken here in the first place, right? Soft. No guns. And even if we did manage to make a run on the hover, we'd be coming from *inside* the prison. He'd assume plenty of lead time.

I rolled as softly as I could to the side of the hover. The Stormer's boots, shiny and pristine, were an inch or two from my face.

I palmed one of my blades and then lay there, motionless. No tendons to cut, if it was an avatar. For a moment I hesitated, and then I thought: *What the hell. I'm on the rail.* If my card got pulled, it got pulled, and there was probably no way to stop it. Sucking in a painful, chest-burning breath, I rolled out from under the hover into the open air, pushing myself to my feet just as a third explosion sent another fireball into the air. *God bless the dwarf,* I thought, and launched myself at the Stormer, knocking him backward into the drop bay and pushing my knife into his face as hard as I could.

There was a little blood—cool and fake, but convincing enough for a second, and then white coolant bubbled up, turning the whole mess pink. It shivered once beneath me and went still, and I lay on top of it, panting, leg aching, vaguely disappointed. I wanted gore. I wanted blood. Fucking avatars.

I held my breath, chest twitching, and listened.

Rolling off the Stormer, I stood up and palmed another of my blades and crept forward toward the cockpit as my eyes adjusted to the gloom of the drop bay. The pilot was still seated, busy working over a digital tablet, her small hands dancing through a series of complex gestures. I didn't pause to contemplate or admire; I stepped steadily behind her and grabbed her helmet with one hand, jerking her head upward and stabbing up through her chin, hard, something brittle and completely inhuman snapping as I yanked upward with all my strength.

Then silence broken by the thin sound of me breathing through my clogged nose.

I turned and stepped back to the drop-bay hatch, hunching down to sit, with my legs dangling over the edge and the dead—if *dead* was the right term for an avatar—Stormer next to me. I relieved it of its sidearm—a piece-of-shit generic that felt too light and insubstantial in my hand, like it would peel open and take my hand with it if I ever dared fire it. Not long ago the System Pigs had had the best of everything, and that meant Roon automatics. If this was the shit they were issued now, it was no wonder they were fighting a sudden civil war.

I dropped to my feet awkwardly, my bad leg buckling a little under me, making me wave my arms around to get my balance. The noise rushed back around me, screaming and shouting, gunfire, a rhythmic, steady booming noise I couldn't identify. The rhythm of it took over and I moved toward the two remaining Stormers using it, feeling ridiculous but not caring—it was the universe, the cosmos pulling my strings, and I was just a fucking puppet flopping my way toward two more murders, although I hadn't decided if avatars counted as murder. Marin would just pump out four more bodies to replace these, built from spare parts or poured into molds or whatever. I crept forward until I was a foot or two away, the muzzle of my new gun just half an inch away from the back of one Stormer's head. My hand, I noted without emotion, shook slightly.

Fast. I squeezed the trigger, felt the surprisingly light kick of the gun, swiveled precisely, and squeezed the trigger again, and both Stormers dropped one after the other.

It felt good to be back in the cut, rolling along. I turned and pocketed my gun, heading back for the hover. As I climbed up into it, I pushed the dead Stormer off onto the ground, then headed back for the cockpit. I just shifted the pilot to the other seat, sweat popping out on my brow, the air of the hover getting closer and hotter as I worked. Then I sat in the pilot's seat and squinted through the windshield, listening as carefully as I could.

I closed my eyes. *Why not?* The universe was protecting me. I imagined Gleason next to me, her tiny body tucked easily into the copilot's seat, saying something mean. *Oh, Avery's cold-blooded. Avery's scary.* Or, *Avery can pull a trigger. Avery's a fucking trained monkey.* I smiled, thinking of her. She was safe now, at least.

I opened my eyes and was startled to see Michaleen, Marlena, and Grisha running for the hover, the skinny Russian hanging off Marlena, blood from a deep scalp wound covering his face. His glasses hung from his nose and one ear, bent and shattered, but the crazy bastard was smiling lazily, like something wonderful had just occurred to him.

I smacked my head against the low ceiling of the cockpit as I stood and made it to the open hatch as they arrived.

"Damn, son," Michaleen said breathlessly, grinning the most natural smile I'd ever seen on his sharp, edged face. "You *are* pretty good dealing the cards, eh? Sure, sure."

"Grisha here left them some surprises," Marlena said, grinning.

"Where's Bartlett?" I asked. Marlena pushed Grisha up at me like a sack of groceries, and Michaleen vaulted into the drop bay like a man of fifty, muttering under his breath.

"He's back there being an asshole," Marlena panted, taking my offered hand and pulling herself up. "And probably having his old badge shoved up his ass. The old woman he moons around got snatched up, taken down—*under* us, man; that's where all this mystery shit happens. He said he had to go after her."

I glanced at the cockpit, where Michaleen had disappeared. "You just left him?"

She was dragging Grisha toward the back wall where the safety netting was. "The *cop*? Uh, yeah, Avery. We left the *cop*. No one was stopping him from coming along."

For a moment I just stood there, slightly hunched in the open hatch. I was calm—I had no worries. I was on the rail. "I'm gonna go extract them."

"What?" Marlena was busy strapping Grisha in. Then she turned and glared at me. "Extract? *Them?* What the *fuck* is wrong with you?"

I shrugged. "We all get out. The cop's part of this," I said easily. I hadn't made any promises, but you didn't just leave someone behind because it was convenient. I didn't say anything about Salgado and our conversation. She'd told me not to worry about her, but I thought it might be good to snatch her back, if only to deny Marin whatever she had in her head. I studied Grisha, who'd gone unconscious. I jerked my head toward the cockpit. "Don't let that fucking midget take off without us," I said, giving her a little smile.

She was still hunched over the Russian, head twisted back toward me. She blinked and opened her mouth and then something took hold of my shoulder and pulled, hard, and I was sailing through the air. I landed on my ass, teeth clicking together on my tongue and filling my mouth with blood, pain shooting up my leg and directly into my brain.

My non-Crusher, the bearded one from the train Bartlett had taken out just a few days ago, stepped quickly toward me, snapping out its shithead-be-good stick with a smart twitch of its wrist. Grinning, it swung and cracked the club against my head, spinning me over backward, my skull smacking against the hard-packed ground.

With a sudden roar, the hover lurched up, an ugly liftoff that had it fishtailing, displacers whining unhappily. My non-Crusher grunted, stumbling as the displacement hit it. I stared up, head swimming, as the hover smoothed out and began rising into the hot, smoky air. Marlena's head had appeared over the edge, staring down, her face a wide mask of surprise, one hand stretched out down toward me.

Then the hover shot upward, shrinking fast. The non-Crusher, fat face bristling with real-looking dark whiskers, appeared in its place. "Welcome back," it hissed, and swung its arm down again.

XV

A MARKO ORIGINAL

I looked around, the silence so thick and dusty it almost sizzled. "No alarms?"

Krasa shook her head, her eye moving around the room in quick flashes. "No need. Our badge sigs won't work anywhere, so no doors will open for us anyway. They know where we are." She removed her badge, tossing it onto the floor without looking at it. It glowed there like a cold ember. "We're trapped in here until the Worms show up."

Marko had removed his badge as well and was holding it in front of him, staring at it.

"Guess you've been de-promoted," I said. I twisted my hands and held them out in front of me. "Maybe we don't need this anymore?"

Krasa glanced at me, her eyes distant. "What does it matter? You're going to be scooped up with us."

"Who is speaking?" Amblen whispered, his voice a hiss all around us. *"Who is there? Dr. Marko?"*

I twisted my wrists, bracing for pain out of old habit, and gave a sharp tug in opposite directions. I felt nothing, though, as one of my hands popped free. I let the bracelets drop to the floor. "We can't just sit here," I said, trying to stay calm and reasonable.

"We can't just *let* them." I'd come too far. I'd been through too much. I'd had too many people die on me. I'd killed too many.

"*I need to be in my* lab," Amblen whispered.

I looked up at the ceiling, imagining Internal Affairs, fucking avatars, making their way to us, burrowing through the steel and rock of the building, spreading webs of wires apart to slide through, their eyes clouded and blind in the darkness. The Worms come to eat Krasa and do worse to me. An uneasy shiver of fear swept through me. If the cops were scared...shit, that didn't leave much for the rest of us. "Where's your lab?" I said to the air.

For a moment there was just the sizzle of that unnatural silence. Then Amblen's voice: "*Who is there? Dr. Marko?*"

"Where's your *fucking* lab, you dead shit, or I'll tear you out of the wall and break your brick in half, okay?"

The sizzle again. Marko looked up at me sharply and blinked, his eyes coming back to life. Then Amblen again, sounding stronger, louder.

"*You're a rude person, whoever you are. Dr. Marko? Are you still here? I will not deal with this person.*"

I opened my mouth, but Marko waved at me and stepped forward, looking around as if Amblen were in the air between us. "I'm here, Dr. Amblen. I apologize for my...assistant. He's not very bright, and things he doesn't understand anger him." I raised an eyebrow at the Techie, and he flushed, turning his back to me. "We need to know where your lab is, Dr. Amblen, so we can take you there."

I nodded to myself and decided to forgive Marko the insult. At least the kid was still working it. Walking over to Krasa, I waited until the last second and then flashed my arm up, intending to slap her across the face. Her arm came up fast and blocked me, and for a moment we stood there, our forearms touching, a few inches apart, her breath coming in short snorts through her nose, her golden eye catching the flat white light and blazing at me.

"Oh, are you awake again?" I said. "Sorry. For a moment there it looked like you were going to pull the fucking covers over your head and have a good fucking cry. They're coming, right? You got, what, a minute? Two?"

She swallowed. "They will take their time," she said. "What's the rush?"

"You going to cry, Krasa?" I said.

Her nose flared. I wondered if that fucking eye of hers could beam out lasers or some shit—if there was any possibility, this would be the moment.

She blinked. "How?"

It was a clipped, businesslike syllable, and it gave me some hope. "Mr. Marko?" I said without looking away. "Any thoughts on escaping this building?"

"None whatsoever," he said amiably. "We're dead."

I made fists. I wanted to hit him a little, knock the life back into him. "Well, let's start small," I said, pushing the words out. "Can you open the fucking door?"

"Sure," he said. "Dr. Amblen? Where is your lab?"

A memory bubbled up suddenly—of course I knew where Amblen's lab was. *Everyone* on the streets knew that or at least knew where it was rumored to be. "The Star," I said. "It's in the goddamn Star."

"The Star," Marko said under his breath. "Sure, of course."

"You might call it that," Amblen's voice complained. *"Street trash call it that, yes. We called it Liberty Island."*

Corny, I thought. "Marko, open the damn door," I suggested. "Let's get moving."

"Sure, sure," Marko muttered vaguely, looking like he was happy to just stand there and stare around, absorbing knowledge from the air or some such shit. I strode over to him and took hold of his jacket, yanking him off his feet like he weighed nothing and tossing him across the room toward the door. He spun awkwardly and danced a few steps, arms out, until he caught himself against the wall.

"Open the fucking door," I suggested again. "Or I'll beat the beard off you, okay?"

He stared at me and then surprised me by smiling. "Good to be working with you again, you psychopath," he said and turned to examine the door, one hand disappearing into a side pocket, searching.

I nodded and turned toward the wall of sockets, taking the brick in my hand. "Dr. Amblen, I'm going to unplug you now."

"*Un*plug? *What the*—"

I tore the cable from the wall, and his voice disappeared.

"Don't do it that way," Marko called from the door, sounding calm but irritated. "You could corrupt his data profile. Scramble him."

I studied the brick. I couldn't feel it, but I had a sense that it was warm. Made me think of someone's brain inside it, like a compacted Monk, and I wanted to put it down and wash my hands. I slipped it into the pocket of my coat and looked at Krasa, scrubbing my hands against my shirt. "Weapons?"

She looked at me for a second and then nodded, kneeling down and extracting a nice-looking small automatic from her ankle holster and handing it over to me.

Krasa pulled her own auto. "I'm not going alive," she said to it, eye moving up and down, admiring. "Let's try, but if it comes to a decision, I'd rather be dead."

"Speak for yourself, *Officer*. How do we get out?"

She started pacing, which I took as an encouraging sign. I felt nothing—no rush of adrenaline, no pounding heart, nothing. Prison had burned it all out of me.

"Got any allies?"

She snapped her hand up and waved it at me. "Fuck, allies. We're all dead. Police. Everyone's a goddamn robot now."

I wasted a second or two staring at her. "I thought System Pigs were tough." I pictured her handling me so easily on the street, calloused hands shutting me down the old-fashioned way. "How'd you become a cop?"

She was looking around as if dazed. "I scored well on a test," she said, finally focusing on me. "When I was a kid."

"There," Marko hissed from across the room. The door sagged open, like it had gotten tired of holding itself shut. "Come on."

Krasa fell into step next to me. "Drop your badges," I suggested. "So they can't trace us."

"We're tagged," Krasa said, her voice firming up as we approached the door. "Subdermal chip. They can track us anywhere in the System."

We stopped at the door. *I* wasn't tagged. And I had Amblen in my pocket—I didn't need two burned ex-SSF leading every fucking Worm in the world right to me. From this moment forward, I realized, my life would be incredibly simplified if I left Marko and Krasa behind. My finger moved to the trigger on the piece-of-shit auto, and then off—I'd made a deal, of sorts, with Krasa. I could walk away from her, give her fair warning, but to just clip her from behind was weak. Grimacing for myself, I took a deep breath.

"This is your building," I said, my voice low as we listened to the foyer's air. "I'm all ears."

"Morgue," Marko said immediately, peering through the crack of the open door. "Go out with the bodies. Dumped into transport every night and hovered over to incineration. Hover's autopilot, all Droid."

Fucking efficient. I turned back and retrieved Krasa's badge from the floor.

"They'll see our tags, asshole," Krasa complained. "They'll dig us out."

"Where are the tags?" I asked.

She moved her eye to me. "Back, over the right shoulder. Deep. You can't miss the scar," she said in a low, steady voice, like she was filling up with herself again, slowly firming up. "Why?"

I ignored the question. "Marko, how do we get to the morgue?"

"Easy peasy. All roads in this building lead to the morgue."

He said it flatly, without emotion, and I got the feeling it was a phrase he'd coined a long time ago, a Marko original. I wanted to twist his nose again.

"All right, get us there."

We pushed into the little foyer and stood awkwardly while Marko, breathing heavily, worked on the outer door with a set of tiny, delicate-looking tools in one hands and a small, wallet-sized unit that buzzed loudly in the other. He touched the tip of a tool to the door, grunted, and then deftly switched tools in his hands and tried again. After about a minute, his grunt was immediately followed by the soft click of the door unlocking, and he quickly stuffed his little tools into his jacket pockets and pulled it a crack. I wondered what would fall out of his pockets onto the floor if I was to grab him by the ankles and shake him.

Pushing the door all the way open, he motioned us after him back into the white, antiseptic hallway.

"Keep your coats closed," I advised, handing the badge back to Krasa, who took it gingerly between two fingers. "Hide those badges. We still need them."

"What are we doing?" Krasa hissed into my ear, her perfume surrounding me for a second. "They're *tracking* us, you fucking street trash. Wherever we go, they'll find us."

A trio of cops approached, and I tensed up. They were young guys, wearing identical white shirts with their sleeves rolled up, their ties loose around their necks, black leather holsters jammed in their armpits. They looked like kids trying to be tough, but I'd been tuned up often enough by youngsters just like them, shiny red-faced fuckers with nothing but energy. They didn't pay us any attention, sweeping past us without even a curt nod at Krasa.

"The Worms don't bother putting out general alerts," she whispered.

When we hit the first door, she gestured us through without hesitating—no way to reprogram every door in the building, I guessed. I was lost almost immediately in the white, unmarked halls, but Marko moved confidently, and after a few turns he gestured open a pair of large doors and waved us into a large, dark freight elevator.

I hesitated just a second—the cab smelled like blood, and the floor was…soft and sticky. I decided not to investigate too closely, keeping my eyes straight ahead. Marko stepped in after us and gestured; the doors slid shut, and the air turned a dull red from the weak light inside the cab.

We said nothing. Krasa and I checked our guns as best we could in the dim light and then held them ready. When the doors split open and that damned clean light flooded the cab again, I stepped forward quickly, pushing Marko out of the way and moving to the side in order to get clear of Krasa's fire, my eyes adjusting to the harsh light immediately, instantly.

It was a large room, aggressively air-conditioned. I couldn't feel the cold, but I could see Krasa's breath steaming out of her as we both relaxed. There was a large bank of drawers across from us, each with an impressive chrome handle and a small Vid screen.

Between us and the drawers were piled body bags, shining wetly in the bare light. They were heaped haphazardly, with empty ones mixed in like rotted fruit.

"Anyone we need to actually keep track of, in the slots," Marko said briskly, moving through the piles toward the opposite wall. "Everyone else just gets dumped in the middle. Our best bet is the bags—no ID on them, they just get dumped and shipped out." I watched him bend down to pick up an empty bag and inspect it, wincing and jerking back as he got a good smell. "Fucking hell," he muttered, and then looked up at me. I was amazed at how far Marko had come. He was almost a god-damn grown-up.

"Trip to the ovens is fifteen minutes, give or take; hover leaves every hour or so," he said. "You got a plan beyond that?"

Every hour—I wondered how many corpses were being generated in The Rock every day. I nodded at Marko. "Chips and badges go into a bag, any bag," I said. "Then *we* get into a bag, too. Sure, they'll trace us here, they'll find the fucking chips, they'll know we were here." I nodded to myself, jamming my gun into my pocket and slipping my blade into one hand. "But they'll never think we *stayed* here. Human nature would be to put distance between those chips and ourselves."

"You can't be sure they won't just search the whole room. Or that they won't just put bullets into every bag," Krasa said, star-ing at her gun.

I nodded. "Sure. You've got a ten-second window to suggest better options." I waited, staring at her, and then nodded. "Then take your jackets off." I examined the knife and its tattered, taped-up handle. "I can't promise to be gentle."

XVI

WONDER WHAT HE USES *NEEDLES* FOR

Someone was singing.

"*Hänschen klein ging allein, in die weite Welt hinein,*" a woman's voice lilted softly, far away, coming to me through layers of pain and darkness. A breathy, girlish sort of voice. I thought of my mother for the first time in decades...I remembered little about her, but this voice, for some reason, brought her back to me. I remembered her fat arms, the fine hairs on them, reaching out for me. That was it. That was all I had.

After a moment I realized I was moving, gliding along.

"*Stock und Hut steht ihm gut, er ist wohlgemut,*" she continued, low and almost sexy, and then drifted into humming, sounding happy.

"You are awake," she said suddenly. "You've been waiting for a long time. That is too bad for you."

I opened my eyes. A shiny electrical conduit snaked above me, bolted into the rough cement. I turned my head and looked around, and as I did so sound rushed back to me, a sizzling silence broken only by the squeaking wheel of the gurney I was strapped onto.

By tilting my head backward a bit I brought her into view: An old woman, midforties maybe, blond hair unnaturally vivid and face unnaturally smooth and refreshed looking. She was wearing a simple suit of black fabric and a bright white lab coat. She glanced down at me and smiled, nodding once and looking back up.

"Why," I asked, my throat burning, "is that bad for me?"

Her smile kinked up in the corners, becoming cruel. "The procedure is extremely *invasive*."

I tested the straps and found them professionally applied, my arms pinned down so tightly I was pretty sure the circulation had been stopped. I remembered Marlena staring down at me and thought her face had been honestly horrified, honestly surprised as that cocksucker Michaleen took the hover up, leaving me to the dogs.

Leaving me to *this*.

I still wasn't afraid. I imagined dying—just everything turning off, suddenly gone, and felt nothing. I didn't worry about dying; I'd been coasting on fumes for so long I think somewhere in the shadowed parts of my brain I'd already decided I *was* dead, in a sense.

But I was *angry*.

The cocksucker had *lied* to me. About everything—about my *father*. I'd known—deep down I'd known all along, but I'd wanted it to be true, to have that connection. I was a fucking punk, but I was going to make Mickey eat it. I strained my arms against the straps; they didn't even budge. I had work to do—it was going to be hell finding one small man buried in the shit of the System, especially with a fucking civil war going on, but if I could just get one arm free, I was going to break this woman's neck and get started.

"Do not struggle, dear," she murmured, not looking at me. "You're *quite* secure."

I believed her. Her face was round and plump, a well-fed face, with a ruddy complexion and a cheerful expression. The bitch was smiling as she pushed me toward *processing*.

"Who are you?" I asked. My voice came out thick and rusty, phlegm pooled in the back of my throat.

Her smile brightened, but she didn't look down at me. Above her, the conduit streamed along, occasionally bending this way and that. "Now why does that matter, dear?"

I made my face into a smiling mask, even though she wasn't looking at me. "I'm taking names for future reference, so I can kill everyone who touches me here." *After I find Michaleen,* I thought.

She didn't look impressed. If anything, her face brightened even more. "Oh, that's *charming*, Mr. Cates. They told me you were a handful. I'm going to have *fun* with you!"

I relaxed my neck and stared up at the ceiling, testing my hands and legs again. I wondered if this was where the rail led to, if this was what the universe had in mind for me. Tilting my head forward as much as I could, I got a quick look at some swinging double doors just before we crashed through them, entering a large room, the ceiling suddenly jumping up another few feet. It was bright and cold; the walls were still the same rough concrete but lined with humming boxes of a dark, rough-looking metal, like something that had been fired until it scorched. Cables snaked along the ceiling, suspended by small clamps and wires, running from box to box. The hum immediately got into my bones and made me nervous, like it was vibrating my DNA.

"They're coming in fast and furious," a male voice said, out of my field of vision. "Assholes brought the hammer down on them, and there's nothing for it but to stuff them down here and speed things up. Order is, process them as fast as we can and try to limit kills."

"Fast as we can," the woman sniffed, stepping away from me. "The problem with the world is that it is not run by scientists. If Director Marin wants things to go smoothly, he should do a better job of keeping the army away from this site. I can't work properly if I've got to have my bags packed for an immediate evac all the time."

"It's a mess, all right," the man agreed. There was a large, bright light above me, making me squint. "I hear they just took Vegas. Just carpet bombed the hover-port and went in, expecting street-by-street resistance, but Marin pulled out, ordering all SSF into the California Department for re-regrouping."

"He got caught out," the woman said with a sigh. "Digital memory storage and synapse replication doesn't make you any *smarter*, does it?"

The man laughed but didn't sound amused. "Be careful, Dr. Kerril. Director Marin has big ears."

"Tut," she said. "If he thinks he's going to process millions of people without me, he's mistaken. I think he knows that he needs me." She sighed. "Well, let's get moving. I've got another dozen already piled up in the waiting room. Word from the mountain is to just liquidate the whole population; the army's too close and the riot's compromised basic security here. It's going to be a long night."

"*How* close? I don't relish ending up standing in front of Ruberto's desk. I hear he's issued a blanket death sentence to anyone arrested in the field. We might not even make it to his desk."

There was a sudden, distant tremor, a dull booming noise, and I felt a soft vibration shiver through the whole room. Everything went quiet for a moment, and then three more tremors followed in quick succession. I felt a fine mist of dust spray down onto me.

"How close?" the man demanded again.

"Show some backbone and get to work."

There were some metallic noises, like metal scraping against metal, and the humming in the air grew in volume, getting thicker. My heart was pounding, adrenaline swelling me, making the straps intolerable. My hat went off to whoever had designed and applied the straps—they were fucking world-class. I made a mental note to find out what the fuck they were made of and have a whole suit made from it.

I swiveled my eyes around, trying to catch a glimpse. "Hey, buddy," I said, keeping my grin in place. "Hey, what's your name?"

There was a pause without any noise at all, and I imagined them standing there making faces at each other.

"He's making a list of people to kill," she said, sounding amused.

"Well, fuck," the man said. "In that case I'm not giving you my *name*."

She laughed, a delightful, musical sound I immediately wanted to hear again. "His name is Dr. Clarence Hiram Kendall, Mr. Cates. Please do kill him if you ever have the chance. He's very annoying."

"You're a cunt."

"*You're* a cunt, Clarence. Just prepare the cocktail for this waste of skin—just make up kits as fast as you can. I've got all fifteen labs humming and they're still coming down."

"Lovely."

I heard her soft flat heels moving away from me, and then the soft sigh of the swinging doors. Moving my eyes and head about, I tried to catch a glimpse of my new friend, but I could only hear him puttering around, clinking things together and muttering something under his breath. I strained my arms until they hurt, grunting softly with effort, but there was no give at all, and I started to wonder if maybe this was where the rail terminated for me. All that bullshit, for *this*. I'd been wading through dead bodies for years for *this*. It made me angrier, and I strained against the straps until my whole body was rigid, sweat beading on my forehead.

"Stop that," the man admonished from somewhere behind me. "You'll just make it more painful for yourself."

I relaxed, and he stepped into my field of vision. He was tall and thin, wearing the same white coat as Dr. Kerril. His eyes were pale and gray, and his hair was a very light brown or blond, making him almost colorless. He held in one hand the largest fucking needle I'd ever seen in my life, and without thinking, I froze.

"Thank you," he said, and without any further hesitation, he plunged the needle into my arm with a professional speed and accuracy I had to admire. I stiffened and then melted, a warm, dreamy syrup seeping into me, soothing my aching bones and slowing everything down. My leg drifted away, somebody else's problem—I could still feel it, throbbing, but it was like I was hooked to it via wires while it lay a few blocks away. I was aware of the pain on an academic level.

"Okay," Dr. Kendall said cheerily, tossing the autohypo onto a workbench. The whole room shuddered again, the booming noise louder this time, and a few things crashed to the floor. Kendall stared around, alarmed.

"Well, fuck," he muttered, spinning and snatching things from the nearest bench. "Better get a *move* on, eh?"

I nodded. Fine by me. Everything was suddenly fine by me, even the large cordless drill he had in his hand when he turned from the bench. He gunned it once, the small roar revving up into a whine and then going silent, and nodded, stepping out of my field of vision. I didn't care. I didn't care about anything. I was memorizing names, on the off chance the rail wasn't ending here, in this underground lab. I wanted to be ready.

"All right, Mr. Cates, I'm going to start drilling. You won't feel anything, of course. Normally this part would be automated, but the robot labs are all in use. Lots of volume, you know. I'm going to strap your head down now."

His head appeared upside down as he tugged a strap over my forehead and snapped it into place, holding me pretty motionless. He lingered, staring down at me. "Think of it this way," he said, sounding kind. "You're going to live forever. Maybe."

"I know your name, asshole," I said, my mouth thick and my words stretched out. "You better fucking hope I *don't* live forever." This seemed funny, so I started to laugh.

He squinted his eyes at me and then disappeared, and a moment later I heard the drill again. Another second, and there was a weird vibration in my head, my teeth, what was left of them, dancing in my mouth. Another deep rumble rolled over us, and everything on the nearby workbench jumped as dust sifted into my eyes, making me blink madly.

"Ah, dammit," Kendall muttered. "Where's the damn cops? The army's here, that's obvious. I don't take sides. I'm a scientist. I was hired to do a job, that's all. Fuck, this is taking forever. There."

The vibration stopped. I noticed a red light flashing over in one corner of the ceiling, steady and ponderous.

"All right, threading...looks good. You're a bleeder, Mr. Cates. I would have thought in your profession you'd have evolved better platelet response. Okay, first feed going in."

Nothing alarmed me. The lights flickered and more deep explosions rippled the dusty air, but I just smiled, my head and limbs held firmly in place. The army was coming. I wondered what that would be like.

"Second feed."

A rolling rumble of explosions shuddered above us, steady, unending. We were pretty far underground, I thought, lazily judging the timbre and tone of the noise. I realized I could smell blood, *my* blood, tangy and familiar.

"Third feed," Kendall whispered, breathing heavily. "There. Okay, running protocols...done, looks clear. Traffic is heavy, but it looks like I've got good contact. Okay. Needles...needles..."

Needles, I thought. *Wonder what he uses* needles *for?*

A split-second image flashed through my thoughts, puncturing the warm, boozy feeling of serenity I'd been surfing on. My heart lurched in my chest, and I strained every tortured muscle against the straps, tendons creaking. Another explosion pushed some cracks into the ceiling, small chunks of rock hitting me in the face.

"Fuck me," Kendall muttered in my ear.

The lights flickered, there was a sudden hum of something powering up, and then voices, distant and rushing toward me, a searing invisible knife in my head. The voices were *in* my head, silent, whispering, a dense knot of words, impossible to pick apart. I felt the table jump under me, a series of loud explosions. One voice resolved for a moment, elderly and amused.

In death, she said in my head, *all things are possible.*

XVII

FLAMES WHERE THEIR EYES SHOULD HAVE BEEN

The bag smelled like rotted flesh.

After ditching Krasa and Marko's badges and chips in a few randomly selected body bags and drawers, we climbed into our own personal slice of death and let ourselves drop into the pile, wrapped up in pitch darkness and the oozing cold sweat of previous occupants. The silence was perfect, airtight and greasy.

Belatedly, I thought, *Well, shit, if they do a heat scan we're fucked.* And then, even more belatedly, I thought, *Maybe we should have just ditched the chips and badges somewhere else, far away from us.* Laughter threatened to bubble up out of me, but I reminded myself that Marko's big brain hadn't considered that either, or offered any better ideas, and managed to get angry enough to stay sober.

We hadn't discussed anything beyond getting in the bags, but none of us said anything, and my world became static.

I counted seconds.

Waiting, again. I'd gotten better at it, impatience burned out of me. Sleep wasn't an option — you never knew what you might say or do while asleep, and a noise at the wrong time would be disaster. So it was the waiting game, the Gunner's special hell.

I'd gotten better at the physical aspects of it; I didn't have the aches and pains and jitters I used to—prison's little gift to me. I knew I could lie in my little pond of pitch-blackness, completely still and quiet, for hours. I had Canny Orel, the legendary Gunner, finally beat—and maybe that's all it took, a little judicious aging. Some key brain cells removed, and you could just sit in the fucking dark dreaming of the yen you were earning all goddamn night.

They came after an eternity, Marin's Internal Affairs, creeping, the soft sound of rubber soles squeaking on the polished floor. Four or five avatars, Droids with digitized human intellects, soft-shoeing around us, heavily armed and so damned silent. They found the chips and badges easily and immediately began making noise as they assumed we'd ditched the trackers and gotten as far away as possible—a natural assumption of human nature. They *sounded* so human—so normal, making jokes and muttering about what a pain in their ass Krasa had turned out to be, calling her a useless bitch and wondering if she was worth even "processing." The Worms stood around for a long time shooting the shit, occasionally poking a swelling bag or popping open a squealing drawer as they made a show of keeping up the search; all while I lay there breathless, clenching my fists, teeth bared to the darkness. I tried to will Marko to stay quiet.

And then, just when I'd bought the whole aw-shucks-we-give-up routine, the deafening report of a good automatic pistol smothered the oxygen in the room. Two squeaky steps, and then another shot.

I listened to the dead air that collapsed around me. More squealing steps; I imagined thick, black soles, steel-tipped shoes, perfect for kicking people until bloody snot spouted from their heads or for fieldwork, stepping through the rubble of downtown or the wastelands of Jersey without getting your feet wet. I saw them replaced every fucking week—fifty thousand yen a *week*—unwrapped in the morning, gleaming and perfect, the old ones, scuffed and stained from bone and blood, tossed into the burner without a second thought.

Another shot, right next to me, a fucking bomb going off. My ear didn't ring or go muffled, and I managed to keep still and not react. A moment later one of them stepped on my leg, putting all his goddamn weight on it. I bit down on my tongue from habit and kept still as the bastard tattooed his tread into my skin; I didn't feel a thing, but the pressure was intense, and I imagined the bastard leaning down to point his gun at my head, his plastic face smirking.

My hands twitched. I shut my eyes and imagined the bullet, splitting skin, cauterizing as it went, shattering bone, and shredding my brain. I lay there forever, face set in a permanent wince, and all I got in return for my efforts was another few squeaks of their shoes.

"Fuck it," a man's voice spat, glass being ground in mud. "They ditched and ran. Fucking cunts."

I memorized the voice. It wasn't hard. I just pictured a volcano vomiting up nicotine-tinged phlegm, and it came back to me immediately.

"Boss isn't going to like it," a milder, almost human voice responded.

"Boss doesn't like anything these days. Fuck it. They're in the building. Tear it up."

After a brief pause, the second voice said, "You heard the man. Tear this shit up."

Footsteps then, the door popping open and then closed. I listened carefully, trying to decide if they'd all left—*how many? Three? Four?* Could have been a fucking dance team standing around with their mouths shut.

The silence felt like heavy gas pumped into the room, settling down on me, pushing the slick walls of my tiny prison against me. I knew what was supposed to happen—within the hour Droids would gather up the bags, and we'd be loaded onto a hover, which would take us crosstown to the incinerators on the East River. Knowing didn't help me stay still and quiet.

I started to picture myself in a field, my usual trick, forcing all thoughts outside the glass surface of my mental bubble. Just as I was succeeding, the image firming up in my mind, I felt a distant but heavy rumble tremble through the floor. It faded fast, and then I lay there trying to analyze it, wondering what in hell had caused *that*.

Just as I started to relax, it was followed by another. It felt like the whole building was shaking slightly.

"What the fuck," I heard Marko whisper, "was *that*?"

I bit my lip. Responding would be stupid — the idea was *less* talking and noise.

"Any ideas?" he pleaded.

"Shut *up*," I whispered.

"That doesn't worry you?" he hissed back. "That doesn't *concern* you?"

"Fucking hell. Zeke, if you say one more goddamn word, I will crawl over there and cut your tongue out, understood? Say absolutely fucking nothing if you understand."

Since I hadn't been shot in the head, however, I had to conclude no one was waiting in the room. Marko stayed quiet for about thirty seconds. I could feel him struggling with his own massive stupidity like a boulder that had rolled on top of him, smothering.

"That is not *normal*, is all I'm saying," he stage-whispered.

I prayed for strength, but before I could make my own mistakes, the door popped again, a buzzing alarm announcing the arrival of the cleanup Droids. The next five minutes was noise: clangings and whirrings and the incessant alarm that crawled under my skin and bit at my nerves directly. I imagined my grassy field again, managing to stay still and calm until I was suddenly shoved, knocked roughly into a short roll and then shoved again and again, teeth-chattering impacts that changed momentum every second, smacking me against the floor, the other bodies, and something unpleasantly hard.

I had a sensation of falling, and just as I wondered if maybe I'd killed us all, a terrible sour spike pushing into my belly and curdling me, gravity smacked me into something that tolled momentarily with a metallic, bell-like noise. I slid a few inches and came to a rest, but before I could appreciate the sliver of peace, someone fell on top of me. And then someone else, a rainfall of bloating, dead bodies in bags, burying me. The weight, the pressure built and built in the darkness, pressing me down into the unyielding darkness. I ground my teeth and made fists, but it grew heavier and heavier, bodies pushing down on top of me. I opened my mouth to scream and the bag was pushed into it, the germy slick material and the cold metal zipper.

A shiver stuttered through me. I tried to kick and swing my arms, but I was pinned in like a brick mortared into place. Suddenly I was back in the coffin, being transported into the Abbey in London when we'd gone after Squalor, 90 fucking percent dead and pain flowing through me, burning every thought into ash. Panic took over, swelling in me like a balloon that filled every limb and pushed them into strained rigidity. I pushed with everything I had, with my arms and legs, and slowly managed to make some room, just an inch or two of inky space, all for me. With gagging effort I pushed the rubbery material out of my mouth, working my jaw and tongue until they ached.

I had the sensation of movement as a steady buzz vibrated against me. I imagined we were being loaded into the transport hover to our fiery fate, a split second of heat and then who the fuck knew—but I was in no rush to find out. Maybe everyone I'd ever killed, waiting for me. Maybe everyone I'd ever failed, waiting for me. That was worse. I saw them all. Waiting for me, flames where their eyes should have been.

Trembling, I moved one arm up, inch by inch, and took

hold of the zipper. As I slid it downward, the body on top of me sagged to fill the sliver of space I'd created, and I had to reset my back against the floor of whatever I was in and push upward again.

"Krajian!" I hissed. I'd meant to shout. "Marko!" My voice sounded like I'd already been buried.

I didn't hear anything for a moment, and then there was the roar of displacement springing full formed all around me, the sickening lurch of being snatched from gravity.

"Krajian!"

I struggled, weak without any leverage, trying to at least bend myself into a shape where I could get my legs under me. A sudden roar of noise—an explosion, not far away—compressed everything inside the hover for a second, and I could tell we'd been jogged off course, spinning a few times before the displacers, whining with that familiar rusty noise, compensated and brought us back into the slot. Just as I got my bearings again, two more blasts, louder than the first, and we were spinning again.

"Fucking *hell*," I shouted, managing to get one of my legs under me. I surged upward and met the sticky, combined weight of all those bags, giving me inches and then solidifying. I growled deep in my chest, pushing up and up and up—and then things were shifting, getting easier.

"Cates," I heard Krasa shout. "Hold on."

Hold on, I thought. A System Pig was telling me to fucking *hold on*.

Her hand appeared, thrust toward me from between bags, and I snatched it without hesitation, without embarrassment. She hauled me up, and I pushed, and with a sudden slippery, sucking expulsion I lurched free, stumbling into her, getting a noseful of her again, clean and simple with a sour undercurrent of fucking terror, maybe an almondy tinge of anger. She steadied me with both hands on my shoulders just as another goddamn explosion went off nearby in the air, and gravity did some flips for a second or two as the displacers hit a white noise level of sound, disappearing above the range I could hear.

"You okay?" she shouted with everything she had, sounding like she was whispering a mile away.

"Did you just ask me if I was *okay?*" I shouted back. "What the fuck are those explosions?"

"What?"

"Those are class-C Disruption Shells," Marko shouted, sounding far away. I turned to find him leaning in, an inch from my ear, surfing with his feet on two shifting body bags and hanging onto a safety strap descending from the ceiling of the cabin. His hair was damp from sweat and plastered against his head, revealing that he actually didn't have that much hair: his fucking head was freakishly huge. I stared at him as he continued. "Standard suppression procedure. Next come the big boys." He nodded, raising his eyebrows. "F-90s, field-contained armaments."

I looked back at Krasa, using her roughly to keep my balance. "Well, fuck," I yelled, putting everything I had into it. "Who the fuck's bombing us?"

She frowned. "Your people!" she shouted back. "The army! The goddamn SFNA is knocking on the door!" I just stared at her and she rolled her eyes as we both almost ate some body bag, the hover rolling beneath us. "The siege! They're making a play for the city!"

"Well, shit," I shouted, looking back at Marko. "Not our problem, then—Zeke, you can get control of this heap?"

He nodded. "It's a simple shell running the show."

"Hit the stick," I howled. He nodded and turned away, but I lunged for him and caught his sleeve, lurching into him.

"Don't crash!" I shouted, grinning. "Or I will slit your fucking throat!"

I felt wonderful. Better than I'd ever felt before. Marko sailed off, slamming into the wall before recovering his footing and lurching away, and I thought it would actually feel *good* to kill someone.

Ooh, Avery's crossed over, I heard Glee whispering in my ear. For a second I thought I could smell her again, feel her in the cabin. *Avery's not even* human *anymore.*

XVIII

I'D BEEN DIGESTED A LITTLE

It sounded like I was at a party. The flurry of voices overlapped each other, tripping on each syllable and blending together into a buzzing sludge of verbiage that made my head pound painfully. My whole body ached as if I'd been stepped on by a giant, crushing bones and grinding my joints into powder.

Somewhere in the distance there was a grinding, screeching noise, the most horrible noise I'd ever heard in my life.

It advised against opening my eyes.

Every now and then a voice would float up near the surface and break out nice and clear. At first I tried to follow them, make sense of them, but nothing connected; no one seemed to be replying to anyone else, so I gave it up. I remembered the terrible pressure in my head as that jackass doctor had begun processing me, and then—

I froze, jerking upright and then collapsing forward as my whole body cramped in protest, pain rippling up from my legs and slamming into my head, where it laid down thick roots, strangling me. I slumped there for a moment, panting.

I can hear you, goddammit; I know you're there

…in a stall just off Taitou Alley, second from the left, ask for Shen…

I don't understand, I just don't understand

...fifty to you, but if we don't tell Gerry about it, it's seventy to you, follow?

...it deepens like a coastal...

They weren't voices. They *were* voices, but inside me, in my head. Dozens, maybe more, men and women, kids and geezers, all just shouting constantly. I reached up and put my hands on my aching head, finding it sticky—*blood*, I thought, recalling something about needles. The swelling balloon of acid embedded in my skull was nearing critical mass, jiggling nauseatingly with every silent bellow from the crowd inside me. Was that what they'd done to me? Sliced my head open, inserted a sac of poison, sewn me back up rough and jagged to wait for the inevitable bursting? It was pushing my eyes out of my head, choking me.

I opened my eyes. The shouting went on.

I've never seen one, but I've seen clips on the Vids about them

...fucking Pigs fucking fucking Pigs

...the Little Prince's security wasn't worth whatever he was paying them

I was still in the lab, still sitting on the slab, but I'd been pushed forward in time—my restraints were torn from the slab, equipment lay smashed on the floor amid a few dead Crushers, men and women in an unfamiliar uniform, and the *extremely* dead Dr. Kendall (distributed liberally around the room), and the walls were scorched in several places. The smell of gunpowder and blood hung in the air, and I became aware of a slight vibration, irregular and faint, slithering up from the floor into the slab beneath me. Working to ignore the voices, I could hear gunshots and shouts somewhere not too far off.

I touched my head again. I'd been hooked up to the brain-sucking machine, but I was still here. Felt like I'd been digested a little, but still alive—whatever had happened here, it had interrupted my processing before they could take an imprint

of me. I swung my legs over the edge of the slab and studied
the carnage, bodies cut in pieces, hunks of meat, pools of blood
everywhere—shredders, I concluded, and not used with much
skill. It was amazing that I hadn't been cut to pieces by accident,
and not amazing at all that I'd been left for dead. Between being
hooked up to Dick Marin's Magical Brain-Sucking Machine and
sleeping through a firefight, I'd have left me for dead, too.

. . . sixteen at twenty-two, thirteen at fifty-one

. . . his blood was hot, hotter than I would have imagined

Slowly, feeling every inch, I knelt down, blood soaking into
my jumpsuit, and leaned in to get a look at the off-white uniform half the bodies in the room were encased in. It wasn't SSF
or ObFu; it was a tough, strangely tacky material that held whatever shape I pinched it into for a few seconds, then slowly resolv-
ing into its original composition. With a grunt I flipped a torso
over. Over the right breast was a logo that resembled the SSF
globe and stars; instead of stars the globe was surrounded by
arrowheads, and instead of ssf the initials sfna were knocked
out in the middle of the globe.

. . . System of Federated Nations Army, jackass

I blinked. I listened to the voices for a second, sifting the
continuous stream, but that particular voice—young and snarling, angry and rough—didn't repeat. I suddenly felt watched.
As I reached back down to feel the uniform again, the shooting
outside suddenly grew louder, underscored by a ripple of small
explosions that made everything in the lab jump.

Head pounding, voices screaming, I looked around quickly.
Whatever was going on here at the prison, it wasn't over. Being
left for dead could turn into being very, very much actually dead
if I was seen staggering around, wearing a bright orange jumpsuit, dried blood streaked down my face. Spinning, I dragged
my gritty eyes around the lab, spotting a more or less whole
Crusher lying on the floor. I limped over, scabby hands tearing
at the jumpsuit and peeling it from me like a second skin, the

dirty, crusty material coming off me reluctantly. My body was purplish and striped with grime; several of my flesh wounds were obviously infected, and suddenly the aching in my head spread throughout my whole body, sinking into my bones like bright, cold blue veins.

Naked, I shivered and knelt down over the Crusher. I tugged its uniform off, revealing a deep, ragged belly wound out of which a nest of red wires and thick white liquid leaked. I was naked with a mixture of blood and fucking coolant puddled around my feet, taking another man's pants off. It wasn't how I'd always pictured I'd go.

I'm so sorry, whatever I did, I don't deserve this

...accident don't happen, motherfucker—I got your number, and I'm gonna pull it someday

...it was like six inches long and smelled like a fucking zoo full of animals had died the week before during a heat wave

...Avery, getting shot naked is the least of your worries.

I paused for a second, a sharp spike of pain throbbing behind one eye. Another voice, boiling up from the mess of noise in my head, had seemed familiar. Like I knew it.

You know me.

"Fucking hell!" I shouted, pushing and scampering back to crash into a loose gurney, which went sailing off gracefully. I rubbed my hands into my eyes, hard, making them ache even more as lights flashed inside my head. What revised hell was this shit? I opened my eyes, expecting blood to be dripping from them onto the floor.

I waited, panting, but the voice didn't rise above again. The noise outside the lab was getting louder, so I forced myself to uncurl and crawl back to the half-naked Crusher. With stiff hands I pulled its uniform off and pulled it on—too big, ridiculous, but I cinched it on me as best I could and tied its boots onto me tightly, my own mysteriously missing. As I stood with some loud popping noises, my head swam as I searched the mess for weapons—six or seven shredders just dropped on the floor. I went through them fast, tossing aside the first three for being gummy with blood and gore. The last was in pretty good shape, with half a clip left. Ten seconds, tops, of ammunition. I stole four clips from the others lying around and did a quick inspection; if the fucking thing didn't jam on a chunk of some dead asshole when I squeezed the trigger, I might kill a few bastards with it.

Skin itching under the damp, reeking uniform, I limped purposefully for the swinging doors. Anything would be better than waiting for the flood in a room without cover or exits. Holding the shredder in front of me, I considered sending a burst through the doors to cut down anyone standing on the other side, but rejected the idea. It didn't feel right to kill people before you even saw them, without giving them a chance to form a fucking opinion about it. I stopped and spun around, transferring the heavy weight of the shredder to one arm as I grabbed hold of the gurney. With a grunt and a massive twinge of pain that burned all the way down my back, I sent it rocketing through the doors, snapping them open for a second, revealing the dark concrete hallway and a single Crusher staring at me as the gurney crashed into him, sending him sprawling.

As the doors flapped shut I saw the Crusher's face: I'd seen it before. Pasty, with a long chin, covered in a thin smear of peppery hair. I rushed forward, unsteady on my stiff leg, and kicked the doors open again, staggering into the hall.

. . . *his name's Guy he's a fucking punk*

. . . *just a dose. I'm sick I'm telling ya*

. . . *je veux juste qu'il tout finisse je veux finir*

"You," I hissed, keeping the shredder in front of me as I stalked down the empty hall toward him. He was getting to his feet, mouth open, eyes wide, the uniform hanging off him as if he'd shrunk five inches in the last hour. The noise of a fight was louder, screams, the heated whine of shredders, bone-rattling detonations that spiked up from the floor into my boots. "I know you."

A smile flinched onto his face. His eyes danced away from me and kept moving from spot to spot. He gestured at his chest. "Great minds think alike."

"This," I said as I got close, jamming the shredder into his belly, "is a Roon Corporation ten-oh-nine model gas-powered explosive shell rifle, commonly known as a Shredding rifle. It will cut you in half so fast you will be alive for a few seconds to marvel at your legs standing there with nothing on top." He danced back a little awkwardly, letting out a kittenish yip of terror. "Now, I said, I fucking *know* you."

His hands flew up, palms out, held up near his shoulders. "I'm Guy Rusbridge," he panted, eyes dancing from the shredder to my face to the floor, over and over again. "Mickey...I met you...."

I paused, memory flaring, and raised the shredder a few inches. "Right." I squinted at him, listening to the approaching noise of combat. I felt a strange lack of urgency, as if I had forever to figure all this out. I brought the shredder back up halfway. "What do you know about that fucking midget?"

"Nothing!" he squeaked, shutting his eyes. They continued to move under their lids, jumping around like he could see through them. "He just called me names and made me stand in line for people." He deflated a little, shrinking before my eyes. "I woke up down here, on a slab. I thought..." He touched the uniform again and opened his eyes again. "Then I didn't know what to do next."

I stared at him, and his face turned even whiter. "The only thing...once or twice he said something...muttered something about Europe." He sank down onto the floor without any hesitation or concern about me. I lowered the shredder as he sat down, pulling his knees up to his chest and wrapping his arms around them. "Mostly he ignored me. When he didn't ignore me, he insulted me." He snorted suddenly. "Which pretty much made him my best friend in this terrible place, you know? Because at least he didn't try to break my ribs every few minutes."

I stared down at him. He was skinny and short and looked even smaller swimming in the oversized Crusher uniform. His fingernails were bloodied and torn, and he hadn't looked me in the eye once.

He looked up at me suddenly, aiming for my chin. "Listen, I still have resources, if I could get out of here. I have access to a lot of yen. And a way off the continent, maybe, if we get that far." He stopped just as suddenly and looked back down at his feet, the sudden flare of hope and energy fading away before my eyes.

"All right," I said, raising my voice over the steady shriek of shredder fire somewhere nearby. "C'mon, let's go."

I pushed him behind me. "Stay back, and if I tell you to do something, *do it*. Except not in a suicidal way, okay?"

"Should I get a gun?"

. . . I got two crates of factory-fresh Roon two-two-threes, last batch out of the old Minsk factory

. . . fucking hell, the food

. . . she'd had her legs lengthened by that sawbones in Helsinki; she was fucking hot

I shook my head, trying to clear it, as a vision of my limbs flying through the air passed before me. "Just stay behind me."

I limped up the hallway. Glancing up I could see the snaking conduit I'd followed before. I didn't remember where it led, but since there weren't any other doors it didn't matter—if we were getting out, this was the way. Creeping forward, I stayed near the wall and listened as intently as I could, trying to form a rough count of guns in front of us.

Avery.

I stumbled and avoided blowing my own feet off with some

difficulty. I recognized the voice—I was sure I did. An elderly voice, a woman's voice. And she'd said my name.

You know me, you silly man. Now, listen. Pay attention: I was conscious when they brought me down, I may be able to help. It's difficult to get through the crush here, so concentrate on me.

I paused just before the hall curved sharply to the right, holding up my hand in the hope Guy wouldn't crash into me. I closed my eyes, and the voices swelled and pulsed inside me. Taking a deep, painful breath, I concentrated and thought: *Hello, Salgado.*

XIX

I DON'T HAVE A SCREEN TO REPRESENT PAINFUL DEATH

"There it is," Krasa said, sounding flat and exhausted. "The Star."

We were almost directly above it, the screens showing us a nice, crisp image of the potato-shaped island obscured by a haze of gray-black smoke. The Star was on the fat end, a squat lump of gray stone with a small pyramid on top that ended abruptly in a jagged heap of rubble. Outlined in foam was the immense thing that used to sit on the pyramid, torn off its foundation long before I'd been born. I didn't know what it had been. Maybe someone did. For as long as I remembered, The Star had been a fortress of sorts — not a particularly hard one to storm, maybe, but effective in its way. Techies had been using it as a data haven for decades now, illicit labs and servers buried deep within it, and while the SSF probably could have taken it down at any time with enough manpower and effort, they'd left it alone. Too much trouble, I guessed. And the Techies always had everything rigged to blank and blow at a second's notice, sometimes even linked to their own vital signs.

And maybe, I thought, someone up on high didn't mind having an unmonitored data haven, either.

Another concussion just a few hundred feet from us sent the hover wobbling again. I was getting used to it, keeping my balance pretty easily, while Krasa went sailing. Krasa looked like she was unraveling, physically and mentally, with one wide, freaked eye and hair everywhere. On the other side of us a sudden roar of high-speed displacement hit our ears a few seconds after three rusty-looking SSF bricks went stuttering past, pushed to their speed limits.

No one said anything. We'd run out of amazement. Someone on Ruberto's side had decided to quit waiting around for the System Cops to finish their program of turning everyone on the force into an untiring avatar, and they were making a real push into New York. The new army had been camped out for months all over the System, outside cities, outside strong points, just sitting there cupping their balls and glaring. I'd expected them to just sit there forever, playing games. Like sending me to try the impossible, assassinating Dick Marin, like I was Canny Orel, some legend who killed world leaders by thinking about it.

Marko had wired up one of the unlicensed Vids beaming from the Appalachians, audio only into an earbud.

"Moscow, too," he said abruptly. "Going after SSF Internal Affairs HQ—where the main Prime is. The SSFA has a fucking tank model!"

Marko was a true geek. He sounded like he was about to stain his pants from excitement.

"Shit, sounds like the snow is fucking them up, though. Fucking trillions in yen, I bet, and they're all sliding around outside Moscow. Fucked. Wait...Utrecht is down, in army hands—wait, almost. Street-to-street fighting, the tanks are making a difference there. Tanks! I didn't know they were developing tanks. Model GH-901."

"Eye on the stick, Zeke," I said. "Remember what I said about crashing."

"Right."

We started descending through a floating minefield, bombs going off in the air around us. Marko called them field contained—the concussion contained in a small area by a powerful, transient force field, concentrating all their power on a small area. The army was pouring them into the air, trying to knock out the SSF hovers, and we'd been lucky so far. Dropping five hundred feet through it didn't sound like a good idea, but I wasn't planning to swim out to the island.

At least the System Pigs would have more on their plate than Krajian and Marko. If we survived the drop, we might have some breathing room while Amblen's ghost gave us the grand tour.

We started to fall as a volley of bombs detonated around us, the hover shuddering and vibrating. A sickening feeling formed in my stomach like a ball of yellowed ice. Marko didn't move or react; his hands moved in a slow-motion series of complex gestures, eyes fixed on the screens. He continued to relay reports from his earbud as he worked, the hover shaking so hard the displays sizzled with static, blinking on and off.

"The Australian Department's all clear," he shouted. "The army doesn't have much presence there. The Japanese Department's also pretty much being left alone. The Balkans is going badly for the army; we're entrenched there and they haven't gotten any traction. Surprise all around—no one saw this coming. We all figured it was going to be years of stalemate." He smiled again. "Fucking tanks."

I left Marko alone with his Techie love for gadgets—even big, skull-crushing gadgets with huge guns mounted on them—while he piloted the hover down. I'd been in enough crashed hovers to never want to duplicate the experience. A trio of SSF bricks buzzed us so close I thought they might peel the metal skin off us, but Marko just kept waving his hands dreamily, and we kept sinking slowly down toward the overgrown little island.

I glanced at Krasa. She was just staring, hanging onto a

safety strap limply. I spent a moment considering ways of snapping her out of it, but gave up on that. I wondered how you went from kicking my ass on the street like a pro to having that empty, hollow look on your face, all because your fucking badge turned red. I would never understand cops. They were aliens.

When we dropped under a hundred feet up, everything calmed and stabilized. The noise of explosions and whining displacement was still everywhere, but we weren't being tossed about like a piece of trash floating on the blackened Hudson River anymore. The last few feet were textbook, smooth and professional. For a second we were all silent, and then Marko glanced around.

"Well, according to scans the power's off," he said. "Which the Vids are reporting throughout the city. So looks like we're going to have to bust our way in."

"Uh-huh," I said absently, leaning forward to study the screens. "Unless you can cocktail up some explosives made from dead bodies, Zeke, I'm not sure how we'll do that."

He nodded. "Officer Krajian, the SSF has had a Red Code for The Star for years now, hasn't it?"

For a second she didn't say anything, and then suddenly snapped around. "What? Yes, of course. We have Red Codes for every major building in the city. In the System." She shook herself and looked at me. "But I don't have access anymore. Neither do you."

"Sure, sure," Marko said, nodding, hands moving delicately. "That slows us down, sure."

I raised an eyebrow a precise amount. "Red Code?"

She nodded, seeming to come back to herself as she spoke. "An infiltration strategy in case of takeover. We need to get into a building that's being held against us, maybe even with some serious force—we have a file of plans to do that. It includes architectural drawings, weak point analyses, and any other usable information. Override codes sometimes for the building shells. If nothing else, it would show us the weak spots we might be able to exploit. But it doesn't matter, as our access has been revoked."

As she said this last she deflated again.

"Okay," Marko said, flipping a hand in the air rapidly. "Call me fucking paranoid, but I've had a couple of fake log-ins set up for *years* just in case. Can't do much, but the SSF thinks in terms of actions, not data preservation, so grabbing a Red Code file is...actually...pretty easy."

With a brisk snapping motion, he nodded and stopped gesturing. Krasa and I both stared at him silently until he looked up at us and blinked.

"Uh, give it a minute. That's a lot of data."

Outside, the bombing went on and on, each individual explosion blurring into the next. I imagined shrapnel raining down on New York, people already half-starved and worn down by siege running for their lives and probably not finding much shelter.

"Okay," Marko said, leaning forward and moving his hands. On one screen in front of him a half-dozen smaller boxes popped up. Before I could make out what any of them were, he was waving his hand elegantly, and the little boxes shimmered, replaced by a new set, which he wiped off the screen just as quickly. He flipped rapidly through dozens of screens, too fast for me to follow, eyes dancing, grunting softly with each transition. I wanted to smack him on the back of his head and make his teeth rattle but held myself back, putting it into an account to pay off later. There'd be time to remind Marko of our proper working relationship when things calmed down. When I didn't need him anymore.

"Sewers," he said suddenly, jabbing a finger at the screens. One of the smaller boxes expanded to full size—a schematic, blurry and scratched like it had been made from ancient plates. "More specifically, tunnels left over from either constructing the sewers or maintaining them. See—big enough to wriggle up through, most of it dried out. Comes up…here, looks like it used to be a lavatory or something, though it's fucking huge."

I leaned forward to squint at the screen. "Fucking sewers," I said. "There'll be defenses."

The Star wasn't owned by anyone, but Techies had been using it for years now, and in their own loose way they'd run the place. I didn't doubt if you lacked the secret handshake or the fucking password, the whole place would collapse around you while some Techie in Singapore watched via remote random-packeted Vid feed, laughing their ass off.

Marko nodded, sweeping the schematic off the screen before I could stop him, popping up four more boxes in a neat arrangement. "Sure, but the power's out. These may not be completely up-to-date, but from what I can see, they have trunk lines, which you can't cut individually. Good work except you have to add local modulators or else your whole enterprise gets fried. But if the whole grid's out, they're out. Major backup generators here, here, and here, but looks like they had to pick and choose what they kept hot in this scenario, so the pipes look clear."

I nodded, taking his word for it. "Okay. What if the power comes back on while we're in the pipes?"

He nodded. "I don't have a screen to represent painful death."

The urge to smack him returned in force. I suspected it might be something I'd have to live with for the rest of my life. "All right, then. Let's not wait around for the power to come back online. Let's get wriggling." I looked at Krasa as Marko stood up, going through his pockets rapidly. She was staring at the screens again, arms loose at her sides. I knew the expression—exhaustion, ennui, despair. I'd seen it up close plenty of times in my life and every day back at Chengara Penitentiary. With her ten thousand–yen haircut and fancy coat, the expression looked worse, like she'd peeked over your shoulder and seen Death riding up on his pale horse.

I turned and moved for the drop cabin to get her out of my sight. If Krasa was going to self-destruct, I wanted her upwind.

The sewer pipe had been underground, originally, but was now half exposed, a semicircle of rusted pipe big enough for a man to crouch and crawl his way into, then widening until he could stand up straight. I paused for a moment, staring at the inky blackness within the pipe, wondering if I was doomed to spend the rest of my short, unhappy life crawling in and out of narrow, horrible spaces. The tunnel narrowed and split off into dozens of smaller feeds, but Marko had sketched the route for me, and there were no defenses or obstacles to slow us down. The route ended in a small junction, where a rusting ladder embedded in the wall led up to an encrusted grating, dark and foreboding. It popped up easily enough, and I pulled myself up into a dark, damp area filled with broken tile and porcelain fixtures, most of which looked like they'd been torn off the walls and hurled at the floor with force. I smelled mold in the air, and I could hear a thin trickle of water somewhere.

Krasa followed, and I helped Marko up one-handed, lifting him into place, not a stitch of his prissy little middle-class suit out of place. I smiled and brushed him off a little with mocking care as he whipped out a razor-thin little handheld that spread open three different ways, tripling in size instantly. He spun around, holding it up.

"No power, no signals. I can't get heat sigs, but it's pretty quiet." His little eyes, buried among the thick curls of his hair, swiveled around and finally landed on me. He looked five years old suddenly. "The, uh, only way out is, uh, that way."

He gestured with his handheld over my shoulder, and it suddenly lit up red and started beeping.

"Fuck," he muttered, gesturing at it. "It's buggy."

"All right," I said, letting my eyes linger on Marko for a

moment as he pretended to be engrossed in making his handheld behave. "Follow me, then." I pulled my gun and turned. The walls of the room had once been tiled white, but most of the tiles were broken up on the floor like a ruined beach, and the walls were bare concrete and silky webs, dust and cocooned dinners hanging everywhere. The only obvious exit from the room was a darkened archway, square tiles hanging from it at crooked angles.

"Take the first junction right," Marko whispered behind me.

"Don't whisper," I said. "Assholes whisper when walking into a bunker wired up with who-knows-what. If they can't hear us whispering, the tech in this shithole isn't worth our time."

I took the first right and the rough floor began sloping upward. Our environment, while remaining infested with webs and dirt—and suddenly, the dried shells of dead roaches like leaves under our boots—dried out rapidly as we rose upward. Marko guided us through a maze of corridors, all cramped and filthy, and we rose steadily until I stepped warily into a wide, open space of rough-hewn rock and uneven floor, unfamiliar shadows formed by mysterious light. It looked like someone had formed the room out of the rock without the benefit of explosives, maybe with a dull teaspoon chiseled against the stone for centuries. Then the shadows resolved themselves into oblong black boxes, linked by thick, winding cables, and large, dead Vid screens fastened to one wall, a bank of inputs and instruments beneath them. Fragile-looking chairs were tucked neatly under the consoles. The light leaked from weak photocells on the wall behind me, emergency disks that clicked on spilling back artificial moonlight, giving the room a pale, terrible glow.

"This is his lab?" I asked, looking around. The shadows formed by the irregular walls were pitch-black, impenetrable. On one wall a square of metal had been bolted. I leaned in, squinting, and saw it was a plaque, the block lettering covering it like squarish bugs. "And what the fuck," I said, "does *brazen giant of Greek fame* mean?"

"Wait," Krasa said, her voice low and phlegmy, like she hadn't spoken in years.

"We'll have to ask Amblen," Marko said, bustling past me and approaching the screen-covered wall. "And for that we need power."

I opened my mouth to ask the little shit where he thought we'd be getting power *from,* when Krasa suddenly stepped forward just as a shotgun blast sucked the atmosphere away and made us all crouch down, the silence sucking all the air out of the room and leaving us panting.

"Stay down," a voice said.

My eyelids fluttered, my brain slowing down again, just a twitch in my thoughts, everything getting gooey and stretched out. I snapped back a moment later, everything rushing to catch up, like I was falling toward the present down a narrow tunnel. The voice had been familiar, a man's deep voice, and the sound of it was like a nail in my brain. I went still.

"I see you," Krasa whispered. I turned my head and we looked at each other, her golden eye glowing softly in the washed-out light.

"My Russian friend is behind you," the voice went on. I heard the scrape of boots to confirm this, and then a second set of feet moving. "He's honor challenged and will shoot you in the back of the head first and wonder if he should have hesitated later."

From the deep shadows off to the left of the Vid screens, a man stepped forward, shotgun—an old, wood-stock contraption from a previous, golden age—held easily in front of him. He came into the weak light and we looked at each other, staring.

"You," Krasa said slowly to the man, swallowing thickly. "You are Avery Cates."

"The one and only, sister," the man said. His eyes landed on me—*my* eyes—and his face stiffened. "What the *fuck,*" he whispered. Then he cocked his head a little, eyes shifting to the side.

"What?" He looked back at me. It was *me*. It was my face, my body. "A fucking avatar," he said slowly. "They made a fucking *avatar* out of me."

"Fuck you," I said slowly, fighting through the weird syrup my mind had fallen into.

Marko was looking from the newcomer to me and back again. "Well, fuck, if you both—whatever you are—got out of Chengara at the same time, where the hell have *you* been?"

The bastard kept grinning at me. "Took me a while to get off the continent. Then, Venice mostly." As I struggled for something to say back, his face crumpled, eyes closing tightly as he started to tremble. He brought his free hand up to his face and touched his forehead lightly.

"Shut up," he whispered in the silence. "Shut up, shut up, shut *up*."

PART TWO

XX

CRAZY WAS GOING TO HAVE TO WAIT

For a second after I spoke to Salgado, the voices faded a little, muting, and I wondered if maybe I'd just gone crazy. Maybe I was in a little room somewhere, screaming and tugging at my bonds, still insisting I could see the ghosts. Then, weak and low at first but gaining in volume, Salgado responded.

You're in a pickle, son.

I opened my eyes again. I had Dolores Salgado in my head.

Keep talking to me. It's easier if you concentrate on me.

I smiled despite myself. *Am I fucking crazy, Dolores? Even if you're a fucking figment, I'd appreciate an honest answer.*

"Mr. Cates?" I heard Guy say behind me. I turned my head a tick or two.

"Don't speak."

The voices swelled up again, swamping her and filling me with a hundred fragments, screams, mutterings, curses. I closed my eyes again and tried to focus my thoughts. I imagined a glass wall between me and the voices, and that helped, for a second.

Don't listen to the old lady, Mr. Cates. She's playing you. I should know. She's been playing me for years.

I shuddered and squeezed my eyes shut tighter. Another voice I recognized. A voice I didn't want in my head.

Curious, this. You must have been partially through the encoding procedure, hooked up to the network and momentarily two way on the data stream—up and down—when you were disconnected prematurely. Fascinating. There was a white paper on this possibility when we were vetting the original research, but I had to suppress it. The researcher sadly had to be liquidated.

I opened my eyes. "Guy," I croaked. "If I asked nicely, would you kill me?"

"What?"

His tone of alarm was so sharp and panic-stricken I smiled. "Forget it."

. . . five gets you twenty. Twenty gets you killed. . . .

. . . eu penso I'm inoperante—eu penso I'm inoperante. . .

It might have been my imagination, but the swirl of voices seemed lessened somehow.

Are you paying attention, Mr. Cates? Undersecretary Salgado—excuse me, former Undersecretary Salgado is a cunning little minx. I wouldn't follow her lead, I were you.

I tried imagining my glass wall again. Had I gone crazy? Was this what crazy was like? I'd always imagined you *knew* you'd gone nuts, somehow, that you marveled constantly at the crazy batshit things you were doing.

You're not crazy, Mr. Cates. I'm here. We're all here. Though some of us were marginal and are fading. It's fascinating—I am aware of them fading.

Shut up, Marin, I thought, hard. *Shut the fuck up.*

Amazingly, they all did, for a second, a blissful beat of silence inside me. And then the crowd rushed back in.

I nodded to myself. Crazy was going to have to wait.

Taking a deep breath, I leaned forward until I could see around the corner. I moved slowly; people had the urge to snap into view fast in these sorts of situations, but jerky, fast movements attracted nervous eyes. Slow was the key. You edged into view and became just part of the background, something static.

Holding my breath and trying to keep the pane of glass up in my head, I edged forward, mouth open.

In the hall around the corner, five soldiers in their weird, off-white uniforms were crouched behind four overturned gurneys, already chewed into twisted sculptures by the shredders. They all had shielded face masks on, giving them each one large eye, with two short flexible tubes popping out from the mouth area and snaking to disappear inside the rest of their suit. Except for the three dead soldiers locked in eternal surprise on the floor, they might not have been human in those things. No one was firing, but the noise was still loud, and I figured this was complex-wide, an invasion. Down the hall was another set of swinging doors, one of which was missing a large chunk of itself. Through the gap I could see the dusty blue uniforms of Chengara's guards.

Slowly, sweating in my filthy stolen uniform, I leaned back and turned to look at Guy. He stared at me in terror. Turning away, I stepped out into the hall, oriented myself, and launched myself diagonally across its width, eyes locked on the white uniforms. I squeezed the trigger and the shredder jumped in my hands, sending out an invisible wire that chewed up everything in its path. Half a clip of ammo was ten seconds, tops, but the soldiers on the far end were already twisting around to face me by the time I crashed into the far wall, letting my rubbery legs go out from under me. I'd missed one—through the dust and smoke I saw him rolling away, a white blur.

As my ass hit the floor, the wall where I'd been a second before exploded into dust and sharp chunks of concrete. I threw myself forward, smacking flat onto the floor and scrabbling to get my legs under me, lumbering blindly forward with my shredder still in one hand. I saw the soldier sitting on the floor, swinging his gun toward me, and with a yell I tossed mine at him, smacking him in the chest as he fired off another burst.

I veered, staggering into him hard and falling down on top of him, letting my knee get between us and just letting gravity yank me down.

Without pausing, I took hold of the tubes coming out of his cowl and pulled his head up, then smashed it down onto the floor as hard as I could. His whole body twitched beneath me, and I grabbed his shredder, glancing at the glowing ammo count as I pushed myself back to my feet, my leg burning. Panting, I slapped the shredder with my palm and staggered through the gurneys.

Down the hall the Crushers, three of them, pushed open the doors and stood there grinning. They looked like human beings, just regular assholes, and I marveled at the fact that they were all avatars, artificial and creepy. These three would have passed for human anywhere—everything about them, from their flop sweat and unshaven faces to their bellies hanging over their belts, screamed *Crusher*, second-rate cop wannabe.

The tallest one was ginger haired and looked like his arms were too long for his body, like a fucking monkey, based on some shit kicker whose family had been eating dirt for generations, producing thinned-out genetic material like Bubba here.

I concentrated on moving easily. Avatars didn't feel pain.

Actually, they can be programmed to feel anything we want, Dick Marin thought cheerfully at me. *Pain might be useful under certain scenarios.*

Pain is a programming error, a new voice—quiet, annoyingly calm—said above the buzz. *Pain should be commented out.*

Hell, Cates, Marin snarled. *You attracted all the fucking quacks to your brain.*

As if on cue, the crowd of voices rose up in triumph, loud and muddled. *Slimmer than before,* I thought.

"That was ass-kick amazing," Bubba drawled, his vowels all weird. "We didn't think any of us were still up and runnin' back there. These cocksuckers came blastin' in like hotshots and got cut off. One of 'em was wounded, and they kept tellin' us they had to get him out for MedVac."

"Medical evac," one of the other Crushers spat. "Fucking weak meat."

"Rules of war or some such shit," Bubba sighed, shaking his head. "All right, gear up—word is these fucks have broken through and are working their way down. We're pulling out. Which means we got to claw out of here before we get swamped by these pieces of shit."

"MedVac," I repeated, and whipped my shredder up, squeezing the trigger. My last few seconds of ammo spun Bubba into two halves, each tumbling in an opposite direction, the blast sawing through him and cutting down the other two as well. The noise of combat was a little further away now, muffled by some walls and doors and lots of the stiff, scrubbed air.

I limped back to the soldiers and examined them.

You have destroyed these men, the new voice whispered. *They are now beyond redemption. The others will live on, as it is meant for us to do.*

He's a lot of fun, huh? Marin sneered. *I used to hate taking meetings with him, back when he was corporeal. This kind of prophecy horseshit, all the time. That's how Squalor talks.*

"Son of a bitch," I whispered.

It might have only been seconds, but stored intelligences operate at incredible speeds, and it wouldn't take long for you to subconsciously sort us out and grab onto familiar, uh, faces, Marin added. *This is* fascinating.

Prophecy cannot be—

Shut up! I hammered the thought as hard as I could. For a second, all the voices cleared up again.

Kneeling down I pulled one soldier toward me by her boot. Working with stiff fingers, I undid the weird little clasps that seemed to just cling to each other without any visible fitted parts and pulled her uniform off—it was a single piece of the white material. When I had her naked and bloody before me, I kept my eyes off her and examined the uniform; it was shapeless and limp, heavy and damp looking. With something akin to pleasure, I peeled off the rank blue Crusher's uniform and stepped into the army kit. The white material flowed around me, stretching here and tightening there, until it was the best-fitting set of clothes I'd ever worn. It felt like a million tiny hands were on my skin, sizing me up, tasting me.

The cowl hung off my neck behind my head. I had a strange feeling it *wanted* to be lifted into place so it could attach itself, but I was suddenly worried I'd never get it off, that it might seal me off and suffocate me, so I left it hanging.

I found one more corpse that hadn't been chopped up by the shredders and pulled its uniform off as well. The two dead bodies were pale and shriveled, and I stared at them for a moment. The new army wasn't avatars; it didn't feel like that made them the good guys. Something glittered on the woman's face, and I knelt down with a grunt and a wince to get a better look. Her eyes were silvery, almost with a soft glow. Augments. I looked up and stared at the scorched wall for a second. Fucking Augments—did that still make them human? Was there any fucking difference?

When I limped around the corner, Guy was right where I'd left him, staring blankly at his hands. I tossed the uniform at him. "Change," I said.

He blinked and picked up the uniform slowly, stared at it for a second, then dropped it and got to his feet with epic, imperial slowness. "How do you do...something like that? Like all those people?"

I shrugged, testing my weight on my bad leg and pulling the sidearm that had come with the uniform. I turned it over in my hands: not bad, I decided. I racked a shell into the chamber and was satisfied.

"Practice," I said. "You ever kill anyone? To get in here? To *survive* in here?"

He laughed, staring down at himself as the uniform visibly adjusted itself to him. "I was a broker. I made money. I made money for a lot of cops, and one of them decided I belonged here." He looked up at me. "Hell, I even had a sponsor, trying to get me out. I almost thought he could. He's got pull, you know? Deep pockets. I had a lot of his investments, and with me in here he lost control of them. He needed me; I don't have any illusions—but I hoped he would get me out."

I nodded absently. "You actually thought you were getting out?" Smiling, I pushed the gun at him and fired a single shot into the meaty part of his leg. The army uniform, I figured, was engineered to be bullet resistant, but at this range there was no such thing as bullet*proof*, and Guy's feet flew out from under him as if someone had tugged the floor away. He crashed down, screaming and writhing. I stared at him for a second: he was weeping, big fat tears streaming down his face. I felt sorry for a moment; I didn't like being the first time this poor son of a bitch got shot.

I holstered my gun and stepped around him to gather a handful of his cowl and uniform and started dragging him behind me, slinging my shredder over one shoulder. As we turned the corner, I saw through the swinging doors on the other end, a knot of white uniforms prowling their way carefully toward us, and I steeled myself, pulling the cowl over my face.

"Sorry, Guy," I said, my own voice sounding too close and too desperate. "But in a situation where I have to choose sides, I choose the side that's got MedVac. You ever survive a hover crash?"

He squealed something unintelligible. I was the worst thing that had ever happened to him, I knew. I was used to it.

"I have," I advised him. "It's not as hard as it seems."

XXI

DESPERATE FOLKS, I FIGURED

I kept my grip on the shredder laid across my knees and kept up that posture of relaxed nonchalance that took every vibrating shred of energy I had to make natural. Next to me, Guy had passed out—or died, though I was pretty sure I knew my arteries well enough to not have murdered him—which at least stopped his unsoldierly *screaming*. But I didn't relax, because I was sitting in a jelly of fucking *wrong*.

The noise was incredible. The hover was mostly cargo hold with a tiny cockpit and nothing else. It was *fast*. The bay doors were wide open, and the ground far below us was whipping past in a vaguely purple blur, all the air in the world scooped up and hurled inside the bay to buffet us, sucking away sound and oxygen, leaving me choking on wind.

But I didn't dare grab onto the safety straps, because no one else was. I crouched against the rear wall of the no-frills bay, which was just struts and sheet metal, freezing cold, vibrating beneath us like it was coming apart. Bright red packs of fabric were tied to the safety straps, fluttering and jumping manically behind the soldiers. My knees ached and my back burned; my head buzzed with voices and my heart pounded the way it did when I was about to be shot at, but I kept myself stock-still and resisted the urge to look at everything and everyone.

They were looking at me, though. Except for the crazy ass-hole on the big gun, laughing uproariously as he sent hundreds of rounds down at the ground, the *chug-chug* chainsaw of it blending into the noise and giving it some rhythm, some bottom. The gun was mounted just inside the bay and moved with oiled ease in response to the soldier's movements, swinging up and down and side to side to cover any vector you could put eyes on, including straight up or down. He was just sweeping it back and forth with his fingers mashed on the triggers, laughing in great, breathless spasms. I had an idea that if he could have spun the gun all the way around, he would have cut us all to ribbons, and laughed the whole time.

Field-contained armaments—sneak up on you, and then BAM *you're not just dead, you're dissolved.*

Dumdum shells, turn a building into cheese

Mr. Cates, you should have been a poet. You missed your calling.

The fact that Dick Marin could hear my thoughts made me feel nervous and exposed, and every time one of the voices broke through and unleashed a stream of words inside my brain, I had to bite down hard to resist twitching, shaking my head violently to dislodge it, like a bug eating its way from one ear to the other.

All of the soldiers were wearing their uniforms, the same bizarre, clingy, almost sentient white material. They'd pushed their cowls back and they all stared at me with bright, silvery eyes. Augments, for sure; I'd seen glowing eyes like that in various hues plenty of times. Back in the old days lots of hard cases got Augments done in back rooms and sewer tunnels, burning through monthlong infections and endless complications for some advantage over the System.

I didn't know what their eyes meant, what exactly had been done to them, but I could see it wasn't the only thing. They each had an identical scar on their temples, like two stylized letter S's next to each other, pink and angry looking. They were sweaty, red-faced human beings, no doubt—not avatars—but each one had a short black cable running from their cowls into the back of their neck, right where their skulls attached.

I'd left Guy's cowl in place, hiding his head, but I'd left mine hanging. I stared back and wondered just how badly I was fucked.

There were five men and two women, all kids, fucking children. Hair shaved off completely, sweat glistening everywhere. Each was wounded, red blood staining their uniforms—one girl with an ear that was just a flower of pulp and blood, one guy cradling an arm that looked like it had been completely severed inside the sleeve. None of them complained or winced or looked even close to being in shock. The ones with working limbs still clutched their own shredders, and I was careful to act like my own gun was welded to my knees.

They were skinny and bruised looking. Poor, I figured; I'd seen enough of the type. Hadn't eaten well, sick all the time. Maybe even jumped at the chance to earn five hundred yen a week getting killed. One of them, a man with a starburst of dried blood on his face and a leaking belly wound that had left him pale and shivery, looked at my hands and then back at my face. He had fine, red eyebrows and a sharp, long nose. He glared at me with fierce, burning eyes—made even worse by their silver, glinting color. It was like an alien looking at me, something I'd never dealt with before.

"Mr. Cates."

I glanced down at the floor. I could feel the atmosphere around me getting thicker and thicker and had a pretty good idea what was going to happen when we got to our destination. It didn't involve a conversation.

"Mr. Rusbridge?" I shouted back.

"I'm dying, I think. I am dying."

"You're not going to die, Mr. Rusbridge. It's a flesh wound. You'll bleed for hours and be in a lot of pain. Trust me. I'm a professional."

"No, I can feel it. I'm dying."

"You're in shock. Although we're both probably going to be dead in a few minutes, so let's not spend our last moments of brotherhood and friendship arguing, eh?"

"I'm dying."

Aside from the crazy Gunner, none of the soldiers had moved. "Okay, Guy, fine. You're dead. Sorry to have killed you."

"Listen to me: there is a boat."

I blinked. "A *boat*?"

"In Galveston. That is in Texas, Mr. Cates. Speak to a woman named Merris. You'll need access to my files—"

I looked back at our comrades-in-arms, listening to Guy's rasping voice with half an ear. It was always amazing what people told you when they thought they were going to die.

I considered my options, which were clarifyingly few. I could not, I assumed, allow the hover to land where it was intended to land. Guy and I stood out, that was clear, so any hope of melting into the fringes and disappearing was out. The cockpit looked pretty secure; I'd been in enough hovers to judge a hatch and this one looked to be magnetically sealed and most probably fail-safe—the pilots would starve to death in there before I managed to get it open. So somehow hijacking the hover was impossible, assuming I could manage to subdue seven injured soldiers.

I ran my eyes over them again, licking my lips. Their absolute stillness while they bled, while tendons and shattered bones poked out of their uniforms was fucking terrifying. Even System Pigs screamed when you tore them up.

My eyes shifted to the bright red packs tied off behind them. I turned my head slightly, just enough to catch a glimpse of that color dancing behind me and Guy, and looked back at the soldiers.

"Hey, Ginger," I said. "If my friend and I wanted to get off before our final destination, would you have a problem with that?"

He stared at me, moving his jaw a little from side to side. "Only if you try to take one of those parachutes with you," he shouted effortlessly. "Those are property of the System of Federated Nations Army. Otherwise, be my guest."

A funny one. I gripped the shredder and wondered. For all I knew they were filled with Augments—muscle layers, nerve accelerators, tendon replacements. All apparently legal in the army. I wasn't sure I'd be able to cut all seven down before one or two of them got up on me—and I wasn't sure I wanted to do that anyway. So far they'd done nothing to impede me.

I considered him, all of them. Where in the world did the Joint Council Undersecretaries get an army in such a short time, men and women willing to have Augmenting procedures and be thrown into a war with the SSF? Desperate folks, I figured. The one resource the System was actually making more of. Food was scarce, energy getting thin, and factories went under constantly—but desperate folks were on an upswing.

"How much," I shouted, "would two of those parachutes cost?"

The kid squinted at me, the first involuntary reaction I'd gotten out of any of them, and I got optimistic. I had yen. I was still sick with yen. Marin had paid me for the Squalor job, and I'd promptly moved that yen from the original account and spread it across a dozen hidden places, nooks and crannies of the System. Even with the economy in free fall I was fucking rich. Why not make some use of it?

. . . need a fucking wheelbarrow for all the yen

. . . I should never have paid you, Cates.

. . . I'm starving starving STARVING

The soldiers didn't look at each other, but the kid's eyes started to move a little, crazy, tiny little circles, and I realized they were talking to each other. Mentally. Not Spooks, though; they didn't have the look. I glanced at the rugged-looking black cable popping out of his neck and running to the cowl and figured there was an Augment there, too—something I'd never heard of.

"Seventy million," the kid said, face blank and expressionless. "And you can jump. One forty," he added with just the slightest hint of a smile, "and I'll order Gordy here *not* to shoot you out of the sky when you do."

"Done," I said immediately and took my hands off my shredder as a sign of good faith.

The kid nodded and raised his hand to his face, spit into his palm, and held it out toward me. Fucking hillbilly. I did the same and we shook, and then he produced a battered and scorched credit dongle. It looked old.

"Can you scan a print?" I said. "I don't have a piece on me."

"Sorry, hoss," the kid said, his face snapping back into cold, tight expressionlessness.

"Cates," Guy said, surging up and grabbing my arm. "Here, give it to me."

I looked at Guy as he slid his cowl up. He didn't look good, clinging to me like it was the hardest thing he'd ever had to do. He was gray and thin, looking unhappy and stretched. "What?"

"Give me the dongle," he shouted.

"The man said *one hundred forty million*," I shouted back.

He pulled himself up by my arm into a sitting position. "Give me the fucking thing!" he hissed, panting, sweat pouring off his face.

I looked at the kid and shrugged my eyebrows. The soldier handed it over and I held it up for Guy, who stretched out a shaking hand toward it, thumb out. After a moment, the dongle lit up green, and I blinked, startled.

"Subdermal chip," Guy panted, sinking back onto the floor of the hover. "Oh, fucking fuck me."

"You have a hundred forty million yen?"

The soldier leaned forward and snatched the dongle back

from me before Guy could gather himself to respond. He glanced at it and secreted it in his uniform. "Gordy," he shouted, looking at me. "Stand down, brother."

Immediately the crazy asshole on the big gun let go and stepped back from it. He was still grinning like a fucking loon.

The kid glanced at him and then back at us. "All yours."

I nodded and stood up, tearing two of the red packs off the wall. They hooked right into the uniforms elegantly, the materials almost connecting themselves, almost seeming to move beneath my hands as I worked the metal clips. I rolled Guy over onto his belly, ignoring his screams, and attached his. Then I looked back at the calm, quiet line of soldiers—one of the girls had lost consciousness and might have been dead.

"Make a hole?"

For a second I thought I was going to get charged an extra thousand yen for this, but then the kid nodded and they all shifted a little to their side, opening up a narrow space. I left the shredder where it was, made sure I still had the automatic that had come with the uniform, and knelt down to pick up Guy, holding him in my arms and staggering for the bay door, wind pushing back at me, my body aching and protesting every inch. I stood for a moment at the edge. The ground below was blurry and indistinct; I had no idea where we were. Feeling certain that every extra second spent on the hover would be regretted, I closed my eyes and made sure I had a good grip on Guy, who was dead weight on me. I thought it best if I never met soldiers again.

Mr. Cates, Marin whispered, *I know I am legion and all that, but I'd much prefer* another *of me die.*

"I'll try to arrange it as soon as possible," I muttered, and stepped off into the air.

XXII

EVEN THE HUMAN ONES

"Mr. Rusbridge?"

I blinked, wondering if I'd been talking again, accidentally responding to the few dozen voices that still clung, tenacious, to my brain. Most of them had faded, but a few lingered and three—Salgado, Marin, and Dennis Squalor—had firmed up and become my own personal ghosts. Marin theorized that because I'd known the three of them, in some sense, I'd subconsciously concentrated on them and kept them "alive" while the rest were being dismantled, brain cells being cleaned out and reused for more important things, like drinking and trying not to throw up simultaneously.

Kept alive? Marin whispered archly. *I'd hate to think we have to rely on your concentration skills for that.*

Shaking my head, I tried to focus. The dented and rusted metal cup of—well, I wasn't exactly sure what it was, though it was harsh stuff and I was pissing drunk after two of them—seemed to float just above the rotten, damp wood of the bar, up and down, up and down. Behind the bar was Bheka, tall, skin so brown it was almost black, skinny as hell and always grinning. Bheka was leaning on the bar with his arms spread wide, squinting at me with a worried expression.

"You okay, Mr. Rusbridge?"

I slipped one hand into my coat pocket, finding my lucky charm. The charm was perpetually damp and cold, slick and slimy. I'd paid some yen to a twitchy geneticist to have it preserved, but it still felt like it was rotting.

Savage, Squalor hissed.

Pay him no mind, Avery. Salgado sighed. *Being in Mr. Squalor's bad graces puts you in my good ones.*

I pushed them all aside, something I was getting better at as the number of voices dropped. "No," I answered, truthfully enough.

The bar was above the waterline, and that was about all you could say for it. It floated on the edges of the city, softly rising and falling, everything sliding first this way and then the other, nothing firm, nothing solid. I hated it. I hated it more than anything I'd ever hated before in my life. Which was saying something since I'd recently spent over six weeks hating a tub of roaches named *The Goose,* an ancient salvaged hull more rust than metal refitted with whatever its crew—a group of dour Scandinavians who claimed to speak no English and who seemed to resent my presence despite my yen—had been able to steal. Which wasn't much.

Bheka's eyes flicked over my shoulder as someone walked in behind me, and I spun, hand closing over the gun in my pocket. The newcomer was a short, thin man obscured by layers of oiled coat and a huge hood, water running off him in sheets as he inspected the damp seats. I turned back and Bheka looked back at me.

"Need something, Mr. Rusbridge?"

I shook my head and Bheka moved away, disappearing through a tiny door behind the bar, and I forced myself to raise up the cup and take a deep drink of the horrible liquor, sweet like fruit juice but slimy and bitter. My stomach clenched up in protest; I didn't want to think too hard about what it was or how it was made.

I kept one hand in my pocket, on my gun.

Savage, Squalor whispered.

I heard the new customer behind me get up and slosh out of the bar, which was hitched up to a long, ramshackle pier made of rotting wood and rusted brackets, the whole thing moaning and shuddering under you as you walked. The thing went on forever, encircling what was left of the city and occasionally sending a spur of rotted wood meandering inward to connect up with some submerged building or other permanent-temporary piece of floating real estate. I'd been in Venice about half an hour, and I hated it already.

I was alone in the place, and liked it that way. Trying to breathe through my mouth to suppress my sense of taste, I took another gulp of my drink.

Revenge, I would have told myself a few years ago, didn't pay well. Not worth it. Here I was a few months in trying to track down Michaleen Garda, and all I had to show for it was a fever, feet that hadn't been dry in weeks.

The door opened behind me again, and I spun, bringing the gun up, clicking back the hammer. It was still wrapped in tough, transparent plastic, protected from the endless damp.

The man standing in the doorway looked local, based on the expensive and neat-looking rain gear he was wearing. He looked fucking dandy, with a neatly trimmed beard and nice, white teeth, clean fingernails held up for my inspection.

"Ah! You must be Mr. Rusbridge, no?" he said, inclining his head a little. He'd been met with guns before; he was careful to keep his hands up and in clear view no matter what else he did, and he didn't seem at all insulted by its presence. "Welcome to *Venezia,* Mr. Rusbridge. It is good to finally meet you face-to-face after so many years of correspondence."

"Mr. Faliero?"

"Of course!" He looked at his hands. "May I?"

I nodded, stuffing my gun back into its pocket. "Sure. Buy you a drink?"

Faliero dropped his hands, water streaming down his sleeves onto the floor, and made his face into a cheerful mask of horror. "In here? Mr. Rusbridge! Please be friendly." He let his square face shift back into a smile—a loose, easygoing face, plump, his skin shining with something beyond health, his beard expertly groomed. The mustache was bushy and had devoured his upper lip, making it seem like he spoke without opening his mouth. "I'd like to introduce my bodyguard, Horatio."

Faliero stepped in and a tall, slightly younger man shouldered his way into the bar, sending the whole place rocking as he added his weight. He was expensively dressed in a shiny black suit that glistened as he moved and a sumptuous leather topcoat that seemed to repel the rainwater away from him. His arms looked like tiny little oak trees inside the coat, and his hands looked like two hands each. I looked down at him, though, and he glared at me with the pissed-off stare of the man born short.

I sniffed the air. "You brought me a fucking Pig, Faliero?"

Kill him! Squalor suddenly shrieked, making me flinch.

Gall, Marin said musingly. *I never understood why he wastes his time on shit jobs like this. Yen, I suppose.*

Faliero's grin leaped back onto his face. "Oh, call me Mari, Mr. Rusbridge. Everyone does. And Major Gall here, while, yes, an officer in the fine System Security Force, is, for tonight, here as my bodyguard."

Gall reached up and removed a metal toothpick from his mouth. "Calm down, old man. I won't run you for outstandings." He leaned against the bar, keeping me in a line of sight clear of his employer, and made a big show of cleaning his fingernails with the toothpick.

"Okay?" Faliero said, wagging his bushy eyebrows at me, mustache wriggling as words magically appeared in the air. "Cops make you nervous?"

"Nauseous," I corrected. Gall glanced at me and then back at his fingers, and I felt better. A major. I'd never met one of the demigods of the SSF before. It was disappointing. "Aren't you assholes busy with the fucking civil war?"

Gall appeared engrossed in something he'd discovered under his thumbnail. "That shit's being taken care of, no worries, Mr. *Rusbridge.*"

"Now, Mr. Rusbridge," Faliero said, looking closely at me. "You do not look well."

I nodded. "Boats do not agree with me, apparently. No matter how old I get, Mr. Faliero, I never stop learning something new about myself."

Faliero's eyebrows, which were impressive, shot up. "You traveled here by . . . *boat?* You can actually do that?"

"During time of war, when getting an intercontinental hover might as well be getting a hover to the fucking moon, yeah, they do that. Neither the army nor the SSF is checking the water, yet."

"Yet," Gall murmured.

"*The Goose,*" I added. "Out of Galveston, Texas. Sixty-five thousand yen for a berth, which was a wooden pen in the hold, a jar of n-tabs, and free rein to piss or puke over the side any time I wanted. Took me to Liverpool, and I've been hitching rides on boats ever since. I fucking *hate* boats."

"Yes. This is . . ." He trailed off and looked back at me. "Should I continue to call you Mr. Rusbridge? Guy *is* dead, isn't he?"

We all are dead.

I glanced at Gall again, but this time the cop didn't react. His coat hung open and I could see two holsters, one under his shoulder and one on his hip. A fucking cowboy. I made a mental note to run first and worry about him later if things got sticky. Then I nodded, looking back at Faliero. "Yes."

"Did you kill him, Mr. . . . . Cates?"

I smiled, heart pounding. Being famous was a tremendous

pain in the ass. I turned back to the bar and retrieved my drink, determined to act like it was the best-tasting swill I'd ever had. I took a deep pull and nodded, turning and leaning back against the bar. "Not on purpose."

"Ah." Faliero nodded, looking amused. He looked down at his shiny shoes. His pants were gathered a few inches above the ankle and tied off with extravagant ribbons. When he looked down like that, his whole face disappeared, becoming two eyebrows and a mustache. "But you have control of Guy's identity and accounts. As you contacted me under his secure account. You have access to his funds?" He looked up, and there was no more smile. For a second it was a very hard, unhappy man looking at me. "Much of which are *my* funds, you understand?"

I drained my drink, which immediately tried a jailbreak. I swallowed with effort, squinting through sudden tears. "I understand that Guy managed funds for people. I understand some of his clients were heavy hitters—police, politicians." I winked. "Anonymous men of means. Men who make their living keeping their ear to the ground and profiting from information. Mr. Faliero, information is what I'm looking for, and you're the local expert—at least the only expert I found in Guy's address book."

He nodded his head like I'd given him a compliment.

Prick, Marin snorted. *He* looks *like a prick, doesn't he?*

"Poor Guy had an experience that didn't agree with him—"

I will never get that image out of my head, Salgado said quietly as someone unknown hummed tunelessly in my head. *Disgusting, and so* cruel.

"—And—and—I happened to be on hand, and we'd developed a sort of bond. Plus, I was the only other person alive within a hundred miles, so Guy didn't have too many choices. I also understand that when Guy was arrested, he was in the midst of a major transaction for you, and his disappearance has left a large amount of your yen outside your control." I smiled. "And you'd like it back."

"Yes," Faliero said, looking up again and smiling. "You understand everything. You can understand my joy when I received a message from Guy. You can understand my continuing interest even when it became clear that the person contacting me was *not* Guy. And thus you can understand why I would think to bring Major Gall here." He looked around the place again. "Well. Shall we repair someplace more appropriate? I have a boat waiting." He frowned. "The smell in this place, Mr. Cates, will settle into my clothes and I will have to destroy them."

I considered. On the one hand, my murder would be tempting to Mr. Faliero, I was certain—I'd met enough men just like him, rich and ruthless, and they were usually hiring me to kill someone. On the other hand, he didn't know how I had access to Guy's information, and he wouldn't take any chances until he knew more. It wouldn't preclude him from grabbing me by the ankles and shaking me until something interesting fell out of my pockets, though. I'd survived a lot of cops in my time, but they still scared the shit out of me. Even the human ones.

"Okay," I said.

"It's all about money," Faliero said as we made for the door. I hung back, encouraging Gall to step in front of me, and he did so with a knowing half grin, rolling the pick around his mouth again. "You know how many people are still in this shithole?"

He paused outside the bar, letting me look past him at Venice, a shallow spot in the ocean with a few dozen tops of buildings jutting up, mossy and crumbling. Most of the city was underwater these days. Bridges going from rooftop to rooftop had been thrown together decades ago and left to rot; some had already sagged back into the water. In the near distance, a tower still thrust up a few dozen feet over everything else. A huge Vid screen had been attached to it, silently beaming cold light out onto the water. The whole place smelled like piss.

Some of the buildings had additions built onto their old

roofs, shiny modern boxes strapped onto these rotting old buildings, and some of the folks had tugged big floating platforms next to their buildings and built on *those*. Weak, wet lights flickered everywhere, like tiny nearby stars. It all looked ready to be washed away.

"About twenty thousand," Faliero said, answering his own question. "It costs. Pumps, boats, manpower, importing supplies. You live here, my friend, you need *yen*. And Guy managed my yen." He turned and started walking down the plank toward the pier. "Ever since those cocksuckers invaded fucking *Russia* — Russia! If there's a short list of places you do not bother to invade, Russia is fucking top three, no? Does no one read history? My yen is worth half of what it was a month ago. And dropping. The funds you have under your thumb, they are *necessary*."

As I stepped onto the pier behind them, there was a painfully loud roar behind me and then a punishing, hot wind pushing against me, making me stumble as it shoved me this way and that. The whole night lit up, and a second later there was a crazy rhythm of hollow drumbeats as chunks of debris rained down from the night sky. I twisted around, squinting. The bar was a fiery wreck, black smoke billowing up from what was left of its floating base.

Well, shit, I thought. *That's fucking strange.*

"It'll sink, fast," Gall said conversationally.

"Perhaps I forgot to mention," Faliero said with a sigh. "Mr. Cates, rumor has it that someone has bought a contract on you."

XXIII

YOU'RE GONNA NEED THE HAND

The sun had come out, and I deeply regretted it.

The sky was cloudless and immaculate, a sheet of blue over our heads that took sunlight bounced off the dark, dirty water and sent it right back at you. I could feel my skin getting red and purple, blistering, my brain baking inside my soggy clothes, sending stinking steam into the air around me. For two days I'd been living with Faliero while he and Gall tried to gather up my price for release of Faliero's money: information on Michaleen Garda, his present location, and anything else they could give me. Two days of queasy, rolling life, the whole world bobbing up and down around me. Everything damp, everything smelling like sewage, the rotten water getting everywhere and hanging in the air heavily, soaking into you. And me reluctant to take off my coat, to sever ties with my lucky charm, so I kept bloating with stink and damp, soaking it up and turning into one walking rash. Faliero said it took yen to live in a place like this, and I believed him. I just didn't understand why you'd *want* to.

Faliero's place was opulent enough, in its way. The platform on top was just a landing point and outdoor space; below there was one whole floor—huge, fifteen rooms and each one bigger than any apartment or crash pad I'd ever lived in—and below *that* were two floors. The first floor, above water, was relatively comfortable. Below that everything was dark, lit by harsh white light, and *damp*. And I mean fucking *damp*. I woke up in my little room — watched, of course, on closed-circuit video that had been inexpertly hidden behind a mirror — in a puddle of myself every morning.

I leaned over the railing and stared down at the inky ocean. For a few feet you could see the city beneath us, the crumbling stone facades from centuries ago, old shit. It was being eaten up by algae and seaweed, disappearing into theory and speculation maybe four or five feet down, the cloudy sea its own atmosphere.

Touma was supposed to do something about this twenty-five years ago, Salgado muttered darkly. *Incompetent piker. Twenty-five years ago there were options to salvage Venice.*

Why in the world would we save *it?* Marin snickered. *Because it is old? Dolores, I expect a higher level of thinking from you. I've got sixty million people starving to death because of you jackasses from the Joint Council, and you want me to spend one hundred seventy trillion yen to stop this pile of shit from sinking?*

No, it's much better spent turning us all into monsters.

I pushed them away, opening my eyes and blinking. I heard steps and glanced at Gall just as Faliero joined me at the railing. The cop looked fresh and comfortable, wearing a new suit of deep purple fabric that looked like it breathed well. He was smoking a real cigarette, making a show of paying me no attention, and I longed for a gust of breeze to send some smoke over to me.

"Do not be fooled, Mr. Cates," Faliero said. He spoke perfect English with no hint of an accent, which meant it was probably the second or third language he knew. "As I said, it takes money to live here, now. A few years ago the Joint Council decided not enough people remained here for it to be a maintained System Subdepartment. The bribes we paid to forestall that! You would be impressed." I felt his eyes on me for a moment, and then he turned away. "Then again, perhaps nothing impresses you. Those who are bored, it is said, are boring."

I ignored this. He was standing inches away and if I'd wanted I could flip him over the railing. He'd probably clip the stonework of the original building his new complex had been built on top of — an impressive thing, from what I could see, one of the few buildings that managed to rise a little above the waterline — and then smack into the water painfully. The trick was to pull your limbs in close and stay aerodynamic, and Faliero looked like a guy who hadn't had to think physically in years. It was always good to know where you were, to imagine scenarios.

I knew my escape routes. Two days of being Faliero's guest hadn't changed my opinion about him or his bodyguard: they'd both shoot me in the head as soon as they were done with me. I kept gazing out at the sea. The whole city was a series of platforms connected by narrow footbridges here and there. Each of the buildings was ringed by a wooden pier of some sort, and boats drifted past us constantly.

"Most of us have a level or two below water," Faliero went on, impressing me. "That must be pumped constantly to be usable. It is...costly. So you see why I am eager to transact our business."

I watched a small boat, huge solar panels like wings spread out in the back, inching its way around the corner of a far-off building, smaller and less opulent than Faliero's. Some of the structures were sad, ramshackle affairs of rotting wood and sprung nails, dirty and even sinking into the water. Some, like Faliero's, were marble and gilding and looked solid, like they would last forever, being built up one level at a time to stay ahead of the rising sea. All of the exposed roofs, every flat surface, was red in color, like drying blood. It was hard to believe that anyone had ever lived here in numbers, that people had been *born* here. The air was rotten and the sun reminded me of prison, and the idea of a whole dark city beneath my feet made me nervous.

"Then transact it," I said tiredly, blinking the dazzle out of my eyes. "And quit *talking* about it."

"A bad habit of mine, I know," Faliero said cheerily. I wanted to put my boot in his mouth, make him taste it. "I will be up-front with you: we have been unable to discover the current location of this person, this Michaleen Garda, you desire to find."

"An alias, you know," Gall said quietly over the lapping waves, flicking his cigarette—half-smoked—into the air. My eyes followed it as it sailed down to the ocean and noticed the boat with the solar panels, bumping into the pier just below us and cutting engines. "I pulled a few favors even—but nothing." He shook his head. "I ain't giving secrets away when I tell you the SSF is going through some strange fucking times." He shook his head again and extracted a black cigarette case from his coat. "Anyway, I put together a dossier on Garda. You ain't gonna like what's in it. But we can't tell you where he is exactly now."

I nodded, eyes on the little boat. A short, thin figure emerged from it, holding a line, glanced up at us, and then bent down immediately to tie the boat off. "Sure, I get it. You're selling a load of shit, and now I'm just waiting to hear what the price is."

"Now, Mr. Cates!" Faliero exclaimed. "Please, be calm. We do not come to the table empty-handed. We do have information."

I watched the figure on the pier, my heart rate kicking up. Off in the distance rhythmic cries rose up on the thick air.

"The market," Faliero said softly. "You can buy almost anything down by the Campanile, if you have the yen."

I looked up and squinted at the tower that still poked its nose up out of the water, adorned with the largest Vid screen I'd ever seen. It was peaceful standing there with these two strangers, with the sun baking me to sleep. I thought I might just let Gall sneak up behind me and slit my throat. It would be easier than raising my arms. I flashed to Pickering's, me on the floor, laughing as the Pigs came in, waiting to be killed and *wanting it*.

I shivered and looked down at the pier. The distant figure

was walking away rapidly. I watched, my heart rate picking up again. I looked back at the boat, which was almost directly below us. I looked back at the person running down the pier.

"We will tell you what we know," Faliero said smoothly. "As a sign of good faith. Then you can decide whether the information is worth payment. You are known as a man of good judgment and fair dealing. Major Gall?"

I translated this in my head: *We will tell you what we know in the hopes that you give up your advantage, and then we can tie something heavy to your feet and drop you into the water.* I didn't hold it against them. I turned around and pushed my hands into my pockets. I saw Gall straighten up and orient on me but ignored him. He was just doing his job, and I had people on the list before him.

Gall stepped forward, producing a small data cube and holding it up so it glinted in the sun. "He was in Europe. Vienna, to be exact. And Dublin, London, and Nuremberg."

I shook my head. I'd been to all those places.

"SSF has a standard Observe Order on him and any of the aliases he normally uses. But things are a little...disorganized now, and he slipped past us." He took his eyes from the cube and looked at me. "You don't know who the fuck he is, huh? Why in *fuck* are you after this guy?"

I spat, watching the glob plummet into the water. "He left me for dead. And he played dirty, and broke the rules," I said. I saw my father again, that missing-tooth grin. For a few weeks he'd been closer. Now he was almost gone again.

With a snort, Gall tossed the cube toward me. I twitched but held myself in check and watched it land about a foot away, bouncing once and then coming to rest right next to Faliero's feet. Gall smiled slightly, turning back to the railing as the older man leaned down to retrieve it.

"We offer no tricks, Mr. Cates," Faliero said, holding the cube and a small reader out to me. I freed my hands and accepted both, snapping the cube into place and glancing down at the tiny bluish screen. I saw the boat below us in my mind and swallowed back an upswell of panic. He was being honest enough; a bullet in the ear was not exactly a *trick*.

"You won't like it," Gall said as I quickly scrolled through the data, which seemed legitimate. "We can't get much more on him, aside from the fact that he's been exclusively using the Garda name for a few years now and doesn't appear to have shed it, so any current records will be under that tag—I doubt you'll find anything on him under any other name."

I didn't like it. I stared for a moment, shock shivering through me, and then looked up, pocketing both reader and cube and touching my charm for its soothing effect on me. "You're sure?"

Gall nodded, sending a plume of white smoke into the heavy air. "I'm sure." He stared moodily into the distance. "Fuck it all." He glanced back at me. "By the way, rumor is *you're* in New York. All the cop nodes are buzzing that you showed up in New York a few days ago. Speculation is you're either putting up your shingle for work in the old neighborhood, or you're back to hunting cops." He looked back at the water. "I hear you killed a lot of cops."

He didn't seem particularly outraged. "A few. I still got a bunch on my list. Along with your boss and an Undersecretary someday. Ruberto. Anyone who fucks with me, I'll get around to."

Gall smirked, picking tobacco from his lip. "My boss. Ruberto. Fuck, Cates, don't you know who Ruberto *is?*"

I shrugged. "Just another asshole who thinks he can make me dance. Anyway, I haven't been to New York since I got pinched to Chengara, though. Your intel's fucked."

He shook his head. "Then someone's using your name."

"So, fair payment," Faliero interrupted, sounding impatient and annoyed. A man unused to being made to wait while his employees chatted shop. "That which is not even yours, Mr. Cates?"

I nodded, turning back to Faliero and picturing the pier, the gap between the ancient building and the wooden walkway, the boat tied off almost directly below us. The Venetian was grinning at me in his fatherly way, a fucking asshole, thought because he could spell *yen* and didn't have to wear the same damp clothes every day he was a fucking prince.

I brought out my lucky charm, holding it carefully in front of me, close to my body, for a moment. Through the thin, transparent material, it looked fresh and new, almost exactly as it had the day I'd cut it off Guy's dead, sunburned body in the Hill Country of Texas. The fingers were curled slightly, but you could see every fine hair, every wrinkle, every splotch of dried blood.

Tossing the hand at Faliero, I spun and pulled myself up onto the railing. I didn't see any point in hanging around to see how they were going to react. I looked down past my grimy boots; I probably had a five-foot margin between me hitting the water and me breaking every bone in my body on the pier. The idea of that brown, greasy water on my skin, soaking into me, made me cringe, but I had a strong suspicion I was very quickly going to want to be anywhere but up on Faliero's roof.

"What is this?" I heard him whisper behind me.

"There's a subdermal chip under the thumbnail," I said, closing my eyes. "Trace the ping, and you'll find his servers. Everything's keyed to his DNA and fingerprints, so you're gonna need the hand." I took as deep a breath as I could manage, my chest burning. "You're gonna want to run now," I added. I didn't much care for Mr. Faliero and his pet Pig, but I thought fair warning was in order. "Looks like my friend with the explosives is back."

"What?"

Mr. Cates, Salgado whispered, *you do know how to swim, yes?*

It does not matter, Squalor said. *He is dead already.*

Feeling strangely comforted by that, I stepped forward and allowed myself to drop off the railing. Faliero's shout followed me down. I kept my legs together, arms at my sides, and looked down just as the water leaped up at me, sending a jolt of searing pain up my back as it closed around me, water pushing up into my nose. Everything went silent for a second as I sank down, an ancient, hidden street somewhere below me.

Above me, the world turned into fire and noise, flames flowing overhead like a second ocean, and I was slammed back into the building beneath Faliero's home by the shock wave.

XXIV

FLOAT BACK TO SAFETY ON MY BLOATED, BUOYANT CORPSE

Breaking the surface, vomiting thick, black water, the first thing I felt was the heat, close and immediate. I clung to the pier in the desperate hope that it wouldn't collapse immediately, and twisted around for a moment, snuffling in air and blinking. Faliero's building had taken a shot; the area of the roof where I'd been standing a moment before was a memory, the charred flower of a stalk of fire that still licked the building. The water where the boat had been tethered was burning, and the pier was collapsing in slow motion, sections of it sinking down under the water every few seconds.

I have been trying to decide, Marin said jovially, *if you are incredibly brilliant or incredibly lucky. Right now, I am leaning toward lucky.*

Fuck you, I thought. I'd been avoiding speaking directly to them, in hopes of discouraging their presence, but I couldn't resist. *You were dying and they vacuumed your brain into a hard drive, and now you're the King Worm.* That's *fucking* lucky.

Hanging on weakly, I sputtered and dragged in wet, foul air. I thought of Marlena, almost felt her next to me, almost heard her snoring. I could smell her, her skin and hair. I saw her face, peeking out at me from the hover as it shot into the air. The expression on her face stayed with me. I knew she'd been horrified, knew she'd been tricked just as I'd been tricked, and I realized Lena had been the first person I'd felt was a friend since Kev Gatz.

I turned my head, water burning my eyes, the slippery, greenish wood of the pier vibrating under my arms like a living thing thrashing against restraints. I froze, blinking; the hooded figure from the boat stood not too far down the pier. The motherfucker had stopped to watch. I stared back at him, rage licking up my arms like electricity, setting my hair on end and drying me off magically. Revenge had been keeping me alive for months, and now it lit me up from the inside like a small sun.

"Mother*fucker*," I hissed, dragging myself up onto the pier, which continued to shake and sink, sections of it sliding under the greasy water even as I pulled myself up onto it. The hooded figure startled, hands flying up before he caught himself and spun, launching into a run. Unbidden, my face spread into a grin, and I reached into my coat to extract the piece-of-shit auto wrapped in plastic. I hadn't killed anyone on purpose in months.

Managing a tortured, staggering gait, I began to run, almost falling over, arms windmilling. I imagined what I looked like, Avery Cates the Gweat and Tewwible, awesome in his deadly skills.

After a few seconds I started to warm up, getting loose, and picked up a little speed as the man in the hood veered to his right and leaped up onto one of the ladders that hung down from the buildings. I considered taking a shot at him, but he was too far for any kind of accuracy, and with me staggering about it would be useless. Already breathing hard, I kept my eyes on him.

When he was halfway up the ladder, he stopped and stretched out an arm in my direction, and I realized he was going to take a few long-range shots at *me*.

The shots sounded puny at this distance, and I just put my head down and kept running, see if the cosmos wanted to kill me off just yet. I wasn't back on the rail yet, but it was close. For the moment, at least, I had a clear path in front of me and just one choice: forward or back. I liked that. It brought me back to the good old days of scratching out survival in old New York, everything easy, everything white and black.

One slug hit the pier ahead of me, sending up a spray of splinters, but my new friend had given up and was laboriously pulling himself up the ladder. I was gaining on him. Venice was going to be a hard place to hide from me, I thought. The pier — if it didn't get sucked down into the water by the ongoing collapse creeping along behind me, the planks under my feet still humming and popping as I ran — was just a straight line looping around the place, with stairs or gangplanks or ladders reaching down from the various man-made islands toward it. Bridges made of rope and wood had been slung in a few spots, looking about as sturdy as spiderwebs, but mostly connected one building to another. There was no cover, no alleys or shadows, the sun falling down onto us like heavy gas and getting sucked up by the black water, everything glare and sparkle, impossible to focus on.

I reached the ladder just as he disappeared over the top. I skidded to a stop, my feet trying to go out from under me on the slick wood, catching hold of the ladder with one hand and bringing the gun up. Panting hard, I squinted up into the omnipresent sunshine and tugged at the ladder, making it shake.

Two, three seconds — and there the cocksucker was, appearing over the edge with his peashooter, thinking he'd have a safe shot down at me. All I could see was a backlit hood. I squeezed off two shots, the plastic sheath around my gun dissolving in my hand, melted plastic burning into my skin, and the head whipped back.

Putting the gun between my teeth, breath whistling in and

out of my nose, I leaped up onto the ladder and began pulling myself up, wishing fervently that I'd thought to grab a pair of sunglasses somewhere, somehow. I'd been squinting into the sun for so long I thought my pupils had to be gray and pale by now, bleached.

As my head came level with the edge of the roof, my lungs bursting and my hands rubbed raw, there was nothing for it but to throw myself up over the edge awkwardly, scraping skin off my face as I landed bad and rolled. Spluttering, I sat up, swinging the gun around in a sloppy arc.

This was a much smaller platform, and was obviously used mainly as an entryway to the rest of the building; the city stretched out around it, the sky everywhere. A lone structure stood about twenty feet away, and a sloppy trail of fat blood drops led straight to it, almost lost against the rusty color of the roofing. Great stagnant puddles of water were everywhere, incubating future species and pumping damp rot into the air just in case you wanted to breathe today.

Coughing, I heaved myself up, tearing the plastic bag from my wrist and lurching forward. I could hear myself panting, hear the scrape of my boots and the constant muffled flutter of the wind. I hit the wall of the little shack and rolled to my right, one hand up to shade my eyes and the gun up by my belly. He was almost to the opposite end of the roof, clutching his side and giving it a lopsided roll that would eventually lead him in circles, if uncorrected.

I stretched the gun out and stared down its nearly useless sight. I could have blown his head off at this distance, but I put one into the roof near his feet instead as a warning shot, bracing myself for him to spin and throw some shots back at me. Instead, he didn't pause or hesitate, running pell-mell for the edge and leaping off. I saw his arms windmilling briefly before he dropped past my line of sight.

Scrambling the last few feet, I threw myself down flat and

tried to see everything all at once. It was a straight drop down into the water below, but the shallow outline of a submerged building spelled broken legs. I couldn't see him anywhere—I twisted my head around, breathing hard, the sun pounding on my neck and pushing me down, crushing me flat.

I felt my chances slipping away. Faliero was probably dead, and while I had my data it didn't tell me where the dwarf was, only where he had been. If this cocksucker was connected to the midget and he slipped away, it would be months or years before I found the thread again. He *might* just be some random fuck who wanted me dead...but I had a feeling he wasn't.

Jump. Marin chuckled. *Why not?*

I forced myself to stay put and keep looking—impatient assholes would take the leap, letting adrenaline and desperation guide them, but I was fucking ancient and I knew better. It was bitter, but I fucking knew better about just about everything. I stood there with a half-dozen weak, dim voices buzzing in my head and kept my eyes on the water, the glare slicing into my brain and setting it on fire. Two, four, six heartbeats, the wind fluttering around me—and then he popped up, twenty feet out, just a head that sank below the surface again immediately. He popped up again and began thrashing about, doing something he may have thought was swimming but looked a lot more like drowning.

I whirled, lungs on fire, and managed a lurching run back toward the ladder. I half fell down, landing hard on my ass on the pier, the huge yellow sun leaping into my eyes and blinding me. Rolling, I pushed myself up and started running again, running in the uncanny silence of this fucking dead city, one big open sewer where the people were just too stupid to move the fuck away.

As I cleared the building I saw him, shouting and flailing. I stumbled to the edge of the pier and dropped my hands to my knees, sucking in the fetid air and watching him drown. Then

I closed my eyes, listening to his choking, phlegmy cries. Fucking hell. You walked up to a man, shot him, slit his throat—you took action and you did it on purpose. You didn't stand idly by while they fucking smothered.

"Fucking hell," I panted. My heart was thumping hard in my chest as I straightened up and peeled off my coat. I hadn't been dry in weeks. Why start now? I dropped onto my ass again and yanked my boots off with two savage pulls, sucked as much of this disgusting, heavy air into me as I could manage, and rolled forward into the water like I enjoyed it.

I'd learned to swim, like I'd learned everything else, running from the System Pigs in old New York; sometimes diving into the East River had been the easiest way to get out from under a pack of cops bent on assfucking you. It wasn't pretty, but I could move myself through the water without drowning, and that was all that mattered.

When I got to him, he grabbed onto me like I was a vision of the messiah and tried to push me under him, figuring he could float back to safety on my bloated, buoyant corpse. I got my hands on his head and shoved him down, holding him under until he started to get a little weak, then let him pop up, took hold of his hood, and began towing him back to the pier. He just floated there behind me, spluttering. At the pier I pulled myself up and reached down to grab his arm, guiding his hand to the edge of pier and holding him there until he took hold. I got to my knees and pulled him up, rolling him onto his back. His hood had fallen back, revealing his white, round face. I sat there, staring for a moment, and then looked away, panting.

"Hello, Grisha," I said. He looked worse than when I'd last seen him in Chengara, and he'd had a head injury then. Now he was thin, his face tight against the bones, and wet like a drowned rat.

"Fuck." He coughed. "You. Let me catch my breath, and I will continue killing you."

I wanted a cigarette badly. I thought of Gall on Faliero's roof, all those good cigarettes, blown up. "Why have you been trying to kill me, Grisha?" I managed, dropping onto my back and just breathing, eyes closed. If the skinny little bastard had enough oomph left in him to shiv me, so fucking be it. I'd been stabbed by worse.

"Why?" He dissolved into painful-sounding coughs, the kind that usually brought chunks of bloody pulp up. "Why?" he repeated hoarsely. "You betrayed us. The little fucker explained it to me. When I discovered you were alive, I thought that unfair. You being alive."

The little fucker. "You mean Uncie Mickey?"

Grisha spat black water onto himself. He looked darker than I remembered, baked. "I don't know this term *Uncie*, but yes, Michaleen." He sat up and spat oily water onto himself, panting. I sympathized. With a bellyful of that swamp, vomiting was a step up. He snorted. "The great Avery Cates, eh? Now we know how you have lived so long. You abandon your friends whenever it is convenient." His face was dark and impassive. "I awoke bloody and alone in the drop bay of the hover. No Marlena, no you. I took up a spanner from one of the tie-down boxes and crept into the cockpit, where I found the little man, furiously ransacking the console for spare tech." He looked away and spat again. "He explained all to me, about the *great* Avery Cates."

I sat up a little, a sizzle of electricity animating me. "No Marlena? What happened to her?"

Grisha slumped down again, breathing hard. "Do not pretend, Avery. Have at least that much courage."

I went cold, and began dragging myself onto my feet so that I loomed over the Russian. Staring down at him, I let my hands curl and uncurl. "What did that little bastard tell you, when you *surprised* him with a *weapon* in your hand, huh?"

He lifted his head again and squinted at me. The sun had

warmed my damp clothes, and steam was starting to rise from us. Behind me, a small secondary explosion made the fragile pier shimmy under us. Grisha considered me for a long moment, not looking afraid at all. "He told me you had betrayed us. That when you had taken the hover as planned, you killed the Christian and then attempted to leave without us. That when we arrived, you killed Marlena and took our hover. That only sheer luck had provided us with another in the chaos." He nodded. "I told you once that I do not forget, Avery."

I stood breathing hard over him. I'd been happy to track down the short fuck because he'd betrayed me, because he'd left me to be mechanized, because he'd used the ghost of my father against me. If he'd killed Marlena, too, I was prepared to kill him *twice*. Without warning, anger swelled up and took hold, and I dropped to my knees and grabbed Grisha by his coat, yanking his face up close to mine.

"You don't *forget*, you stupid fuck? You don't *think*, either. You get the drop on Michaleen and he spins you a story, you let him walk away, and he's fucking *laughing* at you. That little bastard played us all. The only reason *you're* alive is you woke up before he got around to killing you." I let him drop, his head smacking into the wood. He just stared up at me. I leaned back onto my legs, breathing hard. My voice quavered slightly and I swallowed something thick and bitter back. "He fucked us, Grish. And I've been trying to pay him back the favor."

We stared at each other for a few heavy breaths. Grisha hadn't twitched. He was like no other Techie I'd ever met. "All right, Avery," he said slowly. "All right. I have no strength left. While I regain strength, explain to me."

I reached into my pocket and produced the data cube, holding it up to the sun. "I'll explain it all to you on the way to New York."

PART THREE

XXV

SURVIVES THROUGH MYSTERIOUS MEANS

Shut up, I thought, and for once, they did.

I opened my eyes and looked around The Star again. The cop with the golden eye looked like she was going to fall asleep; she just sagged there like there was no point to resisting gravity anymore. Mr. Marko—Mr. fucking *Marko*, who'd been plotting to kidnap for days now—kept staring from me to the avatar like he was afraid we'd explode if we touched each other. The avatar—*my* avatar, with my thoughts in its head, my ugly mug on its face—looked short to me, like they'd gotten my specs from some old SSF jacket and a number had been blurred.

Behind them, Grisha stood calmly, autos in each hand. Grisha was a Techie in some ways, but he was a Techie who'd somehow learned how to survive in the world.

Survival is not permanent. You all will wither from the earth.

I shook my head a little and waited a second, but Squalor declined to say anything else.

"Mr. Marko," the avatar said, sounding like me, like how I'd say it. "Have any light you can shed on this bullshit?"

Marko started to reach into his pockets, and Grisha stepped forward to push one of his guns into the Techie's back. "Do not forget me," the Russian said, his face impassive.

"Be careful, Zeke," I said. "Make me regret being nice to you and I will shave you bald, understand?"

Marko closed his eyes. "I'm just reaching for some equipment." He opened his eyes again. This was a slightly older, thicker Marko than I remembered, like he'd picked up a few years since I'd last seen him. "To scan…them."

Grisha glanced at me, and I shrugged my eyebrows. I'd come to trust the skinny Russian, despite the fact that he'd spent a few months trying to kill me. Grisha was a man after my own heart in a lot of ways—my long-lost brother, just smarter than me.

Michaleen. Thinking of the short little old man made my hands clench into fists. I'd found out plenty about little Michaleen Garda while I'd been hunting him—enough to be pretty sure if I ever found him, my chances of walking away from the meeting were pretty slim. But I wanted my shot at revenge just the same. Fair play or no, I had my doubts that Gall had given me everything the SSF had on the dwarf, and I wanted to dig into the police servers and see where it might lead. And so back to New York we'd come, for the one man I knew of that was the perfect combination of plugged in to the SSF databases and terrified of me: Ezekiel Marko.

Marko, I thought, owed me—he'd pretty much left me to die in Bellevue all those months ago. He owed me, and if he didn't see it that way, experience told me I could *make* him see it that way. Like a gift from the cosmos, here the motherfucker was.

I looked back at the avatar, tightening my grip on the stock of the shotgun. The avatar was silicone and alloys, circuitry and nanotech. It was fake and controlled, and it was *me*. I wanted to destroy it.

"You have an Ambient Analyzer?" Grisha said, prodding Marko in the back. "You have multi-signal sweep?"

Marko nodded. "Left pocket. Model TR-998."

Grisha snorted. "Nine-nine-eight is trash. Nine-nine-six last decent version."

Marko nodded, smiling slightly. "I know! It was a forced upgrade. They literally confiscated all our originals and replaced them."

Grisha snorted again. "Sure, I know the procedure. Go ahead, scan."

Marko reached slowly into his pocket and pulled out a small, thin square of metal that looked like tarnished silver, a small, bright screen embedded on one side. He made some tiny gestures over it with one finger and then held it up, squinting. Behind him, Grisha leaned forward and mimicked the squint, his whole face puckering up as they examined the readout.

Marko swallowed and looked at me. "Holy fuck," he said simply. "It's an avatar. *He's* an avatar, I mean," he added, pointing at the other me in the room. "You're human," he added, looking back at me.

The cop closed her eye. "I know." She opened it up again and looked at me, glowing in the dark room. "No heat signature. Ruberto sent it. To kill Marin."

Marko stared at her. "Well, fuck me then, right? You were going to tell me this, when? Don't answer."

I'd never seen a System Pig look so useless and beaten. During the Plague, I'd seen Nathan Happling covered in blood and tied down in a hover after being burned out of the SSF, and he'd been ready to crack heads and call people names. This one looked like she might curl up and go to sleep.

Marko looked at me. "Are *you* going to kill me?"

I tore my eyes from the avatar and looked at him for a moment. "Mr. Marko," I said, "you're too useful to me at the moment. Besides, as far as killing you goes, you're so low on the list you'll probably die of natural causes before I get to you."

He nodded. "I will certainly try to."

"Kill Marin," I said, stepping out of my shadows. The whole place was dark and damp and felt like it had been carved out of bedrock despite the machined look. It smelled of sulfur and piss, a place that had been used as a hideout for decades now. My voice sounded muffled and flat in my ears, as if it had nothing to bounce off of, buried under tons of rock. "Good idea, but I've got more pressing things right now, so Marin is going to have to wait."

The avatar frowned. "Wait a fucking sec—"

I brought the shotgun up like a club and swung at it, hitting it with everything I had, the whole thing vibrating in my hands as the gun made contact with my face. The avatar went down like a real person would have, but I'd seen avatars in Chengara take bullets. I'd seen Janet Hense fly around the room taking on a Monk and come out of it without a scratch. I leaped down onto the avatar and brought the stock of the shotgun down again, and again, arms aching and breath searing in and out of me like fire.

At first it played dead, sputtering up its fake blood and twitching limply. My fourth shot rewarded me with a thick cracking noise, and then the white coolant started to bubble up, and the avatar went into some sort of automated defense mode, reaching up and taking hold of my neck with surprising, painful force. A second later it altered its grip and I couldn't breathe, pain stabbing up into my head. I swung the shotgun down again, smashing the stock into its face, and with a final twitch that came close to snapping my windpipe it settled back into a gurgling, gently twitching pool of liquids. A faint smell of ozone made me gag as I sat back and struggled for breath.

"Oh, fuck," Marko groaned. "That's Avery Cates, all right."

I stared at the wreckage while I sucked in air. The technology was amazing; aside from the coolant staining everything, it looked like a human being, broken and bloodied. I'd felt better, for a moment. But I knew that an imprint of me was still out there. Whoever created this one could pump out another avatar, or a dozen more, any time he wanted. And there I'd be, doing things I'd been programmed to do, and people would think it was *me*, really me.

"No Marin," I said, climbing to my feet. "Not yet." The King Worm was on my list, of course, but Michaleen was first. Michaleen had punched the throttle. Michaleen had left me behind. I leaned against one of the dark, cold control consoles embedded in the rough, clammy rock of the space, breathing hard. "I mean, that's a fucking *year* of planning, minimum. What were you geniuses going to do?"

For a moment the cop and Marko stood there, staring. I gave them their moment—they'd been following a fucking android around, after all. Finally Marko looked at the cop, but she didn't look back. She just stared at the floor, chewing her lip like she was trying to figure out how, exactly, she'd come to this—standing in some old, wrecked data haven, having a conversation with a man she thought she'd met days ago.

"Okay," the cop said. "Tell him."

Marko started speaking. It was, as always, one of those plans that would never work, filled with death-defying holes and plenty of blanks where you might as well write in *Avery is shot at by an infinite number of people but survives through mysterious means.* When I heard Gall's name I twitched, but I didn't let Marko finish—I waved my hand, and he shut up instantly.

"Like I said: fuck Marin for now. Grisha and I, we're after someone else." I pointed at Marko. "That's why we came to New York. To grab you."

His little eyes blinked in the midst of his hair. "Me?"

I nodded. On the floor, the avatar continued to twitch and gurgle. The distant rumble of explosions above was faint but audible, and the console vibrated slightly under my hand. "I've been searching for someone for *months.* I've tracked the little shit all over the fucking System, but I don't think I've been within a mile of him the whole time." I'd realized that Michaleen was probably the biggest fish I'd ever gone after. And I wasn't even getting *paid* to kill him. I pointed at Marko. "My mark is connected. I've been chasing shadows, so I need data—I need to know what the SSF has on him. They had him in Chengara, so they've got a line on him."

"Avery tells me you are old friend," Grisha said, grinning at the back of Marko's head. "He says you will be happy to help us take a look at the SSF databases."

Marko squinted at me. He looked like a man who hadn't known what *happy* meant in years. "How'd you find me *here?*"

I shrugged. "I didn't. We came here to use it as a base of operations." I smiled, spreading my hands. "*You* found *me.*" I looked at the cop again. She was still staring at my avatar, chewing her lip. She worried me. She was police, but the general lack of contempt and violence was unusual and made me anxious.

Marko shook his head. "Mr. Cates...I'm not sure..." He sighed. "Officer Krajian and I...we've been burned. We barely got out of The Rock alive." He glanced uneasily at the cop. "And...it's got to be Marin. He's got to be *stopped*. What he's doing—"

I considered this, looking past Marko at Grisha, who rolled his eyes at me in disdain. I struggled to keep my face straight. "Mr. Marko, you're telling me you won't *help* me?"

The Techie suddenly took a step forward. "No!" He swallowed, bringing his arms down with care. "I'm just warning you it won't be as easy as plugging in. I'll have to exploit my way in, find a back door. It might take a little time. And I'll need some equipment." He glanced over his shoulder at Grisha.

Marko was a pain in the ass but knew what he was doing, and if he'd been burned, if the Worms were after him as well, then he was motivated. When properly motivated—usually by serious fear of his own demise—Marko had done some pretty great things. I eyed the brick that Marko claimed contained Miles Amblen, supergenius. I'd heard the name, of course—I'd heard Ty Kieth say it enough times—but it didn't mean anything to me. If a magic voice was going to help us, then so be it. I had magic voices in my *head*. What was one more?

Maybe everyone's crazy, Salgado suggested quietly. *Everyone hearing voices.*

"Don't mind Grigoriy," I said, panting as I forced my leg to straighten out despite its emphatic desire to not do so. "He's been living out of his coat for a little too long. You can relax, Grisha," I added. "I don't think Mr. Marko is going to cause any trouble."

Grisha nodded. "And her?"

I looked at her. I didn't trust cops. Marko and my…twin had trusted her, at least this far, but I wasn't inclined to do the same. Before I could say anything or make a move, however, she straightened up, seeming to bloom back to life right in front of us.

"I will help," she said slowly, putting that horrible Augmented eye on me. "Call me Krasa," she said. "I'll help. I have nothing else." She smiled at me, and I found I didn't like her smiling. "Maybe I will get lucky and be killed in the process."

I smiled back. "Sure. Most people who work with me do."

XXVI

A FUCKING PERSON OF IMMENSE INTEREST

I listened to the low roar of a war going on outside. It was like something deep in the earth below us was struggling upward, ramming its giant shoulders against the bedrock every few seconds. Every now and then dust sifted downward onto us, making me blink.

It still felt like the most peaceful place I'd been in months. It was dark and cool, and for the moment it was just me and the cop, sitting in the dark.

"I worked you, once," Krasa said suddenly.

I didn't look at her. "Every cop I meet says that."

"For a while you were a priority," she said, voice low. "After the Monk Riots, when all those creepy cyborgs went apeshit and we had to put them all down. Cops started getting killed in New York, and for a year or two Marin had us running double teams on you, trying to track you down."

Smiling faintly, I shrugged. "Marin made a mistake. I guess he thought I'd just retire and drink myself to death."

It was strange, having a quiet conversation with a System Pig. She sat stiffly, staring at the floor, her hands limp.

"We got close to you. Flushed you out of some rathole downtown. That was years ago—when things were normal. Now, I don't even know what it means to be a cop. Most of us aren't even human anymore. My partner was a *great* fucking cop, a legend. Used to be very high up, got some very swanky assignments, bodyguarding Undersecretaries, shit like that. Knows people. But he kept fucking up. Was always pissing people off, not obeying orders he thought were bullshit." She looked at me. "But a *great* cop. If we'd had a dozen more like him, things would be different. He never thought much of Director Marin. And when all the orders we ever got started coming only from Marin, my partner didn't like it. He started digging, looking to see what had happened. And what did that get him? First, broken back to captain and assigned to me, to street level. Then he kept digging into things, no matter who warned him…and now he's gone. One of the best cops we had, just *gone.*"

With a sudden hum, the lights faded back on. All around us, consoles started clicking back to life, surprisingly loud in the enclosed space.

I groaned, pushing myself up onto my aching legs. She looked up at me, and for a second there was a glint of something alive in her eye.

"If my partner had been there, that day we flushed you," she said, nodding, "we would have nailed you."

We stared at each other, each of us with a pleasant, near smile on our faces. As Marko and Grisha stormed back into the room, I watched the light in her one eye fade, like whatever piece of her that had just flared up was burning off, disappearing back into darkness.

"We good?" I asked without looking away from her.

"We're hot," Marko replied. "Good is a whole other category. Let me get my bearings. I've never been in the fucking Star before."

I turned away from her to look at Grisha. "You?"

He shook his head. "No. Give us a few moments, Avery, to

familiarize ourselves." He shrugged. "Most of this tech, I would think, was stolen from SSF and other government agencies anyway. We should be familiar with most of it."

Marko sat down in one of the thin chairs, and I waited for it to collapse under his fleshy presence. He began gesturing.

"Most of the data in here is *seriously* encrypted—some is even being shredded off the drives as I speak. But access to the comm ports is not restricted, so we can still use this as a dummy terminal."

"Sometimes when you talk," I said cheerfully as the wash of jargon swept past me, "I just want to pinch you, you know that?"

He half turned to speak back at us. "I should talk slow and in small words, huh? Basically, you're welcome to use the tech here as long as you don't try to touch anyone's stuff. It's a hacker's code—free for all as long as you play by the rules. So I think tunneling out to the SSF servers won't be a problem. Getting into those servers and finding what we need—*that* will be the problem."

I studied the Techie. "You're surprisingly…happy, Mr. Marko."

He nodded. "You know what, Mr. Cates?" he said without pausing in his work. "My whole life I've wanted to walk away from the job. Ever since I tested into it in the first place. I never wanted to be police, even TA police. I'm ten fucking years old, they give me a test, a bunch of silly questions, a bunch of stupid games, and suddenly they announce I'm going to be a TA in the SSF. So I was. And I have fucking hated it—except playing with the tech. I wanted to ditch. But I was afraid. And now it's happened—I've been forced out—and I'm not dead. I didn't immediately explode or have an aneurysm or anything like that. I'm *free*."

I thought about pointing out how often *free* turned into *dead* in my world but decided not to rain on Marko's parade, since he was busily gesturing at the console before him. Grisha's wire glasses—still cracked—reflected the dim screens as he followed along.

After a moment, Marko started talking again for no reason I could discern. "Like any self-respecting Technical Associate, I have several exploits carefully set up for just such an emergency. Fake accounts, open nodes, that sort of thing."

Grisha nodded. "Very nicely done, Mr. Marko."

Marko smiled as a familiar logo of a globe surrounded by stars sizzled on the screen in front of him. "And here we are: the System Security Force." He leaned forward. "Okay, we don't have a lot of time. The network speeds are terrible—looks to me like a major conduit has been cut, probably by the army—and my back door won't stay open for long. We've got maybe five minutes before they start back tracing." He spun suddenly in his seat and looked at me. "Who are you looking for, Mr. Cates?"

I walked over to him, stepping over my avatar, which had finally gone quiet a few minutes before. "The name he gave me was Michaleen Garda. He was in Chengara." I grimaced. "I don't know much else you can search on." Gall had said he'd been using that name exclusively, that any records would be tagged with that.

"Okay. Chengara was its own data island...here," Marko said and began humming tunelessly as he moved his hands. "Okay, cross-referencing on the name. Varying the spelling. There he is—crap."

Grisha and Marko looked at each other for a moment.

"Crap?" I asked. "Is that a fucking *technical* term, Mr. Marko?" I hated Techies. They always knew things ten seconds before you did.

"Michaleen Garda is just an alias, I can tell you that," Marko continued, looking back at the screens. "Because the name is an empty reference with a pointer tag. That means his actual file is referenced under something other than that name. But they

purposefully filed him under Michaleen Garda in Chengara.
Because he must be a fucking Person of Immense Interest." He
pointed at a screen as if it were supposed to mean anything to
me. "His actual file is attached to the private physical drive of
the Director of Internal Affairs."

"Marin," I said, frowning. I glanced back at Krasa, but she
was staring at the floor again as if it held the answers to all her
problems. "So you have to get into his data."

Grisha snorted, and the two Techies exchanged another
look. "This is the *private physical drive* of the Director, Mr. Cates.
His Prime. *The* Director. If anything in this world can be said
to actually be Richard Marin anymore, it's his Prime unit. The
Prime has a huge database that is physically separated from the
rest of the network. I've never seen specs, of course, but there are
rumors, and the main rumor is that it contains a complete copy
of the entire SSF database, plus his own private data. It is *not connected* to the SSF nodes, so…well, I simply can't get into it. Not
without physical access to the Prime. Which is in Moscow."

He said this last with the calm serenity of a man who was
pretty sure he'd made his point. I just kept staring at him. "You're
telling me Marin has a database no one else can access?"

"This is Marin's *brain*. Okay? He's got hundreds of avatars
pumping data at him every second. He accumulates data at an
amazing rate. Most of it can just be pushed back at the SSF servers for storage, and he can call it up any time he needs to, but a
lot of it needs to be his eyes only, you know? The Prime is always
in Moscow because that's where his fucking servers are, and
they are the size of a very large building."

I thought about this. One way to secure data was certainly to
deny any access to it whatsoever. "Marin talks to his avatars," I
said. "Get to it through one of them."

Grisha and Marko looked at each other again, and Grisha
straightened up. "Not *impossible*, Avery," he said slowly. "But

difficult. Marin is on own network, yes? Proprietary protocol. The avatars are capable of pushing data up to the Prime and accepting data and commands downstream *from* the Prime. They cannot, by design, push commands back to the Prime, so you cannot somehow forge a packet that would cause the Prime to simply transmit this data to you. Such packets do not exist in his protocol. You can *request* data through an avatar. If we could acquire a Marin avatar and somehow keep it from triggering its own panic codes—which would remove it from Marin's network immediately—and then somehow bypass its internal security to induce it to make such a request, we might fool the Prime into delivering specifics on the little fucker."

"I assume," I said slowly, "that the Prime is pretty well defended in Moscow?"

Behind me, Krasa snorted, but I just watched Grisha and Marko both break into wide smiles.

"Oh yes, Avery," Grisha said. "The Prime is very well defended. Aside from well-armed units and fortifications, there is also Internal Affairs, yes? His Worms. Avatars, very fast, very strong."

"Not to mention," Marko said with a happy cheer I wanted to smack off his face, "this little war you might have noticed. Moscow's been under siege for weeks now. They're fucking eating each other in that burg, they've been cut off by the army for so long."

"I have heard this, yes," Grisha said, shrugging at me. "I would not recommend going to Moscow."

I nodded, just to see the look of dismay flash onto Marko's face. "We'll go if we have to, but let's try the easier way first. If we got a Marin avatar, could you hack it?"

The smiles faded, and they looked at each other again.

"We *do* have Miles Amblen," Marko said slowly.

Grisha blinked at him and then looked at me. "Probably not, Avery. But we could try."

"Then let's try that before we steal a flight to fucking Moscow of all places."

"Okay," Marko said, exhaling an explosive breath. "We have Amblen and his lab. How do we get a Marin avatar?"

I smiled. "I'm Avery Cates, standing here with two recently burned System Cops," I said. "Let's go get arrested."

XXVII

STILL STANDING IN DEFIANCE OF THE KNOWN LAWS OF THE UNIVERSE

Getting arrested was proving more difficult than I would have imagined.

There was a war on, of course, and the spanking-new army that the Undersecretaries had lavished yen on for the last year or two was building pontoon bridges across the Hudson and East rivers, not to mention bombing the fuck out of what was left of New York. Which wasn't much to begin with. A year ago I'd been a Person of Interest, number two on the SSF Wanted List behind Cainnic Orel. A year ago getting one of Marin's avatars to show up to personally — well, sort of personally — put a boot in my ass wouldn't have been that hard. Now, Marin had bigger problems.

I kicked at a chunk of rebar-sprouting concrete and squinted through the smoke rising out of what was left of The Rock. The night before had been an endless carpet bombing, and I'd spent it huddled in the goddamn sewers with Grisha, Krajian, and Marko, listening to the Techie whimper every time the whole world shivered and rained dust down onto us. Grisha had gone to sleep, breathing deeply, calm and unconcerned, leaving me and the cop to stare at each other from across the narrow strip of oily water that flowed down the old pipes.

"You okay?" I'd asked, shouting over the concussions.

She'd stared at me for a moment like she'd forgotten I was there. "No" was all she said. I wasn't sure if I liked her way of saying absolutely nothing and staring at walls like they were moving just for her. On the one hand, it made conversation difficult. On the other hand, I'd never really wanted to talk to System Cops anyway.

We'd come up in the morning covered in white dust to find the whole fucking island beat to hell by Ruberto's forces. As I'd stood there near the old Stadium, coughing up a small ton of dirt, a line of Stormers, four across and shining in their white uniforms, turned a corner and jogged past me, paying me absolutely no attention as they ran.

When I'd turned, I'd found Grisha next to me, stretching and yawning like a man who'd slept well. He blinked and nodded. "Fucking war, eh?" he said with a nod. "Center cannot hold."

That had been the morning. We'd migrated uptown, finding our way blocked by rubble twice, Midtown decimated. I'd seen downtown torn to pieces by Marin after the Plague, all the old, narrow streets razed, letting sunlight and oxygen into spaces that had been richly rotting for decades, putting down invisible roots. But that had been methodical, one block at a time, flushing the population that had clung to life and tearing down their ancient nests. This was overnight, the core of the city flattened, Cop Central reduced to dust and smoke. I could feel the heat thrumming up from the melted ground through my battered boots.

Across the field of pulverized city, the fucking old church was still standing. The beat-up Monks used to hang around it all day begging, and it looked exactly as it always had, two spires of blotchy stone, delicately carved circular windows above the three massive doors. It was as if the church had been built right after the bombing.

"Just think of all the cops flat like paper under this," Grisha said, spitting prodigiously onto the rubble. "That must cheer you, no, Avery? Man who once tried to kill every cop in New York."

"Fucking hell," I muttered, gesturing around. "There won't be much for Ruberto to *run* if he keeps this shit up."

"The System is big," Grisha said somberly. "You're stuck in New York too much, you think Manhattan is all there is."

I grunted. Marko was struggling toward me, picking his way across the ruins like he had the ankles of a little girl.

"Mr. Cates," Marko panted, his hair waving gently, majestically in the wind. "I have a suggestion."

I nodded. "Well, looks like we're not going to destroy any civilizations today, Mr. Marko, so I have some unexpected time on my schedule." My lungs burned from the bitter smoke, and I convulsed into a coughing fit, bones rattling and blood stopping up in my head like jelly.

You won't destroy it, Avery, Dolores Salgado said. *Everything must be organized somehow. Tear this down and what then? A hundred little Systems separated by imaginary borders, like we had forty years ago. That wasn't working out too well, either.*

Shut up, I thought back. It was my standard response.

Marko was panting, the fat bastard. Sitting behind a desk while I'd been roasting in the desert. It made me want to pull his card a little, have some fun. "Look, you're playing by old rules," he said. "This is a civil war, right? Marin's avatar or avatars—they're not going to be worrying about law and order. Maybe a year ago you were a priority of some sort, but fuck, look around—the King Worm doesn't give a rat's ass about you. We're going to have to go *to* him."

I squinted at the damn church. The Techie was probably right. I looked him over and then glanced at Krajian. She walked around like the living dead, like the glowing red badge she'd lost had been her soul, now withered and blackened. But she still walked. She put one foot in front of the other and cleaned her gun every night, and once or twice when she'd been spooked by something, I'd seen her display the sort of reflexes that still made me fear the System Cops. My avatar had been impressed with her and had trusted her to a point. But she stumbled around in a daze and gave me one-word answers to every question—what was she doing? She didn't seem to give a shit about anything, about killing Marin or getting revenge, or anything. When I'd asked her point-blank why she was still with us, she'd chewed her lip for a long time and then sighed, saying simply, "I've got nothing else to do."

I just hoped when bullets started to fly, old instincts would kick in.

"Avery?"

Blinking, I looked at Marko. His face was eager, cheerful—this was, I realized, Marko's Happy Place. He was support staff through and through, and it didn't matter much to him really who or what he was supporting. He was happy just to come up with helpful ideas and supply needed information. "Go to him," I said.

He nodded. "Yes. We need to get on the offensive. We know where one of him will be—the front. He's the general. He's leading the police, and he can afford to be on the front line getting mauled because he can always send in a replacement, or maybe he's got a fucking warehouse of himself somewhere in the city. So let's go to the front—I'd suggest the Battery, where they've got some guns set up against the army's air force. There's a big concentration of SSF there, because it's a likely place for a landing. If a Marin is anywhere on this island directing things, it's there."

I looked around. It seemed reasonable.

"Makes sense," Grisha said over my shoulder. "He will be well protected, of course. We may have to wade through many layers of his Worms to get close to him. Once we are close, we have small field-limited Electro Magnetic Pulse device—this is easy, this is schoolboy project—knock the avatar off its feet before it can self-destruct or dump its core to the wire, and then we drag it to our lovely home where Dr. Amblen can help us dissect and reprogram it. Better plan than wandering city, dodging bombs, and starving to death, no?"

I kept my eyes on Marko. I liked Grisha's mix of tech-savvy and common sense—rare in a Techie—but sometimes he got nervy. I didn't think I could twist his nose like I did Marko—at least not without getting my hand slapped—but I was occasionally sorely tempted to try.

The Battery had been a melted-asphalt stub at the southern tip of Manhattan ever since I could remember, a patch of glassy black land lapped at by the oily bay water. The Star was almost a straight line south from it, the city rising up to the north like weeds reaching up for the sky.

A few hundred feet from the SSF's position, we crouched behind a rusting chassis of some prehover vehicle, a baked-on brownish red frame of metal that some enterprising souls had used as a shelter from time to time, leaving behind a faint smell of piss and some of the usual debris—rotting, half-dissolved nutrition tabs, broken knife blades, plenty of old blood almost the same color as the rust. Getting down this close hadn't been difficult—the cops we did spot on the deserted streets weren't interested in us. I had a feeling we could get surprised heisting a safe out of a building or murdering some uptown Vid celebrity in cold blood and the Stormers would have just hustled past us. We had a good view of the operation, which was impressive. I'd never seen so many cops in one place—but then it was easy when you could manufacture them.

We were pressed in behind our cover. I could smell Mr. Marko, and I did not enjoy the experience.

The SSF officers were still not uniformed, though they wore armbands with pips to denote rank. The Stormers were everywhere, and most appeared to still be human—smoking cigarettes with their cowls slumped down around their shoulders, squinting in the clear, thin sunlight that spilled down around us. Off to my right and south, far away, a thick plume of black smoke was rising into the air, rippling and twisting as it went. I wondered why so many of the Stormers were still human but figured Marin had started with the officers and would work his way down.

The guns had been erected in a loose semicircle just above the yellowish stain of high tide. They were huge, scuffed gray contraptions, their barrels big enough for me to crawl into if I'd been inclined, and they moved with greased ease, up and down, side to side, spinning on their bases to cover 360 degrees of sky, all in response to the subtle weight shifts and gestures of their operators, who wore black uniforms and heavy shielded helmets. If Ruberto tried to take Manhattan from the south, he was going to get a kick in the balls.

"I don't see Marin," I said quietly, the wind in my ears. "But he's got to be there." I pointed at a temporary shelter that had been erected just behind the guns, a hard-shelled dome with a single entrance guarded by two identical-looking men with solid, wide builds and wraparound dark glasses.

"Yes," Grisha said, squinting. "Of course—with a full detail of his Worms packed in there like insulation."

I scanned the Battery again. "A hover—we'd need a hover."

"Maybe," Grisha said. I settled back down and leaned against the steel frame, feeling limp. We were just a few hundred feet from the most SSF I'd ever seen in one place, but there was a strange lack of urgency. It was like we were watching a Vid, comfortable and safe somewhere far away. "But there would be no pursuit, I think. The EMP" —he held up a fist-sized sphere of bright, chromelike metal—"will knock avatars within a few feet off-line for some hours. Even if we prevent the Marin unit from self-destructing and blanking its drives, once off-line it will be deleted from the security database and thus will not be able to handshake with the system again, and will probably dump core and self-destruct when it comes back online—all things we hope Amblen will be able to help us resolve. As a result standard procedure dictates pursuit is unnecessary."

"Okay," I said slowly. "We still need transport. We'll need—"

"What you need," Krajian said suddenly, standing up next to me and drawing two automatics from shoulder holsters, "is a distraction."

I stared up at her. "What the fuck are—"

She stood there for a moment and then slammed the guns back into place. She glanced down at me, and her face had lost its tightness. I hadn't even realized how twisted and cramped her face had been until she looked down at me, half-smiling. She looked *happy.* "Your window won't be long. Don't miss it."

I stood up. I didn't know her. I didn't know anything about her beyond thirty minutes of combined conversation and the fact that my avatar, a version of me, had trusted her. She just smiled back at me while I stood there, my mind a blank. I didn't have any words for her.

"This is fine," she said, and a shiver went through me. "Everything is fine."

Without another word she leaped up on top of the rusted hulk and then down onto the ground. I jumped after her, coming up halfway before Grisha's hand on my shoulder pulled me back down. I whirled and had a hand on his throat without even consciously thinking about it.

"What the fuck," I hissed at him.

"She is going," he whispered back, choking. "And I do not

think trying to stop her will be useful. Think, Avery: We have the EMP, and I do not doubt Officer Krajian's distracting abilities. We should perhaps try to exploit this."

I clenched my teeth. "No. We can't—"

"She is police. Stop her is what we cannot do, Avery. Be ready!"

Everything is fine, I thought, my hands balled into fists.

The cop was striding down toward the mass of cops, her coat thrown back, her head held high. She was a little grubby, but she *looked* like a cop. She was all perfect, arrogant confidence and wound-up violence, marching down toward them all without a second's hesitation. She veered toward the shelter and no one seemed to notice her or be alarmed at her approach—here was the cop I'd kept expecting, here was a woman to worry about, to keep in sight. I watched over the rim of our rusted shelter as she strode right up to the twins guarding the shelter. None of the other cops paid her any attention.

Stopping in front of the two guards, she paused for a few seconds, turning her head to look around quickly—getting all the players fixed in her mind. Then, just as the two guards were rousing themselves to tell her to go fuck off, she reached across herself, drew both guns, and shot them both in the face.

"Ah," I heard Grisha grunt appreciatively.

She spun, putting her back to the door of the shelter and picking off three nearby officers with exactly three perfect shots. The door behind her snapped open, and she spun back again, firing six times into the dark maw of the entrance before throwing herself into a neat roll, coming up on her feet like a dancer a few feet away, guns extended.

The cops still hadn't reacted. She took out three more with quick, precise shots, her face impassive, her eye glowing.

"Now, Avery," Grisha said. "Now, Mr. Marko."

The two Techies stood and moved a few steps away, but I

found myself transfixed by Krajian. *Everything is fine,* I heard her say, echoed by my own voice.

The cops were finally moving, taking cover where they could find it. It was chaos—most of them weren't sure where the shots had come from, and even the ones who had an eyeball on Krajian couldn't be sure she was alone.

Grisha was back at my side, panting. "Avery!" he shouted. "She has chosen this! We cannot do this without you!"

I allowed myself to be pulled up and staggered after him, pulling my own gun from my coat. The glassy ground made a strange, hollow thump as we picked up speed, running for the temporary HQ. The world bopped up and down as I limped as fast as I could, breathing in short, painful gasps, trying to keep her in sight as we scrambled. She was still on her feet as we made it to the open entrance, but two more of Marin's remarkably similar bodyguards emerged as we skidded up to it. They were locked onto Krajian and she might have taken a few to the head, but they didn't see us and putting one each in their ears was like old habit, reflex, an easy rut to fall back into.

Marko and Grisha pasted themselves against either side of the entryway while I faced outward, watching. Krajian had been winged, blood soaking one sleeve of her coat, but she didn't seem to notice, rolling a few feet to her left and coming up in a perfect crouch, spitting shots at a group of cops who were hiding behind a tall pile of barrels and crates just above the high-tide mark. Her smile was still dreamy, pleased, *happy.*

Somewhere nearby, I heard the familiar warming-up whine of Shredding rifles.

"Now," I shouted over my shoulder, "would be a good time."

Grisha shouted back, "EMP in!"

There was a soft, barely audible *ding* from within and then the sound of anything running on current shitting the bed and hitting the ground.

Then, Marko's voice over my other shoulder: "Three…two… one…ah, shit, here I go!"

His voice disappeared inside the shelter. *Good luck, Zeke,* I thought, hoping Marko found a space filled with deactivated avatars and not pissed-off human beings. I spied two Stormers creeping up behind Krajian, who was still standing in defiance of the known laws of the universe, and I took the opportunity to help her out by putting them both down, *boom-boom,* easy at this range and with no one realizing I was there yet.

"Down!" Marko's voice emerged from behind me. "Give me a hand. Marin weighs a fucking ton."

"Faster, please," I shouted, taking a useless shot at the officers crouched behind the supplies. Shredders suddenly leaped to life, but miraculously Krajian didn't turn into a vaguely pink jelly as their roar screeched around us; they were aiming in the wrong place.

Krajian took the opportunity to limp over to the piled-up supplies. As I watched in disbelief, the grunts and curses of the two Techies emerging behind me, she calmly stepped around behind the cops kneeling there and shot them all in the back, steady shots, rapid and exact.

"Hurry up, now," Grisha shouted as a hand tugged at my shoulder. He sounded winded. "Time to go!"

I started moving backward. No one had even noticed us. Krajian stepped from behind the shield of the supplies and looked in our direction for a second. I couldn't see her eye. Her face was blank, bloodied from a gash in her forehead. Her arm hung limp at her side, the sleeve drenched in blood, and another wet-looking stain had swollen up in her midsection. Her skin was white, drained and ghostly, like she'd died five seconds before but hadn't noticed yet. I imagined we locked eyes.

"Everything is fine," I whispered, and imagined she could hear me.

I stumbled backward, gun held uselessly before me. The

ground in front of her erupted as if underground explosives had suddenly gone off—the shredders finally finding the mark. Just before the shredders cut her into three almost equal pieces, she took a bead on a white-uniformed Stormer running across the field and sent him sprawling face-first with one easy shot.

I turned and ran after Grisha and Marko, who were carrying an inert Dick Marin between them, like hunters returning with their prize.

XXVIII

I THINK OF HIM AS LITTLE DICK

I sat shivering with my back against the cold, damp wall of the old sewers. A small nova lamp gave us some bleak white light and harsh shadows, and the walls shivered at irregular intervals as the F-90s dumped destruction down on Manhattan. My lungs burned, and I was shaking a little, feeling feverish. I kept seeing Krajian, pouring every coming decade of energy and violence inside her into one five-minute spread. I counted twenty-three cops. Twenty-three dead, most from near-perfect headshots. She'd walked onto a field filled with hundreds of cops—officers of her own rank and skill level, Stormers with their shredders ready—and killed twenty-three before they'd taken her down. For those last moments, Krajian had reminded me of Janet Hense, whom I'd admired as sort of the patron saint of hardass, emotionless bastard cops until I'd found out she was an avatar, one of the earliest ones. Maybe. Who knew how long Marin had been quietly grinding his force through his big avatar machine?

I looked down at *my* avatar. My face was bloated and ruined, slack and damaged. Grisha said it was still functional; they'd put it into a "stasis" mode. I wanted my imprint burned out of it, destroyed, and Grisha kept telling me it was low on the priority list. Looking up, blinking Krasa out of my eyes, I guessed I agreed.

A dozen feet down the tunnel, Marko and Grisha were hunched over our second avatar, the Marin. Three voices drifted back to me—Grisha's throaty growl, Marko's soft, rounded words, and Amblen's artificial, generated voice that still managed to come off dry and unamused.

Marin's avatar was a perfect copy of him. Or a perfect copy of the avatars I'd already seen—who knew what the hell Marin had actually looked like before he'd been converted into a digital intelligence. It lay there with its chest torn open, a slight grin still on its smooth, waxy face.

I looked back down at the muddy stream running through the old tunnels. I felt terrible—raw and scraped and shivery, like I'd spent too much time out in the open eating nutrition tabs and drinking runoff, gritty water scratching at my teeth. Shortly after our raid on the cops down at the Battery, the army had thrown another carpet-bombing party, and The Star had been turned into a smoldering crater right in front of our eyes, the heat wave intense enough to reach us across the fucking river. So we'd hunkered down in the sewers, the good old familiar sewers, clogged with shit and mud.

I thought of Marlena. I'd gotten used to having her warm body next to me at night, crowding me. I thought of her less and less as days went by, but she still popped into my head now and then. I wondered where she'd gotten to, if she'd even survived. If Michaleen hadn't just shot her in the head when they'd cleared Chengara and pushed her out the drop bay.

A particularly thunderous round of distant, muffled explosions sent a rain of grit down on us. Marko and Grisha threw themselves over the sliced-open chassis of the avatar, cursing. The Russian stood up as far as he could in the tight tunnel, rubbing the small of his back, and turned to stumble over to me, sitting down hard right in the muddy stream and shaking his head. My ruined avatar lay between us.

"You are maybe hoarding cigarettes I do not know about?"

I shook my head. "I've quit, until I can find more."

He nodded, rubbing the back of his neck with a hand that had a thin layer of dried white coolant on it. "Me as well, yes."

I glanced at Marko, who was staring into the Marin avatar's guts like it might hold the secrets of the universe. "How's it going?"

"Ah, not well, Avery. We have managed to keep unit from damaging itself and have disabled internal security. We have been able to reprogram the implanted algorithmic intelligence—Marin—to take orders. This is easy. We cannot, however, do anything with the external security requirements. Encryption I have not seen. Encryption *Amblen* has not seen. So we cannot connect it to its network, or it will simply be remotely disabled. Useless. Amblen says there are ways to solve this using molecular memories and reverse compression routines, but we do not have the equipment or the power lines or the"—he paused to throw his hands around in frustration—"conditions for such work."

I nodded, feeling nothing in particular. "So it's a bust."

Grisha shrugged. "Not completely. We have the unit in working condition. Another stored personality could be implanted into it, and no doubt Marin who was functional until a few hours ago has useful information, yes? And we may yet find ourselves in better conditions, able to continue trying to crack it."

I smiled again. "Better conditions? Sorry, Grigoriy, but in my experience the conditions go in one direction: fucking downhill."

He smiled, teeth white in the gloom. "Yes." He looked back over at Marko and the avatar. "How does some…thing like that become most powerful…thing in System?"

That's easy enough, Dolores Salgado suddenly spoke up in my head. As she told me the story, I translated it for Grisha.

"Easy: You take a broken, half-dead failed System Pig and test a frightening new technology that's pretty much fatal ninety-nine point nine percent of the time on him and make him into the first avatar. Then you put programming into his digital brain to make sure he behaves, and you make him Director of Internal Affairs because you're scared to death of your own fucking police force and terrified to give anyone that kind of power—but you can secretly control him through his programming. Then he figures out how to engineer a crisis that allows him to suspend his programmed limits. Then he forgets to terminate the state of emergency, forever. Easy peasy."

Easy peasy, Marin echoed in my head. *Unlike what you're attempting over there, which won't work.*

Grisha smirked. "So what does this creature do with such power? Free the slaves? Make reparations? No. He—"

Marko suddenly stood up and stomped over to us, squatting uncomfortably next to Grisha, careful that his pants remained dry. The ground beneath me shifted violently for a second or two, and more dirt drifted down. Marko's glasses caught the glare of the nova lamp and appeared to be made of white light.

"It's, uh," he said, nodding his head once in a definitive way. "It's asking for you."

I squinted at him. "Excuse me?"

"Marin. The, uh, avatar." He pulled his eyes up to mine for a second and then looked back down at the ground. "It's asking for you."

"The fucking avatar," I said, "is asking for me."

I looked at Grisha, who shrugged his eyebrows at me. "The fucking avatar is asking for you, Avery. You afraid of the fucking avatar?"

I pushed myself to my feet, leg and back barking, and winced. "Fuck yes," I said, staggering off.

The avatar looked just like him, or at least as I'd seen his avatars look, except for the torn-open abdomen, the wires and black boards spilling out of it, and the pool of off-white coolant around it. As I approached, it grinned and turned its head toward me in a stiff, jerking motion.

"Hi, Avery," it said, voice melted and distorted.

I squatted down and reached out, took hold of its glasses and pulled them off, revealing a pair of perfectly normal-looking green eyes. They immediately crinkled up as it grinned at me.

"New model, of course," it said in the now-familiar gurgle of a damaged Monk or avatar. "The eyes are made from a special polymer we actually can't make anymore. They're in short supply, and we've been forced to have a strict recycling policy."

I put a smile on my face. I'd been making my face smile for so long it was automatic and meant nothing. "Whose are these?"

Its grin snapped on in the familiar, sudden manner. "Original issue, Avery." It cocked its head a little, a spurt of coolant drooling out of its chest. "You know, I was told you were dead. I wasn't surprised. I am surprised now. Are you seeking revolution, still? Is this another scheme to destroy the world? Tell me otherwise, Avery. Don't be a striver."

Do I really talk like that? the Marin in my head said.

"I'm looking for someone."

Its smile widened. "Who?"

I shook my head. "I need you connected to your central database, your main unit. The Big Iron. I need real-time information, and I need you to be able to reach out your whole long arm and sift it all for me. Besides"—I tapped my head—"somehow I have you in my head, after you tried to *process* me in Chengara. I think of him as Little Dick. He's actually kind of chatty and answers questions. I guess he doesn't have your programmed restrictions in place."

Marin said nothing for a few beats. If it hadn't been shielded and torn open, I'd have thought it was listening to its own data stream, collating real-time data from a thousand sources a second. Then it cocked its head again. "Little Dick. That is *amusing,*

Avery. But I know what you're going to ask me. You are sadly predictable—after our last transaction—in which I *honored* our agreement, I'll remind you, you spent much time and energy prosecuting revenge against *me*. Revenge is in your genes. And I can tell you even without being whole that I don't know where they are."

I nodded. "Sure. But you have the whole SSF. You have every fucking System Pig in the world. Every SSF database, scan check, snitch, and paid informant. When I have you connected, and persuaded, you can find him." I reached out and put its glasses back on carefully. "I like you better this way."

"Even if you somehow communicate successfully with my Prime, Avery, and somehow compel me to help you—which would require a degree of ruthless efficiency I have yet to observe in you—there is no guarantee that I will be able to locate him."

With a grunt and a loud pop from my knees, I got to my feet, ducking my head. "Director, you don't know everything. And I know a little more than you think."

It twitched, its whole chassis undulating in one quick movement. "Why, Avery—incompetent, yes, but as always, full of surprises."

I walked over to the two Techies. "Well, boys," I said. "Pack that fucking thing up and let's make some plans. We're going to Moscow."

Marko looked up at me with a pained expression. "Ah, shit."

XXIX

AN ESTIMATED LIFE SPAN OF UNTIL THE UNIVERSE CONTRACTED INTO A HEAVY DOT

"What is that *smell?*"

As was becoming my standard policy, I ignored Mr. Marko and kept the avatar between us. Marko had a dispiriting habit of stepping into my line of fire at awkward moments, so I liked bouncing him off obstacles.

"Come," Grisha said without looking around. "I know of a place."

I hugged myself tighter against the endless wind and tried to remember the last time I'd sat in a heated room, comfortable. Shit, before the Plague. Me and Belling and Glee in the back room at Pickering's, sweating our way through a bottle of gin and collecting gold badges. Then one day I'd been snatched to Newark, and I'd been freezing, burning, aching, and bleeding ever since.

I glanced at the avatar. It was grinning. Motherfucker couldn't feel cold.

Stay strong, you're doing god's work, Squalor muttered.

I shut my eyes and pushed them all back, re-creating my mental bubble. Even then I could feel them grumbling, pressed against its glassy walls, watching me. I opened my eyes again and took one last look around.

"Impressive, isn't it?" the avatar said in my voice. "Very old, those walls."

I didn't look at it, keeping my eyes instead on the red brick walls across the square, impressive enough except for the two big gaps where the bricks crumbled away, like a shell had exploded, revealing white rock beneath. Hauling two man-shaped lumps of alloys and silicone, one functioning and one basically luggage, halfway around the world hadn't been easy. The hardest part was listening to this one prattle on and on, liking the sound of my voice.

I didn't want my imprint functioning. The idea of another me…of *me*, floating around out there, separate and becoming alien with each passing moment, was unacceptable. Grisha and Marko had argued hard against it, but I'd forced them to rip the brains out of my avatar. We'd kept the physical unit, though; I didn't care about that. They could make all the dummies that looked like me that they wanted, and I wouldn't care. It was the *me* inside that made me angry.

Dick Marin was famous, so we'd switched his imprint into my avatar and we'd been carting the Marin unit, empty and lifeless, around in the large metal cube that floated behind us, its mini-hover engines sputtering and jerking, making the cube drift wildly, a few inches up, a few to the left, then settling down again. It still made almost no noise as it floated, though.

Shivering, I stamped my feet into the crusty yellowed ice that coated the cracked pavement, looking around. It was an impressive sight, so much open space being wasted. Five hundred people could live on this space, I thought, though why they'd ever want to escaped me. Moscow was more or less deserted, as far as I could tell anyway. I looked to my right.

"What's that?"

It was a ruin, the remnants of a colorful facade hanging onto the walls for dear life. Several intact spires sprouted from it, topped with half-destroyed domes that rose to a strange point at the top.

"A church, Mr. Cates," the avatar said. I admired the workmanship on the avatars—this one actually looked bruised and beat-up, like a real human being that looked just like me had taken a few shots. Its mouth didn't work so well anymore, so it spoke with a rubbery tone. "We keep meaning to tear it down. The locals get ornery when we try, though, so it's been easier to just leave it."

I looked around the square, thinking, *Locals?* We'd seen signs of people actually living in this frozen hell, but I still refused to believe it.

Fuck, it was cold. I stared at the ruined church for a while, an inky outline against the rotted ice of the street and the rotted atmosphere beyond, all subtle shades of yellow, some of it almost white. Russia made me think fondly of Chengara, of the endless baking sun that stayed with you even at night, radiating out of the sand and stone.

I looked back at the ruined red walls. An impressive tower sprouted up across from us, soaring up and ending in another jagged edge. From what I'd heard the Russians hadn't gone into Unification willingly. "So this is the center of the universe," I said. "Why here?"

The avatar cocked its head slightly, as if listening intently to someone else, someone invisible. "It's a fortress, of course," it said. "It's been here for a very long time, Mr. Cates. And—" It paused, a slight smile pasted on its fake face. It was strange to see my own face and body doing things I'd never do. I kept wanting to smack myself. "There's no reason to believe it won't be here long after *you're* gone," it finally finished, turning on a sudden, unfortunate grin. "Besides, it's got a nice history of autocracy." The avatar's smile inched up a bit on the annoying scale. "That's—"

"Don't," I said, holding up a hand, "fucking define it."

The avatars were made by the System, so naturally they were a fucking nightmare, filled with all sorts of technological chains, overrides, and surveillance. All the System Cops, their meat bodies long ago burned in huge, nighttime incinerators, were not much more than robots in a lot of ways—the brass could flick a switch and shut them down anytime they wanted to, or beam commands into their virtual underbrains and make them march up and down, whatever. With Amblen's help, Marko and Grisha, muttering to each other and sweating like pigs, had taken my avatar apart and put it back together again with a new brain—still a slave, but a slave to us.

"Come!" Grisha shouted, further away than seemed possible. "It is not safe to stand here, in the open."

"Seriously," Marko echoed. "What is that smell? It's like…like…"

"Quickly!" Grisha shouted, giving the Techie a shove.

I fell in behind them, the avatar doing likewise. The crusty ice cracked and crunched beneath me as I limped through the abandoned streets. Moscow had the look of a deserted corpse, licked clean long ago.

You are an insect. I am an insect. Scuttling about. But you and I have time. You killed me? Yet I am here. Time. We are masters of it, and thus can do anything, if only we have patience.

I closed my eyes for a second. I had a working relationship with two of my ghosts. I wished Squalor would stop popping up to preach every half hour, snippets of the *Mulqer Codex* whispered in my inner ear, like a line of ants crawling up my auditory nerve.

I imagined the glass walls again, me on one side, everything else on the other. After a few blessed seconds with only the sound of our feet tearing into the snow, I opened my eyes again and turned my head to look at the Kremlin as we crawled past it. Yellow ice like scum clung to the roof of the building rising above the walls.

We'd started smelling Moscow before we'd seen it; a char smell that clung to everything, greasy and thick. Getting back into Europe hadn't been too hard—I'd done it often enough now—especially with everything gone to shit with the war. Getting from Europe to Moscow had been a fucking death march. The old rust bucket SSF hover we'd boosted out of Liverpool had never been intended to operate in this kind of cold, and three hours out of Dover it had frozen solid and dropped us just outside of Helsinki, just a few miles from the front line of the civil war. The army had swept through northern Europe, Marko's weak, staticky Vid reports told us, and then hit the snow and the gathered might of the SSF Northern Europe and Russian departments, and there things had stayed for weeks now, everyone cheerfully freezing their nuts off with half a mile between them, each line spread so thin we'd had no trouble at all slipping through them. No trouble stealing one of the army's fancy troop transports, either, a huge hunk of metal with tracked wheels like a tank that chewed up the ice and moved at the stately pace of twenty miles an hour, at best, without heat. Crunching through northern Europe, we'd come across more abandoned matériel than seemed possible, pristine tech and vehicles just left on the sides of roads like presents. Grisha had driven, and I'd had to send Marko up front every now and then to clear the frost from Grisha's eyes.

Now we'd made it, and I thought we might freeze to death before we got any work done.

The avatar liked to remind us that it had an estimated life span of until the universe contracted into a heavy dot and crushed everything down to infinity, and I liked to remind the avatar that we were working on changing that. So far all I got was that fucking smile, so goddamn familiar, even on my face.

Grisha led us along the river heading west for a bit, then turned north again, circling around the walls of the Kremlin. He turned onto a wide road, filled with rotting barricades from

riots past, everything encased in layers of cloudy ice. The buildings on each side were gray and brown boxes, mostly windowless, some half-destroyed by explosions. This wasn't age; this
wasn't time. This was recent, and violent. Moscow hadn't been a
happy city not too long before. Now it appeared to be an *empty*
city, though Marko assured me that Marin's Prime, step one in
an exhausting chain of events that would lead me to Michaleen
Garda so I could strangle the old man, was still in the Kremlin.
You didn't up and move a server farm the size of an entire neighborhood just like that. At least not with half the SFNA deployed
a few hundred miles away.

Most of the buildings sported complex graffiti, usually in
red paint. One stylized group of words repeated constantly,
several times per wall. I studied them as we crept past. To me
they looked like *neogeon*. They were paired with drawings, surprisingly beautiful and detailed anatomical studies of human
body parts: a severed head with veins and tendons dragging
beneath it, eyes up and mouth open as if in an expression of dismay; a foot, long white bone jutting from the ankle and tapering
to a jagged edge; an eye, muscles and nerves trailing behind it
like a squid. The art was all fresh and skilled. The fucking Ivans
liked their art.

"Hey, Grisha," I shouted, my voice echoing grandly down
the canyonlike road. "What does this mean?"

Moscow was huge but felt tiny. Every move you made came
right back at you, amplified, like we were under a glass that
moved with us, keeping us exactly in the center.

The skinny Russian stopped and spun on his heel, storming
back toward me, face red, snot running freely from his nose as
he crunched and struggled. When he was just a few feet away,
he raised his hands.

"Be *quiet*, Avery," he hissed. "Fucking hell. It is not *safe* to
draw attention to us."

I looked around: ice and air, dead concrete. The whole city

was made of frozen rock and empty spaces, it was just a bad, burned-fingernails smell held together by habit. "Grisha," I said easily. "Don't tell me what to do, okay?"

Grisha stopped suddenly, his breath panting out of him. He stood there for a moment and then spun away again. "Quickly," he muttered, his voice carrying easily on the thin air and bouncing off the buildings. "Quickly."

We crossed a wide, gray stone bridge over the river, the wind howling and underscoring the creepy silence of this almost-abandoned city. Where exactly an entire city of people disappeared to when everything around it was fucking wasteland, I didn't know. I walked as fast as I could, feet sinking into the crunchy ice and leg aching, and caught up with Grisha, sending Marko fading back to join my avatar—my face, dented and mashed from our first meeting in The Star, with Dick Marin's brains inside—with a look.

All the buildings were massive, huge square hulks rising up on either side of the street, all with complex, fancy facades, columns and fluting, and intricate masonry everywhere. They'd all been brightly colored at one time, with flecks of yellow and red paint still clinging here and there, but time had worn them down to a near-uniform gray and brown. The streets were paved and in good shape, the only sign I'd seen so far to prove that this city hadn't been abandoned decades ago. But I'd been to Newark and Paris; I knew what a dead city looked like. Moscow was too clean, too neat. Buildings hadn't collapsed, and there weren't fields of debris and trash the size of city blocks. It was sterile, clean and neat, as if everything and everyone had been plucked up and teleported somewhere else, instantly. Burned out. The ice clinging to every surface, dripping down like teeth from the vacant windows and cornices.

The streets were too wide, too. They didn't offer any cover.

As we crossed another huge, empty intersection, the distinct noise of gunshots startled us. After the absolute lack of noise, the three shots froze us all in place, heads whipping around just in time to see a group of people, distant to the north, like tiny shadows flitting past us. They kept coming and coming, bursting from behind one monolithic building and disappearing behind the next. As we stared, a small group stopped and stood in the street, staring back at us.

"Fuck," Grisha growled, rushing back toward us. "Move, move! Come, come! This is not good, Avery. Not good."

He turned and marched off, and Marko, the avatar, and I slowly turned to follow him. The dim figures were too far away to be of immediate concern, and I had no desire to actually meet people who lived in this dead fucking city. My nerves were sizzling, and I spent the next ten minutes twitching this way and that, spinning at every sound of cracking ice and almost murdering Marko every time he cleared his throat. The Techie was thin and sweaty, and had been for days now, looking like some sort of prototype of himself.

Outside an abandoned cube of a building behind a sagging chain-link fence, Grisha stopped and flagged us to follow him. Over the narrow and uninviting front door the awning still held rusting letters: гостиница. In my mind I pronounced it *rock-hila*.

"This was hotel," Grisha said as he pulled the creaking, rusted door open. "Back when there were visitors to Moscow."

Back when there were people, Salgado suddenly whispered.

I took his word for it as I stepped inside, smelling mildew and rust. Maybe before the civil war there'd been visitors, but now with the System of Federated Nations Army locked down a few hundred miles away across the snowy desert, it was just an empty box without power, heat, or charm. And the SFNA was making sure it stayed that way.

We entered a small foyer of some sort, a grimy-looking desk front and center. Spikes of ice hung from the desk, evidence that in the warmer months our hotel leaked like a gutshot. The walls were all peeling green wallpaper, brittle and frozen, and the floors were bare concrete with a million tiny tacks in place where carpet had once been. I realized bitterly that I was going to have to keep my boots on all the time, my feet turning into white mold within them. Getting shocked out of sleep and running down here onto this would be a fast way to infection and amputation.

"Close the door!" Grisha snapped as the floating cube struggled in behind us, scraping the walls and making my skin crawl. "Quickly, we must explore and fortify."

I turned and walked deliberately back to the front door, slamming it shut. It banged loosely and jumped back at me. It was a good, heavy metal door, but the lock had been torn out and there was no obvious way to secure it. "Who are you worried about getting in here, Grisha? Those nice folks we saw running?"

"The good people of Moscow, yes," he snapped. "Come, let us explore. We must find a strong room."

Before I could say anything else, he strode purposefully out of the room, his rough bag slung over his shoulder, his fingers poking out of his black gloves like sausages. I looked at Marko, who stood blinking by the desk, running his hands over the console embedded in it as if it spoke to him.

"You have a spot welder kit?"

He nodded, eyes locked on the dead console. "Of course."

I took two steps and grasped him by the shoulder, spinning him around roughly, getting a spluttered grunt as a reward. "Seal up the door, Zeke. Be useful. That should be your fucking motto, you know. Be fucking useful."

I found Grisha in the next room, which was a small office, windowless and tight, crammed full of a desk and a large black cube from which cables snaked to and from the walls.

"Why don't they just bomb the shit out of Moscow?" I wondered aloud. "Why starve it like this, freeze it out? A couple of hours of dumping ordnance on it, and it's not here anymore."

Grisha was looking at the walls critically. "They wish the Marin Prime as a prize, maybe," he said. "Or maybe the SSF big guns keep their hover fleet at bay, who knows?" He stopped and looked at me. "You have a plan, Avery? For getting to the Prime? You get in, we find a way to access the data, we find the midget. Very good. But how?"

I wanted a cigarette in the worst way, even if it made my lungs bleed. Instead I rubbed my cold hands together. "We're going to walk in."

Grisha leaned forward, squinting at me. "Using Marin avatar? Will not work, Avery. Even assuming we can reconstruct damaged security modules in unit—which I doubt since even with Dr. Amblen's help we barely managed dirty hack we did in New York—there is no doubt it has been listed out of commission and is no longer on trusted list. We will not bluff our way past automated systems that way."

I nodded. Blue light began flashing into the room from the foyer, and I could hear Marko muttering angrily. I knew if I could hear him clearly, I'd be forced to hurt him. "We're not going to bluff automated systems. Marin's got a weak spot, whether he realizes it or not." I stopped to beam a smile. "The Technical Unit."

He blinked. "Yes?"

I started to pace. "Marin's been afraid to process the Techies into avatars, right? Afraid they'll lose whatever spark humanity gives them that lets them innovate and hack, right?"

Grisha nodded slowly, eyeglasses shining and making him look blind. "Yes. The Technical Unit is largely unprocessed."

I snapped my fingers. "Social engineering, Grigoriy. The Techies in the fucking Kremlin are *humans*, and they can be conned. Fuck all his security. We walk in, looking like a bunch of hardass System Pigs, dressing the part, with Director Marin *himself* in tow, and we fucking snow them under. The usual tap dance—you'll be cleaning toilets in Chengara this time tomorrow, you piece of shit; you want *me* to contact your supervisor? Shit, we'll have them crapping their pants, and they will *let us in*." I smiled, putting it on my face like a tool. "They will *guide* us to his office."

"Perhaps," Grisha said slowly, nodding. "We will need luck in who we encounter, but…perhaps. Marko with his SSF contacts can maybe do some research for us, find out who is on duty here and who might be a wise choice for confronting. Then, maybe." Grisha raised an eyebrow and looked at me. "Who will…populate the avatar? Marin himself?"

I scowled. The light suddenly stopped. "Fuck no. Who knows what tricks that bastard has up his sleeves. He stays out of his own unit."

Very wise, Avery, Marin chuckled. *Very wise.*

Grisha's face folded into a slight, subtle smile. "You?"

I held up a finger. "I thought I made it clear that my imprint be destroyed, Grish—if I find out—"

Grisha put up his hands, his smile blooming. "I tease you, Avery. It is easy."

I kept my hand up. "Do it again, Grisha."

His smile faded. "I apologize, Avery. If not you, and not Director Marin…?"

I lowered my hand slowly. "We're going to ask Dr. Amblen a favor."

Grisha cocked his head, considering, and opened his mouth to say something when a hollow, heavy booming noise filled the air. We heard Marko's startled squawk from the other room. I exchanged a look with the Techie and retreated back into the foyer, where Marko was slowly backing away from the door, which was shaking and vibrating, the fresh welds still glowing in places. He still held the small gun in a limp hand at his side.

"That's a good weld, Zeke," I whispered.

"Thanks," he whispered back. "What is that noise?"

From outside, a sustained howling had begun, a crowd of people shouting at the same time. It was loud and angry and unintelligible, and it almost seemed like the noise was battering the door, a living thing pounding on it.

"Grish," I said slowly, reaching into my coat and pulling out my gun.

Grisha nodded for no reason. "The war has been hard on Moscow," he said quietly. "Moscow is starving."

"Who the fuck is out there?"

He shrugged, wriggling out of his bag and pulling out his own gun, checking it professionally. I loved Grisha. I was going to marry him. "The good people of Moscow," he said. "Cannibals."

XXX

I WAS FOURTEEN AGAIN

"Wait," Marko said, slipping his torch into his pocket. "They want to *eat* us?"

"That explains the smell," my avatar said.

That explains the smell, Marin echoed in my head.

"Come," Grisha hissed. "This hotel is good place, but I have not been here in a very long time. We must secure it. I recommend we remain on the first floor and block the escalator and elevators. Not functioning, of course, but still access points. Come!"

A whole city cut off from the rest of the System by an entire army. Nothing in or out. The undead Director of SSF Internal Affairs and his zombie staff sitting in a fortress with dozens of emergency generators underground, keeping him warm and sizzling on the network. Everyone's last stash of nutrition tabs gone weeks ago; people sent out to find supplies disappeared forever. We'd gotten in, of course, but then the army's whole idea wasn't keeping small parties of assholes from getting in or out, it was all about keeping huge shipments of supplies from getting in, or a huge server farm from getting *out*.

The limitations of meat, Squalor whispered, a worm in my brain, chewing. *Better that they pass, so that the saved may inherit the earth.*

I checked my gun quickly and felt myself up for ammunition. "Grisha, give me the layout, fast."

He didn't hesitate as he dug through his bag. "Five rooms on first floor: this entryway, small office in rear you have seen, to left and right are escalator and elevator banks, and also behind us supply closet. Closet has two windows, high off floor."

I nodded. "Fuck the soft spots. Back in the office and make a choke point."

He shook his head. "You are good at slitting a single throat, Avery, but if we do that we will only be able to fire one at a time and we will be overwhelmed — the door to the office is too wide. We do not know how many are out there."

Eyeing the office door — wide enough, indeed, for two or even three people to push through in a pinch — I listened for a moment. It was one blurred noise, rising and falling, like fingernails on my spine. "No more than five hundred," I offered, blank faced.

"You take one bank," he panted, standing up. "I take another. Mr. Marko takes the storeroom, and we sincerely hope the welds on the front door hold."

Marko spun around. "What the fuck? You're kidding, right?"

Grisha stepped forward suddenly and slapped Marko across the face, a hard backhand that spun the Techie around, making him stagger until he found the wall to catch him.

"You have a gun, you fucking complainer," Grisha shouted. "Make use of it."

I found I was smiling broadly. My heart was pounding, and I felt like my thoughts were lasered in, ticking along at a million miles a second. It had been a while since I'd had some easy, guiltless fucking carnage. I'd felt complicated for years. It all fell away, and it was just me, a gun, and the determination to survive. I was fourteen again.

I spun and jogged over to Marko, who was leaning against the wall rubbing his chin with a look of such stupid amazement on his face that my cheer doubled, swelling inside me. I grabbed his shoulder and pulled him with me, making for the storeroom door with him limply in tow. I kicked the door open and peered inside: rows of shelves reaching up to the ceiling, the two windows grimy and dim squares of feeble, icy light. Anyone coming in would first have to smash what looked like thick, robust panes of glass and drop a good ten feet to the floor, where they would be momentarily blind and off balance.

"Look, Zeke," I said, forcing myself to speak slowly. "In this case a choke point—the door—will work; it's a narrow opening. They're going to hit the floor shaky and blinking. They're going to have glass in their hands where they steadied themselves." I took his arm and raised it up, bending it at the elbow, positioning it. "Be relaxed, accept the recoil. Take your time—they can only come at you one at a time. Don't be fancy, just hit them. You don't need headshots, you don't even need to kill them. Writhing bodies on the ground will actually be to your advantage, and despite what you might think, most people when shot—even in the fucking leg or arm—go down like pussies and start screaming. It *hurts*. Okay?"

Marko's eyes were wide. There was a particularly loud boom against the front door; and he flinched, then nodded, taking a deep breath. He looked down at himself and fumbled in his pocket for a moment before bringing out the Roon I'd let him have. Wasted on him, of course, but it wouldn't jam, and the smooth action would help him stay calm. "Okay. I think."

I took the gun from him, just reaching out and plucking it from his grasp, which worked more often than you might imagine. I popped the clip out and checked it: full. Slapping it back, I handed it to him. "Make sure you have clips. Don't forget to reload. Don't wait to be clean out; pick a moment of slack when you can pause for ten seconds. Don't *forget* to reload, okay?"

He nodded again, accepting the gun. "Okay. I have five clips in my pocket."

"Make sure you can reach them. Make sure they're the only things in that pocket. Be calm. Take your time. Don't be picky."

"Okay."

I nodded and stormed away. "I've got the bank on the right," I said. "If you get swamped, scream." I glanced at my avatar, grinning at me with Dick Marin's evil energy. "You don't fucking move. Stand in front of the door, be an obstacle."

Dick winked at me with my own eyes and stepped forward.

Can't eat me, the Marin in my head said.

"Can *eat me*," I reminded it.

As we passed each other, heading for the opposite elevator banks, Grisha and I exchanged a stiff, curt nod. Breath steaming from me like exhaust, a light grit crunching under my boots, I stepped out of the foyer into the elevator and escalator banks. Two grim, dented brown elevator doors were on my left, pocket doors that slid into the walls. I ignored them. Even though it would be trivial to open the door once inside the cab, getting from the second floor down into the elevator cab and then triggering the emergency release on the doors would be slow and difficult. If I were starving, half-mad, and ready to tear some people apart for sustenance, I wouldn't be in the frame of mind to go through that kind of trouble, not when I could scramble down the wide-open escalator.

It was a risk, but I moved past the elevators and stared up the escalator. It was new looking, free of rust. It looked like you could just fire it up, scrape the ice off, and press a button, and it would begin to silently and endlessly rise up and sink down forever. Each track was wide enough for two people to stand abreast or one person and their luggage. I didn't think this leaky hellhole was the sort of place to have a few Droid bellhops to haul your crap up to your room. The tracks rose up on a fairly steep angle, leaving a lot of dead space on the sides. I dashed around the side of the far escalator and pressed myself into the hollow formed between the rising escalator rail and the rear wall. Crouching down, I'd be completely out of sight to anyone tearing down the steps until they were in my line of fire. It was risky; if any of them proved to be calmer than expected, they might make their way down the elevator shaft and hit Grisha and Marko from behind, or if they were faster than expected, I might miss one pouring down the escalators.

I bent down as much as my back would allow and gripped my own Roon, forcing myself to wait. A professional, one that lived past his teen years, learned how to fucking sit still and make like a rock. It was usually the main difference between survival and death.

I made like a rock.

The noise outside had taken on a different flavor, echoing distantly with the tinge of murder, as if the crowds of people had floated up into the air and hung there, snarling and dripping sizzling spittle down onto the street. They were everywhere, all around me, encased in concrete and harmlessly terrifying.

I imagined my glass shield in my head, even though no one had spoken inside me in a long while. I didn't dare hope that they might have gone away, been flushed down whatever drain stole my memories and made it possible for me to sleep. I concentrated on my breathing, counting seconds and trying to slow myself down a little at a time, fighting the urge to suck in gasps of air.

Up above me, unseen, there was a hollow crash, and the howling was suddenly all around me, echoed back and forth, bouncing off the walls. I took a deep breath and put my finger on the trigger, blinking once, deliberately.

The first two came down the escalator in huge bounds, three steps at a time, landing on the floor in front of me at a run. They were just blobs, wearing heavy winter coats that were like gigantic, blubbery exoskeletons, ripped and torn in places. I exhaled and squeezed the trigger twice, and all I got were two silent puffs in the backs of those pillowy coats. The two Howlers went down, belly flopping onto the rough floor and skidding a few feet.

Three more were right behind them, windmilling their arms and screeching as they invaded. I took the first two *bam-bam*, right in the square of the back, but the third—not even noticing the bodies on the floor—almost made it around the corner before I managed to orient on him and catch him down low, knocking his feet out from under him.

I reminded myself of my advice to Marko: Don't be fucking fancy. I didn't have *time* for fancy.

One more, wearing what looked like several suits of thin clothing, maybe every stitch he'd been able to find. He was skinny, his head looking way too big for his body as he stumbled to a halt at the bottom of the escalator as he almost tripped over the bodies lying there; a quick shot and he dropped, weightless, floating to the floor.

A wave of them then, six at once, all bunched up as they leaped downward, howling, crashing into each other at the bottom. There were two men in the bubblelike winter gear, seeming to float along, and four women in multiple layers of rags, their skin gray, their hair falling out. As they bunched up, startled, at the bottom they whirled to face me, snarling. I fired twice out of reflex, knocking the two men onto their asses, blood spurting up from the floor in a weak fountain, and then I hesitated; the stretched, skeletal faces of the four women were scabbed and stained with dried blood, their teeth greenish and jagged.

One of the girls shouted something, and they launched themselves back toward me. I forced myself to stand still, hitting each one in the abdomen, their howling transforming suddenly into a keening scream. I found I preferred the former but didn't have time to think on it anymore: Three more Howlers were already racing down the escalator, the lead one screaming something and gesticulating at my hiding place. I skipped forward, spinning to run backward just before they vaulted over the side to land right where I'd been, each of them filthy, dried blood all over their faces and the fronts of their ragged clothing. Their fingers were blackened and curled into permanent hooks, and none of them looked particularly hearty or energetic as they struggled to their feet after the fall.

The first one up took a second to find me as I glided as best I could in a wide curve away from them, lining up with the escalators. He was older, maybe my age, with a severely broken nose and a thick white beard under all the scabbed residue. His eyes were dull, landing on me and just sitting there like bugs, no spark of surprise or joy or hatred. They simply registered me and stayed with me. He said something, and the three of them came at me with no art, no creativity. They just staggered at me, running dead on, and I hesitated. I watched them run, mouths open, tongues lolling. Then I saw shadows up at the top of the escalators, the next round, and I put three bullets in them, the old man dropping just four or five feet away from me, his feet sliding out from under him as his face exploded.

Staring at him, I dropped my clip and fished a fresh one from my pocket. I realized everything had gone quiet.

I looked up, bringing the Roon up with me. I had a clear line of sight up the escalators; all the way at the top was a knot of them, gray and rail thin, some enveloped in the huge, puffy winter gear, some just wearing every scrap they'd found, looking like scarecrows. My breath piled out of me in thick white jets as we stared at each other. I counted fifteen.

Fucking hell, I thought. *I'm about to be fucking swamped.*

One of them took a slow, careful step down. She was tiny, short, her limbs stubby. She would have passed for a child from behind; from the front she passed for about a century old, with a leathery, tanned face and limp, gray and white hair that had grown wildly, frizzing out at the ends. She had the same dull, empty eyes as the three I'd just cut down, eyes that just sat there, dumb and implacable.

She said something in that blurry language. Russian, fucking hell—no one could be civilized and speak shit like this.

I didn't move or say anything.

She squinted down at me, gestured with one arm toward the bottom, and repeated herself. Then she closed her eyes for a moment and took a deep breath. When she popped them open again, she stabbed a black finger at the floor.

"Bodies," she said in her reedy, weak voice. It sounded like *boh dees*.

I blinked and glanced around again. One of the trio who'd just come for me was dragging himself toward me by his fingers, leaving a thick trail of blood behind. Everyone else was still. I took a step back from the escalator and nodded once.

"*Da*," I said. Grisha had taught me that much. I held up five fingers, and the crone nodded.

Well, it's easier than bracing you, Marin chortled inside, seemingly loud and crisp after so much interior silence. *Hell, Avery, you just fed these folks for a week.*

This is modern man, Squalor chimed in. *This is the disease in action. When we are all freed, there will be no need for food, and thus no need for sin.*

Five of them came, limping down the escalators while the rest stayed up top, staring at me listlessly. The silence was complete, suddenly. As the five reached the floor, I began backing away on a curve, angling my way so that they stayed in front of me until I was in front of the doorway back to the foyer. They each took a corpse, getting their hands under their shoulders, and began dragging them back up the escalator. As each made it back to the top, a new recruit would glide down and retrieve one more.

When they finally got to the crawling guy, he'd managed

about six inches. They just grabbed him under the shoulders like everyone else, and he let out a long, raspy moan, then fell into silence as he was dragged up the escalators. When all the corpses had been collected in this way, the rest of them just turned and walked off, disappearing into the shadows of the second floor. I considered going up there to make sure they'd left the building but turned instead and headed for the foyer, where Grisha was already standing.

"They just faded back," the Russian said. "They just gave up."

I nodded. "Let's barricade the elevator banks," I suggested, moving my finger from the trigger to the side of my gun. "And set up in these three rooms. Though I think our friends the Howlers are going to have a little party these next few days; we shouldn't get much trouble from them."

Grisha spat on the floor. "Yes, unless there are other *Howlers*, eh?"

I shrugged. What could you do? "Come on. We've got to shave Marko's head."

Grisha blinked. "Why? Will not help with Optical Face Scan."

I nodded, heading for the storeroom, where Marko still stood in the doorway, his gun up and ready. "Just in case some human Techie in the Kremlin recognizes the infamous Ezekiel Marko."

Marko jumped a little and turned, momentarily pointing the gun right at me. I sidestepped a little and reached out, pushing his arm down.

"No one came through the windows," he said, sounding tired. "I didn't shoot anybody."

I winked. "That's okay, Zeke," I said. "I did."

XXXI

THEY ALWAYS CAME BACK

Moscow was the future.

The city hummed around us like an open line, background static and white noise. You could wander the city for hours and not see anyone, not even a sign that anyone had ever been there, and then suddenly turn a corner and find dead bodies, blood frozen around them like melted red plastic, neat fillets cut out of them, their organs gone.

Eventually, when Marin had converted everyone into his little puppets, this would be all the cities, just empty corridors. Would Marin even need everyone to be turned on and moving around? Or would it be easier to just have everyone shut down into power-saving mode? Or stored on the Big Iron, nothing more than programs?

Shit. It would be like an eternal prison, locked down inside yourself. I was on the rail too much as it was, but at least I wasn't a damn Droid.

We crept along the frozen river. It would have been better to arrive in a hover, like the most powerful...thing in the System actually would, but getting a hover into the wasteland between Ruberto's army and Moscow was not within my feeble powers. So, we improvised. The only thing I had going for me was the as yet uncharted stupidity of your average highly trained System Techie.

As the Kremlin came into view, a collection of distant spires and walls on top of an icy white bump in the landscape, I stopped suddenly, cocking my head. Grisha, Marko, and Amblen—inhabiting the Marin avatar with a sullen lack of grace—caught up to me, all of them looking like new and better people in the expensive suits we'd scavenged from stores, all abandoned and icy, their wares left undisturbed since, I assumed, you could not eat them. My own avatar, empty and dead, we'd left in the hotel. I found myself picturing it, staring up at the ceiling with my ruined eyes.

"Problem, Avery?" Grisha asked, looking around with his sharp eyes.

I pushed my eyes around the landscape, the rotting buildings and snow-choked streets. There was nothing there, no movement, no shape that shouldn't be there. But I'd...heard something? Smelled something? I wasn't sure, but my underbrain had twitched. I'd learned to listen when that happened.

"No," I finally said, turning back. "I'm imagining things, I think."

We started off again, soft crunching and wind, four black figures. I felt small. Moscow, so huge around us. The System so huge around Moscow. And both decaying, falling apart. As we stepped past a row of collapsed buildings, rubble and ice, I wondered if anything I'd ever done—Mitchell Kendish, Squalor, the cops in New York, the Plague, everyone directly or indirectly murdered by me—mattered. If we all weren't going to be erased, not only killed but plowed under by a million years of slow growth, sandpaper winds, and dry rot turning everything we do into an indistinct mush. I'd been plotting for years, with nothing to show for it—Pickering's gone, Glee gone, everyone I'd been trying to kill for years still moving around as they pleased.

Grisha faded back to match my pace. "I see it, too, Avery," he said. "We are being followed."

I startled; I hadn't *seen* anything. "Fucking hell, Grisha," I muttered. "Where were you ten years ago? We could be running this whole world by now, you and me."

"Ten years?" He smiled slightly. "Ten years ago I was in tiny office, designing nanocircuits. I never knew what they were for—I received only as much spec as needed for the part." He shook his head. "No, I would not have been of much use ten years ago." He cocked his head. "*Three* years ago, perhaps. You do bring a certain something, do you not?"

I allowed myself a smile. "A tolerance for pain, so far, seems to be my only marketable skill."

He shrugged. "Do not underestimate that. But it is your inability to cheat which makes people follow you."

Bullshit, I thought.

Bullshit, someone echoed in my head.

"Marko," I said softly. "Any ideas who's back there?"

He pressed a finger against the bud in his ear, a habit I hadn't had time to break him of. No matter how often I'd slapped him, he still did it and might as well have placed a bright sign on his head saying EARBUD with an arrow. "I'm getting a single-step pattern. One person, I'd say. Light-footed, knows how to move quietly. Not heavy. One fifteen, one twenty pounds. If I had—"

As I looked at him, a pink puff appeared briefly behind his right shoulder. He jerked and cried out, hitting the icy ground hard.

I reached out and took hold of Grisha's shoulder, dropping down onto the ice and pulling him down with me. "Sniper!" I hissed. "Stay down!"

Grisha hissed something into the snow I didn't catch, wriggling to flip over onto his back. "Worms?" he panted. "More of Marin's little robots?"

I started to shake my head when I noticed that Amblen, in

Marin's avatar, was still standing. As I pushed myself toward him, reaching out, the side of his coat silently exploded into a jumble of frayed threads. He didn't even flinch. Dick Marin's body stood there in the street like a statue, a slightly constipated expression on his square face.

"Down!" I hissed. "Dr. Amblen, *down!*"

"I've been shot," Amblen said. "But I don't think it matters."

I finally hooked a hand onto his ankle and pulled, sending the avatar crashing to the street. "Override code sixty-forty-tenner-forty-alpha," I panted. "Stay the fuck *down*."

"As you suggest," Amblen whispered back.

I rolled onto my back and pulled out my automatic. "Mr. Marko, you okay?"

"No, I am not *okay*," he complained, his voice strained and tight. "But I won't bleed to death *immediately*, which experience tells me is all you fucking care about at the moment."

"Good," I said. I pictured the street, the river, our little piece of the city. The collapsed buildings we'd just passed gave way to a group of semicollapsed ruins, but the first floor offered decent cover and small chance of being buried alive in crumbling masonry. The silence that smothered us when we stopped talking was immense, thick, like a gas. "Can you move?"

"Yes," he said. "Yes, damn you, you fucking...*fuck*."

"On our left, building with no facade," I whispered. "Stay down. We need cover. Amblen, override code sixty-forty-tenner-forty-alpha, stay down and follow us."

"As you suggest," Amblen said amiably.

We crawled, tensed for the next puff of snow or fabric or blood that would be our only indication of another shot fired. The sound of scraping ice and our breathing seemed incredibly loud as we wriggled over the ice and rubble, finally finding shelter behind a semicrumbled wall of cinder blocks and the last vestiges of a stucco facade. I lay there for a moment, leg aching, and stared at the thin trail of pinkish blood Marko had left behind.

You see how existence is a wheel. You put death into the engine, and death comes out of the engine. You have killed so many as they begged for their lives, no doubt this is how your own end will be. Now or later.

I closed my eyes. *Shut up,* I thought.

As usual, when one of them woke up and started talking, the others were roused. I didn't understand it. They were walled off—I couldn't examine them or see their thoughts. I could speak to them, in a sense, and they to me. They could answer questions, and usually did. And I couldn't stop them from talking to me. I could ignore them, push them back until they were so far away I could *almost* pretend they weren't there, but they came back. They always came back.

Well, Mr. Cates, I can't say I'm surprised. You're a quarter mile from my seat of operations! You didn't expect I'd never find you, did you?

Shut up, I thought again.

Death, the first one whispered, *is not inevitable. But you may have missed your own path to immortality.*

"Avery?"

I opened my eyes and looked at Grisha, whose face had the familiar expression of worry. I was losing my mind. I didn't blame him, and struggled to concentrate. "Sitting here waiting is a death sentence," I said. "I'm going up and out to take a look. You stay here and keep these two alive."

"*Now* you want to keep me alive?" Marko panted.

"There may be more than one," Grisha advised. "They may have spotters. You may be shot the moment you poke your head out."

I nodded. "Maybe." I gestured at Marin's avatar. "He was standing there for what, ten seconds? Sounds like a single shooter reloading a precision weapon."

Grisha chewed on that for a moment and nodded. "Yes. But there may be others *without* precision weapons, yes?"

I nodded back, checking my auto. "In that case, no problem."

I stood up and ran my eyes over the interior of our little shelter. Fragments of a second floor were still in place, supported mainly by the rubble beneath them. I saw daylight not too far above that and judged I could get up there, even with my leg feeling like someone had jabbed an ice pick into the nerve. As I moved upward onto a small mountain of stone and rebar, I heard Marko coughing behind me.

"Well, shit," he spluttered. "This plan's going *perfectly*."

I found the climb up easier than I'd expected—the rubble was at a decent incline and was stable enough that after a few wary seconds I threw caution to the wind and just started pushing myself up, my leg complaining. I was standing on the scrap of floor left on the second story in just a few moments, and on the side of the building, miraculously, was an almost perfectly preserved balcony, crusted in dirty ice. I stepped onto it slowly, senses straining for any sign of collapse, and then crouched down so that my eyes just cleared the railing. I had a good view of the road we'd been following and the river. I scanned carefully, blinking the glare out of my eyes, and then froze.

Unbelievably, a single figure was making its way rapidly along the road, jogging with something long and thin in its hands. I stared for a moment, wondering at the existence of someone skilled enough to even get a shot close to us at that range but stupid enough to come jogging up the road in plain view.

No one on my payroll would be that stupid, Marin said in my head. I had no idea how old the imprint of the King Worm in my head was, how recent its information was.

"You're right," I whispered.

A second later, a creak of the blasted roof above made me freeze.

"Don't move," she said.

The voice was so familiar it was as if months hadn't passed since I'd last heard it. I saw her face again, twisted up in horror, in regret, in emotions I wasn't even sure I could identify. My heart lurched into a furious pounding. I opened my mouth to say her name, but my tongue was too thick and I just hung there.

"Drop the cannon."

I doubted Grisha or Marko could hear us below. I could make noise, but she might get hurt in the ensuing chaos. I set the automatic down on the balcony floor, wind whipping up and spraying ice dust around me. I swallowed what felt like a rock in my throat. "Marlena," I said, my voice raspy, unwilling. "You're—"

"Shut your fucking fake mouth, you fucking robot," she hissed. I heard a hollow popping noise and then the unmistakable hum of something powering up. "They told me what you were. They told me this would shut you down pretty good."

Here we go, I heard Dolores Salgado whisper. *Clench your teeth, or you'll bite your tongue off.*

I started to say something else when she smacked something against my back and pain ran into me like electric current, setting every individual cell of my body on fire.

PART FOUR

XXXII

STARTING TO BLACKEN ON THE EDGES

I awoke to a sensation of movement—rapid and bumpy, my stomach lurching against gravity, my shoulders biting into tight straps painfully. A sizzling echo of pain remained under my skin, dull and fading but hinting at something terrible, as if whatever had been used on me had singed my cells, my atoms.

It took me a moment to realize that my eyes were still closed.

I was inside a small vehicle, something I'd never seen before. We were ground level, the landscape streaking past the windows that lined the sides. The interior was divided into two halves separated by a sturdy-looking metal cage; my half contained two hard chairs outfitted with straps and handcuffs—one of which was my current perch—and nothing else aside from the smell of piss. The front was filled with a huge bank of controls, all backlit blue and red, glowing in the dusky light of the interior as if the vehicle were burning within, and a single seat situated in front of a round stick that turned smoothly from side to side. Sitting in the seat was Marlena.

I studied her for a moment. She looked as I remembered her—skinny as hell, without a curve to her name, but graceful in her way, compact and minimal. I hadn't seen her since the hover had lifted off from Chengara, leaving me lying there about to have my brains sucked out of my skull, her face leaning out over the edge of the hover's hatch. I could picture her in that moment, her exact expression, and I still thought it was completely raw shock and horror. She hadn't wanted to leave me behind. Her ink looked like shadows clinging to her skin.

"What the hell is this thing, anyway?"

She didn't react. After a moment she said, "Ground transport. Solid fuel cell."

Inefficient, Squalor grumped in my head. *Ancient tech.*

I turned my head to watch the world rocketing by. "What is this, the fucking dark ages?"

She shrugged, her shoulders moving under her skin. "Hovers have a tendency to get shot down these days. Things are pretty hairy out there, Plastic Man. Once we hit the shore I was given this thing to stay under the radar, you know? Right now the fucking government is knocking everything out of the sky."

"So Marin gave you *this*?"

Hell, I didn't even know we had stuff like this! How long have I been off loop, anyway?

"Fresh out of the factory. I think there's only five or six of these in the whole System. It's all-terrain—you can drive underwater in it if you have to. The Pigs are cranking out some seriously amazing shit because of this war."

I waited a few seconds to see if she was going to start talking, but she just moved the wheel a little this way and that, course correcting. "Why?" I finally asked.

She didn't answer right away. The off-rhythm thump of the ground beneath us was soothing. "Because you're a fucking robot that looks like someone. Because you shouldn't be shopping his face around. And because they're paying me a lot of money to scoop you up and offered me a full walk, my file deleted."

She said it all in a bland, flat voice.

"I'm not an avatar, Marlena."

Sure you are, Avery! Marin barked cheerfully. *We all are!*

She snorted. "You're a fucking Droid. A new model of Monk. They…" She paused for a second or two. "They ripped his brain out of him, and they made…you."

She'd been sold on me as an avatar, and I didn't think there was much I could say from my present position to change her mind. Of course I was dead—just about everyone processed into an avatar died. Surviving the experience almost never happened.

Nine hundred and ninety-nine out of a thousand perish, Squalor breathed.

Almost never, Marin agreed.

"Who hired you?" I said instead of arguing.

"Marin's people," she said immediately. "They're paying us an *immense* amount of money to gather you up. It hasn't been easy. Don't you stay in one place for any length of time?"

"Not anymore. I don't have any place to stay."

We rode along in silence for a while. I mulled it all over—that last night, the chaos of the riot, the hover lifting off without me, the underground lab, Ruberto's soldiers busting in. I let the atmosphere in the cabin settle down, get calm and smooth, and then asked her my question.

"Do you know where Michaleen is?"

"That fucking piece of short shit," she spat immediately. "No. Wish I did. Filled Grisha with sunshine about you betraying us, but I knew better. Set that hover down in Mexico and said he was stepping out to check on the displacers. I gave him five minutes and went out to maybe beat the truth out of him, and the motherfucker was gone, like a ghost. Like he'd dug a hole and climbed in. Fuck, if that son of a bitch showed up in front of me now, I'd slit his throat twice without thinking. He *killed* you. Just like he'd pulled the trigger himself."

I tested the straps a little, seeing if they had any give. They were pretty advanced, though, giving when the vehicle lurched and I was carried along by momentum, but refusing to move at all if I just tried to lean forward. My hands were bound in the usual silicone bracelets I was already almost free from, twisting my wrists out of her sight. I tested the straps again and realized their variable give was tied to momentum—if I tried to move slowly, carefully, they gave a little, and I could spool out enough slack to duck under.

"I'm not dead, Lena," I said with an involuntary grunt. "I'm not an avatar."

One hand popped free from the bracelet, and I let it drop to the floor of the cage.

"Keep saying it," she replied.

I squinted at her through the cage, making sure her eyes were locked on the instruments and the windshield, and began to slowly stretch out the straps, pushing them away from me with care. Keeping my eyes on her, I ducked my torso under one, then the other, letting them slide back into the seat. Bending down a little, I freed my feet from their strap and sat up again quickly, trying to stay still and stiff as if I were still strapped in. I traced her shoulders with my eyes, remembering what she smelled like, sweat and something sweet underneath I'd never been able to place.

I wasn't going to hurt her if I could help it.

You can't help it, Squalor hissed. *Insects destroy. Consume each other.*

I ignored him, ignored them all, chattering away. I sat still for a few moments, looking around. I was free, but I was still in the cage. As discreetly as I could, I put my hands into my coat, feeling around, wondering if she'd been lazy about patting me down, too. She hadn't left me my gun, but she'd left my blade in my boot—she'd rushed, maybe worried over voices in the rooms below, maybe anxious to get me in the cage before I came to. Maybe, in the back of her mind, knowing that for people like us having something—*anything*—to defend yourself with made all the difference. I slid it from the boot carefully and sat up again slowly.

Her eyes flicked to me and then away. I cursed under my breath and tried to brace myself just as she wrenched the wheel all the way to the left, sending the vehicle into a spin. I was torn from the seat and slammed against the side, cracking my head against the roof, the blade flying from my stiff fingers and rattling around on the floor.

Suddenly, we'd stopped, silence smothering me, and I sagged down onto the floor, one leg hooked on the second seat painfully. She looked back at me, and for a second our eyes were locked on each other. I thought, suddenly, that I saw something there, some softening, some flicker of doubt.

Then she leaned forward and slapped a big red button on the control panel.

Instantly, my whole body lit up in orange, ragged pain. Everywhere my skin touched the interior of the vehicle, I sizzled and spat like someone was running live current into me. My teeth clicked down hard onto each other, my tongue slid back into my throat, and my lungs seized up like rusty motors.

"You're half-smart," Marlena said, unstrapping herself and turning around to watch me twitch. "This heap's designed for transporting avatars. I've been working this for a few months now, shacking up at the facility when I'm not out snatching a list of artificial folks they've lost track of. I'm getting good at it. That'll fry your systems good, but you'll come back online in a bit good as new. And when you come back online, Averybot, you're going to be secured again, and I suggest you just enjoy the ride this time, unless you want to go through this again."

The facility. It didn't sound hopeful.

I couldn't respond. Black spots appeared before my eyes as all my muscles felt like they were going to snap at any moment. Marlena was in my line of sight; she stared back at me, her face tight and annoyed. After a moment she leaned over and slapped the red button again, and I gladly shut my eyes and passed out.

I woke up strapped into my seat again, but without the sensation of motion. I squinted my eyes in an attempt to focus; Marlena wasn't in the front half of the cabin. I was alone in the vehicle, still sizzling in perfect silence, my whole body feeling bruised. I considered trying to move, but my muscles felt like they'd been melted into glass, brittle and liable to snap. I considered speaking, but my tongue felt like it had swollen to about six times its normal size.

I considered just sitting still and seeing what happened, and liked that option.

Disappointment and frustration filled me like pus. I wondered if Marko had lived, where Grisha had gone. I'd been so *close*, so goddamn close. Standing right outside his fucking house, ready to go in and get some answers.

It drained away a second later. Fuck it. It would have ended in disorder and disappointment anyway. With me half dead and everyone else all the way dead. With nothing changed. With Dick Marin still on top of the pyramid, with me still on the rail, with no idea where Michaleen was.

With a soft hiss the back door of the vehicle was pulled open, and a moment later the straps snapped open and retracted, letting me sag forward in the seat. Hands reached in and pulled me out, rolling me roughly out the door and onto my back, where I lay on the hot, dry ground, the thick air pushing down onto me in a terrible, familiar way. Eyes closed, I could feel the sun on my face, burning, and I imagined myself turning red already, starting to blacken on the edges.

I opened my eyes and struggled onto my belly, raising my head up. I squinted through the clear, painful glare and saw it, the train tracks half buried in sandy dirt, the arrival pen still holding the weirdly eternal bodies of several Stormers, their white uniforms tattered and flapping weakly in the wind, their silicone skin and alloy bones untouched, perfect in their ruin.

"Welcome back to Chengara, Averybot," Marlena said. I turned my head to glance back at her and saw the stick, the Taser, coming down. I shut my eyes and made sure my tongue wasn't between my teeth.

XXXIII

AND YOU DIDN'T EVEN KNOW IT UNTIL A FEW MOMENTS AGO

I opened my eyes slowly, imagining I could hear the seal that had formed over them breaking open, a tiny ripping sound. My vision was hazy at first, all painful bright spots and murky shadows, but after a few blinks the small world around me clarified.

Dick Marin — or a version of him or maybe the real deal, the Prime; who the fuck knew? — sat in a simple metal chair across from me, smiling. I imagined he'd been sitting there for hours with that smile in place, just a holding pattern, taking up a tiny percentage of his total consciousness as it monitored this one node on the network a thousand times a second.

"Hello, Avery," he said.

He was wearing a snazzy black suit, the fabric shining in the dim light, tailored perfectly to his body. His hair was cut severely short and parted with razor accuracy, and his sunglasses were custom jobs, thin and delicate, wrapped around his temples like a visor embedded in his skin. In his cold, plastic hands he held a prop: a digital clipboard, thin and gray, its screen of digital paper shimmering.

I tried to speak and found my tongue too swollen at first. I worked it around, looking for some saliva to get things moving.

Marin waited patiently, his eager smile seeming to encourage me. As I struggled I looked around—we were back underground, I was sure, based on the sealed feeling of the room, the texture of the half light around us. Something about the way the air smelled, too, reminded me of those terrible moments after my failed attempt to escape.

"You're looking well, Dick," I managed to mumble.

He laughed, the same sudden release of noise I remembered, and then he stopped, just like that. "My goodness, we've gone through a lot of trouble to get all of you Averys back under control. I'm glad to see your sense of humor made the transition across the singular divide."

I nodded. "I get it," I slurred. "I'm an avatar, right? I just *think* I'm human."

Marin cocked his head. "You doubt it? Of course you do. You've always been an egotist, haven't you, Avery?" He made a show of referring to the clipboard. "Let's see. You're one of thirty-two released into the wild. We've retrieved twenty-seven and destroyed four." He looked back at me, his smile adjusted down a notch. "That leaves you, the last one. And of course, you're the unit we *need*."

I blinked. "Released by who?"

"By your esteemed former boss Ruberto, of course. He obtained your unfinished imprint from this facility—where you died, by the way, just a few hundred feet from here—when he took it by storm in the action last year. We have since reclaimed this facility, but he did claim a great deal of valuable intelligence from it. One such asset was you. He created thirty-two of you and sent you all out to cause disruption—your one definite skill. Some to try and assassinate my Prime, some to simply set off bombs and recruit other troublemakers, assassinate high-ranking police, et cetera." His smile brightened a few clicks, lighting me up. "You all thought these plots were your own idea, of course. You're skilled at what you do, Avery, and you were difficult to contain. We even had to consider and engage freelance talent."

He's lying, Dolores suddenly whispered to me.

Always am, Little Dick confirmed, sounding cheerful. *You just never know about* what.

I nodded slowly. "Marlena."

Inexplicably, Marin made a gun shape with one hand and pointed it at me. "Exactly. We didn't think much of her, either, but talent is short in these desperate times, and she certainly got the job done. I assume she had . . . intimate knowledge of you and exploited it. Took the job cheap, too, apparently as a grudge. She didn't appear to like the idea of you as an avatar."

I tried to shift in my seat, but I was tied down to it too tightly. My feet and hands both burned with the phantom fire of limbs long gone numb. It was a much better job than Marlena had done on me. "So why am I the special one?" I asked. I didn't know what Marin was doing with this you're-an-avatar bullshit, but the ache in my hip and the razor slice I got every time I took a deep breath argued against it. Having few other options, I thought I'd play along a bit, see what the King Worm spat out at me.

He leaned forward a little. "Something odd happened to you during processing, didn't it?" he said quietly. "Because of data corruption and severed transfer lines, there were actually several imprints of you on file, which isn't supposed to happen. You are the only unit created using the first imprint. The other imprints, numbered two through seven, are degraded copies and contain varying degrees of neural information describing the personality and data of 'Avery Cates,' ranging from sixty to ninety-six percent completeness." He glanced down at his clipboard. I wondered if these tics were on-purpose showmanship to act human or if they were remnants of the time, decades ago, when Marin had been a real live person. "Two of those partials were functional enough for Ruberto's use in creating his Cates units. His people apparently didn't know how to use refining algorithms to round off the missing spots and used the imprints as is, with even their date and inception stamps intact." He looked up at me again. "Now you, you're from imprint one. Imprint one scans out at one hundred and fourteen percent complete. Which is, of course, impossible." His grin disappeared. "My Techs didn't even know the Amblen Rating went beyond one hundred."

I tried to grin experimentally, and it seemed to go well. "So I'm smarter than you thought?"

Marin let out another sudden, barking laugh, his expression unchanging as he opened his mouth and threw his head back. It was disconcerting—a blank, unhappy expression and this harsh, braying laugh. It stopped as suddenly as it had begun, and he snapped back to staring at me blankly.

"No, Avery, you're not smart. Look where you are! Dead, and you didn't even know it until a few moments ago. In my power simply because I ordered it. No, smart is not the concept I was looking for. You are . . . saturated."

I nodded. "Fuck you, Dick. I'm not an avatar. So you've either made a huge mistake here, and boohoo for you if you did, or this is the weakest trick you've ever tried."

"Why?" he said immediately. "Because you feel pain? Because you bleed? Because you *feel* human? Hell, Avery—you're programmed to feel these things. I could program you to feel like an elephant, if I wanted."

A cold spike sent ripples through me. It *might* be. I might be an avatar, convinced by programming and firewalled data that I was human. My heart lurched into motion, pounding in terror—was I a fake? A copy of a copy? A Monk without even that last shred of humanity left to him? A fucking puppet?

My heart pounding. Even that might be faked, a data stream feeding into a processor loop, sending operation codes to activate subroutines and functions.

That's all you are now, Squalor suddenly whispered at me, sounding almost sane for a change. *That's all any of us are. The only difference is the hardware.*

Don't believe it, Salgado repeated. *A trick. A technique. If Squalor were coherent, he would tell you this is impossible.*

I am coherent, you terrible woman, Squalor huffed. *I see more clearly than you. Certainly it is not possible. The human mind is infinite. The intelligence and personality matrix is artificial and will not accept an imprint of over one hundred percent. The human mind has endless capacity. That is why I rejected Amblen's designs and integrated the brain into* my *design.*

I closed my eyes and imagined what Gleason would have said, her soft, sarcastic voice so real I wondered for a second if I had her inside me, too, or if maybe I'd finally gone bonkers, resurrecting everyone inside me: *Oh, Avery's going batshit,* she would have said. *Avery's cracked under the* pressure.

I opened my eyes and put a blank expression on my face. I nodded. "Go ahead. *Prove* it to me."

He didn't move for some time, just staring back at me with a half smile on his face, perfectly still. I wondered if he was conferring with his Prime or gathering data from hundreds of other Marins throughout the System. I could ask him about Michaleen, but I had no way to compel him to answer me or to verify that the answer he gave was accurate. And I didn't like him knowing anything about me.

He stood up suddenly. "I don't need to prove it to you, Avery. Your belief in your own reality is immaterial to my needs. You're back here as the only inmate of Chengara Penitentiary. This facility was designed and maintained as a place where people who *knew* things could be warehoused until we could extract their consciousness and peruse them at will. A database was being built from all these combined minds, you understand, and eventually—thirty, forty years from now—we would be able to simply search and find out everything you people knew on some subject or other. You were here because you knew things that might have been *potentially* useful, Avery. But others were here because they knew *specific* things. Because of Ruberto's raid, this project was terminated prematurely, and we did not secure all of the information we'd planned on."

He turned and started walking briskly away. "*You*, Avery—this specific unit—are here because somehow when you were processed, something went wrong and you ended up with something extra, didn't you?"

I think he means us, *Avery*, I heard Little Dick whisper in my head.

"You're back here, Avery," he said over his shoulder as a heavy-sounding metal door snapped open on his approach, "because now you know something *specific*. You certainly don't know what it *is*, but that is why you're here. So we can extract it from you . . . or whomever we need to extract it from." He stopped short of the door, standing aside as a second figure stepped into my roomy cell. "I'd like to introduce you to your interrogator, Avery."

The newcomer turned to approach me, and a shiver went through me. Not surprise, because while I hadn't considered the possibility, it now struck me as perfect, the obvious choice. I saw my own face approaching, with a perfect little hitch to his stride as if his hip bothered him—it was me again, sprouting up like a fucking mushroom whenever I tore him out of the ground. Another goddamn avatar of me, walking the System.

He looked clean and well rested, the artificial bastard. I couldn't move my numb hands, or I would have clenched my fists. Instead I watched him pick up the chair Marin had just vacated, spin it around, and sit down in an easy motion with his arms crossed over the back. He didn't say anything, just gave me a grin and a wink. If I could have moved, I would have launched myself at him, biting and tearing.

"I'll leave you to it, then," Marin said flatly, stepping out. The door swung shut automatically behind him, ending in a deep, echoing click that hinted at a magnetically sealed portal.

I looked up at myself. The avatar leaned back and reached into its coat, producing a small black case. It popped it open and set it down on the floor between us with a deliberate, slow movement. I glanced down at it, surprised, somehow, to find a single shiny-new autohypo and a large clear bottle of slimy-looking liquid. I looked up again, and my avatar had rested its chin on its hands, a hint of a smile—my smile—on its face.

"Tell me," it said in my voice, a perfect replication except for the complete lack of fear, panic, and desperation, "about System of Federated Nations Undersecretary Dolores Salgado."

XXXIV

THE BEST IDEA I'D HAD IN *YEARS*

I drifted in and out.

I opened my eyes to find myself sitting in front of me, with that same static smile as if it'd been in low-power mode for hours. Cold water dripped from my nose and hair, the shock of my revival rippling down through me, humming in my bones. The grunt with the bucket was just stepping out of the cell, so I figured I'd been out about a minute.

I shook my head, feeling my brain rattling around as if it had become unglued. I was naked. I couldn't remember the last time I'd been naked—decades ago, at least. I watched the avatar put down the electric prod it had been using creatively and sat there struggling to suck in enough air to survive on, waiting for the next round.

The rounds tended to end with me passing out.

"I know what you're thinking," the avatar said. It was amazing, and terrible, to think how perfectly it imitated me. I thought of the unit back at The Star, how beat-up it had been, so believably bloody and bruised—no wonder everyone had bought it as me, prowling around New York again, covered in shit and trying to find a way to kill someone. This one was so shiny and perfect no one would have believed it for a second.

"You're thinking you don't *know* what we're trying to get out of you, right?"

I didn't react—or didn't think I reacted; my nerve connection to my face had been shut down in self-defense a long time ago, and I may have been making faces and weeping openly for all I knew. I'd tried asking Salgado—or the version of her somehow locked up in my brain—what they wanted, but she'd gone mute, refusing to answer. Which was typical. When I was trying to act sane in front of everyone, she'd chattered on and on. Now that her voice in my head might actually do me some good, give me something to barter with, she was gone.

"The answer, brother, is that you appear to have a near-complete imprint of Undersecretary Salgado in your memory somehow, and while you may not know what we're looking for, *she* does. And we believe that whatever we do to you, she will experience also. You don't have enough memory capacity to house complete imprints—the people living inside you, Avery, are using your own subsystems. They exist as separate intelligences only in the abstract, in the higher level operations. So, for example, if I do this—"

It suddenly leaned down and plucked the electric prod from the floor, spinning neatly and jabbing it into a well-worn area approximately near my crotch. Pain flooded me, intense and jagged, but only for a second, not long enough to knock me out or make me shit myself again.

"She experiences it as well. So, you see, we're torturing you to torture *her*. Eventually, even though you don't know the information, she will tell you, and then you will tell us."

I tried opening my mouth to say something, but this proved more difficult than I'd imagined.

"What's that?" my avatar said, leaning in and cupping one perfect hand to its perfect ear—a sculpture of my ear that should have won awards. "Why bother torturing you if you're just an avatar? Glad you asked, Avery. For one thing, you don't *think* you're an avatar—you don't believe it—so this is just as effective as if you were really flesh and bone in front of me. And we can't just suck out your digitized intelligences and sift them because they're so fucking mangled and tied up with each other we'd just destroy whatever one-in-a-million balance you've got going in there. No, sorry, brother, it has to be the slow, old-fashioned way." It put a cold hand under my chin and tilted my head up, peering down at me. The stubble on its face, a mix of black and white whiskers, was stunning. Vaguely, I wanted to know where the factories were that built these things in a world where I hadn't been able to buy a decent handgun in years.

My avatar flipped the prod into the air and caught it deftly behind its back, whirling and raising it up into the air. "Let's stop—"

I opened my eyes to find myself sitting in front of me, with that same static smile as if it'd been in low-power mode for hours.

"Thought I might have short-circuited something that time," my avatar said, grinning.

My head was ringing, a persistent static noise deep inside, embedded in my cells. I let my head drop down and studied the floor blearily. My chair was seated on a shallow pool of thick liquid. My blood, I realized stupidly.

"Guess we have to wake you up," my avatar said. I pulled my head up with immense effort in time to see it pulling the black case from its coat. I couldn't remember what it was, at first. Just a black case that I'd seen before, that made me uneasy.

Dolores, I whispered to myself, my own thoughts lost in the static. *If you were maybe thinking of telling me what the fuck they want to know, now might be a good time.*

There was no response. I wondered if maybe I'd been crazy

all these months, hearing voices. My head was all echoes and cobwebs, now.

The avatar stood up with the autohypo in its hand and leaned down to twist one of my arms painfully, exposing the bruised vein. It pushed the hypo against my skin, and there was the tiniest prick—just a drop of extra pain in the ocean of misery.

"There," my avatar said. "No rest for the wicked, huh?"

My heart lurched in my chest, and my whole body went rigid, straining me against my bonds. My tongue snaked back into my throat, choking me, and I shut my eyes tightly as they bulged against my eyelids. Suddenly shivering, fire flowed through me, pushing every tendon rigid and turning every nerve on full throttle. The chair beneath me creaked as I surged upward, trembling.

My avatar knelt down in front of me. "I was just thinking about how everyone around you dies, huh, Avery?" It held up one hand and began ticking off fingers. "Pickering—dead. Kev Gatz—dead, and we never treated him very well, did we? Melody, dead. Gleason—ah, poor old sweetheart. Vicious and near feral, but cute in her way, huh?" It winked at me leeringly. "At least *we* thought so, huh?"

My heart managed an extra beat and I pushed hard, trying to leap up out of the chair and smash into this fucking demon. I wanted to rip its head off, gouge out those shining, expensive polymer eyes.

"Too bad they all died before this technology was perfected. They could be here now, with you. Dancing. Singing. Telling jokes. Beating the shit out of you."

Too late, I thought. *Glee and Kev already did that part.* What was it about the fucking cosmos that it always wanted to bring my ghosts back, one more time, expressly to assault me?

"Have you asked her yet?" my avatar suddenly said, cocking its head in a way I was pretty sure I'd never done in my life. "Salgado, I mean. Have you tried just *asking* her directly?"

I nodded. "She told me to go fuck myself. Untie me so I can get started on you."

For a moment the avatar froze the way I'd seen Dick Marin do a dozen times, just hovering there with one expression on its face, its eyes glittering and seemingly alive but everything about it suddenly completely still—no breathing, no twitching skin, no movement of the irises. Then it ticked its head in the opposite direction and smiled, the expression flashing onto its face as if it had always been there and I just hadn't noticed before.

It moved fast, swinging its fist around toward me like a cudgel, knocking my head around hard. I felt a tooth torn from its roots, flying out of my mouth damp and warm. The ringing in my head swelled up like a thousand street bands tuning up for different songs all at once.

It didn't pause, swinging the fist back again and hitting me just as hard. The chair lifted up off the floor for a moment, and I half spun, bodily, purple light flashing inside my head, and I was suddenly and completely blind.

Detached retina, I heard Dolores whisper. *Maybe something worse. Or better.*

What does he want to know, you goddamn ghost? What the fuck does he want to know?

No answer. To that, the only fucking piece of information I wanted, nothing.

"Well, Avery," I heard the avatar say, and I could hear the fucking *grin* in it—wide and shit-eating and nothing at all like what I would ever put on my face. "My fists weigh a fucking *ton*, and there aren't many people who can take two punches and stay online—but can you take—"

I opened my eyes to find myself sitting in front of me, with that same static smile as if it'd been in low-power mode for hours.

I blinked. My eyesight had returned, but it was blurred and

jumpy, everything smeared with something thick and sticky. I
squinted at the figure across from me as I shivered in the chair,
my body just shaking uncontrollably. It wasn't my avatar. It
was Dick Marin. A Richard Marin who'd been through some
rough times. An attempt had been made to spruce it up a
bit—repaired skin that didn't quite match in tone and quality,
a newish suit that had once been very expensive and impressive
and was now merely a very nice old suit, a pair of wraparound
sunglasses that showed a tiny but noticeable crack in the left
lens.

It cocked its head at me. "Awake at last? Fucking hell, I look
like shit."

I tried to blink. One eyelid came down first, slowly, and then
the second, which decided to stay down. "What?"

"Fuck. You look like a complete fucking burden. This is
going to be a pain in the ass."

I shook my head, trying to spill the ringing out of it.
"What?"

Suddenly, it reached out and took hold of my nose. A fresh
bloom of jagged, sparkly pain barely registered in me, a distant
flash, like thunder on the horizon. I'd been trying to retreat into
my old quiet spot inside my head, a glassy sphere that kept noise
and pain out, leaving me safe. But I hadn't been able to summon
it for a long time. It kept shattering inside me.

"Stop saying *what*, okay? And then we'll be friends."

This was me inside a Marin avatar. It made no sense. I realized suddenly that I didn't like myself very much. I was kind of
an asshole.

"What," I said.

The avatar—my imprint inside Dick Marin's chassis—-
twitched its head. "Good." It waited a moment and then
removed its hand from my nose, its face turning serious.
"Grisha sent me. To retrieve you." It smiled again, suddenly
sunny. "It's amazing, really. Russian bastard tries for *months*

to kill us, now he follows us like a fucking lost puppy, right?"
It shook its head. "Never met a Techie with his kind of chops.
Fucking Grisha could have been an *operator* back in New York,
you know?"

I nodded. "Yeah," I said as slowly and clearly as I could.
Slowly I felt myself flowing back, like blood into a sleeping limb.
The ringing in my head was receding slowly, although I kept
shaking. "I know."

It nodded. "Okay! Okay. Let's get you up. Get you dressed.
Medicated. I've got stimulants and coagulants and anti-
infectious cocktails. Even if you're bleeding internally, you'll feel
better. Though I can't prevent you from actually dying, sorry.
I'm double layered, and if I wasn't air-conditioned, I'd be sweating my balls off. Come on. It's not far."

It leaned in, and with three quick tugs I was freed of my
bonds. I immediately fell sideways onto the floor. This seemed
like the best idea I'd had in *years*, and I decided to stay there.

"Ah, hell," the avatar said, reaching under me and easily lifting me up, approximately upright. "Shit, I did *not* need
to see that. All right." It let me slide back to the floor, and my
heart swelled with gratitude. "Easier to dress you down there
anyway."

I was too tired to be humiliated as the avatar tugged dirty,
unfortunate clothes onto my bleeding, shivering form. "All
right," it said, standing up and examining me with hands on its
hips. "We need to move. Our window here is about five more
minutes. Come on, you sad sack of gristle."

Roughly, my arm was stretched out again, another autohypo
jabbed into the bruised crook of my elbow. Another barely noticed
prick of pain, and warmth seemed to flow from my arm into the
rest of me. "How did you manage to get in here?" I gasped as it
lifted me up and pulled me toward the door of the cell.

"Same trick you thought of back in Moscow," it said immediately. "We dressed me up and sent me against the fucking

Techies. They let me waltz right in. We got schedules and maps, so we're set. If we keep moving."

"Who," I struggled to say. "Who gave you the maps?"

"We also have a Pusher helping us out. Greasy little bastard, makes me glad I don't have a brain for the first time. Here we are," it said as we found the cell door. The avatar gestured and the door fell open an inch or so. It reached out immediately and pulled it completely open, shoving me through with a sudden, rough push that sent me windmilling on rubber legs into a concrete hallway, scratching my hands on the rough, unfinished walls as I tried to steady myself. My legs were shivering uncontrollably, but I felt surprisingly better, stronger.

"Keep going straight," the avatar said, pulling the door shut behind him. "Try not to fall."

I concentrated on moving myself forward aided by the occasional shove from behind. I'd quickly come to hate the avatar. When I found out which one of my pet Techies had saved my imprint from The Star, I was going to twist their nose until they fucking *screamed*. I wasn't sure Grisha would let me get away with it, but if he'd secretly sucked a copy of me out of that robot and hung onto it all this time, I was prepared to take my chances.

The hall terminated at a shiny metal elevator door. The avatar gestured and the doors slid open, revealing a clean, polished interior that looked like it had been installed a few minutes before—not even a smudged fingerprint—an elevator used exclusively by avatars with their plastic hands.

A shove sent me sailing into it. My legs collapsed under me, and I crashed awkwardly into the back wall. I lay there as the avatar stepped into the cab behind me, gesturing the doors closed. The elevator immediately began to rise, pushing me down into the floor.

"As soon as I have a few weeks to recover," I panted, "I'm going to tear you into small components and melt you."

"My alloys have a pretty high melting point," it said, sounding cheerful. "And some materials used in my construction don't react predictably to heat." It turned its head halfway toward me. "But since you really can't get any uglier, why not take the risk?" It turned back to stare at itself in the shiny doors. "I like this chassis. Much better looking. We are one ugly bastard, don't you think?"

There was a soft beep, and the elevator settled to a stop. The doors split open again. Grisha stood outside the elevator, a Shredding rifle ridiculously strapped to his back, bigger, almost, than he was, and a cheap-looking auto in his hand. Otherwise, he looked exactly as I'd left him in Russia—dirty and wearing a heavy coat that must have been punishing in the desert heat. He didn't look like he'd been sweltering in the sun for days—which was to say he wasn't dead.

"Good to see you are not dead yet, Avery," the skinny Russian said, stepping backward quickly. "Come, we must move fast. The psionic cannot hold the guards for much longer."

The avatar spun and pulled me up again, every bone in my body stabbing into something soft and puncturing it. I thought I might be able to walk but decided not to advertise the fact until I knew the full facts of the situation. I let the avatar drag me painfully along a brief corridor that ended in a set of battered-looking double doors.

"Grisha," I managed to cough out. "Grisha! Did you rip my imprint and hang on to it? Because I'm going to strangle whoever did."

"In that case," he shouted over his shoulder as he arrived at the doors and pushed them open. A blast of skin-melting heat pushed its way into the hall. "In that case, Avery, it was Mr. Marko. Now, hurry, please."

The sun hit me like scalding oil, immediately dripping down over me and baking my skin, sweat popping out everywhere. I squinted my eyes against the blinding white glare, but

I could make out the familiar rounded shape of a hover, painfully reflective in silver, with odd markings on the side I didn't recognize. As we got close I realized that four Stormers were standing at attention around it, perfectly still, cowls down and mouths slack, staring. Pushed. I'd seen that expression enough when rolling around with Kev Gatz.

There was no drop bay. The hatch popped open as we approached, and Grisha bounded up into it, turning around to take hold of me as the avatar passed me up. I was pushed down into a plush seat, and I heard the hatch snapping shut behind me.

"Are we good?" a voice said, oily and assured.

"Yes," Grisha said breathlessly. "We are good. Easy, as you said."

I squinted around. We were in the nicest hover cabin I'd ever seen, carpeted with rich-looking chairs arranged around bolted-down tables. A bar had been set up in the back, and a very tall, very tanned man in a very nice suit stood there with a deep drink in one hand, rings glittering expensively in the soft light. Cool air caressed me gently, pulling the fresh heat away from me. I thought perhaps heaven was a brand-new military hover, and I'd finally managed a way in.

The tall man unspooled himself and walked over, throwing himself down into the seat across from me. I scowled at him. He smelled too clean and looked like he ate regularly. Not my kind of people. I probed a raw spot in my mouth where a tooth had been lost; the pain was numbed, fading throughout me into a dull pulse. I sucked in a deep breath, blinking my eyes clear.

For a second, just a second, I felt a whisper in my mind, a soft brush of someone else's thoughts—someone's thoughts *outside* of me. My scowl deepened. He was the psionic, then. He was their Pusher. And I didn't think an avatar could sense psionic activity.

Clever boy, Marin singsonged. *You're a real live boy after all!*

"It's him, all right," the tall man said and put the most insincere smile I'd ever seen on his face, his teeth too white against his tan skin. "Mr. Cates, it's a pleasure to see you again."

I swallowed dust and sunlight. "We've met?"

He blinked, then let loose a calculated, insincere laugh. "Oh! Of course not! My apologies." He leaned forward, extending his hand. "Name's Neely. I work with Cal Ruberto."

Don't trust him, Dolores Salgado whispered in my head. *In fact, if you get a chance, throw him out a window.*

XXXV

NONE OF THAT PRETENDER BULLSHIT

I kept blinking my eyes, trying to get the gloom and glare out of them, struggling for control. I squinted owlishly around, hoping I looked mysterious and calm instead of batshit and broken. I saw Marko sitting in one of the plush chairs and tried to give him a smile, unsure if I'd pulled it off. The glassware at the bar—delicate, expensive things that looked old, from a previous era—rattled gently as I heard the dim roar of displacement behind insulated, soundproofed walls. Then my stomach—already shaken loose from its moorings—sank into my ass and stayed there as the hover rose into the air.

I looked at Grisha again, then back at Marko. They both looked back at me blankly. After a moment, Marko smiled, a slow, uncomfortable change of expression that made me wish I had the strength to smack him.

"So how, exactly, did this *happen?*" I asked.

Grisha shrugged. "Mr. Neely showed up in Moscow shortly after you'd been snatched," he said. "Looking for you."

"If we'd gotten there a few hours earlier, we might have prevented your being taken altogether," Neely interjected, sitting back and steepling his hands. "Since our goals temporarily coincided, I suggested to your colleagues that we pool resources at least this far."

The tan man smiled at me, those white teeth like search-lights popping out of his mouth. I started coughing and put some theater into it to buy time. I was feeling a little better—just getting up and moving had helped, and whatever miracle drugs the avatar had pumped into me were doing their work—but this didn't feel right. I'd spent a lifetime feeling my way through situations, getting betrayed and stabbed in the back. You developed a taste for the bitter upchuck sizzling in the back of your throat that always preceded a real good assfucking, and I had half my organs clawing up my throat.

I cleared my throat forcefully. "Why? Why come looking for me?"

I wondered why Neely wasn't Pushing me. I was pretty sure the last way to describe what was happening was a *rescue*, so why wasn't the bastard just putting me in a mental headlock?

Probably he doesn't know how that will affect us, Dolores whispered to me. *We're an unknown quantity. What if we resist? What if our presence makes you immune? What if we all snap like brittle glass and you're scrambled? He can't take the chance.*

I felt her go silent again before I could respond.

Neely's smile didn't falter. "Frankly, Cates, when we acquired your imprint and hatched this little plan, we didn't realize ... what had *happened* to you. Aside from being a citizen of the System and thus under the protection of its duly elected officials, you're, shall we say, *valuable*." He spread his hands in an elegant gesture. "I won't lie. The same hidden knowledge that brought you to Chengara under Director Marin's ungentle attention makes you valuable to us. The difference is, we're *asking* you to help us. We're *asking* you to tell us what Undersecretary Salgado knows."

My bullshit meter exploded. I didn't know who the fuck this Neely character was, but I knew just from looking at him that he was not the sort of man accustomed to *asking* anything.

I ran my dry tongue over my cracked lips, wincing at the sudden pain. "You got any gin back there, slick?"

Something passed over his leathery face, a fast contortion I couldn't quite catch. He regained control right away, glancing down at his lap and coming up smiling. "I apologize, Mr. Cates. You have been through an ordeal." He stood up and pointed at me. "Old-school: warm and straight, yes?"

I nodded. "Piss warm if possible."

He turned for the bar. "At any rate, Cates, for you the war is over, of course, whether the old bag decides to tell you her secrets or not. We'll put you anywhere in the System within our power." He glanced over his shoulder at me, a glass in his hand. "With your verbal pledge to not act against us, of course."

I looked at Grisha. He stared back at me without expression. I looked at Marko, and he was still giving me the off-center smile that made him look like he had a brain disease. I turned to look at Neely's solid back. This was nothing like Kev had been, or even the government Spooks like Bendix I'd run into during the Plague. This was a fine touch for a Pusher. Neely had two people on a slow burn and wasn't even breaking a sweat.

He spun around with two glasses filled four-fingers deep, took three steps, and held one out to me. I reached for it, humiliated to see my hand shaking. I put the glass up to my nose and breathed it in, the smell familiar but different than I was used to. Less bathtub and more gin, I supposed—filtered, cleaned, and professional. I swallowed it all in two gulps, the fumes rising into my head and making my eyes water. It was terrible. It tasted like someone had boiled gin down to a mathematical equation and had a computer construct a glass of it, molecule by molecule.

"Thank you," I breathed, feeling steadier. The healing power of booze. "So, let me get this straight: you've rescued me."

Neely nodded, pointing at me again. "Yes! Because that is what constitutional governments do—they protect their loyal citizens."

Fucking hell, I thought, *this guy's not used to operating without his Push.* He was all elbows and creepy smiles. "And you think it'd be nice if I told you something I don't even fucking know."

He sank back into the seat across from me. "Yes!"

"And then I can go anywhere I want as long as I promise not to fuck with you."

He nodded crisply. "Yes."

I took a deep breath and tried to get a quick snapshot of my physical state, a sense of what I'd be able to do. It came back pretty thin. Every joint ached, my muscles trembled, and the ringing in my head had blossomed into a thick cloud of fog. I wasn't sure I'd be able to get up out of the chair, much less do anything else. But there was the choice, because I had a strong feeling that if I stayed in the chair now, I'd never get out of it.

I was off the rail, and I didn't like it.

Exhaling slowly, I put my hands on the seat of the chair and pushed myself up, trying for a smooth, slow motion, trying to make it seem easy. I managed to get to my feet while keeping my face smooth and unworried with effort. I felt Neely's narrow eyes on me as I made for the bar, taking small steps but managing a steady gait, and at the bar I fell forward into it at the right moment to mask my unsteadiness. I picked up the bottle of gin, half-full and made of thick, heavy glass. I weighed it in my shaking hand, struggling to slow my breathing down to a normal rate. I turned and leaned back against the bar for a moment.

"I can't promise not to fuck you, Mr. Neely," I said, breathing deeply again, holding it for a moment as my lungs burned, and then launching myself back toward him. "I'm a Gunner. I get paid to fuck people, and if you start turning down jobs because of vague promises made under duress in hovers, you pretty quickly get a reputation as a useless motherfucker, and jobs dry up."

Neely smiled as I approached. "I am sure we can work out some sort of agreement that satisfies honor amongst thieves."

He is *a fucking prick, isn't he?* Marin whispered to me suddenly. *The great Sekander Neely. One of the first babes snatched up*

*for the project, M-rating off the charts. He's famous. I've never actually
seen him before. Are you aware that your eyesight is not very good, Mr.
Cates? Of course, I'm used to digital optics.*

"Honor amongst thieves?" I said, forcing a smile onto
my face. "What the fuck do you know about honor amongst
thieves?" I took a second to steel myself, trying to summon every
drop of energy I had left; then I flipped the bottle up, caught it
by the neck, and smashed it down on Neely's head with everything I had.

As he fell out of the chair, blood spurting, I felt the light-
est touch of his Push again, but it faded away immediately as
I gladly dropped to my knees next to him. Panting painfully, I
took hold of his blood-damp hair and yanked his head up, pressing the jagged edge of the broken bottle against his neck hard
enough to draw an extra trickle of blood.

I remembered the first time I'd played that trick, feeling
happy. Neely's strangled grunts filled my ears, and his warm
blood covered my hand.

You're a true professional, Avery, Marin chortled silently inside
me. *No complicated tech for you, huh? No ancient martial arts. None
of that pretender bullshit. Just a broken bottle and a complete lack of
empathy for the rest of the human race.*

I ignored the whisper in my mind, panting spittle down onto
Neely's damp head. "You don't like not being able to Push me,
huh, you fucking dandy? Fuck you. You're under orders. Send
him back."

Neely gasped and twisted under me. My vision swam, but I
pushed everything I had into my one arm and tugged harder on
his hair. "Who?" he hissed. I noted that neither Marko nor Grisha
had moved. Neely was the most powerful Pusher I'd ever even
imagined. I'd *broken a bottle over his head* and now threatened to
slit his throat, and he could still maintain his Push on them. If he
hadn't obviously been ordered not to try anything with my delicate, special little brain—any doubt that I was an avatar tossed

in the garbage with that one tiny flicker of his Push against my thoughts—I wouldn't have had a chance.

"Your fucking boss. I don't deal with fucking flunkies, seconds, or dressed-up secretaries."

He twisted his face around and slid his eyes toward me. "Oh, fuck you, you goddamn monkey."

"Mr. Cates," I heard a new voice say from the direction of the cockpit. I turned and looked at a tall, black man—the darkest man I'd ever seen—hunching a bit to fit under the ceiling of the hover, his belly an amazing sight, swollen and preceding him by several orders of magnitude. He was dressed in an even nicer suit than Neely's, looking hand tailored and possibly made out of pure gold. His head was shaved and waxed, shining in the warm light. I put him at fifty or sixty, though he had the ageless look of the rich with their endless stem cell treatments and surgeries—despite the very edge of a nasty surgical scar peeking up from his collar. He walked gracefully over to Neely's vacated chair and lowered himself down with regal grace, then looked down at me with an expression of immense disappointment.

"Release Mr. Neely," he said in a low, rich voice. "And we will talk."

And I heard Dolores Salgado again, whispering, *Forget Neely. Throw* this *son of a bitch out a window.*

And then Marin again, sounding muted for a change. *Damn,* he whispered to me. *Look at that. I haven't aged well at all.*

XXXVI

I WANT TO BE *ERASED*

I stared at Ruberto longer than was wise. I still had Neely's hair in one hand and the bottle against his neck in the other, but I'd lost all power and gone limp. If Neely had surged up, he could have thrown me back against the cabin wall like I was made of paper.

What did you just say?

Marin stayed quiet. I remembered the Worm in Moscow, Gall, spluttering, *Don't you know who Ruberto is?*

"I think I understand your kind, Mr. Cates," Ruberto said, sighing deeply, as if the disappointment of such understanding was more than he could comfortably bear. "You are looking for a deal, yes? You have something we want, and you would like fair compensation. In spirit, I agree with you. I am sorry if it appeared we were trying to, as you might say, *screw* you."

Ruberto had a slight wheeze, like a distant tide.

Well, I'll be damned. That would explain a lot of bullshit, Salgado muttered.

Is that what you know? I demanded as I struggled to control my breathing. *Is that what they want from you?*

She didn't know that, Marin said, somehow conveying smugness in my head. *No one knew that. It was the perfect crime.*

We assumed, Salgado went on. *We convinced Captain Marin to*

participate in our little pilot program to have his brain sucked into a
quantum drive. Two hundred volunteers, one hundred ninety-nine died
leaving no usable brain imprint behind. Marin's imprint was the only
viable one. We assumed his body died as well—the body always dies.
And then when we needed a Director of IA, we had this imprint we
could program and nudge, control.

Didn't die, Marin said gleefully. *Even I didn't realize it at first,*
but I survived. Just like you, Mr. Cates! We're brothers in a sense. When
I realized, I found myself and . . . elevated myself. Changed the appear-
ance of my avatars to confuse the issue. Bit by bit, slowly, I created new
files, a new name. I created Cal Ruberto, and I made him—myself—an
Undersecretary in time.

"Mr. Cates?" Ruberto said, cocking his head. Like a bird.

Easier than it sounds. They thought I'd died during the process—I
was the first subject who even left a usable brain imprint behind, and
no one even checked the body—my body. Why would they? Everyone
died. Like you, Avery, they left me for dead, scooped up my imprint,
and a few months later hit on the brilliant idea of making me their
lackey—Director of SSF Internal Affairs. So I could tame the beast
they'd created. They added all sorts of programming to my imprint, to
control me. Meanwhile, my body, my physical self, managed to survive.
Crawled back into the the System and disappeared for a while. When I
found myself again, what was I supposed to do? Let me languish?

I sank back onto my ass, releasing Neely, hating the feeling
of Dick Marin in my head. The Pusher didn't scramble away or
anything; he got to his feet slowly, wiping blood from his eyes
and slicking back his hair with one hand, flicking a pattern of
dark blood onto the floor of the cabin. He took a deep snorting
breath and spat blood, stepping to stand behind his boss and
stare at me.

"A deal," I said hoarsely. I felt like I couldn't breathe deeply
enough, like my lungs were bottomless, just letting the air pass
through. I wiped my chin with one sleeve. "All right. Make me
an offer."

You have nothing to barter with, Salgado said tersely.

My bullshit meter was still off the known charts. I stared back at Neely and Ruberto—Marin—and asked myself what was wrong with the whole scene, why everything felt off. I didn't know. All I knew was that this was all bullshit.

The gin in my gut had soured and was making me woozy. The adrenaline dump had perked me up, though.

"An offer," Ruberto repeated, glancing down at his hands. "Mr. Cates, it would be helpful to know what it is you *want.*"

"World peace," I said breathlessly, swallowing vomit. "Education for all the children. Jobs for everyone. Go on, get creative. Let's start with letting my friends have their minds back."

Ruberto raised an eyebrow, and his eyes swiveled to Grisha, who still sat calmly, a neutral expression on his face. "We can discuss that. At present I am worried that their reactions may be...unproductive."

Ruberto, Marin, Dolores hissed in my mental ear. *This is a conspiracy. They've been working angles. Marin alive! For decades! Everything makes sense now. Everything.*

I shrugged at Ruberto. "Okay. Let's talk money."

The Undersecretary narrowed his eyes at me. "Money? Mr. Cates, you are still a very rich man from your previous exploits, despite everything."

I was buying time. For what, I didn't know, but I figured if the only thing selling was time, I'd better buy as much of it as I could. "You Undersecretaries are doing such a great job, I think I need about six hundred thousand yen to buy a pair of shoes these days, and the way you fuckwads are shelling the countryside it looks like things are getting worse. We're going to start hitting buffer overflows on our credit dongles."

Ruberto's plump lips pursed, and then he nodded. "Perhaps we can work out a payment—do you have a number in mind?"

Don't deal with Ruberto, Cates, Salgado whispered. *You can't*

*trust him. He's setting himself up as king of a new System ever since he
claimed control of the new army.*

I blinked, trying to keep my face blank. "I thought you were
making the offers, Cal," I said, tossing the bottle neck over my
shoulder. "But we can come back to that. Obviously, I want my
file vacated. I don't want to just be released, I want to be *erased*.
I don't want to be anyone's Person of Fucking Interest anymore,
okay?"

"How about we just chuck you out the hatch and be done
with it?" Neely growled.

Ruberto held up a hand languidly without looking at his
flunky, and Neely took a deep breath, clamping his jaw shut
tightly.

"All right, Cates. I cannot speak for Director Marin, of course,
but I will excise you from civilian and military data banks. Anything else?"

I smiled at him. It was almost fun to test how desperate they
were, how much they'd offer me. "I have a question I've been trying to get answered for a while now. I'm looking for some—"

"Fuck this. He's playing with us," Neely suddenly growled.
I could feel the hover's momentum changing, my stomach flipping again: we were landing.

"Playing with us," Ruberto echoed, sighing deeply.
"Perhaps." He stared at me for a long time, both of us just
breathing—him slow and steady, me in wincing little yips and
snorts—and I thought this motherfucker was nothing like Dick
Marin. At least, the pureed, stuffed-in-a-can Marin I'd always
known. But I guessed having your brain sucked out through
a dozen needles and slammed into a storage brick might have
some side effects.

This is how you take over the world, Salgado said. *We thought
Marin was doing it—seize the SSF, start making avatars, and then
bring the hammer down. But that was messy. A war broke out, and we*

were not without resources. But now imagine you're fighting both sides of the war! Every battle, every defeat and victory planned and orchestrated. And in the end it won't matter who wins, because you're leading both sides! But Ruberto could never seize complete control. They need to get rid of the other Undersecretaries.

What do you know? I demanded.

For a second there was no response. *I know that Marin did not suspend all of his programmed overrides. I know that there are bare-metal panic codes built into his design. I do not know the overrides myself. But I know the identity of the one person who does.*

Marin suddenly spoke up. *Bullshit. You know what, Avery? I always hated that fucking bitch. Just an endless headache, that woman.*

Dolores had sunk deep again. I clung to my one blessing in the last half hour: at least Dennis Squalor, also embedded in my head somehow, had been quiet as a saint.

Ruberto suddenly leaned forward. "All right, Mr. Cates. We can defer further negotiation until later. We have settled some terms, and you have my pledge that we will settle more. But first, perhaps, you could offer up something to prove you have the information we require?"

I glanced at Neely, who was staring at me in a fixated way I recalled well from my previous encounters with psionics. He already knew what I'd been trading in: bullshit.

I gave him my best grin, twisting my face into the familiar shape with some effort. "How about we see if I can't get my hands on your neck and snap your windpipe before your monkey there can stop me?"

For a moment, we were all suspended and silent. I expected violence, or a sudden icy fist in my brain, taking control and pulling on my tendons like puppet strings. Neither happened, and then the hover settled onto the ground, the displacers going silent and the woozy feeling of resisting gravity and momentum evaporating.

"I am sorry we could not come to an accommodation, Mr.

Cates," Ruberto said, standing up and shooting his cuffs. He smelled pleasant, and his skin had a nice tan pigment, like good leather. "Your associates will have to debark as well. Sekander, see to everything."

"Yup," Neely said tersely. He jerked a thumb toward the opening hatch. "Let's go, smart-ass."

I struggled to my feet. "Smart-ass? That's the best you can do?"

"Be careful, or I might take you for a ride," he growled, following me toward the exit. "And if your mind pops like a balloon, I might just say you fell, broke your neck, really a shame, the world's a sadder place."

I pushed my shoulders through the hatch door and blinked down at the trio of smartly dressed men waiting on the hot, sandy dirt. I recognized two of them. The one on the left was Horatio Gall, looking none the worse for having been murdered in Venice. The one in the center had a familiar jagged scar on his round face and smiled up at me with his left arm still hanging limply at his side.

"Hope you enjoyed the ride," Howard Bendix said, his smile tugging his puckered face into a terrible expression that had nothing to do with humor. "It may be the last air you get for a while. Follow us. And don't forget *I* don't have to be careful of your precious brain."

As if to prove it, an invisible fist pushed me hard from behind, sending me onto my hands and knees in the hot dirt, my palms scraped raw. My eyes watered from the dust as I raised my head and looked past the telekinetic. The abandoned-looking entry to Chengara rose up behind him, like I'd never left in the first place.

XXXVII

AND THOSE WERE MY *ADVANTAGES*

At the door to the cell I was suddenly lifted up off my feet and thrown against the far wall, hard enough to set my head ringing again. I fell awkwardly onto the chair I'd previously been tied to, my wrist and side bursting into fresh pain, rolling off onto the floor.

"I take it back, Mr. Cates," Bendix said from the hall. "You're not lucky at all, are you?"

I found myself laughing, spluttering against the gritty concrete floor. "Always nice to see a familiar face, Mr. Bendix," I breathed into the floor. I wasn't sure he could hear me, and a moment later the door was shut.

After a moment, I pushed myself back onto my ass, stretching out my bad leg to ease it a little. I sat there in the dark, waiting for my breathing to slow down, my fists to unclench. I didn't try to think. After another moment, I closed my eyes and took as deep a breath as I could manage. I cleared my mind, imagining a field of grass at night in a high wind, no other sound but the rustle of the blades. I struggled to create a complete scene: The smell of the air, the push of the wind, the sense of nothingness above me, and something unseen and huge crashing endlessly through the trees toward me. I hadn't been able to manage the vision for a long time, peace escaping me even during those long months in the prison aboveground, with nothing but the boiled sky and the baked ground and hours and hours of time spent waiting for something to happen.

I found my way to it now, pushing everything out behind an imaginary glass wall, clearing the core out and leaving me encased in silence.

I sat there for a long time, my aching leg forgotten, not sure what I was going to accomplish with this peaceful state. But I clung to it. I was afraid if I let it slip away, I'd never get it back again.

Avery.

Marin's ... voice, for want of a better word. I considered pushing him away, out past the borders of my peaceful little node, but decided to let him talk.

Avery, maybe it's time you and I came to an understanding.

Silently, I nodded. Whoever was watching me on whatever closed-circuit Vid screens they had set up in the place probably thought I'd finally gone crazy. "Sure thing, Dick," I said aloud, smiling. "Are you real? Are you really stuffed in there, somehow?"

I'm real. Out of date, a little — my Prime has accrued several years' worth of experiences since I was separated, of course. But I am a complete and functioning imprint. I don't know how this works, either.

I nodded again. "Maybe you were shoved in to torture me."

Sure. I could start singing, maybe, or reciting numbers.

"Or just commenting on every fucking thing I do until I want to stick an ice pick into my ear to shut you up."

Ah, hadn't thought of that, Avery! You are truly an entertaining individual sometimes. I am almost glad I've kept you alive all these years.

"Kept me alive? Mr. Director, with all due respect, I had something to do with it, too."

No, Avery. If I'd decided you'd lived past your usefulness, you would have been dead a long, long time ago.

He wasn't lying, I could tell. Somehow I knew that he wasn't lying—maybe he was *wrong*, but he believed it. "Okay. You haven't pulled my card, and I am eternally grateful, Mistah Directah, suh," I said amiably. "What understanding are you talking about?"

Somehow you've found yourself in a position where I can actually use you, Avery. You can do a job for me. I haven't been networked with my Prime for some time, of course, but I am confident this decision would meet with approval. I could feel him grinning. I didn't understand how that was possible, but I knew he was smiling. *So tell me, Avery, are you available for some freelance work?*

"Fucking hell," I murmured. "Are you kidding me?"

I am perfectly serious, Avery.

I struggled to maintain my sense of peace. I was negotiating a job with a ghost that lived in my head. I was in a prison Dick Marin fucking *owned*, and I was negotiating with his ghost for a job. The glass wall between me and chaos shimmered and vibrated.

"What could you possibly offer me? You're not connected, as you just admitted. You can't make any offers on behalf of…of yourself."

True. But I can guide you out of this prison. I had this place built, Avery. I can tell you exactly how to escape. That is my offer.

My eyes popped open, and the imaginary sphere of calm burst into tiny fragments.

I can make no guarantees to you, because I cannot issue orders to staff and you may be apprehended in the attempt and killed, as standing orders require. Pass codes may have been changed—well, I certainly hope they have been changed!—and any number of factors are outside my sphere of influence, which is, I might admit, confined to you. So I offer nothing guaranteed. I merely offer the information you might use to obtain your freedom.

I stared at a random spot on the dim wall across from me.

Take your time, of course. There's no need to rush. I am sure my counterparts are not contemplating more invasive forms of torture, or your summary execution.

I licked my lips painfully, wondering if I could trust him. It. Whatever—the voice in my head. How did I know this wasn't a setup?

At least you're not wondering if you're crazy anymore. That's progress. Do you really have any choice, Avery? If I am lying then, yes, you will either be killed or perhaps tricked into revealing something. Although I don't think you actually know anything to reveal. But let that drift. If you sit here and do nothing, you will almost certainly be tortured again or killed or both—as we both know too well simply dying is no longer a guarantee of release from the miseries of existence, yes? For the moment they hesitate to try digitizing you again, for fear of destroying the only extant copy of Salgado we know to exist. But if you die and your brain begins decaying, there would be nothing to lose, and they might succeed. Simple logic points you toward accepting my offer. At least it is a chance. If you are missing some diabolical wrinkle that will serve to betray you, well, at least you go down swinging, eh?

I half nodded. "Grisha and Marko," I said slowly, feeling my way through it. "They come out, too."

Complications, Avery. I would have thought an old hand like yourself would be a little more sensibly ruthless. But they may be useful, I admit—and how you execute this adventure is entirely up to you, of course. No one is paying attention, but we all have our vanities. Yours is that you are a fundamentally good person, yes? Poor old Avery. As you wish: your odds go down, but I can advise you on how to retrieve your . . . friends? . . . and escape with them, yes.

I had no weapon, my physical state was weak—although the cocktail the avatar had administered was buzzing inside me, giving me artificial energy and numbed nerves, something to claw onto and ride. And I was locked in a box a hundred feet under a cruel desert. And those were my *advantages*. "All right, you cocksucker. What is it you want me to do?"

Kill Ruberto, obviously. On your way out, so to speak.

Mild shock rippled through me. "Ruberto's *you*," I said. "Why would you kill...yourself?"

He was me. Now he is someone else. We remain...brothers, I suppose, and we have been partners in this adventure, yes. Working secretly together, we engineered the state of emergency and the removal of my programmed limitations. Working secretly together, we engineered the sad decline in relations between my police force and the civilian government. We engineered the creation of an army and the declaration of a civil war. Ah, but here's the rub: I don't need my sad wetware body anymore. My supremacy is in the bag, you understand. If Cal Ruberto remains alive and in charge of the forces at his disposal, this will undoubtedly devolve into a struggle between us. We're both me, Avery, and I want to be the one in charge, you see? Eventually one of us will have to go.

"You could just wait him out," I suggested. "He's going to die someday."

Too risky. What if they invent goddamn immortality in the meantime?

Or just stuff him into an avatar, too. I considered. If I killed Ruberto—assuming I was even able to—it would leave the King Worm as unchallenged master of the System. I wasn't sure I wanted that. I had no love for Marin and would be glad to put a bullet in *his* head, in fact.

"I also need a guarantee of safety once I leave Chengara," I said slowly. I had a vision, bright and cheerful, of the three of us stepping into the sun and being gunned down by Stormers.

Can't do it, Avery, Marin said. *Sorry. I have no way of communicating with my Prime. I can offer him no updates. Whatever deals we make are between you and this version of me alone.*

Honest, at least. "How do you know Ruberto's still here? He probably took off to the front."

He's here. You're a priority, Avery. Salgado had the highest clearance, and she used it—that old bat knows a surprising amount of information no one else even bothered to research. He's going to personally oversee the rest of your dismantling. He's here. I can even guess where he is.

I closed my eyes again. My choices had narrowed down to a manageable two: Stay in the cell and wait for one of Ruberto's creatures to go a little too far one day and kill me, or take Little Dick up on his offer and become one of Marin's employees again. Take on a murder in return for compensation, just like the old days. It wouldn't solve anything, but once again I'd been pushed inevitably to this point, inch by inch, every other option closed off.

"All right, Dick," I said quietly. "We have an agreement."

I was back on the rail. And it felt good.

XXXVIII

TWO, I'D BEEN FUCKING LUCKY

All right, Avery. Stand up and go to the door. The panic code is alpha-septimus-delta-nonus. Got that?

"You have panic codes...in a prison?"

I stood up carefully, giving my leg time to adjust. I was stiff and aching all over but felt surprisingly steady.

Rule number one, Avery, is always have a panic code. You never know when you might end up in your own damn prison, eh? Rule number two is be the only person extant who knows the panic code, even if you have to eliminate the engineers who designed the place for you. Now, there's at least one guard outside the door, maybe two, avatars, not meat. I'm afraid you're going to have to kill them with your bare hands. Rule number one does not instruct us to keep a cache of weapons inside the cells of your own damn prison, unfortunately.

I'd killed people—regular, flesh and blood people—with my bare hands, and it hadn't been easy with *people*. I turned around slowly, squinting through the gloom of my cell. The only thing in it aside from me was the metal chair. I stepped over to it and picked it up, lifting it to chest height. It was heavy, a well-made piece that was probably pre-Unification.

No, Marin said tersely in my head. *Made in Bristol. Though I admit that factory has since been shuttered due to malfunction, as have a lot of factories in the last ten years.*

I flipped the chair over and examined it, tilting this way and that to catch the feeble light. I tested one bolt, and it gave slightly, slicing into my fingers a little. I sat down on the cold floor and began working the bolts, biting my lip and cursing every time a bolt slipped out of my stiff fingers. Moving my fingers carefully, precisely, wiping the blood off every few seconds to keep them dry, I worked the damn nut off the first bolt and then the second, and with a loud clang the leg fell off and hit the concrete floor. I set the rest of the chair down and held the leg in one hand, judging its weight and balance. It was a terrible melee weapon, difficult to hold and awkward to swing. But it was heavy, and I thought it might just cave in some alloyed avatar skulls.

I stood up and crept back to the door, holding my new club in front of me. "Do I just speak the panic code, or do I have to gesture something, or what?"

Speak it, Avery.

I took a deep breath and stepped close to the door, pressing my back against the wall so that when it opened inward I'd be hidden behind it. A simple trick, but it worked often enough to make it worthwhile, and I had a pretty limited arsenal of tools to work with. Beggars couldn't be choosers.

I whispered the bullshit Marin had given me and was mildly surprised when the door sagged inward slightly with a loud click. I held steady, keeping my grip on the chair leg loose and easy, breathing shallowly and resisting the urge to shift my weight. After a moment, the door began to crowd against me. I waited, listening to gritty footsteps as they moved past me and stopped a foot or two inside the doorway. I stood there with my breath held, listening, listening…and there was the slightest scrape.

I pushed off the wall and slammed into the door, sending it crashing into the guard, knocking it into the opposite wall. With a grunt, I sprang back and sidestepped, letting the door swing back from the Crusher, which was on its knees, pushing back from the wall. I raised the leg over my head and brought it down on top of its uncovered head, rewarded by a distinct dull crunching sound.

A blurry movement to my right made me whirl, bringing my makeshift club up in a wide arc, making contact with something that sent the club flying out of my grip as I lost my footing, my bad leg betraying me. I went stumbling backward and landed hard on my ass again, a sharp lance of bright red pain splitting my spine into two brittle spikes.

I rolled sloppily to the left and dragged myself up, stumbling backward into the wall. I panted there, clinging to the cold stone. Nothing moved. I limped forward: the first guard was where I'd left it, slumped forward against the wall. A second set of legs lay halfway inside the cell, splayed and still. Staring, I sank slowly to the floor, panting, my vision swimming and my head pounding. Everything grayed up, and I felt nauseous, my back and leg pulsing with a dull ache that felt permanent. I hugged myself tightly, breathing fast, trying to get enough oxygen to clear my head.

After a moment I concluded this was impossible and pushed myself back upright, head pounding and legs shaking. Breathing heavily, I limped over to where the chair leg had landed and bent down with a grunt to retrieve it.

Well, that was exciting. Maybe the current models are a little too humanlike. Problem is making the casing too thick makes the units too heavy, and they suck up power like sponges, resulting in overheating and frequent power-down modes.

"Fuck," I panted, "you." I walked over to the door, spots before my eyes, and stepped over the prone form of the second guard. The bare hallway was otherwise deserted. I inspected its deceptively Crusher-like uniform. One Taser stick was all I got for my trouble, but I swapped it for the leg without hesitation. "Now what?"

Assuming you don't have some sort of infarction—surely physical fitness would come under the heading of professional interest, Avery?

"Big talk from a fucking data file. Now what's next?"

After some consideration—especially of your physical state—I now think your chances of success in this endeavor are greatly enhanced if you have your fellow prisoners, so we should gather them first. They will almost certainly be one level below you if the staff here has followed standard procedure. We can either take the elevator—my preferred choice—or there is a large wire conduit you can access from the floor outside. I only mention the conduit because you always seem to choose the dirtiest and least comfortable approach to any problem. I wondered if perhaps it was congenital or a compulsion of sorts.

"Fuck you," I repeated. "What makes you think the elevator's safe?"

What makes me think? Avery, this is my *prison. I wrote the guard rotations. But wriggle down the conduit if it makes you feel more manly.*

I wanted to hit someone. Instead I started off down the hallway, taking the first left at the junction as instructed by Little Dick. It terminated at the dull silver doors of an elevator. Marin described the simple gesture for summoning the cab, and I managed it on the third try. Distantly below me something rumbled into life, and I snapped out the Taser, getting a nice electric sizzle from it.

A second later the elevator doors split open, revealing my old pal Mr. Bendix and a youthful, round-faced boy of maybe seventeen, by his look also a psionic. They were both wearing immaculate blue pin-striped suits with coats cut long in the back, though Bendix made it look like the clothes had grown onto him like a pelt whereas the kid looked like he'd borrowed some larger, more confident man's wardrobe for the day. Bendix wore a single black glove on the hand of his withered arm, managing to make it look kind of sexy.

There were a couple of reasons I was still alive. One, I'd never imagined that just having a gun in my hand made me danger-ous, or smart. Two, I'd been fucking lucky. And three, I learned my lessons once and remembered them.

And Bendix had taught me the only lesson worth remember-ing when it came to the fucking telekinetics: once you got him down, don't let up. The trick was *getting* them down. I launched myself forward and crashed into him, knocking him back into the rear of the elevator. A second later that familiar invisible fist slammed into me and tore me free from him, and as I sailed upward I managed to swing the Taser out and caught him on the chin with a glancing blow. He screeched, and I dropped to the bottom of the floor with a grunt.

I jumped up, my instincts five years younger than my ach-ing body. My bad leg gave under my weight, sending me into a lurching fall right onto Bendix. He threw his arms up across his face, and I slammed into a wall of air, tossed weakly backward. I stumbled on my bad leg again and spun myself, crashing into the other psionic, who squeaked slightly and stiffened against me. For a second, I felt that terrible sensation of someone's mind touching mine, invading, clamping down hard on my motor functions.

"No!" Bendix rasped hoarsely from behind.

Immediately the mind retreated, and before either one of them could recover, I jabbed the Taser into the kid's neck, giv-ing him a full shot, and then spun him around like dead weight while he was still shivering, using our momentum to send him hurtling toward Bendix. The kid suddenly stopped and rose into the air, and I let gravity pull me down beneath him, stab-bing the Taser forward and landing a clean blow on Bendix's exposed calf. I gave him all the juice I had in the stick, and he went rigid immediately, blood spurting from his mouth where his teeth had clamped down on his tongue. The kid fell on me, crushing the wind out of me and knocking the Taser free from my grip.

I lay there, unable to breathe, with a hundred pounds of useless psionic pushing toward the ground through me. I heard the elevator doors close with a smooth *whoosh* of displaced air. On the floor next to me, Bendix had begun to convulse.

After a moment I sucked in a tattered stream of air, forcing my lungs to expand, and rolled the kid off me. Sitting up, I managed a deep inhalation that started me coughing, and a rope of spittle trailed from my mouth to the floor as I staggered for the walls, steadying myself enough to gesture the elevator into motion. I rode the elevator down one level in perfect silence except for my sucking breath, three seconds of my life. When the doors opened, the hallway looked exactly like the one I'd just turned my back on. I grabbed the Taser and left Bendix and friend inside. I didn't have anything to bind them up with, and the time spent was probably wasted anyway—Marin and Ruberto would have dozens of Spooks on staff here. One more or less wasn't going to make any difference.

Left, right, pass two junctions, left, and there'll be another pair of guards to handle.

I started walking. "I get the horrible feeling I'm going to be breaking out of Chengara forever."

My soggy boots sucked my feet loudly as I walked down the empty, cold hall. Adjusting my steps to try and minimize the noise, I wondered how anyone found their way around the place, as it was all unmarked corridors of concrete and steel bathed in shadow-intolerant white light; I kept repeating Little Dick's instructions as I walked, counting junctions and turns until I judged I was just around the corner from where my two errant—and unfortunately loyal—Techies were locked up. I leaned against the wall and slowed my breathing, listening for any sign that the guards had heard my approach. Odds were, considering my general state of grace and balance—not to mention the charming *wheeze* I'd developed—they'd only heard me if they were listening. And awake.

There was no sound, though. I frowned, forcing myself to wait another half minute, holding my breath until the blood pulsed in my eyes. I stretched my neck and took a deep breath, then stepped out into the hall, prepared to do my best imitation of a run.

The hall was empty.

The cell door was closed. I crept closer to it, Taser held loosely in my hand. "Well, Mr. Wizard," I whispered. "Any ideas?"

Only that I'm going to have to wire in some pain circuitry in order to punish goldbrickers, he groused silently inside me. *Any chance you'd be interested in a job as a security tester? This is embarrassing.*

There was nothing for it but to keep going. I felt ragged and torn up and tried to steady myself as I prepared to use Marin's code to open the cell door. Before I could, the door swung inward, slowly, and a moment later Grisha's face appeared. He stared at me for a second, eyes wide in shock, and then he pushed the door open all the way, grinning. Behind him, Marko stood with a Taser in one hand. Two bodies lay on the floor of the cell between them.

"Mr. Cates!" Grisha said cheerfully. "Did you know there are *panic codes* hardwired into this complex?"

XXXIX

ALL ITS LIFE, ONLY WAITING FOR ME TO ARRIVE

"We're going *down?*"

I prayed for strength, because Marko was talking.

"Isn't escape and happiness *up?*"

We'd arrived at the elevator doors, which I gestured open. For a second the three of us just stared at the two prone Spooks.

"Avery has been busy, yes?" Grisha said, slapping me on the shoulder as he pushed past me. I made a vow to always somehow locate the skinny Russian for future descents into hell. If I had to deal with Marko every time the cosmos put me back into the slot, I was just going to let the next motherfucker I came across kill me and be done with it.

I limped after Grisha. "Yes," I said.

"Wait a second," Marko said, frowning as he stopped short of entering the elevator. "We're riding the goddamn *elevator?*" He looked at me. "You don't think that's a little *obvious?*"

I turned to face the Techie. Both he and Grisha didn't look too bad, like they'd been shoved from the hover into their cell and then forgotten. Marko's hair was starting to fuzz in all over his face, making him look like a blotchy, slightly rotten peach. Silently, I gestured and the doors started to close.

"Fuck!" he squealed, dashing into the cab. Behind me, Grisha chuckled softly.

"Ezekiel forgets his place," the Russian Techie murmured. "What are we doing, Avery?"

"Killing someone," I said.

"I am glad of it," he replied calmly.

I *loved* Grisha.

"Who?" Marko said, biting off the word unhappily.

"SFN Undersecretary Cal Ruberto," I said as the elevator trembled to a stop. "I have it on good authority that he's here on the seventh floor."

"Aw, *shit*," Marko groaned. "Every time I think, *Hooray, Avery just saved my life*, it always instantly turns into *Aw, fuck, Avery's gonna get me killed*."

"No one's forcing you to follow me around," I said mildly, hands twitching. "You can go on back up and wander the fucking desert, if you want. Me, I'm getting out of here alive. The price of the ticket is Ruberto. Do what you want."

"Slow down," Marko complained. "What's the goddamn *plan*?"

I turned and took a step toward him as the elevator continued to sink. He shrank back a step, so I took another, enjoying the sudden look of pale horror on his face. I backed him into the wall and stopped, keeping my arms at my sides.

"The plan is simple, Mr. Marko. I'm going to let divine fucking guidance—with which I am currently *overflowing*—show me where the Undersecretary is. Then I'm going to kill him. Then I'm going to let divine guidance show me the way out. You"—I lifted one arm and pushed a finger into his chest, making him flinch with a grimy little surge of joy inside me, ugly and dumb—"may be of assistance."

I stared down into Marko's bloodshot eyes, our breathing loud in the cab. After a moment, Grisha cleared his throat.

"In other words, Ezekiel, Avery will tell us as soon as he figures it out, no?"

Fucking Grisha. Marko visibly braced himself and swallowed. "All I want," he said slowly, "is to get out of here and be dropped off somewhere within fifty miles of *anywhere*, and I won't bother you ever again, Avery."

I grit my teeth, and Marko suddenly shut his eyes as if bracing for a slap. I forced myself to turn away. I wondered why Dolores Salgado had been so quiet, why she wasn't chattering away, warning me of dire consequences and unintended results. Her silence, once I noticed it, bothered me.

"What of the psionic?" Grisha pressed. "The Spook. He is possibly best I've ever seen. Could easily incapacitate all of us, I think. You have a plan for dealing with him?"

For a second or two, we all just stood there in silence. I was still looking at Marko, and he frowned back at me, his eyes shifting to my forehead.

"The cell doors...do you think..." He looked past me at Grisha. "Do you think the avatars in this place have panic codes? If we had an avatar, fully digital, no *brain*, the psionic wouldn't be much use against *it*, now would he?"

I waited, but Marin said nothing about this.

"Interesting," Grisha mused. "Possibly. However, even if this is the case, it does not help us much."

The elevator had rumbled to a stop.

"You've hacked an avatar," I reminded him.

"Yes, with tools and time and the help of Dr. Amblen. We have none of these things at present."

I was getting annoyed at all this. "You didn't have them in your cell, either."

"Mr. Marko was part of the teams that helped design protocols in this complex," Grisha said, waving his hand as the elevator doors opened. "He has a bad habit of hacking the SSF data banks and knew of the panic codes and wondered if they perhaps had not been changed. This proved a lucky truth, but I doubt we will get so lucky again."

I leaned out of the cab quickly and caught a glimpse of an empty hall, smooth concrete floor and rough walls carved out of bedrock. A sensation of crushing weight settled on me. Death was all around us. At any moment we could be discovered, and I was tired and weak.

"Not *all* the avatars," Marko whispered. "There's at least one in this complex that's already been hacked."

I took a step back into the elevator and gestured deactivation, which closed the doors and kept the cab sitting where it was. "The Marin unit, which has *me* inside it." I turned to face them. "That reminds me that someone in this elevator used the imprint of *me* I explicitly ordered them not to. But we'll pay that invoice later." I looked up at the ceiling of the cab. "Mr. Wizard," I said, ignoring the look shared by Marko and Grisha. "Any idea where that avatar might be?"

Are you sure it's been kept in this complex? Last we saw it was on the hover. It may have been removed. However, since it was one of my units, they may assume it contains an imprint of yours truly and thus would wish to download its data net and sift its contents. In that case it can probably be found in the lab, also on this level. You will likely remember the lab well.

I remembered cables snaking along the ceiling, the old woman singing to me, the needles. I remembered, all right.

"Let's see if we're lucky again," I said, gesturing the doors open.

"Avery," Grisha hissed at me as I stepped out into the hall.

Left, Avery.

I spun and began walking.

"Avery! I do not wish to burden you with silly questions, but perhaps you can realize that speaking to the ceiling and then announcing you have all the answers needed is not *reassuring*?"

"Fuck reassuring. You're in Chengara again, Grisha. You feel reassured? No? Pick a fucking direction and start walking, then. You'll be at the same fucking level of security as you are following me."

A cloud of tense doubt trailed behind me like exhaust. I glanced up and saw the cable wriggling along the ceiling as I limped, Taser gripped tightly in one hand. The rail had angled downward, and I was riding gravity. Maybe I had a tumor. Maybe there was a lump in my head speaking in the whispered, imagined voice of Dick Marin and maybe my limp was it pressing against some nerve bundle. But fuck if it didn't feel good.

I heard a rustle of fabric and then felt a hand on my shoulder. I took hold of it and spun, taking the arm with me and bending it around painfully, pulling Grisha tight against me. He grunted in pain and didn't struggle.

"Avery," he gasped, "how do you know where we are going?"

I took a deep breath and released him, letting him stumble forward a few steps before I pushed past him. I didn't have time to really explain Little Dick and the voices. "I've been down here before, remember?" I said.

We passed doors on either side, but no other personnel. They'd cleaned up after the invasion, all the bodies and debris cleared away. The emptiness was alarming; I wondered where in hell everyone *was*.

You're the only prisoners in this complex at present, Avery, Marin whispered. *How many people do you suppose it takes to contain you?*

"More than you've got, apparently," I whispered back.

We turned a bend in the corridor, and at the end of a long stretch of floor were familiar, battered swinging doors. A sign over them read LAB-009 in faded, chipped letters.

There are three holding cells off this lab, Marin noted. *If your pet avatar was retained, it is likely in one of those.*

I crashed through the swinging doors, the sound exactly as I remembered from my last involuntary visit. My scalp itched where the needles had been stabbed into my brain. Then I stopped, my footsteps echoing away into silence—the space was empty, just a round high-ceiling room of concrete, several hanging light fixtures crowding the roof, and the walls puckered with sockets of every imaginable kind, waiting for cables to snake into them and bring the place back to life. It smelled clean, aggressively clean, like someone had set a small chemical fire in the place to burn off any trace of dirt or evidence.

Looking around, I saw the doors Marin had mentioned. The gestures to open them—complex and dainty—came to mind unbidden, supplied by my ghostly adviser. Without a word to Marko or Grisha, I limped over to the closest one and gestured savagely. The door remained shut. I took a deep, shuddering breath, swallowed down the coughing fit this tried to inspire, and forced myself to repeat the gesture calmly, slowly, precisely. The door slid into the wall instantly, a faint rush of stale air pushing against me. Within Chengara, for the time being, I was fucking god.

The avatar of Dick Marin stood in the doorway smiling, as if it had been standing there for all its life, only waiting for me to arrive. It didn't look at all like Cal Ruberto. Somehow I could tell with just a glance that Marin's personality wasn't inside it. Something in the eyes, the kink of its mouth. I couldn't believe it was *me* in there, but it wasn't *Marin*, either.

"About fucking time," my ghost said through Dick Marin's face, twisting it into an expression I'd never seen on the Director. "Are we *finally* going to kill someone?"

XL

I'LL PROBABLY HAVE YOU CRUSHED INTO A CUBE AND CARRY YOU AROUND AS A SOUVENIR

"Rule number one," I said to myself, "is I am in charge. I'm the fucking *Prime*, get it? Don't improvise, innovate, or interpret."

The avatar cocked its head and looked at Marko. "Am I always such an asshole?"

Marko nodded glumly. "Pretty much, yep."

"Rule number two is don't fucking talk to them," I hissed. "You're here for one single purpose, and once that's done I'll probably have you crushed into a cube and carry you around as a souvenir."

The avatar frowned. "Keep it up, Meat. I'm starting to dig being digital. It's got its advantages, first of which is that nothing hurts, like when I do this."

It reached out for me, fast, and I just managed to dodge its hand, slapping it aside and stepping away. "Mr. Marko, do we have control over this unit?"

"Yes! Yes," Marko stuttered, for some reason stepping forward. "Periscope depth, Mr. Smith."

The avatar went still. "Ah, nuts," it whispered.

I looked at Marko. "Periscope depth?"

He shrugged. "I wanted something that doesn't come up in normal conversation."

"Okay. What now?"

The Techie sighed. "Mr. Smith, transfer and duplicate administrative privileges to Mr. Cates, standing before you. Indicate compliance."

"Done," the avatar said, its voice flat.

"Mr. Smith," Marko continued, rubbing his eyes, "stand by for voiceprint of Mr. Cates."

"Standing by."

The Techie motioned to me. I turned to face the avatar—which stood without expression, blank and motionless. I opened my mouth, unsure of what to say, and managed a grunt to clear my throat.

"Voiceprint captured," the avatar said.

"Very well," Marko said, sweeping his arm toward me. "Return to normal operation. Cates, feel free to issue orders."

I nodded as animation flowed back into Marin's plastic face. "Don't fucking touch me," I said.

It cocked its head toward me, scowling. "Nuts."

I jabbed my finger at it. "Don't harm me in any way. You are a suicide bomber, okay? Your job is to walk in and handle the fucking Spook—a Pusher. Your job is to walk over to him and break his fucking neck, okay? No matter what else is being thrown your way."

Dick Marin's face folded up into a mask of shock. "A *suicide* bomber? You're fucking shitting me. *Suicide?* As in, I've hung on by my fucking fingernails for decades living hand to mouth, and now I'm going to dash into a room and get turned into a fine red—uh, *white*—mist so you can hide behind my ass?"

I nodded, grinning. "Something like that."

The avatar shook its head. "You're a fucking prick."

"Let's go," I said, turning away and heading back for the swinging doors. I wanted out of this room as soon as possible.

This was where I'd been split off into who knew how many versions. This was where I'd lost control of everything. I didn't know if there really were dozens of avatars of me running around or if that was just another lie meant to get me in line. It didn't matter—one was bad enough.

As I crashed back through the swinging doors, I took stock. I had two human Techies, one useful in a fight and one not; one unhappy imprint of myself in Dick Marin's body; and three Tasers. I was hundreds of feet under a desert and listening to voices in my head. The corridors with their rough rock ceilings and walls and the smooth, machined flooring seemed heavy and sagging, like the whole prison had been hollowed out of the earth above us and was going to collapse in at any moment.

Don't worry—Ruberto's overconfident. He thinks he owns this place. He thinks we're brothers. Now, guns.

A thrill went through me. I'd known there were guns in Chengara—I had vivid memories of those silent puffs of dust from the snipers—but I hadn't known if the hardware was still on premises. "Mr. Wizard, you're melting my heart."

Turn right and take six steps. Munitions Closet in left wall. Light arms only.

I gestured as instructed and a hidden panel slid back into the wall, revealing a nice selection of standard cop iron: five Roon automatics, light and balanced, and two gleaming sniper rifles that looked never used, as well as plastic boxes of ammunition.

"Happy fucking birthday," the avatar said. I took charge of two autos and Grisha, Marko, and the avatar took the other three, Marko appearing to have indulged in absolutely zero efforts to familiarize himself with handguns since I'd last seen him misuse a weapon. I considered taking it away from him but decided to let him keep it—there was no reason to humiliate one-third of my army, and fuck, maybe a few badly placed bullets would make all the difference. I'd seen Techies manage lucky shots before.

We loaded up on ammo and left the snipes. Loading as we walked, no one said anything as I led us down the corridors again, listening to Marin's one-word directions and giving every impression of knowing where I was headed.

Stop.

We had turned a corner and now faced a double-wide doorway, unmarked, the sort that would be sucked into the wall when triggered. I stopped immediately and put out my hands to block the other three. "Well, Mr. Wizard?" I said, looking up at the ceiling. I enjoyed worrying Grisha.

There will be two perfunctory guards outside his office, Marin hissed inside my head. *Be ready for them.*

I nodded and leaned in to my three followers. "Two avatars guarding the door. I don't know what's inside. I can gesture the door open. So, we rush the guards and take them down—you're in the lead on that too"—I hesitated a moment—"Mr. Smith."

The avatar nodded. "Naturally."

"Then we're in, and we have to move fast, so let's be clear on our roles." I pointed at the avatar again.

"I know," it said immediately, forming its hand into a gun and pointing it at me. "Suicide by Spook."

I nodded. "I'm on Ruberto. You two are gonna have to take on whatever else might be in there. I don't care what you do, or how, but keep it off me until I'm done, okay? Or else you're never getting out of here."

"Got it," Grisha said, grinning. "Suicide by miscellaneous."

Marko moaned. I smiled at Grisha and reached out, patting him on his bristly cheek. "If I had a pass to sell, Grigoriy, I'd sell you one. Let's go."

The avatar stepped forward as the three of us raised our guns.

Don't fuck up. That would be disappointing, Marin whispered, somehow conveying mild annoyance with the thought—I was just a fucking tool for him, disposable. If my head got blown off in there, well, it was back to the drawing board for Dick. If he ever even found out about this little plot of his.

The avatar glanced back at me for a second, our eyes meeting. For one strange moment I almost imagined there was some hint of a soul in them, some spark of myself staring back at me, hating me the way I hated Marin and Ruberto and everyone who viewed me as a tool, a means to their end. Then it nodded and turned back to the doors. I waited another stunned moment and then gestured the doors open with a jerky motion of my hand, following Marin's instructions. They parted so quickly it was almost as if they'd dissolved into thin air, and then we were running down a short corridor toward another pair of avatars dressed in Crusher uniforms.

They reacted instantly. One second they'd been leaning against the wall on either side of the doors, the next they had Tasers in their hands as they braced themselves.

"Headshots!" my avatar and I yelled simultaneously as we both stopped, planted our feet, and took aim. Grisha ducked down as low as he could while moving forward, but Marko kept running full speed and upright at them. I squeezed the trigger, and a second later a second shot exploded next to me, and both guards dropped to the floor.

"Keep moving!" I hurried forward, pushing Marko aside and stepping over the two guards. I gestured at the door savagely, and nothing happened. My pulse pounding, I lowered the gun and forced myself to take a deep breath, moving my hand through the gesture slowly, all the rock above my head making me feel compressed and tight, like I was in an invisible box.

For a second, nothing happened, and panic seared my nerves, jolting my heart into a lurching, stuttering rhythm. Then the door dissolved just like the others, melting into thin air, and the avatar was instantly in motion, dashing into the room beyond before the rest of us could react. I lurched after it, displaying exactly zero of the speed and agility the avatar had just shown. With Grisha and

Marko on my heels, I speed-limped into Ruberto's office, made it four or five steps, and stumbled to a halt.

For a second, I was dazzled. We were in a jungle.

The air felt warm and wet, heavy like we'd been thrust into a sponge. There was a sweet, rotten scent to it that made my nose twitch. A random and natural-feeling breeze pushed back against me, thick and elastic. I glanced down, but instead of a thick bed of vegetation, there was just the blank white floor. The walls were covered in a thick, dark green tapestry of vegetation that almost seemed to twist and move in the wind.

Dimly, I saw the avatar leaping, seeming to fly for a few feet before landing on top of Neely, knocking the Spook down with a screech.

A simulation. It was all just light and effects. I pushed my eyes around, straining, and saw the outlines of the walls. And there, a few steps away, was Ruberto, sitting at a very normal desk that appeared to be in the middle of a jungle. Only a few seconds had gone by, and the Undersecretary still sat there with his hands frozen in midgesture over his desk, his plump little mouth open, glistening. His eyes were locked, wide in shock, on the writhing forms of Neely and the avatar, both of whom had hands on the gun, pushing it this way and that. Amazingly, there was no one else in the room. But then the prison was more or less deserted, and all threats safely locked inside cells.

I forced my legs into motion, ignoring the stiff pain. Vaguely I thought of instructing Marko and Grisha to just shoot Neely in the head if they could and save us a bit of trouble, but before I could act on the thought, Ruberto's desk was rushing toward me, and I had to concentrate in order to leap on top of it without crashing down on my useless fucking leg and probably shooting myself in the foot.

I managed it with a little flash, landing well and bringing my gun around perfectly to slap against Ruberto's nose as he swung his head around in sudden panic.

"What!" he gasped, pushing his seat back from his desk. Behind me I heard two shots. I didn't turn to investigate; if Neely had gotten the upper hand I'd find out soon enough.

"Dick sold you out," I said, clicking back the hammer. "So sorry, Cal."

He pushed both hands up at me. "Wait!" he said, sounding suddenly reasonable, like he'd gotten his balance back just like that. The palms of his hands were pale, almost pink. "We can—"

I squeezed the trigger, and he flew away from me, landing on his back near the windows.

"We can't," I whispered.

Mr. Cates, Marin breathed in me, *you are a marvel.*

The jungle flickered and disappeared without ceremony, and suddenly we were standing in a bare concrete room. I turned halfway around and found Grisha and Marko standing pretty much uselessly just inside the door, the avatar straddling Neely, whose tanned head had rolled to the side, his wide blank eyes on me as if he were trying to touch my mind from beyond death.

I looked back down at Ruberto's desk. A glint of reflected light caught my eye, and I bent down to retrieve a silver cigarette case. Flipping it open revealed a dozen perfect smokes, and my heart sang.

Then the lights went out. A second later, before I could turn and shout, the door slammed shut behind us, and the sudden quiet was shattered by the sharp wail of an alarm.

Perhaps I did not mention, Marin said quietly, *that Cal had his biometric readings tied to the security shell of the prison. This will complicate things.*

And then, like dust rising from the floor when you enter a long forgotten room, there was Dennis Squalor in my head.

It is no matter. He was saved long ago.

XLI

REACTING TO THE POWERFUL RADIATION OF THEIR THOUGHTS

Cocksucker, I thought.

I looked over at the Techies and met Grisha's gaze. We stared at each other for a moment.

"No Mr. Wizard, Avery?"

Our deal was made honestly and remains in effect, Mr. Cates. If you can escape this room and evade capture, I will certainly attempt to guide you to a hover, which can take you to safety.

Oh, fuck you, I thought, jumping down from the desk and looking around the office, which now appeared barren, the walls scuffed and pitted with impact craters. There was nothing in it besides Ruberto's desk, two corpses, and us. *Can you get us out of this room?*

No. I'm sorry, Avery. In an emergency like this the security status of administrative offices change, and all gestures and codes are wiped clean.

I nodded. *Then shut the fuck up and leave me alone until you can offer me something useful,* I thought. I started walking toward the avatar. "No Mr. Wizard, Grisha," I shouted over the alarm, which was like a solid wall of sound, irritating my ear nerves directly. "Can you and Mr. Marko try your hand at opening the doors?"

"I am not his fucking sidekick," Marko shouted. "I scored over six hundred on my T6, dammit."

I barely picked out Grisha's response: "Yes? Very good, Ezekiel. I scored a seven hundred and twenty-five myself."

I ignored the sudden cotton ball of awkward silence behind me as I stopped at Neely's body. "Don't move, Mr. Smith," I instructed the avatar and put my gun against its head.

"Avery," Grisha shouted immediately. "We may yet need the extra resources that unit represents."

The avatar remained kneeling over the Spook. "Don't," it said, so low I almost couldn't make it out over the alarm. "I'm *you*, you jackass. I don't want to die."

I laid my finger across the trigger. I *hated* this thing. It had my memories, my mannerisms, my secrets—and it was just a mass of wires and boxes, cobbled-together tech from the research of two or three geniuses. I hated it and wanted it gone, erased from the cosmos, like I thought it had been weeks ago. I didn't care if there were other copies of me out there, digital or avatar. I didn't care that Marin might wave his hands at any moment and make a chorus line of me appear, singing and dancing. I wanted *this one* gone.

My hand shook.

"I might still be useful, jackass," it said without moving its head. "He's not the only Pusher in this burg, right? And I look like the King Worm. That could come in handy, too. Don't be an idiot."

"Avery," Grisha said from the door behind me. "Listen to it. Destroy it later. There will be time."

I swallowed something hard and jagged, felt it travel all the way down into my gut, and slowly lowered the gun. "Fine," I said. I hated that the avatar *felt* something. That it wanted to continue to exist.

"Good," Grisha shouted, sounding out of breath. "You do not seem concerned about our situation, Avery."

I shrugged, sitting down on the floor with the avatar. "You'll either get the door open or you won't," I said. Turning, I saw the two Techies standing in front of the door with their arms hanging down loosely at their sides, studying the door as if they expected invisible ink to start fading in, reacting to the powerful radiation of their thoughts. "What the fuck," I said tiredly, extracting one of Ruberto's cigarettes and tapping it against the fancy case, "are you two *doing?*"

"We have no tools, Cates," Marko snapped without turning around. "We have *nothing*. You think we can just stand here guessing at all-clear gestures?"

"Hell," I said, struggling to my feet with the cigarette clenched between my teeth. Leg aching and lungs suddenly burning, I stumped over to the desk and kicked it over, stumbling backward and almost falling onto my ass. I walked over to it and bent down, taking two of the drawers in hand and lifting them up and out, tossing them aside and letting their contents spill everywhere. I repeated the process three times, dumping out the drawers, and then bent down and lifted the desk back into position. Its surface was one large screen, gesture controlled and currently a deep, angry red to reflect the alarm state of the facility.

I looked back at the Techies. "See if there are any *tools* in this shit, and I know I'm just the fucking trigger squeezer here, but maybe you should be trying to hack this terminal as well. There are *two* of you."

They looked at each other for a second.

"Fuck me," Marko growled as they both spun and trotted over to the desk. Grisha dropped to the floor and began sorting through the junk. "Try a Poison Push," the Russian said. "If the terminal is connected to standard SSF shadow net, it might catch an unsecured node you can drill through."

"We locked down that exploit three months ago," Marko muttered, shaking his head. "It was a fucking superhighway for Black Box Techies. I've got a dirty trick—"

"Try a flood attack to gain physical control of this terminal," Grisha shouted. "I don't think the systems in this prison have been updated in several months."

Marko shook his head. "Physical control, yes, but I've got a better way." He dropped to his knees and reached an arm into the desk itself, grunting as he suddenly tore a fistful of wires free, their plastic connectors empty and dangling. The desk went black with a flash. He pushed the ball of wires back in, his cheek pressed against the side of the desk as he strained to reach back inside its guts. "Fucking ports. They're pouring human brains into fucking Droids, but I'm still on the floor shoving jacks into fucking ports."

Grisha paused to look up at him. "Cold case attack," he said, sounding impressed.

"I've got it down to a science, my friend. Fifteen seconds and I'll be tunneling anywhere in the System."

Grisha sat up and wiped his brow. "Stop talking then, and do it."

Marko devolved into mumbling, straining with his head mashed up against the desk until he suddenly grunted a higher note and slumped back, his face ruddy and damp.

"Fucking ports," he repeated and then leaped up, studying the desk's surface and moving one hand in tiny, complex patterns. I could see the solid black had been replaced with what appeared to be solid red, but Marko seemed excited by this turn of events.

"So let me get this straight," I said, watching him. "You're going to open that door *there* with that terminal *here*."

Marko shook his shaved head, which sported a bald spot at the very top, usually hidden by his diffuse cloud of hair. "I'm going to open that door over *there*," he said with raised eyebrows, his eyes locked on the screen, "from a terminal in…Havana, it looks like. The boards in these dummies are all pulled from the same inventory, and most of them blank out their security pins when the juice gets yanked directly, and you usually have a few seconds to enter some root commands before the pins reload and go live again. If you manage that, you can start routing packets anywhere you want. So I'm going around the fucking world to reach that door right there."

I nodded. "I didn't ask for an explanation. I asked a question. The answer to which is, I guess, *yes?*"

He didn't answer, preferring to just frown at the screen and wave his hands.

I looked at Grisha. "You find a lighter in that mess?"

He spread his hands with a weak smile. "Sorry, Avery."

"Cock*sucker*," Marko suddenly hissed, snapping one hand up from the desk's surface screen as if he'd been burned. "Changed out the tables. Never mind."

"Avery," Grisha said, standing up slowly. "What are the chances, I wonder, that a dozen avatars will rush into this room if and when we open that door? Assuming they do not open it for us once they are in position?"

Could happen, Marin whispered. *I do not know the current head count on duty at this facility. Certainly there must be some excess capacity in the staff, and they are almost certainly being routed here as we speak.*

"Mr. Smith here," I said, gesturing at the avatar, "is going to be ready for that. You, on the door. Be ready for anything that comes through."

The avatar didn't move for a second and then hung its head and pushed up onto its feet, checking the gun with precise, memorized movements of its plastic hands. "You're just going to keep throwing me in front of the fucking train, aren't you?" it muttered, voice low and steady. Without looking at me, it turned away and stepped in front of the door, holding the gun loosely down in front of itself, as if it didn't care much if it managed to get it up in time or not. As if it was considering suicide. I stared at its back for a moment, remembering the weeks just after the Plague when I wandered New York in a fog, half expecting to be killed at any moment and not particularly caring. I remembered when the System Pigs finally came for me, their lists in hand, and how I just sat on the floor of Pick's old place, unconcerned about my fate.

"I'm in the node," Marko announced. "Trying an old backbone password I've had in my back pocket for fucking *years*...okay, I've got a low-level pathway in, trying to leap permissions—"

"Try spoofing the packet," Grisha suggested, sounding like he was ordering a cup of coffee.

Marko waved one hand behind him in irritation. "I know how to leap perms, goddammit," he muttered, his other hand moving independently, fingers and wrist in constant motion.

The alarm seemed to be speeding up, getting louder. We had a chance—with a skeleton crew of guards and Little Dick whispering in my ear, we had a real chance of getting to the surface—but with every second spent trapped in this fucking office with the cooling corpses of Cal Ruberto and his flunky our odds were dwindling. To keep myself from urging Marko on the only way I knew how, I clasped my hands behind my back.

"Perhaps—" Grisha started to say, and the alarm suddenly stopped.

"And *that's* how it's done!" Marko shouted in the sudden vacuum.

I looked up just as the door slid open, a shadowed figure framed against the corridor beyond, where emergency lights were flashing in a slow, steady rhythm. The avatar and I both snapped our guns up at the same time, as if we'd practiced it.

The avatar was blocking my line of sight, though, and dumb instinct made me hesitate, my finger slack on the trigger, while it fired twice.

The figure framed in the doorway dropped to the floor, was still for a moment, and then began flailing, a hoarse scream hitching out of it in unsteady breaths. The avatar stepped forward immediately and knelt next to the twitching form, starting to reach out a hand and then pausing. After a moment Dick Marin's face looked back at me, blank, mouth open.

"It's Marlena," it said.

XLII

BECAUSE YOU'RE A MISERABLE BASTARD

For a moment I just stood there, gun still up in front of me, the alarm still ringing in my ears like a phantom noise. It transformed, mutated, and became the hacking, dry-throat screech of the figure on the floor just outside the office. The avatar continued to stare at me slack faced, frozen between us, as if a fatal error inside its wiring had bricked it.

I walked slowly over to the door. I wanted to move faster, push myself into my patented unsteady lurch, but my body wasn't responding. She was screaming, kicking at the floor and flopping this way and that, her hands pressed against her belly, dark, rich blood bubbling through the laced fingers.

"You fucking shot me!" she screamed. "You fucking *shot* me! I'm shot!"

She looked angry. Her skinny, leathery body was all sinews and tendons pulled tight, ropes under her inked skin. She was pale, and her whole face was shadowed, making her look dead.

I stepped around the avatar, which was still kneeling there immobile, and realized I still had the gun in one hand. I let it drop slackly into my pocket, and she looked up at me, suddenly going limp as a fresh river of blood seeped up between her fingers. She squinted up at me, her face tight.

"What the fuck are you *doing* here?" I asked, pushing the words out with difficulty.

"Had to...was calling it a day...getting paid...came down to see the boss...." She swallowed with obvious difficulty, twitching. "Are you—shit, Avery, I—" She closed her eyes. "I fucking left you *twice*."

I turned. Grisha and Marko were crowding the door along with the avatar. Grisha nodded at me. "Avery," he said. "We must be moving." He looked past me, down at Marlena. "I am sorry, Lena."

"Ah, fuck it," she whispered, voice shaking. "I fucking always knew I'd go this way."

I nodded again, looking around at each of them, my head picking up its own strange momentum and just moving up and down, up and down. I saw her face peeking over the edge of the hover, felt her weight against me in the cot at night, heard her soft snore. "Right," I said. "Grab her. We're taking her with us."

"What!" Grisha barked suddenly.

"Oh, Ave," Marlena moaned, her voice still shaking. She'd stopped moving, and her hands were slack on her belly. A weak stream of blood leaked out of her, and she lay on the floor as if something heavy and invisible were sitting on top of her. "Oh, shit, I'm dead. I'm dead."

I kept nodding for some reason. "We all go, right? You," I said, pointing to the avatar. "Carry her. Be gentle."

"Fuck you," the avatar said through Dick Marin's mouth. Its face was working through several expressions at once. The thought that the machine might be feeling my emotions made me angry. "Tell me to be gentle."

"Avery." Grisha pushed between me and the avatar, getting closer than I normally would have allowed. I held myself back. "Avery," he said. "I am sorry for Lena, I am. I am sorry for *all* of us, yes? But she is dead. She will bleed out and die, and in the meantime we will be slow because of her. We should not bring her."

I smiled, lifting my Roon from its pocket and clicking back the hammer. "We're taking her."

The avatar had already knelt down next to her and was murmuring softly as it slid its hands under her skinny frame. The amount of blood that had pooled beneath her was startling—it looked like a deep, wet, black pool had opened up underneath her. "Damn right," it muttered.

This is touching, Marin whispered to me, *but foolish. But you've been astoundingly foolish many times in my experience, Avery, and somehow you manage to survive your own mistakes. When this little war calms down and I have the time and resources, I may do a little study on you and your roachlike ability to survive. In the meantime: out. You want to head back to the elevators. Take this corridor until it terminates.*

"Straight on," I announced. I knew Marin would keep his word—the letter of it, at least—and guide us to an escape route. Whether we'd actually be able to escape was another matter. "Grisha, take up the rear. Marko and . . . Mr. Smith, you're in the middle."

Marlena screamed as the avatar stood up in a smooth, fluid motion, and I clenched my teeth and started off. Grisha could follow or not as he wished—he was a big boy and could handle himself. I was getting out of this shithole, and when we were in the air and leaving it behind, I was going to push Dick Marin's avatar out the hatch and watch it hit the desert below.

Oh, Mr. Cates, you are full of mischief, aren't you?

The dry old woman's voice. I blinked. *Well, hello there, Dolores,* I thought, sweeping my eyes this way and that as I walked. The corridor was narrow and hot, with minimal lighting. We passed doors on either side, all shut tight, a diffuse red glow making them look forbidding. I assume it indicated they were locked down. *I thought maybe I'd lost the brain cells you were making your home in, Your Grace.*

I did not and do not approve of your course of action. But I suspect it may have some unexpected consequences for Director Marin. We have been cut off inside you for too long, and I believe he has miscalculated. He expects that Ruberto's death will result in the collapse of the government forces and an easy road to dominance for him. I suspect otherwise.

The corridor seemed endless, stretching out in front of us in red-tinged gloom. *Well, that's grand. Good for you. If you'll excuse me, Dolores, I'm fucking busy here.*

Wonderful silence filled my head as we walked, our rough breathing, Marlena's hitching cough, and the avatar's heavier than normal steps all we could hear. The corridor took a sudden turn to the left, just as suddenly ending at a bank of two elevators, each gleaming, new-looking steel and each lit up a soft, soothing green color.

"This is an uneasy coincidence," Grisha said sourly. "Everything *but* this elevator is locked down?"

I listened to Marin. "Mr. Wizard points out that this is an administrative level, and the only way up or down is via elevator. *Trust* me, Grisha. Please."

The Russian grunted but said nothing more. I wasn't used to having Grisha pushing back against me.

I started to gesture at the elevators. "All right, then—"

Without warning the elevator doors opened with a slight hiss of escaping air, and instantly I felt like something very large and very strong—tentacles, perhaps—had seized me from behind and begun to squeeze. My eyes bugged out of my face and my mouth opened, tongue wagging uselessly as I stared at Bendix and the round-faced kid, each puffy and bruised from our last encounter but still wearing the hell out of their fucking suits.

The kid was staring at me with yellow, slitted eyes, like he wanted to make my brain explode into greenish chunks, was just waiting for the order. Or for Bendix to turn his back for a moment.

"Now—" Bendix said.

From behind me the gunshot sounded like a bomb going off in the tight, murky corridor. A large red welt appeared on the round-faced kid's forehead, and his legs gave way, dropping him to the floor of the cab where his head bounced with a hollow clang. Bendix flinched and spun to stare down at the kid, and the tentacles disappeared.

I launched myself forward with everything I had, my bum leg twitching unreliably under my own weight and twisting me around so that I smacked painfully into the Spook off balance, my gun jammed between us and aimed approximately at my own liver. We grappled for a second or two as I strained every muscle I had, determined to get out, to get the *fuck out* of this fucking prison for once and for all. Bendix smelled bad up close. His breath in my ear was like rotten meat, and his skin smelled like old fish left in the sun.

He grunted, and I was pushed away from him violently, rising up and slapping into the ceiling of the elevator, making the whole car jitter and swing. I remained pinned against the roof of the elevator, my arms held stiffly up by my ears, pain shooting through my shoulders as I imagined my tendons creaking, the bones developing hairline cracks—the fucking Spook was going to break my arms.

"Mr. Bendix!"

It was Dick Marin's voice. It was Mr. Smith, down below, me inside a Marin body—I could see it, standing just outside the elevator, still holding the limp form of Marlena in its arms like she weighed nothing. Just behind it was Grisha, gun still held up by the avatar's ear, held stiffly and shaking slightly, caught in Bendix's invisible tendrils. I pushed as hard as I could against

Bendix's mind, but all I got was more sweat dripping off my nose.

"Mr. Bendix!" the avatar repeated. "Have you lost your fucking _mind?_"

Bendix didn't move. I remained pinned above him, staring down at his unmistakable bald spot, a glowing circle of pale skin in the midst of his dark hair.

"Drop that asset immediately, Mr. Bendix, or I will see to it that you are reclassified into our custodial department to spend your few remaining days on this planet shifting metric tons of fucking garbage around dumps. Do I make myself clear?"

The avatar cocked its head to one side suddenly, and a little thrill went through me. For a second it had looked just like the fucking Director of SSF Internal Affairs himself.

Bendix seemed to twitch below me. "What?"

"I'm going to have to review the entrance exams again, as it appears more morons than tolerable are slipping through," the avatar said. "I am ordering you to release Mr. Cates and cease being an _unbelievable pain in my ass._ Now, in small words to make sure we're clear: Do. You. Under. Stand?"

Everything was silence. I imagined I could hear Bendix's eyes swiveling in their sockets as he reviewed the scene. Grisha and Marko were still in their suits—disheveled and sweaty, but they'd both worked in the machine and knew the blank expression of the underling, the very still way you stood when more powerful people were in the room. They would pass. The avatar looked like Marin and talked like Marin—I'd spent enough time with the King Worm to do a five-minute impression. Except for the dying woman in its arms, it might have _been_ Marin, which was the ugly and unfathomable possibility Bendix was considering.

As if on cue, Marlena moaned. Bendix oriented on her, and I felt the invisible hand slacken just for a second, getting spongy as Bendix's attention wandered.

The avatar dropped Marlena, just letting her fall at its feet like a bundle it had been carrying too long, bringing its own gun up faster than I ever could, faster than I ever *had*, even when I'd been young and limber and reckless. It fired twice, its aim perfect, and Bendix slapped back against the rear of the elevator as I dropped from the ceiling, landing hard on my bad leg. A red spike of pain shot up into my brain, and everything went hazy for a moment.

When my sight returned, Dick Marin's face was hovering directly over me, smiling. I could feel the very slight vibration of the elevator as we rose upward out of the prison's guts.

"She's still alive," it said. "Had to be done."

"I'm still going to brick you when we're free of this place," I said softly, forcing myself to sit up. I still had my gun in my hand.

The avatar nodded. "I know. Because you're a miserable bastard. And because I'm *you*."

The elevator stopped, and I heard the doors behind me open with a soft, serpentine hiss, heat slapping me on the back like something solid. The avatar looked up from me and its expression blanked instantly.

"Oh, sh—" I heard Grisha say, and then the loudest noise I'd ever heard in my life swept into the elevator like a wave and smacked me back against the rear wall.

XLIII

IMAGINING THAT I ALWAYS GOT TO *DECIDE* WHO I KILLED WAS JUST ARROGANCE

I bounced off the wall with my own unexpected inertia, landing flat on my back, my head bouncing hard on the floor, making my vision swim again. The heat was suddenly a living thing in the elevator with us, the crank air we'd been living in a memory, and a hazy one at that. Blinking my stinging eyes, I twisted around, slapping my hands out for my lost gun.

"It's a fucking war zone," Marko said in a strangely level, calm voice.

I squinted into the bright, hot light just as several shining silver hovers flashed past the ragged hole above us. The elevator spilled out into a crawl space that had once been just deep enough for a normal man to stand up in, located just below the prison's common dorm room, which had been completely torn away. Scraps of the joists still remained, and a few sharp-edged pieces of cinder block jutted up here and there, but otherwise it was as if the old dorm area had been torn off cleanly, leaving behind the exposed subbasement.

Something smashed into a guard tower off in the distance, an explosion of rock and dust and smoke followed a second later by a high-pitched whine and the concussion. Another silver hover shot over us and through the dissipating cloud of dust that had once been the tower.

What the fuck, Marin hissed in my head, *is going on?*

Looks like things have slipped beyond the King Worm's control, Salgado whispered, somehow conveying glee. *He thought Ruberto controlled everything. Start a war and think you can control it? Foolish. Considering the function of this place, we have long wished to destroy it to slow down Marin's ability to transform his people into avatars. Ruberto vetoed this in favor of occupation, but it appears hotter heads have finally prevailed. Marin will not find it easy to rebuild his labs elsewhere.*

There was return fire from the ground, streaks of white soaring into the sky impossibly fast, intersecting with spiraling, swooping hovers a mile up. I'd never seen hovers move that way, zigzagging and rolling, darting through the air. The new military was setting the standard.

An explosion nearby made the whole world tremble again, and we all instinctively ducked our heads a little, crouching down inside the elevator. As I was considering the wisdom of remaining inside an elevator while the general area was being bombed into oblivion, Grisha turned and grabbed onto my coat, pulling me close to shout over the roar.

"Well, Mr. Wizard? We cannot *sit* here?"

Another bone-rattling explosion, and the elevator lights flickered off for a second, then back on again. We had to move quickly.

Well, Mr. Wizard? I thought. *We had a deal.*

If the hover is no longer in place or is damaged, Marin whispered back, *I cannot be held responsible. That said, I am an entity of my word. You will have to climb out of this debris and work your way around the rear of the installation.*

I nodded. "Up and out," I shouted, pushing Grisha toward the doors. I stood up, the elevator wobbling this way and that as

I shifted my weight, and pushed forward, taking the lead. Marlena hung limply in the avatar's arms, bleached and limp, her ink looking like something beneath her skin leeching out of her, some sort of terrible worm. I forced myself to look away and get moving.

"Up and *out?*" Marko shouted. "Do you see the fucking *impact craters?*"

"They're not looking for us," I shouted back, climbing into the ruined crawl space. "This looks like a shutdown operation—tear this fine complex off the earth, make sure it's unusable. You stay in one place, you *will* die. Keep moving. If I happen to leave you behind, Zeke, you will be on your own, okay?"

I heard him panting behind me as I grabbed onto a jutting piece of rebar—warm in my hands—and experimentally gave it my weight. "Okay?" he complained breathlessly. "Like that's fucking *news.*"

As my head rose above the edge of the foundation, the noise and dust slapped at me in sudden fury, making me squint and cough. Through the glare and haze I could see a lot of matériel moving around the prison grounds: hovers in the air—both the shiny new ones the civil government had been building and the dull gray ones the SSF flew—some of the strange solid-cell vehicles like the one Marlena had transported me in (with swivel turrets mounted on the back), and clumps of Stormers in yellowed desert uniforms, their faces hidden by huge black respirators like spiders clinging to their chins. As I hung there, stunned, two shining hovers swooped overhead, low, and just a few hundred feet away the yard began to erupt like a fountain of sandy dirt, a beautiful, perfect line of dancing earth. As the line passed through a clump of Stormers and their vehicle, I watched them each split apart in apparent silence, each of them suddenly dividing like worms, parts of them rising up and floating away. I didn't see any blood, but whether these were avatars or their blood just mixed in with the dirt and dust I couldn't tell. When the line of fire hit the car—a dull metal wedge on four huge black wheels, wires and conduit snaking all over it, the windshield black and blind looking—it split neatly down the middle, just flopping over to each side, two white uniforms strapped inside wriggling like maggots inside a dying fly.

Someone pushed me, hard.

"Avery," Grisha shouted into my ear, sounding washed out and far away. "*Go!*"

Do not fear, Dennis Squalor whispered from somewhere in the back of my brain, the dark and unmapped portion where all the fucking ghosts had taken up residence. *You exist with me now. You have been called home. You are eternal.*

A wide, flat spike of terror suddenly landed in my chest, and I pulled myself up and out with a grunt. Marin began whispering directions to me, and I ran according to his instructions. There was nothing else to do—the noise was constant, and the ground that had once been Chengara's yard kept erupting, spewing up chunks of dirt and rock, the ground beneath my feet lurching this way and that, threatening to roll me. Closing my eyes, I forced myself to stop and spin, dancing back a few clumsy steps as I grabbed a quick glance. The avatar, with Dick Marin's face locked in a mask of concentration that looked completely wrong in his features, was right behind me, Marlena bouncing in its arms. Behind it by a few steps were Marko and Grisha; the Russian had one hand in Marko's coat, urging the other Techie forward. Grisha did not look happy, and I was reminded that he'd followed me around the System, almost killing me twice, simply because he felt betrayed.

I spun again and found myself facing a cluster of Stormers double-timing right at us. I brought my gun up instantly, but they ignored me, splitting apart to hustle around me in a jangly, eerily voiceless cloud, holding their shredders in front of them like totems. They were past me in seconds, a sour cloud of cops disappearing in our wake, completely uninterested in us.

Left, Avery, Marin suggested. *See the hover pad? Better hurry before some Augmented army jock up there needs a fresh target and spies it. Fucking mutants have pretty good eyesight even at that speed, I understand.*

Mutants or Droids—that was our fucking future choice. I swerved as best I could, sweat dripping off me. I considered shedding some clothing, but I had no idea where I was going or if I'd be able to replace anything, and there was no time, no fucking time. Something huge and angry burst a few dozen feet away, the shock wave almost lifting me off my feet, hot dirt raining down on me as I skidded and stumbled, keeping my feet by sheer dumb luck.

The hover pad was just a square of cement set into the desert behind the prison. The walls had hidden it from the prisoners, but there it was, a slab of cracked stone with a single, small hover sitting on it, undisturbed, like a piece on a game board. Dragging my bad leg along like it belonged to someone else entirely, I huffed and puffed, looking up in time to see two hovers collide in the air, both spinning off into wild new trajectories that had the ground in common, both adding a keening new whine to the jelly-thick noise around us that made me hunch my shoulders and put my head down. Fuck dodging the rubble—just keeping my legs moving through the chaos was taking every shred of my will and energy.

As we got closer, the hover resolved into Ruberto's luxurious state boat, gleaming and beautiful, sleek and light. My head began to swim with memories of his wet bar, the thick carpet on the floor, and the smell of that high-quality crank air, the kind they had to pump out of the fucking arctic circle and compress and then feed into the cabin, fresh and cold.

The bulk of the chaos was now behind me, and I imagined us bare and obvious against the ground, specks running like ants—at any moment we would be noticed again and scooped up, or crushed. A strange exhilaration filled me, a lightness and cheer. It didn't matter. I'd made it a lot further than I'd ever imagined. For years now I'd been on the run, desperate, and if the cosmos reached down and crushed me right at this moment, well, at least I wouldn't ever be handcuffed on a fucking hover again.

The hatch was open, the elegant folding stairs deployed. We were in the middle of a desert in a prison with exactly three prisoners—theft had obviously not been much on Ruberto's mind.

I crashed into the steps, my leg giving way, and avoided a painful fall by clinging to the railing and swinging myself around. The avatar was on my heels and knelt down on the concrete, setting Marlena down gently.

"Grisha," I panted, recalling Marko's handling of the hover during the Plague, "get this thing online."

Grisha nodded, his face flushed red, his mouth hanging open loosely. He pushed Marko up onto the steps wordlessly, staggering up behind him. The Techies disappeared into the hover. I closed my eyes for a moment, breathing hard, my whole body burning. The noise sharpened, and I could pick out the sound of small arms, the whine of shredders, the random, shuddering explosions, the soup of displacement roaring behind it all. It was as if the whole world was being torn apart, starting right here in the middle of fucking bone-bleached nowhere, and it was soothing for a moment.

With effort, I opened my eyes to the painfully bright sun and pulled myself back upright, swinging myself onto the bottom step. I turned back to the avatar.

"Well—" I started to say, and froze.

It was kneeling over Marlena, who lay there limp and pale and very, very dead, her open eyes staring up blankly. The avatar kept rubbing its hands on its legs, over and over again, and when it looked up at me, Dick Marin's face was blank, slack, like it had just come off the assembly line in the factory.

"She's dead."

I nodded, stepping down from the steps as the hover swelled into life behind me, the low buzz of its displacement absorbed by the rest of the noise and lost. I stood over them.

For a moment we were both still. I thought of her turning to me in the yard and saying *Wanna fuck?* like most people said hello. I remembered the knife dancing across her knuckles. I didn't feel anything. I'd given up feeling bad for the people I managed to kill by accident. I killed people, it was what I did, and imagining that I always got to *decide* who I killed was just arrogance.

Of course, sometimes I did get to decide. I stared into those fake eyes, Marin's fake eyes.

The avatar and I both moved for our guns. It beat me. It beat me by a second, maybe two, more than enough to kill me. We both pulled our guns, and it had me easy before I had a good bead on it, and it didn't shoot. I had ordered it not to hurt me, after all. Its shoulders slumped and it turned the gun a little, staring at it.

"Well, look at that," it said.

I squeezed the trigger. The shot was swallowed by the maelstrom, and the avatar's head exploded in silence, snapping back from its neck and dragging its body after it for a few inches. It twitched once and then lay still, a small puddle of white coolant springing to life beneath its head.

I turned and holstered the gun, climbing up the steps slowly, taking my time, daring the cosmos to shoot me in the back. As I pulled myself into the beautiful cabin, Marko came skidding out of the cockpit, saw me, and gave me a hasty thumbs-up, spinning around and dashing back, out of sight.

I leaned down and pulled up the steps, folding them into place and locking them down. The hover slowly began to rise, smooth and calm, Grisha's hand competent on the stick. I stared down at her, and as we rose the wind started to lick into the cabin like invisible flames, growing stronger and more insistent. She seemed to stare back at me, her face frozen, her eyes watching as I rose up into the air, as I left her behind in Chengara.

"Fucking hell," I whispered. My hands twitched, and I thought that Marko was lucky he wasn't standing next to me.

Just as she receded into a dot on the ground below and I'd raised my hand to gesture the hatch closed, an enormous sound in the distance brought my eyes back up to the horizon, where a series of flashes trickled left to right, each slowly forming into a brief fireball and then a puffy, seemingly frozen mushroom-shaped cloud.

Well, shit, I thought. *That's fucking strange.*

EPILOGUE

KID, I'M NOT A *COP*

The sun didn't bother me anymore, and besides, it wasn't the melting-flesh levels of hot I'd come to know so well out in the desert, out in Chengara's yard. It was just hot, and the sun wasn't an angry orange welt; it was just fiery yellow and sinking fast behind me. I'd been sweating all day, but then I'd been sweating steadily for the last few weeks, it felt like, and I couldn't even smell myself anymore.

My boots were about to just split open and slide off my feet, exhausted, and my coat had seen better days. I wasn't used to being outside so much—I'd grown up in the city, in crowded streets of apparently permanent buildings looming over you, and even the past few years of constant kidnapping, imprisonment, and hover flight had always had a roof over my head. Shaking Grisha and Marko's hands and making my way from the spot where the hover had finally crashed, plowing a deep furrow into sandy dunes of scrub brush and rocks, had been weeks of sleeping out in the open, being rained on, sunbaked, and starving.

The only thing that had saved me were the towns.

I'd always imagined a big expanse of nothingness stretching out across the country—imagined that most of the System, in fact, was just vast emptiness with a few big cities you'd heard of.

Staggering eastward from the crash site, I'd stumbled on these old, rotting towns, abandoned for decades, dotting the countryside. The first one I'd come across had been called Grafton, or so a sloppy sign on the side of a beaten track had proclaimed. It had been a few ancient, sagging old buildings, the oldest things I'd ever seen, set in a soupy ocean of mud. At first I'd assumed it was just empty, but I'd found five or six people living there, escapees from cities with stories about the civil war, about their homes being bombed into splinters and System Pigs executing entire neighborhoods to save them the trouble of figuring out if they were dangerous or not. They were huddled in a one-room building they'd put some sort of roof on, eating game they'd killed and generally resembling Mud People. Initially they'd been terrified of me—twin army-issue Roons in hip holsters and the good cheer inspired by a few days out in the open had made me less jovial than normal—but then they'd been kind of happy to see me. I had some news, after all, and if I wasn't going to shoot them all and steal their crap—and the word *crap* had been *invented* to describe their possessions—then they were pretty happy to let me get in out of the rain and have a bowl of some of the most disgusting meat I'd ever seen. I'd been able to trade about a million yen for a handful of nutrition tabs, too, though they'd tried to insist on seeing what I might have to trade first before accepting the cash.

Since then, I'd come across two or three other places like Grafton—old places that had been empty since before Unification, now filled with a dozen or two filthy, unhappy refugees from the war. They were all scratching out an existence and rebuilding where they could. Most of them had created little governments, electing mayors or governors or, in one tiny spot boasting a population of thirteen, a duke. They were mixtures of people, by and large, white and black and tan, speaking different languages. Some had been friendlier than others, but I'd survived them easily enough.

This shit wouldn't last. The System was in chaos; the civil war had gotten savage and even in the cities that were still in one piece—according to the good citizens of Shitholes, America—the System Cops didn't have much time for keeping order anymore. But someone was going to win the fucking war, and when they did, they'd start paying attention to the shitholes.

So, I'd stayed long enough to dry off and buy what I could, get some news (a few mobile Vid screens had made their way to the shitholes), ask my one question, and get some sleep. It was tiring, moving from place to place, baking in the day and freezing at night, but I wanted to get back to familiar surroundings. New York was, by all reports, an impact crater these days, but at least I knew something about it, and if anyone had hung on and survived in it through the Plague and the war, it was my people.

The sign outside this particular shithole had read ENGLE-WOOD. I had no idea where I was, and it was fucking amusing that someone thought they knew where they were enough to give it a name. Or maybe, like with most of the shitholes, the place had already had a name, faded and forgotten, dusted off by refugees and adopted from the past. Why not? People liked to think that places had always had names, had always had a spot on the map.

Englewood was a neat little collection of sagging buildings arranged on either side of a wide, cracked memory of a street. Some of the structures had fallen into themselves, just sighing down into a comfortable doze, but some were still sturdy looking, and a few plumes of white smoke here and there attested to another population of grubby survivalists. I pushed my coat back to give me access to the Roons, my heartbeat speeding up as I took in the layout of the place, searching for the shadows and empty buildings that might be my only path of retreat if things turned ugly.

As I stepped from the brush onto the wide street, which just began as if someone had been building a road and then just decided to stop, the quiet brought the hairs on my arms up on end. My leg ached as I limped, squinting through the late-day twilight, my skin itching under my dirty, stiff clothes. The place was obviously inhabited by *someone* — aside from the neat smoke pumping out of some of the buildings, the street was packed and swept, and some of the buildings sported fresh repairs that stood out against the sun-cracked originals. I could hear the scrape of dry dirt under my pathetic boots, and I laid my right hand on the butt of one gun, a familiar sour rush of adrenaline flooding me.

Then I stopped. One of the repaired buildings, out of which a thin trickle of white smoke rose to the sky, had a new sign propped up against the rotted, dangerous-looking front steps. HOMMAAD BOOSE it read in bright red, streaky paint. Or blood, who the fuck knew?

I considered, mouth watering. If these assholes had something resembling liquor on hand, I was prepared to kill for it.

I walked over to the building, eyes everywhere. The interior was dark, with no door in the not-quite-square doorway. I had a sense that someone was inside, and I hesitated: I didn't know the building, whether there was a back way out or if there were people who would crowd in behind me if I entered. I took the time to walk around the whole place, slowly, turning frequently, my hand still on the butt of the gun. I didn't see anything threatening. There was a back door, hanging loose and useless on hinges that were more rust than metal at this point — the sort of door that satisfyingly turned to dust when you slammed into it — and as I circled back around to the front, I figured if I was willing to kill for a stiff drink, I might as well be willing to die for one. Slowly, trying to will my old eyes to adjust quickly, I stepped up and into the place.

It smelled like smoke and dust inside, dry and musty. I could see immediately that someone had been cleaning the place up—the floor was old and rotten but had been cleared of debris and swept sometime in the last century. Along the back wall was a makeshift bar—just a collection of barrels and crates with some planks set on top. All around the perimeter of the room was the junk that had once clogged the floor: piles of wood, glass, bits of metal here and there. None of it meant anything to me, and none of it looked at all recent.

Behind the "bar" was a tall, thin kid, half my age or less, awkward looking. He had shaggy brown hair that was hanging in his eyes and the largest Adam's apple I'd ever seen. It bobbed up and down inside his throat like he was trying to swallow a mouse. His eyes were squinty, narrow and shifty looking, but the way he gripped the edge of his bar told me he was afraid. He worked his throat a bit, watching me approach, and finally managed a full-on swallow and cleared his throat.

"You real, mister?"

I frowned at him.

"Human?" Before I could reply, his eyes rolled up and down me, and he seemed to decide the answer for himself, nodding. "We ain't got nothing to steal, mister," he squeaked.

I shook my head. "I'm not a thief, kid."

Squeaky blinked at me several times rapidly. "Oh," he said, as if I'd just spoken gibberish he couldn't possibly understand.

I nodded. "You sell liquor here?" He stared at me for a few moments, so I jerked a thumb over my shoulder. "The sign outside?"

He blinked again, and once he'd started it seemed difficult for him to stop. "Oh! Yes, uh, that is, I make some pretty good stuff in the back. Trade for it, mostly."

I nodded again, stepping forward. "I've got yen."

He watched me approaching with some alarm. "Yen? Uh, we don't, uh...well, I guess." His eyes lighted on my hand resting on the gun for a second and then whipped back up to me. "Uh, I guess we can take yen. Hiller makes his way north to the city sometimes, and yen still means something there." He squinted a little, suddenly getting some pluck. "It would take, uh, a *lot* of yen, though."

I nodded a third time, turning to scan behind me briefly. Yen was only worth anything by the fucking metric ton these days. "How much? Do you get many folks through here?"

He shook his head. "Some. One or two a month maybe, usually comin' from Vegas. They fucking melted Vegas into the desert, you know? Not a fucking building standing." He considered as I leaned against the bar, my coat pushed aside to keep one gun clear. "I'd say two million yen a glass," he finally said and then started blinking again. He was tense, and I figured if I made any sudden moves he'd probably jump six feet into the air.

"Fine," I said, fishing in a pocket. I'd gotten a new credit dongle from a corpse I'd stumbled across in the first week of wandering, black and bloated and sheltered in a little copse of brush. Dongles were easy enough to wipe and reprogram—all you needed was your fingerprint and your code, and I was surprised to find out how much of the fortune given to me by Dick Marin himself in exchange for destroying the Electric Church was still there. Worth much, much less, but still there. I handed the dongle over to him, and he stared at it for a moment, as if he couldn't remember what it was.

"Oh! Right. Hold on. I've got a reader here somewhere. I'll get your drink first."

He dashed into the back, and for a second I wondered if I'd just been robbed by the worst thief to ever walk the earth. A moment later he returned, though, juggling a dirty-looking jar filled with cloudy liquid, an even dirtier-looking glass, and an old, battered credit reader. He slapped the glass onto the bar and placed the jar next to it, indicating with a jerk of his head that I should help myself. I unscrewed the greasy cap and gave the stuff an experimental sniff, burning off a few nose hairs in the process. I poured the thick stuff into the glass, half expecting it to dissolve, and felt a stab of joy. *This* was almost like old times. If it turned me blind, it would be *exactly* like old times.

"What's your name, then?" the kid said, scurrying back to return my credit dongle. I'd bought a drink and failed to murder him in the first three minutes, so now he was friendly and relaxed. "You looking for a place to settle in?" He looked at my guns again. "Be warned: we got some trouble here, you know?" He looked back at me. "Fucking Monks and avatars. Fucking Droids with brains, harassing us."

I nodded. I'd heard tales—just like some people had hit the wilderness trying to stay one step ahead of the war, there were old, broken-down Monks and your occasional damaged cop avatar wandering around, too, generally murdering people and burning shit down. "Cates," I said. "Avery Cates. Not from around here. Not staying, either." I swallowed the stuff in the glass and had to stand still for a moment fighting my gag reflex. It tasted like the kid had made it from his old underwear, just squeezing out the juice into a jar. But it burned nicely and settled into a terrible, sour ball in my stomach, lighting up fires that had been dormant for too long. I gave him a smile and poured myself a second glass.

The kid held out his hand suddenly. It had been so long since anyone had been polite to me; I just stared at it for a moment before taking it carefully. He pumped it up and down exactly three times.

"Glad to meet you, then, Cates. You sure about not staying? We could use a…a…cop, I guess. A sheriff or something. Someone who knows how to handle one of those."

He nodded his chin at the Roon at my side. I shook my head and picked up the glass. "Fuck, kid, I'm not a *cop*." I studied the cloudy liquor for a moment and then looked back at him. "I'm just passing through. Actually, I'm looking for someone; maybe you saw someone like him. Short guy, almost a fucking midget. Old. Older than me, if you can believe it. Has kind of a funny accent sometimes. Sometimes goes by the name Michaleen Garda. Sometimes" —I toasted my glass —"he goes by the name Cainnic Orel."

APPENDIX

Final Audio Diary Entry of Lieutenant Thomas Kittinger-98, retrieved from Site ID CH-099-U7 (Chengara Penitentiary, North American Department)

Joint Council File #904TY9
Reviewed by: T. Greene, Joint Council Undersecretary

Background: Despite its widespread and involuntary use within the System Security Force, evidence indicates that a balance is sought between servitude—programmed limitations and hardwired prohibitions—and free will within the avatars being created by the SSF. Reports indicate that Director Marin, himself now fully digital, fears that some indefinable aspect of humanity is lost when the brain is digitized and that this "uncanny lapse" will result in a loss of creativity and inspiration-type thought. As a result efforts are made to leave avatars within the SSF—and now, as the program expands, within the general population—as much freedom of thought and action as possible while still maintaining the control coding required by Director Marin.

This audio diary was retrieved from level four of the Chengara installation while army forces held it briefly earlier this year. A records search indicates that Lieutenant Kittinger was a model officer in the SSF, once posted to New York and fast-tracked for promotion. Subsequent to involuntary processing into a digital intelligence housed inside an Augmented self-powered HUD-AUG-9 unit, however, his performance has become erratic and his failure rate abnormally high, eventually leading to all of his units in active service being posted to guard duty at Chengara.

He is the only digitized officer of the SSF known to have kept a diary. This is the final entry made; other entries are still classified T-1 and can only be accessed by Undersecretary Ruberto.

I wanted to go into medical. I'm not sure why or if I'd ever have had the fucking brains for it, but when I was a kid I always wanted to get into surgery or something. Cut things out of people, see how things work. I wanted to peel open some guy's chest and yank out the ribs and see all that shit inflating and whirring, moving. I liked the idea that we were all just parts, like a hover — you could pull a displacement blade out of one hover and jam it into another. I wanted to make a person from spare parts.

I knew I wasn't going to test into medical, though. The sciences in general were tough; everyone knew that. No one could tell you why or what you were supposed to be good at, but everyone knew the things you had to be good at to muster into anything were unexpected. There were stories. Like a kid who could draw anything, just glance at something and sketch it perfectly, like a human digital recorder, testing into CS8, government services, so he could sit behind a desk all fucking day hating life. Or a girl who could run marathons, just hours a day on the treads without even breaking a sweat, testing into PO9, media, and becoming one of those lame talking heads on the Vids. Everyone knew it made no fucking sense, or it made sense in a brilliant way you had to be a genius to comprehend. This was the conventional wisdom.

No one could tell me what I had to test out on in order to get into medical, but whatever it was I was pretty sure I didn't have it.

I didn't have anything. I lay on my cot in the UA dorm the night before my testing week and stared at the ceiling, heart pounding. Some kids tried to prepare. They studied and practiced. If they were good at something, they practiced that. If they wanted to be good at something, they practiced that. The other wisdom was, since you never knew what would muster you into something, the best you could do was be really good at something so at least if you mustered into an unexpected kind of field, you would muster in at a high level. Even making it into medical would suck if I was only rated thirteen or fourteen. That meant mopping up blood and doing injections all fucking day.

Everyone knew how to game the tests, but you sort of knew no one really knew.

I can't remember anyone's name. That's weird, but they fucking cooked my brain making me into this fucking piece of tech, so who knows. Who knows if any of my memories are real. Or if they're correct. For all I fucking know it's all bullshit. Maybe they just create memories for you; maybe we all have the same fucking memory of testing week, planted in there. I'll never know. But I can't remember anyone's name from the dorms. Lived there for twelve years, with mostly the same kids, and I can remember most of them physically but not their names. I don't know if that's because of the processing or not. I'd never tried to remember them before, not for twenty years.

I remembered their bodies, though. I remembered the black kid, skinny and taut, always in motion, always fucking kicking his legs and swinging his arms, always bopping around. He was my roommate for five years, wanted to be be I5, security. I always told him he was too goddamn scrawny for I5. When I tested into I5, he didn't say a word to me, just turned away, kept walking. I never saw him again. Five fucking miserable years later, I was in fucking Manhattan, taking orders from some fat sweaty asshole named Scagnetti, breaking heads in Chelsea. I never saw him again. He tested into G1. General. He was going to be working in sewers or morgues or digging ditches, probably all of it, every shit job that Droids couldn't handle for some reason.

I told myself I was lucky to have tested into something respectable. A lot of kids thought testing into the I Cat was the best possible result — be a cop, see the world, get to shoot bad guys. Category I was tricky. IE6 *you got to wear a uniform, stand around all day, useless. IE4 and, rumor had it, you got taken away immediately and were never seen again. I tried to figure out what I'd done, what part of the tests I'd somehow aced to get made a cop. There was one where they showed us pictures of flowers, hundreds of us sitting in a big room with a big Vid on one wall. Like fifty, a hundred pictures of flowers, all kinds, all colors. And then we had to write five thousand words on any subject, as long as it was coherent and from a first-person point of view. I remembered being alone in a room with a creepy guy with these big, round eyes, just fucking huge eyes bulging out of his head. Sitting across from him, and he would hold up these black cards, nothing printed on them, and stare at me, and I was supposed to say any word I wanted. I kept throwing random words at him, but he never reacted. He never said anything or wrote anything down. He just went to the next card without even looking at it.*

I remember climbing ropes in a big gym, wearing these really comfortable red pants they issued us. I was strong and I enjoyed climbing; a lot of the kids hated it and didn't do well. Was that it? I climbed fucking ropes well so make me a cop? I'd never understood.

Halfway through, word got passed around that a bunch of kids were breaking out, running away. An excited buzz went through the whole dorm: this was exciting shit. We all chattered about it. Just deciding not to test? Everyone had been tested. We had no idea how you lived if you hadn't tested. Where would you go, what would you do?

The more I thought about it, the more excited I became. I'd never thought about it before. It had simply never occurred to me, to just walk the fuck away. Holy shit. It was like I'd spent my whole life treading water, and then someone came by and said, Hey, look, there's actually no water. You're free. *I was the only one from my floor who showed up that night, sneaking away and walking to the shadowed commons outside the dorm. There wasn't much by way of security—we were kids. I knew it was possible, it would be easy, just pick a remote direction and start walking.*

Looking back, I wonder if maybe letting a few dozen kids sneak away is part of the whole plan.

There were about a dozen of us, maybe a few more. We stood around nervously. We'd never left the dorm—not on our own, unsupervised, not without a destination and a hover. Not without intending to come back a few hours or days later. One or two of the kids tried to organize, to issue instructions, but no one was really listening, and finally one kid just stood up and walked off. The rest followed, alone or in twos, just wandering into the night, until I was the only one left. I was breathing hard, just standing there, but I couldn't see what good it would do. If you weren't tested, what were you? How did you live? Who fed you?

After a while, I went back up to my room and fell asleep.

Every night, exhausted, we sat limp in our rooms or in the hallways and tried to make sense of it. We'd been hearing about testing week our whole lives. No one had ever really explained it to us, but we knew this was where we started everything else.

My roommate, the night before scores were released, you could tell he knew what was waiting for him when they published the lists. We sat there in our room exhausted, talking in slow motion, one of us saying something and the other responding ten minutes later.

"Tomorrow's forever, man," he said to me. "We wake up tomorrow, we find out who we're gonna be. Forever."

I considered this. I remember sitting there chewing over the word forever. It didn't mean anything. I'd been a kid in the dorm forever. There was no way you could change that.

"Forever," he repeated a moment later, and it sounded like sand hitting the floor. He never spoke another word in my presence.

I was a good cop. At first I almost liked it, and I wanted to succeed. I didn't want to wash out and get recategorized. Recat was the worst—it never went well for people. It was interesting; a lot of kids thought they just handed you a gold badge and a license to kick ass and bought you a nice suit. But it was a lot of training first, five years on Desolation Island. At first I almost liked it. It was really physical. In year two we started on SFN Law Codes and I hated it, but passing grade in Law

Code was pretty low so I managed it, but I hated it. I thought maybe we'd get back to learning interesting stuff, but it was all downhill from there, and I hated it ever since. I hated crowd control techniques; I hated the rallies where they shouted at us how fucking incredible we were; I hated being awake for a week straight to prove how hard we were.

It's funny. Not a single one of my friends from the dorm mustered into I5. There were five hundred kids in my dorm. I didn't know every one of them well, but I'd know them if I saw them. I never saw a single one ever again.

I'd never cursed like this when I was a kid. None of us did; we knew the words, but it just wasn't something we did. Desolation Island taught me how. The men who ran it, our teachers, our commanding officers, they didn't like us. We weren't their kind when we arrived, and they didn't like us at all, and they abused us from the first moment. Looking back, it was obvious: they were shaping us, because we all quickly figured out that you could behave more like them and then they were easier on you. The more like them you acted, the more they liked you. On my first day I'd said please *and called them all* sir *and they'd called me a fucking faggot and boxed my ears until I had a persistent hum in my head. When I started telling them to fuck themselves, they still boxed my ears, but they did it with a wink and a jolly smile and started calling me Kitty.* Hey, Kitty, get your pale ass over here and break down this weapon.

They were still calling me names and beating the shit out of me on a regular basis, but now it was with smiles, and you started to feel like you were part of something, that we were all in on it. That these guys had been beaten up and called names and that someday you yourself would be banging some kid's head into the ground, yelling at them to man up.

I got posted to New York. Prestigious. They only post the best to places like New York or Moscow or Islamabad or Bogotá. And I was real good at it, for a while. You felt good, working connections and paying attention, noticing something and making sure it didn't blow up into something bigger. You felt like you were making a difference, even if it was kind of a rough and disreputable job. But I could handle the occasional bullshit you had to shovel because I really thought I improved things, one bust at a time.

So I dealt with the security details for VIPs who made me want to assault them instead of protect them, spoiled assholes who barked orders at me and called me "chum." I put a few shells in a few ears on verbal orders from majors who appeared out of luxury hovers to pass the word, and I didn't feel good about it, but I told myself there was a good reason for it, somewhere. I watched my partners and squad mates getting rich, shaking down just about everyone, a hundred yen here, a thousand there. Bodyguarding rats. And I walked some really bad people in the front door of Rockefeller and out a back door, untouched, unprocessed, and took the bracelets off them and smiled at them instead of kicking them in the balls until they cried and charging them up the ass with a whole fucking bouquet of violations. I did all these things and got sicker and sicker about it, but I still clung to what I thought the job was. I did it. I did it all and laughed with Miggs and Heller and Mage and got blind drunk every night, roaring, trying to make enough noise. But all I ever heard was that kid saying forever like it was a lead weight he was spitting out.

And then Heller disappeared. For a while. For two weeks. We'd been partnered for a few years, and I'd gotten used to the psychopathic bastard and his foul mouth. Got used to him hurting the rats just so he could say he'd marked them. He didn't want to kill anyone, he wanted to mark them all, scar them, be able to look at the lilliputians and know that they'd met him before. I'd gotten used to him, and then one day he was gone, on unspecified leave. Un-fucking-specified leave. The man hadn't so much as taken a lunch in all the years I'd worked with him. He enjoyed breaking heads too much.

And then he came back.

Heller was still Heller. He still told everyone they were a fucking cunt at least six times a day. He still enjoyed breaking heads. My skin crawled standing next to him. The way he sometimes seemed to get orders out of thin air, to make decisions that were completely fucking *irrational, to sometimes use phrases I'd never heard him use—none of it made any sense, but I started to drink on the job. Fuck it. I woke up hungover and started in immediately so I'd be humming nicely by the time our shift started, and two hours in when Heller was tracking down some Taker who had information on the location of a political POI, muttering under his breath like always and terrorizing everyone, I was hammered and didn't notice how he was one fucking step off from normal.*

Every day was a grind, every day was a descent. Rumors started to float about cops disappearing, coming back. Rumors were everywhere, but I barely heard them. And then one night I got woken up at three in the fucking morning by six identical assholes in nice suits with Internal Affairs.

I got killed on my first day after being reassigned to Chengara. Stupid. I'd been wandering around, in a fucking haze, going through motions like they were programmed into me. I didn't know why I was doing half the things I was doing; they just bubbled up from some dark center, moving my limbs. I hadn't gotten around to worrying about it, because it was the only thing that kept me moving. I'd been kidnapped and knocked out, and when I'd woken up I was in an artificial body and some smiling, plump woman with a slight German accent—so slight it was maddening—was telling me to smile and be cheerful, because I was fucking immortal now. So I was on autopilot, somehow knowing everything I needed to know about being assigned to Chengara. I knew where everything was; I knew the routines, the schedules, everything. Even though I'd never been there before.

Two of the inmates started snarling, and without thinking, I stepped between them. The one in front of me tried to shiv me in the belly, but I knocked the taped-up blade from his hand with a neat snap of my arm I was pretty sure I wasn't capable of performing. Before I could goggle at that, everything went black, and I woke up back in one of the labs underground. The other shithead had stabbed me in the fucking head.

No harm done. The same smiling woman greeted me cheerfully and sent me back to duty. Assured me that over-the-air backups meant I had only lost a second of memory, at most, and would suffer no ongoing problems. I was immortal. Endless. Forever.

The only thing even approaching normal was arrivals. That duty was at least slow-paced and continuous. You woke up on the elevator with a half dozen others, instantly alert and alive, and then you made sure there were no slowdowns or fuckups with debarking the assholes from the train. A good hour, maybe more. I felt like I got to think a little. When I rotated off of arrivals, it was a fucking nightmare: waking up in the elevator, you could hear the shouting, and then we were out in the yard, a fucking riot, orange jumpsuits everywhere, sniper fire going off, and it was just old-school shit, beating them back with Tasers.

Standing Order Thirteen instructed us not to kill unless necessary. That made it a little challenging. Though you could game the definition of challenging *if you tried hard enough.*

Then, back in the elevator, and blink—you're out again. And you woke up some random time later and did it all again. Asleep, kicking ass. Asleep, kicking ass. No transition, nothing in between.

At arrivals, I got to chat a little. They said working a normal shift detail was better, because you almost got to be normal. They said that at first Internal Affairs returned processees to their original detail because they thought it would help people cope with the transition, but it turned out that while it did help the processed get their bearings, it freaked everyone else out, so until the majority of the force had been processed they'd started rotating everyone to new duty when their number got pulled.

Well, shit. So now I'm stuck in this shithole. I've got fifteen minutes a day to myself, when I'm lucky. They say they have to switch us on for a little bit every day or we get disoriented. They need us to turn on immediately, so we get these fifteen-minute windows to percolate and clear out the cobwebs, and I use them recording this…diary, I guess. I listen to yesterday's first. I say the same thing all the time. But I still say it. I listen to myself saying it, and then I say it again, because nothing else ever happens. My life is all past now.

Yesterday, and the day before, and the day before, I Tasered some old man by the dole until he pissed himself and passed out. This is who I am. Forever.

Acknowledgments

When my Future Self emerged from his homebrew time machine in my devastated living room back in 1987 and told me to write this book, I was dubious but took notes anyway because it seemed like the right thing to do. Plus my Future Self was pretty drunk and belligerent, waving around a silver batonlike thing that might have been some sort of death ray. The notes remained locked inside a fireproof strongbox for twenty years until that fateful day when my publisher sent a team of thugs to my home to extract signatures on new publication contracts, and I needed an idea fast. I am quietly assured by my Future Self that the publication of this book will lead me to world domination.

Along the way, many folks have helped: First and foremost, my **beautiful wife, Danette,** who alternately kicked my butt when it needed kicking and dressed my wounds when they threatened the writing progress. She remains the most perfect wife, partner, and motivator known to modern science.

My agent **Janet Reid** continues to feign amusement with my ways and negotiates the heck out of everything my name appears on, often appearing in a flash of purple smoke anytime I reach for a pen to sign something. This is sometimes awkward in restaurants when the check comes, though it makes fleeing from expensive meals a little easier.

My editor **Devi Pillai** always starts our conversations by telling me how great I am, which I appreciate, and then starts talking, and somehow by the end of the conversation I have agreed to write more books for her, wash her car, pick up her dry cleaning, and scrub her shower tiles. These books would not be as good as they are without her help and patience, not to mention her ability to control me with her thoughts.

Everyone else at **Orbit Books** for putting up with me and for doing a fantastic job of putting these books together and then convincing folks to purchase them.

And of course, I have to thank everyone who bought a copy of *The Electric Church* or *The Digital Plague*, without whom I'd just be another crazy man on the street corner, waving a stained and torn manuscript about as I drunkenly demand that everyone pay me a dollar.

Finally, if not for the quick reflexes and fearlessness of the world-famous **Lili Saintcrow,** this book would likely never have been written, as I would likely have perished in a Russian prison, disavowed even by my own government. Thanks, Lili!

extras

www.orbitbooks.net

about the author

Jeff Somers was born in Jersey City, New Jersey. After graduating from college, he wandered aimlessly for a while, but the peculiar siren call of New Jersey brought him back to his homeland. In 1995 Jeff began publishing his own magazine, *The Inner Swine* (www.innerswine.com).

To find out yet more about Jeff Somers, and other Orbit authors, register for the free monthly newsletter at www.orbitbooks.net

if you enjoyed
THE ETERNAL PRISON

look out for

THE WAY OF SHADOWS

by

Brent Weeks

1

Azoth squatted in the alley, cold mud squishing through his bare toes. He stared at the narrow space beneath the wall, trying to get his nerve up. The sun wouldn't come up for hours, and the tavern was empty. Most taverns in the city had dirt floors, but this part of the Warrens had been built over marshland, and not even drunks wanted to drink standing ankle-deep in mud, so the tavern had been raised a few inches on stilts and floored with stout bamboo poles.

Coins sometimes dropped through the gaps in the bamboo, and the crawlspace was too small for most people to go after them. The guild's bigs were too big and the littles were too scared to squeeze into the suffocating darkness shared with spiders and cockroaches and rats and the wicked half-wild tomcat the owner kept. Worst was the pressure of the bamboo against your back, flattening you every time a patron walked overhead. It had been Azoth's favorite spot for a year, but he wasn't as small as he used to be. Last time, he got stuck and spent hours panicking until it rained and the ground softened beneath him enough that he could dig himself out.

It was muddy now, and there would be no patrons, and Azoth had seen the tomcat leave. It should be fine. Besides, Rat was collecting guild dues tomorrow, and Azoth didn't have four coppers. He didn't even have one, so there wasn't much choice. Rat wasn't understanding, and he didn't know his own strength. Littles had died from his beatings.

Pushing aside mounds of mud, Azoth lay on his stomach. The dank earth soaked his thin, filthy tunic instantly. He'd have to work fast. He was skinny, and if he caught a chill, the odds of getting better weren't good.

Scooting through the darkness, he began searching for the telltale metallic gleam. A couple of lamps were still burning in the tavern, so light filtered through the gaps, illuminating the mud and standing water in strange rectangles. Heavy marsh mist climbed the shafts of light only to fall over and over again. Spider webs draped across Azoth's face and broke, and he felt a tingle on the back of his neck.

He froze. No, it was his imagination. He exhaled slowly. Something glimmered and he grabbed his first copper. He slithered to the unfinished pine beam he had gotten stuck under last time and shoveled mud away until water filled the depression. The gap was still so narrow that he had to turn his head sideways to squeeze underneath it. Holding his breath and pushing his face into the slimy water, he began the slow crawl.

His head and shoulders made it through, but then a stub of a branch caught the back of his tunic, tearing the cloth and jabbing his back. He almost cried out and was instantly glad he hadn't. Through a wide space between bamboo poles, Azoth saw a man seated at the bar, still drinking. In the Warrens, you had to judge people quickly. Even if you had quick hands like Azoth did, when you stole every day, you were bound to get caught eventually. All merchants hit the guild rats who stole from them. If they wanted to have any goods left to sell, they had to. The trick was picking the ones who'd smack you so you didn't try their booth next time; there were others who'd beat you so badly you never had a next time. Azoth thought he saw something kind and sad and lonely in this lanky figure. He was perhaps thirty, with a scraggly blond beard and a huge sword on his hip.

"How could you abandon me?" the man whispered so quietly Azoth could barely distinguish the words. He held a flagon in his left hand and cradled something Azoth couldn't see in his right. "After all the years I've served you, how could you abandon me now? Is it because of Vonda?"

There was an itch on Azoth's calf. He ignored it. It was just his imagination again. He reached behind his back to free his tunic. He needed to find his coins and get out of here.

Something heavy dropped onto the floor above Azoth and slammed his face into the water, driving the breath from his lungs. He gasped and nearly inhaled water.

"Why Durzo Blint, you never fail to surprise," the weight above Azoth said. Nothing was visible of the man through the gaps except a drawn dagger. He must have dropped from the rafters. "Hey, I'm all for calling a bluff, but you should have seen Vonda when she figured out you weren't going to save her. Made me damn near bawl my eyes out."

The lanky man turned. His voice was slow, broken. "I killed six men tonight. Are you sure you want to make it seven?"

Azoth slowly caught up with what they'd been saying. The lanky man was the wetboy Durzo Blint. A wetboy was like an assassin—in the way a tiger is like a kitten. Among wetboys, Durzo Blint was indisputably the best. Or, as the head of Azoth's guild said, at least the disputes didn't last long. *And I thought Durzo Blint looked* kind?

The itch on Azoth's calf itched again. It wasn't his imagination. There was something crawling up the inside of his trousers. It felt big, but not as big as a cockroach. Azoth's fear identified the weight: a white wolf spider. Its poison liquefied flesh in a slowly spreading circle. If it bit, even with a healer the best an adult could hope for was to lose a limb. A guild rat wouldn't be so lucky.

"Blint, you'll be lucky if you don't cut your head off after all you've been drinking. Just in the time I've been watching, you've had—"

"Eight flagons. And I had four before that."

Azoth didn't move. If he jerked his legs together to kill the spider, the water would splash and the men would know he was there. Even if Durzo Blint had looked kind, that was an awful big sword, and Azoth knew better than to trust grown-ups.

"You're bluffing," the man said, but there was fear in his voice.

"I don't bluff," Durzo Blint said. "Why don't you invite your friends in?"

The spider crawled up to Azoth's inner thigh. Trembling, he pulled his tunic up in back and stretched the waist of his trousers, making a gap and praying the spider would crawl for it.

Above him, the assassin reached two fingers up to his lips and whistled. Azoth didn't see Durzo move, but the whistle ended in a gurgle and a moment later, the assassin's body tumbled to the floor. There were yells as the front and back doors burst open. The boards flexed and jumped. Concentrating on not jostling the spider, Azoth didn't move, even when another dropping body pushed his face briefly under water.

The spider crawled across Azoth's butt and then onto his thumb. Slowly, Azoth drew his hand around so he could see it. His fears were right. It was a white wolf spider, its legs as long as Azoth's thumb. He flung it away convulsively and rubbed his fingers, making sure he hadn't been bitten.

He reached for the splintered branch holding his tunic and broke it off. The sound was magnified in the sudden silence above. Azoth couldn't see anyone through the gaps. A few feet away, something was dripping from the boards into a puddle. It was too dark to see what it was, but it didn't take much imagination to guess.

The silence was eerie. If any of the men walked across the floor, groaning boards and flexing bamboo would have announced it. The entire fight had lasted maybe twenty seconds, and Azoth was sure no one had left the tavern. Had they all killed each other?

He was chilled, and not just from the water. Death was no stranger in the Warrens, but Azoth had never seen so many people die so fast and so easily.

Even taking extra care to look out for the spider, in a few minutes, Azoth had gathered six coppers. If he were braver, he would have looted the bodies in the tavern, but Azoth couldn't believe Durzo Blint was dead. Maybe he was a demon, like the other guild rats said. Maybe he was standing outside, waiting to kill Azoth for spying on him.

Chest tight with fear, Azoth turned and scooted toward his hole. Six coppers was good. Dues were only four, so he could buy bread tomorrow to share with Jarl and Doll Girl.

He was a foot from the opening when something bright flashed in front of his nose. It was so close, it took a moment to come into focus. It was Durzo Blint's huge sword, and it was stuck through the floor all the way into the mud, barring Azoth's escape.

Just above Azoth on the other side of the floor, Durzo Blint whispered, "Never speak of this. Understand? I've done worse than kill children."

The sword disappeared, and Azoth scrambled out into the night. He didn't stop running for miles.